Praise for *The Silent Room*

'Mari Hannah has always had two key specialities: a gift for genuinely ingenious plotting matched by a skill at choreographing suspense sequences that is the equal of more stellar names in the genre. Both characteristics are at full stretch in *The Silent Room*, with everyone involved (notably the warring officers in the Northumbrian police) leaping off the page. But a crime novel stands or falls on how vividly its central protagonist is conjured, and Hannah has come up with a real winner in Detective Sergeant Matt Ryan'

Barry Forshaw, *Independent*

'Former screenwriter Hannah uses her skills well here, creating an action-packed standalone adventure that just cries out to be turned into a TV series' *Crime Scene Magazine*

'Taut storytelling and ravishing dialogue – not to mention Hannah's use of the Northumberland countryside – make this a novel not to be missed' *Daily Mail*

'[a] pacy, standalone thriller ... turns out to be an international conspiracy, with all the delicious twists and turns that entails' *Sunday Express*

'Very creepy. Read it on your commute and you'll be looking over your shoulder all the way home' Claire

The
Death
Messenger

Mari Hannah is an award-winning author whose authentic voice is no happy accident. A former probation officer, Mari turned to scriptwriting when her career was cut short following an assault on duty. Her debut *The Murder Wall* (adapted from a script she developed with the BBC) won her the Polari First Book Prize. Its follow-up, *Settled Blood*, picked up a Northern Writers' Award. She went on to win the CWA Dagger in the Library 2017 and is currently Reader-in-Residence for Theakston Old Peculiar Crime Writing Festival. She lives in rural Northumberland with her partner, an ex-murder detective.

By Mari Hannah

The Kate Daniels series

The Murder Wall
Settled Blood
Deadly Deceit
Monument to Murder
Killing for Keeps
Gallows Drop

The Ryan & O'Neil series

The Silent Room
The Death Messenger

Mari
Hannah

The
Death
Messenger

PAN BOOKS

First published 2017 by Pan Books
an imprint of Pan Macmillan
20 New Wharf Road, London N1 9RR
Associated companies throughout the world
www.panmacmillan.com

ISBN 978-1-4472-9110-7

1 3 5 7 9 8 6 4 2

A CIP catalogue record for this book is available from the British Library.

Typeset by Ellipsis, Glasgow
Printed and bound by CPI Group (UK) Ltd, Croydon, CR0 4YY

For Wayne

who gave me my first break in publishing.

Prologue

Dusk was the perfect choice, heavy on atmosphere, exactly what she was after. To her it was almost as important as what she had in mind to do. The weather was playing its part. Thunder rumbled overhead as she left the village and crossed the bridge, the loch on one side, the swollen River Tay on the other. The folly she was heading for wasn't far, but the riverbank was slick and shiny, heavy going for most people, more so for her. The path was deeply rutted by horses' hooves and the footprints of those daring to venture out. She'd chosen well. It was getting dark. Locals were heading home to eat. The chances of meeting anyone on the way to the kill site were negligible.

She had no qualms. Not one. Her targets deserved to die, in the worst way possible. Allowing them to go unpunished, after what they had done, was out of the question. When she started out on this journey she'd listened to her gut. Surveillance was key. No point in being short on detail. As it turned out, stalking the first one was easier than it should've been. Security wasn't so much lax as non-existent. Diplomat? Ha! Not any more. Killing him made her feel well again. Better than she had in ages.

She thought of her victim now, the surprised look on his face, the horror in his eyes. A couple of months had gone by since his execution, but she'd watched the video so many times that every action, every word was now indelibly etched on her memory. It still gave her a thrill, the way everything had followed her script to the letter.

1

Even though she'd never taken centre stage personally, it was a first-rate job. She could never have imagined such a positive outcome, representing as it did that all-important first step on the road to hell.

It was all mapped out . . .

Her map . . .

Her rules.

Sorted.

She soldiered on, the mud sucking at her boots with every step. Tracking number two had been easy. One slight setback, but nothing she couldn't handle. Annoying more than anything. She'd climbed the fence surrounding his fuck-off estate. Crawled on her hands and knees through woods to observe his house through binoculars, only to find him loading a suitcase into the boot of his car. The bastard had taken off on holiday before she had time to act.

No matter.

In retrospect, the height of the summer holidays was perhaps not the best time. She could wait. She'd spent the time productively: tracking other targets, scouting locations, never idle. And now, after several weeks of waiting, the judge's time was drawing near. According to her unwitting source, His Lordship was due back any day now. She smiled to herself. People were so gullible.

The local newsagent had fallen over himself to be accommodating when she'd called the shop. 'Good morning, I'm from His Lordship's residence. I'm his new PA, just checking that his newspapers have been cancelled until further notice?'

There was a momentary pause.

'There must be some mistake.' The lad on the other end sounded flustered. 'Let me check the ledger . . .' The phone went down onto a hard surface. She heard pages rustling, then he was back on the line. 'Our instructions are to stop them only until October twelfth.'

2

'Oh, I must have got that wrong. I'll consult with the house-keeper and get back to you. If you don't hear from me just leave it as it is. Sorry to have troubled you.'

'No problem at all.'

'I'll pop in one day. The name's Jenny.'

'Alec. That would be cool.'

Would it, really?

Somehow she didn't think so.

Deception worked every time. It never ceased to amaze her how many folks were willing to take her at face value, to accept every lie, every pleasantry exchanged in person or on the phone. Her mother had once told her that her familiarity would get her into trouble one day. How wrong could one person be? It had opened so many doors they may just as well have been left open.

Yes, it was all shaping up nicely.

Shadows were beginning to form as the sun fell beneath the horizon. If someone did happen along she'd play it cool, take out her equipment and set up a photo shoot. Capturing an ancient monument, a throwback from a bygone era, in the atmospheric light of dusk – nothing suspicious in that. She was simply a consci-entious professional, a slave to her art.

If only the same could be said of her co-conspirator. His non-stop whining was getting on her nerves.

'Quit bitching,' she said. 'It's a bit of rain. And it's giving us the best chance we'll ever have to check out the terrain, do a proper walk-through at the temple, with no one around. It can't be far. Come on!'

He hitched the camera case further onto his shoulder, rain drip-ping from the hood of the waxed jacket she'd given him so he'd blend in. Sodden, it would weigh as much as he did. 'This place gives me the creeps.' He looked around as if some unseen enemy was

3

lurking in the half-light. 'You sure we've picked the right site? What if—'

'You want out?'

'I didn't say that. I was only—'

'You're in too deep to be backing out now.' She saw the resentment in his eyes and decided to change tack. 'Look, we've talked about this. Out here in the sticks we'll be too conspicuous if we try following him. The house is out, because it's bound to have a state-of-the-art alarm system as well as live-in staff. At work he's surrounded by cops and security and CCTV. The only time he's alone is when he walks his dog – and this is where he likes to walk him, bright and early every Sunday morning, when he's got the riverside all to himself. Logistically, this is far and away our best bet. So what is your problem?'

He pulled a face: *What do you think?*

'We won't get caught if we're careful and patient.'

'It's too risky. What if his Lab goes for us?'

'Then you'll kill that too.' She glared at him. 'What? You can waste a judge but you're squeamish about offing a man's best friend? Come on, when have you ever seen a Labrador go for anyone? They're more likely to lick you to death.' She walked on, her feet squelching in the mud, his complaints not far behind . . .

'Why bring all the gear if we're just having a look?'

'Because I want to sort out the lighting, maybe shoot some test footage.' Her gaze shifted to the river. 'It's handy having the river close by for disposal purposes, but the noise of rushing water is going to play havoc with the audio. I need to check sound levels, figure out a work-around so it doesn't cause a problem when we're filming. Trust me, I know what I'm doing.'

She pulled up sharp, in awe of the building that emerged through the treeline. It was so much more romantic than the images she'd

4

viewed online: an ornate hexagonal tower, raised up from the ground on a stepped plinth, surrounded by mature beech trees, the branches of which almost met in the middle above a stone cross; a magnificent sight.

The graffiti-covered door stood slightly ajar, inviting her in. Her eyes travelled up to the viewing platform at the top – a tailor-made lookout post. Perfect for her needs. She winked at her cohort, went inside and climbed the winding staircase to take a look, brushing cobwebs and creepy-crawlies from her hair as she emerged at the top, her eyes scanning the scene.

Movement . . .

No shit!

She stepped back from the edge as a ghostly figure appeared through the fading light. The hair on the back of her neck was rising, not in panic but exhilaration. This was no apparition. The judge was moving towards the folly at a pace, his trusty gundog trotting to heel. It wasn't planned but luck was on her side. She alerted her accomplice. Seconds later, he seized his chance.

No one heard her quarry scream.

1

Control patched the call through to Detective Superintendent Eloise O'Neil as soon as it came in. The woman's voice was devoid of emotion as she delivered precise directions to the location. She was savvy too, refusing to be drawn into conversation, seeing through O'Neil's strategy of keeping her on the line long enough to trace her location. The moment she hung up, Eloise was on her feet and heading for the door.

As he followed her to the car, Detective Sergeant Ryan was conscious of O'Neil's concern, but also her excitement. There was nothing more stimulating than taking on a fresh investigation. They had spent the morning viewing a DVD sent to Northumbria Police HQ anonymously. As footage of a crime scene filled the screen, an unidentified female described, in graphic detail, just how she'd managed to achieve such a staggering spectacle of blood spatter on the ceiling and walls, using the eye of the camera to draw their attention to the spot where the victim bled out. She was calm and controlled. No discernible accent. No waver in her voice. She didn't mess up or stutter. Having listened to her on the phone to O'Neil, there was no doubt in Ryan's mind that the caller and narrator were one and the same. He noticed that the time-stamp at the bottom of the screen read Sunday, 8 December: 1545 hrs.

Two days ago.

He blipped the doors open and got in, a list of questions already forming. He held back, hoping O'Neil would offer an opinion first, but she said nothing as he turned the engine over, put the car in gear and pulled away.

O'Neil took out her phone and began typing.

Ryan drove in silence, replaying the DVD in his mind. From the first viewing he'd been struck by the way it had been shot: no shaky, amateurish camerawork, no lens flare from direct light sources, just a long smooth shot panning slowly and steadily across the bloody scene. It seemed to him that the person shooting it was deliberately trying to eke out the suspense, building up to the moment when the lens zoomed in dramatically on a man's shoe, a bloody axe abandoned next to it, the butt-end of its blade illuminated by the overhead light.

Joining O'Neil in a newly formed unit – one that could potentially cross international borders, working on- or off-book on assignments deemed too hot to handle – was a once-in-a-lifetime opportunity. Given the unit's remit, there was no telling where in the world a case might take them. It had therefore come as a surprise and something of a disappointment when his first crime scene in the new job turned out to be a stone's throw from HQ.

'Any thoughts?' he said, dying to get her take on it.

'Plenty.' She kept her eyes on the road.

'Bizarre, wasn't it? The way the camera paused for effect. It felt staged to me. I'm wondering if it's all fake, some kind of sick joke. If it's a hoax—'

'It's not. The woman on that tape means business.'

'So why us and not the Murder Investigation Team?'

'You have one guess.'

'One? Will I be sacked if I get it wrong?'

'That's the deal.'

Ryan put on his best thinking pose. 'This isn't the first DVD?'

'Bravo! You get to keep your warrant card.'

'Thanks, but it's still a case for MIT – unless you know something I don't.'

'Me? I know nothing . . . yet. But I agree with you, there's something odd going on here.' Eloise swivelled in her seat to face him, excited as he was by the mystery surrounding their first investigation. 'While you were working your notice in Special Branch, I was down in Brighton, checking out a DVD that had been sent to Sussex Police. Like the one you've just seen, it showed a crime scene – blood all over the place, weapon on display, no victim in sight. Within hours of the DVD arriving at the Sussex Police HQ, a call came in giving directions to the crime scene. Forensics confirmed the blood was human. I'm no voice-recognition expert but I'm as sure as I can be that the narrator was the same woman who featured on this morning's DVD. Trust me – this is no hoax.'

The crime scene was an unremarkable lock-up on North Shields Fish Quay, eight miles east of Newcastle, not far from the mouth of the River Tyne. The building next door had been completely demolished leaving rough brickwork on the western gable end. A rusted mesh panel secured the window, its weatherbeaten frame showing through the few remaining flecks of blue paint. White corrugated sheeting covering the space that was once the door. It had been prised open to reveal an eerie dark hole beyond.

An empty Coke can lay abandoned near a much larger entrance, this one secured by a grey, concertinaed metal shutter. A sign to the left said: ALL DELIVERIES TO MAIN FACTORY. Underneath the wording, an arrow pointed west. Crime scene investigators were all over it, inside and out, the perimeter guarded by uniformed personnel, a roadblock in place to deter passers-by from wandering in off the street. No body had been found.

Ryan peered inside. What he saw was no surprise: it matched the video he'd viewed at HQ. The men in white suits were packing up their gear, preparing to leave. Now the real detective work could begin.

As he followed O'Neil inside, the Crime Scene Manager approached, her bright green eyes scanning the scene with forensic attention to detail, her expression inscrutable. She turned to face them, unaffected by the awfulness, professionally detached.

'I have work elsewhere. Any questions before I leave?'

'Is the blood human?' Ryan asked.

'Affirmative. You want type?'

His eyebrows almost met in the middle. 'You have it already?'

The CSI tipped her head at O'Neil. 'Cages have been rattled.'

'What can I say?' O'Neil said. 'There's no job more pressing than ours.'

She was right. They were in a different league now. Fast-tracking samples at the lab was not a favour they had to beg for. They were briefed and bound by the Official Secrets Act but with a lot more clout than your average copper. If they wanted to hire in specialist help, they only had to ask. Still, their newfound status would take a bit of getting used to. The thought alone made Ryan's heart beat faster. He was about to ask a question when O'Neil cut him off, indicating with a tilt of the head for him to follow.

Once they were out of earshot, she told him, 'The blood is female, Ryan. AB negative, same as yours.'

Ryan looked at her. 'And you know that, how?'

'Have you forgotten who was standing over your hospital bed like Florence Nightingale not so long ago, hoping you'd pull through? That would be me, Ryan. I want to be ready next time you need a pint or two of the red stuff.'

He gave a wry smile. 'Medical records are confidential, guv.'

'Unless you work for me. I'm in charge of this unit and I've done my homework. When you're special ops it's basic procedure to know blood types and allergies in case of emergency. Mine is engraved on the underside of my watch, in case you need it.' She narrowed her eyes, a playful look on her face. 'There's nothing I don't know about you.'

There was a good deal she didn't know. Ryan had the distinct feeling that the same could be said of her. He rather liked it that way.

2

Despite the amount of blood spilt and the likelihood that the axe found at the scene was the murder weapon, without a corpse the detectives had to assume that the victim might still be alive. An outside chance, undoubtedly, but they couldn't rule it out. Left in situ, the poor sod may have survived, though the rare blood type wouldn't have helped her chances. Transported and deprived of medical attention, she most certainly would have bled out.

'I'd better give Libby a ring,' Ryan said. Libby French was the Home Office pathologist, new to Northumbria, highly experienced. Everything he'd heard about her was encouraging. Like most in her profession, she was meticulous in her approach to her work.

'I have it covered,' O'Neil said. 'She's standing by.'

Ryan bent down for a closer look at the shoe that had featured in the video. It was a man's, grubby, recently scuffed, a brown leather wingtip brogue, hand-stitched round the upper. 'Left foot,' he observed. 'Expensive. More than I can afford on my salary.'

'Same here.' The last remaining crime scene investigator looked up from his evidence collection kit. Though most of his face was concealed, Ryan recognized the bloodshot eyes peering through the narrow strip between hood and mask as belonging to Pete Curtis, a CSI who'd been around since the days they were still called SOCOs. 'Won't be many in North Shields who can pay those prices,' he added. 'None who work for Northumbria Police anyway.'

'Don't suppose you managed to lift any prints?' Ryan could hope.

'Not even a partial.' Pete's voice was muffled by the material covering his mouth. 'It's not been here long – it's too clean for that.'

'Anything else?'

'Someone hightailed it out of here in a hurry. Take a look near the door.'

Ryan glanced in the general direction. Pete was no slouch. There were uneven marks in the dust near the entrance, evidence that would suggest someone moving at speed, scuffing their feet as they fled.

The killer, he supposed.

O'Neil's mobile beeped an incoming text. She turned away to access it. Seconds later, she pocketed the device, eyes trained on the shoe, an avoidance tactic if ever Ryan had seen one.

'I wonder if she left the shoe there on purpose,' she said.

Pete looked up, a question in his eyes: *she?*

O'Neil looked away.

Ryan managed not to react. The content of that message was serious, enough for her to take her eye off the ball. Quick as a flash, he covered for her, his focus back on the CSI. 'That goes no further, Big Ears. It's information way above your pay grade.'

'Understood.' The eyes behind the mask were smiling. 'Discretion is my middle name.'

Ryan could see that O'Neil was cursing herself for letting

her guard down. He'd spent years in Special Branch, working undercover, living with the knowledge that the smallest slip of the tongue had the potential to cost lives, so a high level of secrecy came as second nature. That wasn't something she'd had to contend with in Professional Standards.

It wasn't the first time he'd seen her floundering and he hated to see her that way. From a shaky start – their first encounter had found them on opposing sides of a disciplinary action – she'd grown on him. No, more than that. A strong bond had developed between them, a chemistry that wasn't easy to define. It intrigued and excited him.

He dropped his voice to a whisper, reassuring her that the crime scene investigator was a man who could be trusted.

Her expression remained troubled.

'Guv, is there something you're not telling me?'

'I'll explain later.' O'Neil put her hand on his forearm, preventing him from moving off. 'Thanks, Ryan.'

He threw her a smile. 'Don't mention it.'

'This scene is much the same as Brighton: bloody but clean. Looks like our offender is forensically aware.'

'It wouldn't surprise me. She doesn't seem the type to compromise her safety by leaving physical evidence for us to find. On the tape, she was clinical. Flat calm. Not an agitated killer looking over her shoulder. She sounds like a woman on a mission to me.'

'On the phone too,' O'Neil said. 'I can't get that voice out of my head.'

Ryan could still hear the voice in his own head, but it was vying for attention with thoughts of his new role and responsibilities, the information O'Neil had given him on the way over, her uncharacteristic lapse in concentration a moment ago, and all the while he was trying to process details of the crime scene in front of him and identify any that didn't match the DVD footage. O'Neil's voice took him in another direction . . .

'The time and date on the DVD can't be relied upon.' Her observation was spot on; the perpetrator could have tampered with the camera to throw them off the scent. 'Then again, most of this blood is dry, so it's possible whatever happened in here did take place on Sunday as the counter suggests.'

Ryan nodded his agreement.

Time and forensics would tell.

Being at the crime scene was like watching the DVD all over again. Blinking as a camera flash went off in the entrance to the lock-up, he surveyed the ceiling, visualizing the footage he'd seen at HQ, forcing the stream of thoughts racing through his mind to slow down so he could focus. There was something odd, something missing. He scanned the lock-up. 'She must've been standing right here when she was filming,' he said. 'Give or take a few feet.'

O'Neil agreed. 'The angle is consistent with the video.'

Fortunately, they were standing on tread plates to preserve evidence and avoid contamination. Ryan locked eyes with her. 'I'll say one thing, she's a dab hand with a camera. There was no discernible wobble on that recording.'

'She could have used a tripod.'

'She could.' He crouched down again to examine the dusty floor. 'There's no evidence to suggest that here though.' He stood up. 'She must have an accomplice, guv. Even if the victim is female, wouldn't a woman struggle to shift a dead weight on her own?'

'Not necessarily. Most coppers, firefighters, and half the nurses I've ever met could do it.' O'Neil swept a strand of red fringe from tired eyes. Under that tough exterior, Ryan sensed anxiety, not that he'd ever tell her that. She looked at him, perplexed. 'Why move the victim? It would have been a damned sight easier and a lot less risky to leave her here.'

Ryan frowned. 'The woman in the video said, "They *both* deserved to die." Maybe more than one victim's been moved.'

O'Neil corrected him. 'What she actually said was, "They both deserved *it*," which means we can't be sure we're dealing with murder, serious assault or torture.'

'Either way, we could be looking at two victims.'

'Not from this scene.' The voice had come from behind them.

Ryan and O'Neil swung round.

Pete tore away his mask as he moved closer. The man had war wounds, pain and suffering etched permanently on his brow. He'd seen more blood and guts than any individual could reasonably be expected to stomach in one lifetime. He held a hand up in apology.

'I know nothing,' he said.

O'Neil relaxed. 'One blood type is all you have?'

He nodded. 'If you have reason to believe there's a second victim, you need to be searching for another crime scene.' Hoisting his kit bag over his shoulder, he told them he was done, said goodbye and made for the door, his words echoing in their heads as he reached the plastic sheeting placed over the entrance.

'Hey!' O'Neil called after him.

He swung round to face her.

'What's your name?'

'Curtis, ma'am. Pete to my friends.'

'Thanks for the heads-up, Pete.'

Nice touch.

It was one of the traits that had drawn Ryan to Eloise. She made it her business to get to know those whose expert opinions would be delivered in court. It was everyone's responsibility to preserve the chain of evidence, from crime scenes to the lab, reporting and storage. She didn't want to end up with a dismissal.

'You're very welcome,' Pete said. 'Someone will be back for the mobile lighting. We have all the photographs we need.'

Ryan's eyes flew to the ceiling. There was no overhead light. Rusty wires hung loose where a light had once been fitted. O'Neil locked eyes with him. She knew what he was thinking. This was the missing part of the puzzle he'd been struggling with earlier, quite literally a light-bulb moment.

'Ma'am?' Pete pointed to the mobile lights on tripods. 'You want them left?'

'There's no electricity in the building?'

'Not this century,' Pete said.

O'Neil didn't speak until he was out of sight. Her focus shifted from the loose wiring to the battery pack on the floor and then to Ryan. 'Are you thinking what I'm thinking?'

'The killer must have brought her own.'

'Or, as you said, she had an accomplice standing by with a very large torch. We need to look at that video again.' She glanced at the exit. 'You sure you can vouch for Pete?'

'Relax, guv. He's a man of his word. He worked with Special Branch a lot. He's specialist-trained and vetted.'

'I hope you're right.'

'Trust me.' Ryan paused, considering. 'That's not what's bothering you though, is it? Are you going to tell me what is?'

'You want a list?'

'The woman who sent the DVD is really getting to you, isn't she?'

'Oh, you think so? Whatever gave you that idea? Whoever she is, her game plan is to confuse us, keep us guessing – why else would the victims be removed? She's calling the shots like some wannabe Spielberg, lining up her fancy camerawork and delivering her lines while we hang around like spare parts, waiting for her next masterpiece. Well, she might just have met her match.'

She'd been smouldering like a lit fuse ever since the North Shields DVD was delivered. Now, watching her fury ignite, Ryan had to suppress a grin. If the woman taunting them thought Eloise O'Neil was going to stand back and play second fiddle while someone else ran the show, she'd seriously miscalculated. His guv'nor had a blueprint of her own.

Game on.

3

'Drive me to HQ, Ryan. I need to make some calls.' O'Neil pulled her mobile from her pocket, tapped the Home key, then a number, and lifted the device to her ear. 'This is Detective Superintendent O'Neil, Northumbria Police. Put me through to Detective Superintendent Munro . . . yes, he'll know what it's about.' She sighed. 'Please do, the minute he hangs up. Thanks.'

She rang off.

Ryan didn't recognize the name and she was in no mood to share. As he negotiated the slip road onto the Coast Road, heading for Newcastle, he began to speculate as to whether or not there had been another DVD. Whatever her call was about, it was serious if a Detective Super from another force was involved. He was itching to ask about the text she'd received at the lock-up, but she was making call after call, asking for information that made little sense to him.

This was the fourth in a row . . .

'Nicholas Ford, yes. I must speak with him.' She was getting nowhere fast. 'Yes, you already said that. Has he or has he not viewed the file I sent him this morning? Then go back and tell him it's urgent. I require his feedback immediately.'

Following her rant about Spielberg, Ryan could feel her frustration at the time suck of having to wait on the line or, as she put it, 'hang around like a spare part' yet again – this time for her immediate boss, who Ryan had dubbed the grey man. The Home Office official seemed in no rush to talk to her. The more Ryan thought about that, the more he formed the impression that she was being fobbed off.

'Time to fess up, Eloise.'

'About what?' She didn't look at him.

'This is about that text you took at the lock-up, isn't it?' She didn't answer but Ryan wasn't giving up. 'Guv, Jack kept his cards close and look where it got him.'

Jack Fenwick was Ryan's ex-boss. He'd gone it alone on an off-book investigation and it had got him killed. Ryan had sensed he was preoccupied about something but hadn't wanted to pry.

If he had, Jack might still be alive.

Now O'Neil looked at him.

Ryan held her gaze. She wasn't easy to read. Without a trace of makeup, her physical attractiveness was evident. A natural redhead, she needed no chemicals to enhance what was already there. It was her personality that interested him the most, her keen intellect and ability to punch above her weight.

'You're staring, DS Ryan.' She always called him that when she was taking the piss.

'Am I? Sorry.'

'You have something on your mind?'

'As a matter of fact, I do. If you knew something I didn't, you'd tell me, right?'

Nicholas Ford waved away his aide, reiterating the fact that he was incommunicado and therefore offline to anyone, especially

Eloise O'Neil. He'd already spent the best part of yesterday afternoon in godforsaken Newcastle upon Tyne – the arse-end of the Empire he had no intention of visiting again – in order to inspect unit premises and properly brief her on Brighton. What a monumental pain in the neck that turned out to be. So much so, he couldn't face the prospect of round two.

This morning, he'd changed his plans to stay longer, made an excuse and left the area, telling her that he had more pressing business to attend to in the capital, returning to Heathrow on the first available flight. On arrival at the Home Office, he'd left strict instructions that he wasn't to be disturbed, for any reason, and yet O'Neil had already called twice – imperative, apparently. Then, having done some detective work of his own to establish why she was so demanding of his attention, all hell had broken loose.

The last thing he'd bargained for was that her own force would receive a similar DVD relating to a crime scene in North Shields, which he hadn't got wind of because he was in the air when it came in, too late for him to turn around. Now he was regretting a hasty decision to come south. Had he stayed on in Northumbria, he'd have been able to exert some control over the investigation and O'Neil, whatever way she jumped. And she'd have been in the dark – exactly where he wanted her.

Except that didn't work out either. Things really took a turn for the worse when O'Neil found out about a linked incident in Scotland on the banks of the River Tay in Kenmore. An urgent call intended for him had gone to her, some idiot in the Northumbria Control Room having texted her the details when *he* didn't answer his phone, knowing she'd been involved in the DVD investigation on her patch. Now the bitch was baying for blood.

The conference call had been ongoing for half an hour. Now he'd had time to bone Northumbria Control for passing O'Neil information he didn't yet want her to have – a minor glitch in the scheme of things – Ford was feeling pretty smug. So what if she knew about the DVD received by Police Scotland and the body they had dragged from the river yesterday? He was the boss. She'd just have to suck it up and move on, much as it frustrated her. And it did frustrate her: she was practically apoplectic, fighting hard to keep her temper in check.

Too bad.

'Well,' Ford said. 'What are your thoughts, Superintendent?'

'On what, sir?'

He forced himself to suppress a grin. Addressing him as 'sir' was hard for her to swallow but protocol demanded that she extend the courtesy in her dealings with him. Operationally she was in command but the absence of rank didn't mean she could ignore him.

'The shoe!' he barked. 'Are you even listening to me.'

'I am indeed,' O'Neil said. 'The item is being forensically examined as we speak. I hope to have more on it later.'

'Won't the blood give us gender?'

'The victim is female, sir.'

After being her own boss for years, O'Neil was exasperated at having to give Ford houseroom. In all honesty, she begrudged any civilian involvement in a police investigation, especially at managerial level. This was serious shit, not Marks and fucking Spencer.

She'd commandeered the office made available to him at HQ. When he'd told her he was returning to London, she was pleased to see the back of him, but then things had kicked off when the DVD landed in her lap. She'd not given him a second thought until that text arrived. Now she wanted to punch his lights out for briefing her on half a case. That was probably why he'd retreated to the safety of his own workplace; another poor decision.

It was bad enough having Spielberg's cat-and-mouse games to contend with. Eloise could do without an officious prick like Ford breathing down her neck and making decisions – the wrong ones – on operational matters. A beat of time passed as he digested new developments, his self-satisfied composure beginning to disintegrate. Information was power and she was now firmly in the driving seat. Or so she thought . . . with a face like thunder, no notice or apology, he muted the call and swivelled his chair so that he was facing the other way.

Ford cared less that O'Neil would now have a view of the back of his head as he conferred with his aide. Women who chose career over family were to be avoided at all costs. WPCs, police-women or whatever they were called nowadays were a particular bête noire of his. He'd come across her type before. At the initial briefing in October she'd shown him little respect. In fact, her attitude at times bordered on hostility. He was in charge of this new shadow squad and she'd do well to remember it.

'Did you find out who put O'Neil in charge?' he demanded

to know. His aide, a young man with a bad complexion and floppy hair, sat up, straightening his tie. He was being fast-tracked through the Civil Service and was shadowing Ford, himself a junior minister. It was clear the idiot didn't have a clue.

'Well?' Ford barked. 'You've had weeks to look into this. What the hell are we paying you for?'

'I'll find out.' The aide shot off his chair. 'Was there anything else?'

'Yes,' Ford crowed. 'When you track him or her down, you can tell them from me that Detective Superintendent O'Neil is totally unsuitable. If they argue, tell them she's chosen a second-rate DS just back from suspension as her professional partner. It beggars belief, it really does.'

It galled him to think that O'Neil had been in post before him. Someone should have done him the courtesy of allowing him to sit in on the selection board. Whoever it was, they had made a big mistake and *he* wasn't paying for it if the wheel came off.

O'Neil rubbed at her forehead. What Ford knew about po-licing she could write on the back of a postage stamp. She ran a tight ship and didn't see why she had to answer to a man who'd never so much as seen an angry dog. On that subject, whatever was going down at the other end, it was obvious to her that his aide was coming off worse.

Her poker eyes met Ryan's. He really was the doppelgänger of Henry Cavill, a little older perhaps, deep brown eyes, dark hair with flecks of grey. At her request, he was sitting out of sight. The initial briefing hadn't gone well. Ryan had only met

Ford for the first time yesterday, but he'd taken an instant dislike to him, a feeling that was mutual.

Her attention flashed back to the screen before the agitated aide now facing her realized she had company. The last thing she needed was another slanging match with Ford with a third crime scene to deal with across the Scottish border. So far he hadn't mentioned it. If he thought that she wouldn't, he could think again.

She was just waiting for an in.

As if he'd sensed something untoward going on behind his back, he swung his chair round to face her. His mouth was moving but he'd forgotten to switch on his microphone. O'Neil pointed at her right ear and shook her head. The gesture caused his aide to step forward and advise him of the fact that she couldn't hear a word he was saying. Ford's jaw bunched. He looked like he might explode. Then he was back online . . . his shouty mouth in full working order.

'Is that confirmed?' he asked. 'The victim is female?'

'I wouldn't have told you if it wasn't.'

'Then the shoe must belong to the perpetrator. Maybe he was disturbed and made a run for it, thinking he'd get caught—'

'Not necessarily,' O'Neil said.

His face was a deep shade of red. 'How so?'

'There's no evidence to support that view.'

'Then find some!'

Ryan tuned out the grey man to concentrate on O'Neil. After visiting the North Shields lock-up, she'd used the female locker room to freshen up at HQ, keen to get in touch with Ford at the earliest opportunity and give him a piece of her mind. Minutes later she emerged looking remarkably well-groomed, all things considered, and buzzing with energy. Ryan could see two tiny computer screens reflected in the lenses of her rimless specs. Her eyes were like pools of calm water. Such composure. She was seething underneath.

'Maybe the woman witnessed the offence and knows who is responsible but doesn't want to turn them in,' Ford said. 'Has it occurred to you that she might be an unwilling participant – a mother, sister, girlfriend – now in grave danger or dead? It's not beyond the bounds of possibility that she was forced to record that message, is it?'

'You can't believe that. The subtext of her message was clear. Surely you picked up on it?' He clearly hadn't but O'Neil stuck to her line of reasoning and didn't wait for a response. 'Not only was she justifying her actions, she was enjoying the drama. If not the main player, my gut feeling is she's an equal partner, someone with an axe to grind.'

'This is no laughing matter, O'Neil.'

'I agree. My apologies. An unfortunate choice of words. My point is this. If the woman were being coerced, we'd have heard it in her voice. If I may be so bold, women are just as capable of serious assault and homicide as men, given the right stimulus.'

'Which is?'

'Yet to be determined. There's every possibility that she may be working in tandem with someone else—'

'Finally, we're making headway.'

He had no bloody idea. 'No, sir, we're not. The possibilities so early in the enquiry are vast. I deal in facts, not speculation.'

Ford pushed his chair away from his desk, his piercing eyes looking right through her. O'Neil was suddenly wary. One minute he was on the back foot, the next he'd returned to his arrogant self.

There was a long pause. Unsure whether or not Ford had cut the call, Ryan remained silent in the background. O'Neil took a sip of water from the bottle she'd grabbed on the way in, cleared her throat and waited. A ghostly white reflection from the computer screen lit up her face, highlighting every contour, every blemish, every wisp of hair. But it was her grim expression that worried him. Whatever game Ford was playing, it was giving her cause for concern.

O'Neil ended the impasse. 'In my opinion, there was an undertone of arrogance in the woman's voice, an ego in play. She's not acting on impulse or under the thumb of her accomplice. She was cold and calculating. A person I suspect may be a tad unhinged.' She took a breather, toying with a stray hair that had escaped the pin holding it up.

A sigh . . .

She'd come to the end of her patience. 'Why was I not told that a DVD had been received by Police Scotland on the eighth of October?'

'Aah, you've been talking to Detective Superintendent Munro—'

'Never mind who I've been talking to. That DVD was filmed on a Sunday and reached Munro on a Tuesday, identical scenario to Brighton and now North Shields. You had victim DNA and yet you thought it was a good idea not to tell me about it? I demand an explanation.'

'At that point we had no body.'

'And yesterday you did!' O'Neil was glaring at him. 'When I accepted this job I made it quite clear that I would do so only if I was given free rein. If you want to run the enquiry yourself, be my guest. Alternatively, if you'll allow me to get on, I will feed developments to you as and when I have anything of significance to report. I want full disclosure, on all three incidents, and it had better be waiting for me when I get back to base. Now, if you'll excuse me, I have work to do.'

Cutting the call, she blew out her cheeks.

Ryan gave her a round of applause.

'I knew you had balls,' he said. 'Not that you were suicidal.'

'That's not remotely funny.' O'Neil was expressionless.

Ryan was taken aback. He'd touched a nerve, stepped in something he didn't understand. He hoped he hadn't upset her. That was never his intention. 'Isn't it time you told me what's going on? Who is Munro, and what the hell was in that text?'

'A body was found floating in the Tay yesterday. Police Scotland, Superintendent Munro, was on the blower to Control trying to contact Ford. When they couldn't get hold of him they gave me the heads up, unaware that I (we) weren't in the loop.' Taking her phone from her pocket, O'Neil tapped on the text and held the device out to him. It had come from a name he recognized immediately, a senior staff member in the Control Room. If nothing else, it was succinct: HQ, quick as you can. ID confirmed on Kenmore victim – Operation Shadow. Ryan needed no further explanation. It was the code name assigned to their case.

4

Their top-floor office was accessed via a private lift and secured with a heavy iron door. As protected as Fort Knox, it was far enough from HQ to operate without interference, close enough to call in favours without undue delay. Ryan punched in the code and stood aside as O'Neil entered, his mind still troubled by the revelation of a Scottish connection.

She went straight to her computer. Using her ID, she logged on. Now the cat was out of the bag, Ford had no choice but to cooperate. He'd emailed documents via secure download. She pressed for two copies, passing one printout to Ryan, and sat down to read the other.

His eyes seized on the classification:

OFFICIAL-SENSITIVE

MEMORANDUM FOR: Secretary of State for Scotland
FROM: Lord President of the Court of Session, Judiciary of Scotland
DATE: Monday, 14 October 2013

Dear Sir
It is with great sadness that I report to you the disappearance of The Lord Justice Clerk, my deputy, Leonard Maxwell, Lord Trevathan. He was listed to

preside over a high-profile trial, due to start this morning. He failed to appear and all attempts to raise him have failed.

In late summer, His Lordship organized a prolonged period of leave in the West Country. His housekeeper confirms that he arrived in Cornwall on 20 August, as planned, and was due to depart 12 October. However, he cut short his leave in order to retrieve a briefcase that he had inadvertently left behind; apparently it contained important papers that he needed in order to prepare for the trial. He returned to Scotland on Sunday, 6 October. Sadly, he never arrived at his residence.

Having discussed this matter with the Chief Constable of Police Scotland, I have been apprised of certain details that lead me to fear the worst. It seems that on Tuesday, 8 October 2013, Divisional Command in Tayside received a video recording of a possible crime scene. A subsequent telephone call led officers to Maxwell's Temple (Kenmore) on the banks of the River Tay. Scene of Crime Officers attended. Blood was found. No body recovered. Utilizing all resources at their disposal, in the absence of a missing persons report or DNA match, detectives were unable to progress the matter further. The video lasted only two minutes. According to the digital time-stamp, it was recorded 6:05–6:07 p.m. on Sunday, 6 October 2013.

I pray that I am wrong to link the sudden disappearance of Lord Trevathan to the crime scene at Maxwell's Temple, but the timing and the coincidence of the temple bearing his family's name are of grave concern. I firmly believe that His Lordship has come to harm.

In light of this, I request a special operations unit to examine any further messages, intercept those responsible and facilitate the recovery of the victim, dead or alive. Press blackout and Level 1 vetting of such personnel is essential.

Your loyal servant,

Gordon McEwan

OFFICIAL-SENSITIVE

'Jesus!' Ryan didn't get beyond the first page. He ran a hand through his hair, scratched his head, eyes on O'Neil. 'I'd love to think Trevathan either flipped or pissed off with a call girl, but somehow I don't think that's the case.' He whistled. 'It don't come any more high-profile than this.'

'The victim or the content?'

'Both.' He tapped the letter. 'So McEwan requests a special ops unit on the fourteenth of October. Wasn't that about the time you got the call offering you this job?'

'It was indeed.' She looked like she was ready to blow a gasket.

'So the unit is set up, they take us on, but then someone decides to withhold intelligence from the very people they appoint to investigate? Why? It makes no sense—'

'Unless there's another unit like ours operating in Scotland. They're a separate entity altogether.'

'Yeah, but they're exceptionally cooperative. I can't see them refusing to hand it over. If that were the case, wouldn't Ford have said so, if only to pass the buck? It doesn't hold true anyway, not if they're sharing this with us now. No, the grey man is the sticking point, not them, Eloise.' Ryan stuck his tongue in his cheek, mentally joining the dots. 'The more I think about it, the more convinced I am that this has MI5 or even 6 written all over it. With such a high-profile victim they would get the call initially. They go in, get nowhere. Then the Brighton DVD arrives and they still can't make any headway. By this time the case is getting too hot to handle, so they dump it on you and me. If we succeed where they failed, Ford will be stuck with us. If we screw up because we only have part of the picture, it's curtains for us and he gets to pick himself a new team. Job done.'

'That's not an ending I can live with, Ryan.'

'Nor me. Let's show the bastard what for.'

O'Neil got up and walked away. He watched her go into the kitchen and fill the kettle, then turned his attention back to the letter. There was a clatter as a heavy mug dropped out of her hand, smashed off the kitchen bench and onto the floor.

She swore under her breath.

When Ryan looked up she was on all fours picking up the fragments. 'You OK?'

She nodded, her back to him, shoulders tense. Ryan went back to the letter. She had two mugs of steaming liquid in her hands when she returned. He took one from her, failing to mention that he needed something stronger than a coffee hit. If he was reading her right, so did she.

'What do we know about the trial Trevathan was working on?'

'Nothing.' She sat down. 'Munro said his hands were tied in that respect.'

'Let me guess. It's not relevant to our enquiry.'

'Right on the money.'

'So we're supposed to investigate blindfold?'

'Drop it, Ryan.'

He couldn't. 'Whatever happened to transparency? We're going to need that information—'

'And we'll get it . . . somehow.'

He climbed down, mulling over the problem. This was big – this was very big – and he was beginning to understand why O'Neil was under so much pressure. His silence didn't last. 'We need to get hold of that information. I can't work in the dark, Eloise.'

'It's never stopped you before.'

She was right, it hadn't, and it wouldn't now. Ryan had pulled a few strokes in the past. Stuff he wasn't proud of. Things he'd go to his grave without sharing. Accessing the force's HOLMES database via the back door was one example. It would end his career if it ever got out. O'Neil had discovered his use of an old warrant card to gain unauthorized entry while he was officially suspended. Working in Professional Standards at the time, she could have – should have – busted him. She'd made an exception. That was all the motivation he needed to repay her with a positive result.

One thing was clear. If they put a foot wrong, this investigation could see them both back in uniform. Ryan took a sip of coffee, meeting her gaze over the rim of his cup. She pointed to the papers in his hand, inviting him to read on. He picked up the next sheet: same classification, different author – equally prominent.

OFFICIAL-SENSITIVE

MEMORANDUM FOR: Secretary of State for Scotland
FROM: Chief Constable – Police Scotland
DATE: Friday, 18 October 2013

Dear Sir

Acting on information received from the Lord President of the Court of Session, detectives entered the home of his deputy, The Lord Justice Clerk, Leonard Maxwell, Lord Trevathan. The property was locked and secure. There were no signs of a break-in and no evidence to suggest that a struggle had taken place inside.

The Judge's residence had been made ready for His Lordship's return by his housekeeper, Mrs Margaret Forbes, who lives on his estate in a cottage in the grounds. She was out when officers arrived, but returned soon after.

Mrs Forbes was away on holiday from 4–11 October. She was therefore unaware that His Lordship had left Cornwall early. She was expecting him to return on the evening of the twelfth and had prepared a light supper for him as instructed. When he failed to materialize she assumed that either he'd decided to break his journey at some point along the way, or that his upcoming trial had been delayed and he'd simply extended his leave for a few days without telling her. This had happened before. She thought nothing of it and didn't raise the alarm.

Scene of crime officers collected DNA for comparison with blood taken from Maxwell's Temple. The samples were processed in an expeditious manner and Forensic Services have confirmed that the blood was His Lordship's.

House-to-house enquiries were immediately initiated and POLSA search teams scoured the area. Search parameters included parts of the Mains of Taymouth country estate and all areas bordering the river. Lord Trevathan's Volvo estate was recovered from The Courtyard Brasserie & Bar car park on the A827 road leading into Kenmore, proof that he made it back to Scotland.

His Lordship is well known in the area. I am led to believe that he often parked at The Courtyard for convenience when taking his dog for a walk. This is a busy car park at any time of year, but no one noticed the vehicle tucked away at the rear.

Extensive enquiries have so far failed to locate His Lordship or his dog. According to the clerk at his chambers, the two are inseparable, information that has been corroborated by the Lord President himself.

I will keep you updated as and when there are further developments. Please be assured that our investigations are ongoing.

Yours sincerely,

James Price
Chief Constable

OFFICIAL-SENSITIVE

Attached to the back of the report were stills of the Kenmore crime scene and a comprehensive account of the Police Scotland investigation. From what Ryan could see, they had followed protocol and, on the face on it, done a thorough job.

Ryan asked: 'Did Ford send the DVD footage?' O'Neil shook her head, a black look Ryan knew wasn't meant for him. 'Take no notice, Eloise. He's making us sweat.'

'He's making me puke.'

'Either way, he's picked the wrong fight.'

O'Neil shot him her best smile.

Ryan returned to the crime scene photos. The amount of blood at the scene brought to mind the North Shields lock-up. Lifting his head, he said, 'I wonder what kind of shoes His Lordship wears.'

5

They spent the rest of the afternoon poring over the Kenmore report, drawing up a list of actions, familiarizing themselves with the first offence chronologically, trying not to dwell on, or even admit, that they had been blindsided by a Whitehall bureaucrat hell-bent on derailing their investigation. O'Neil quizzed Munro. Voice-recognition experts had already confirmed a link between the Kenmore and Brighton DVDs. They bore the same woman's voice. It was only a matter of time before North Shields was added to that list.

They could bet on it.

They had one body to examine: Lord Trevathan. On top of that, they had three crime scenes and no clue as to the identity of other victims, but now they were in possession of the whole picture, rather than a partial, and as lead investigators for a series of offences, five hundred miles apart, the Northumbria detectives were hoping to make progress. The only downside was not knowing the nature of the trial the Scottish judge was due to hear in Edinburgh – a priority for them now.

Ryan glanced at O'Neil. The increasing gravity of the case appeared to be getting to her. She was nowhere near as cool as the mint green shirt she was wearing. A contrasting sweater lay draped across her lap.

Drawing his eyes away, Ryan scanned the top-floor apartment. It was brand spanking new, a residential conversion, rather than a traditional office. Unusual because, for all intents and purposes, it was someone's home, not an elite unit's place of work. The first time they walked in there to try it for size he knew that his career move was a good one. It had been hard to go back to the open-plan office at HQ occupied by Special Branch and work his notice.

'What's up?' Eloise was staring at him intently.

He waved a hand, indicating their surroundings.

'This don't come cheap,' he said.

'We got lucky.'

'That's crap and you know it.' His eyes were smiling. 'You got friends in high places I don't know about?'

'Hardly!' She frowned. 'Were you dozing off when I spoke to Ford?'

He threw down a challenge. 'I was just wondering . . . why you? Why here?'

'Why me?' She bristled. 'You don't think I'm up to the job? Join the queue. The grey man obviously agrees with you.'

'That's not what I said.' He eyeballed her. 'It's quite a leap from your former role, that's all.'

'I was headhunted, Ryan, same as you.'

'I'm not getting at you, I just like to know where I stand.'

Much as the idea of being her wing-man thrilled him, his bullshit detector was working overtime. O'Neil should be buzzing and yet since their return from HQ, she'd seemed out of sorts. He figured she was holding out on him and he didn't like it. She demanded transparency. Well, so did he. But he could see that she was in no mood for his questions.

He let it drop.

'Ignore me, I reckon I could slum it here for a while.' He was kidding. The apartment was equipped with everything they could possibly need, professionally and personally – apart from alcohol – including a link to HOLMES, the computer system on which all major investigations were run.

He might even get to use it officially this time.

Ryan was peckish, which was unfortunate because neither he nor O'Neil had had the foresight to stock the fridge with even the basic requirements to satisfy his hunger. He suggested they walk along the Quayside to the Pitcher and Piano. Situated on the banks of the Tyne, the pub was three minutes from their smart new base, an ideal spot in which to review the day's events, decide on a strategy for their case and grab a bite to eat. With any luck it might snap O'Neil out of the mood she was in.

They ate quickly. Ignoring the buzz of those around them, their conversation taking the form of a mini briefing, several lines of enquiry already obvious for the North Shields scene: the Coke can, the shoe, the axe, the type of video camera used to film the crime scene, whether the same piece of equipment had been used for the previous DVDs.

Ryan stopped chewing, put his sandwich down, wiping his hands on a serviette. 'If the details of Trevathan's trial are being withheld, it's probably safe to assume that it's terrorism-related, something that might compromise national security. Which makes our case a lot more complex than we first thought.'

O'Neil nodded. 'And thanks to Ford, we're well and truly at a disadvantage. It's hard to believe that all the time I was working the Brighton case, he never said a word about Trevathan or the Kenmore DVD, even though it would have given me something to work with. And now I'm supposed to go through him to get to the Chief of Police Scotland?'

'Sod that. You're not going cap in hand—'

'Don't fret, Ryan. I went over his head already.'

'Good. What did he say?'

'Price? Nothing. He wasn't available. He'll call me this evening but it might be late on.'

She took out her iPad to check if she'd missed an email confirming a time.

She hadn't.

Ryan watched her open the device's browser. He wasn't close enough to read upside down as she typed into the search bar. 'Can't Ford compel Police Scotland to tell us about Trevathan's trial?'

She peered over the top of her glasses. 'That's a matter for the Lord Chief Justice apparently. Ford said he'd give it a go.'

'That's big of him. Bloody hypocrite. He spent two hours yesterday lecturing us about keeping channels of communication open and maintaining reporting lines – all the while keeping the Kenmore files under lock and key – and yet he doesn't trust us any further than he can throw us. We cannot work this case without full disclosure, Eloise. It's impossible.'

'Looks like we're going to have to for the time being.' She clicked to open a page.

'What time are we expecting the other DVDs?'

'I have a copy of the Brighton footage back at base. Ford said the Kenmore one would arrive shortly. That was over an hour ago.'

The door opened. A crocodile of women wearing high heels

and little else spilled in, probably a works night out. A Christmas tree hat stood out among tinsel headbands and reindeer antlers as the group staggered loudly to the bar. The blonde bringing up the rear clocked Ryan on her way in and tugged at the dress of the girl in front.

'Hey, I've scored. Get the mistletoe oot.'

A roar of laughter followed as she held a sprig of plastic mistletoe aloft, pursing her lips, inviting a kiss.

'Move along,' said O'Neil, smiling. 'He's spoken for.'

Spoken for? Ryan could dream.

He let the girl down gently, a wry smile on his face. 'Thanks for the offer.'

'Your loss, handsome.' She winked at O'Neil. 'Just pulling his leg, pet. Keep hold of him – he's *lush*!'

As the group moved off, the repartee continuing elsewhere, the detectives shared a moment of intense, intoxicating chemistry that caught them both by surprise. It wasn't the first time it had happened. Ryan had felt the connection from the moment they began working together, though it seemed destined to disappear now that he had joined O'Neil officially as part of the new unit. The fact that it was still there stirred him physically.

He looked away.

When he turned back, O'Neil was working on her notes.

He scanned the pub. The last time he was here, it was in the company of Grace Ellis, a retired colleague who'd helped him in his search for Jack Fenwick. Discreet and trustworthy, her special skills would come in handy if O'Neil found it necessary to bring in outside help. Ryan wanted to raise that with her – it was a stretch to think that they would be able to handle an investigation on this scale without it – but he held back. It was too early to throw names into the mix – better to wait it out. He didn't want her thinking he lacked faith in her ability. He had a lot of time for her. She was now playing with her iPad.

'What are you doing?' he asked.

'Research.'

'On what?'

'Maxwell's Temple.'

'I could've saved you the bother. It's a nineteenth-century folly, also known as The Cross, built as a tribute to some countess or other—'

'And when did you discover that?'

'When you were getting the drinks in.' He held up his mobile. 'You're quick or dead in this game.'

Dusk had brought on the lights of the Millennium Bridge. People wandered across it to visit the Baltic Centre for Contemporary Art, or to stand and take pictures of the iconic Tyne Bridge to the west. Beyond it, on the south side of the Tyne, the Sage Music Centre was also lit up.

'Damn!'

Ryan checked the date on his watch.

'Are you bored with my company?' O'Neil said. 'Or am I keeping you from something?'

'You will be on Friday – unless I can have the night off?'

'You are joking!' She dipped her head on one side, peering curiously at him. 'We'll be heading north soon, Ryan. We have scene issues to consider at either end of the country. We'll be working round the clock, camping out at base for the foreseeable future.'

'Don't worry about it,' Ryan said casually. 'Caroline will

understand. Maybe Hilary can go in my place.' Caroline was his twin sister; Hilary, Jack Fenwick's widow.

O'Neil pretended not to notice how distressed he was. Ryan idolized Jack and had done everything possible to find him. Since his murder she'd taken the time to call on and support Hilary and the kids. In Ryan's book that was an action above and beyond a duty call. He palmed his brow, wiping away a thin film of sweat that had settled there.

Ryan moved to safer ground. 'Don't you find it odd that a senior judge of Trevathan's standing could go missing for such a long period of time and not be missed?'

'Not really, no. Judges usually head off to their second homes over the summer recess. With a big case to prepare for, he might have shifted his leave period back a little.'

'Wouldn't he call to say he was on his way home?'

'Call who? His housekeeper was away, remember?'

'Yes, of course she was.' He rolled his eyes at his mistake, but he still wasn't happy. 'I'd love to know why she didn't raise the alarm when he failed to surface on the date he was expected. He was a top judge, if he missed even a single day in court it would have major repercussions.'

'She's the hired help, Ryan! She wouldn't have a clue what he was working on. Reading between the lines of that letter, it sounds like he had previous for changing his holiday plans at a moment's notice. That's the way the other half live, whether you like it or not.'

'Maybe. Wouldn't you think there would have been contact, however minimal, between the housekeepers in Cornwall and Scotland?'

'Ordinarily, yes. But not if his Scottish housekeeper was on holiday.'

They both went quiet for a moment.

O'Neil spoke first. 'Call Mrs Forbes when we get back and ask her about Trevathan's footwear, please.'

'It's on the list.' Ryan supped his pint and replaced it on the beer mat. 'What I don't get is the report on the CCTV.'

'In what respect?'

'Police Scotland clocked Trevathan's car travelling north, established that he was in it, but claim he wasn't followed. He got as far as Aberfeldy before he fell off the radar—'

'And never made it home. That threw me too.'

'That's not what I meant but it's easily explained.'

'Is it?' O'Neil was curious.

'I reckon he took his dog for a walk after the long drive north. Caroline always does the same thing when we've been a distance. As soon as I park up, she gets out, takes Bob for his constitutional before she ever steps inside the house. A guide dog is still a dog like any other. As soon as he gets a sniff of home, Bob gets excited, starts yelping and barking. Trevathan's dog would sense the end of the journey too. By all accounts, they were joined at the hip. If you're a dog-lover, it's a question of priorities: the animal comes first.'

'Suppose.' O'Neil had never owned a dog. She'd never been in a position to give one the time it deserved. 'Why not drive all the way home and walk the dog on his estate? It's big enough.'

'Do *you* shit in your own yard?'

O'Neil grinned. 'Point taken.'

'Maybe they liked the river, the dog wanted out for a wee or the judge needed to stretch his legs. I checked the map. His estate is north of Kenmore. He'd have to cross the bridge to get there. Easier to park at the Bistro where his car was found.'

'Works for me.' O'Neil picked up her beer. 'What were you going to say before?'

'If Trevathan was away and returned early, but wasn't followed, how did the offenders grab him? You just said, Forbes was not at home. No one in Scotland knew he was coming, which sounds like a random attack, so nothing to do with his trial.'

'OK, we'll bear that in mind going forward. Anything else?'

'Well, for a start, I reckon you're right about Spielberg. Watching that DVD this morning, it occurred to me that she was choosing her shots for dramatic effect, cutting away here and there to create suspense in an attempt to increase our anxiety. The lock-up was lit by something and yet it has no power. Photographic lighting would be my guess – a torch would give off too much glare. She could have been shooting a horror movie, the way it was staged. All we're missing is the spine-chilling music—'

O'Neil's brow furrowed. 'Or someone else was directing and she merely did the voiceover.'

'That's another thing – why do a voiceover?' Ryan asked. 'The woman on the tape had no need to speak, so why did she?'

'Good question, bearing in mind her voice is presently the only thing we have to go on. Once we confirm a link to the other two scenes – and we both know that's a foregone conclusion – an analyst will give us an idea of where she's from. It might be our only chance of nailing her.'

'You reckon she's a God-botherer?'

O'Neil narrowed her eyes. 'Why d'you ask?'

'She used the word "evil". I always think it's old-fashioned, almost biblical. Like "sinful". Chance would be a fine thing. Whatever her motivation, I'm guessing it involves some form of abuse. She's paying her victims back for something in her past. She said as much on the tape, didn't she?'

'Or someone is,' O'Neil corrected him.

'You have a theory?'

'Nothing concrete.' O'Neil bit her lip. 'I know Ford is an idiot, but something he said to me struck a chord. I can't remember his exact words. It was about the woman witnessing the offence, knowing who was responsible, not shopping them—'

'And you shot him down. Rightly so, in my opinion.'

'At the time, yes. However, there is another scenario.'

Ryan waited.

O'Neil was still formulating a theory. He was happy to be her sounding board. He might not agree with all or part of it, but it was important to let her finish processing her thoughts. That was his plan at any rate. Seconds later, it fell apart when O'Neil began to hypothesize.

'What if she's not a relative or girlfriend but a stalker turned voyeur, getting her kicks by looking on?'

'At three crime scenes hundreds of miles apart?' Ryan was shaking his head incredulously.

'You're wise to be sceptical,' she said. 'I know it sounds a bit far-fetched, but bear with me. On the way over here you asked why she hadn't gone the whole hog and given us the footage of an offence taking place – assuming her motivation was to shock us. But what if she couldn't?'

'Because?'

'Maybe she saw it happen but couldn't record it, so she returned to the scene with her camera afterwards.'

'Then why is she telling us after the event instead of warning us beforehand? Why not help us put a stop to it?'

'Because she finds it fascinating.' O'Neil paused, allowing him time to reflect. 'Ryan, think about the way she put that tape together. Like a movie scene, you said. Like shooting it was something important to her, something she must get right—'

'She said the victims deserved it. How would she know that if she had nothing to do with it?'

'I don't have all the answers. I'm putting forward suggestions. Stalkers are obsessive. They monitor their prey. Idolize them. Go to great lengths to track them down. Follow them wherever they go. Wouldn't a person like that be capable of justifying anything, even murder?'

'I'm not saying that there's no stalking going on. Just that they're in it together. If it's not revenge, it's a game, a thrill thing—'

'Exactly my point! Remember Wearside Jack, the Ripper hoaxer? He played that game. He was so turned on by murder he wanted to get involved. He taunted the police with letters and an audiotape – "I'm Jack, catch me if you can" – or words to that effect. His message was also sent to an assistant chief, as I recall. He had no connection whatsoever with Sutcliffe, which is what made finding him so very difficult. Twenty-five years it took. Twenty-five! That would see you and I well into retirement.'

'I see where you're coming from, but I still think she's up to her neck in a partnership. Gut feeling? It's a bloke and he's the killer—'

O'Neil looked at him. 'So what does that make her?'

'I have no idea.' That answer would keep them both awake tonight.

6

They left the pub and fought their way through a fog of smokers sitting outside. Girls hung about in ankle-breaking eight-inch killer heels and less clothing than was sensible on a dank December night. They were all tipsy, much like the blonde Ryan and O'Neil had encountered inside. Blokes, well dressed and toned, watched the girls; both genders on the prowl like peacocks on parade.

Tucking her hair into her coat, O'Neil pulled up her collar. 'What I wouldn't give for a night on the razz.'

The comment surprised Ryan.

'What?' she said. 'You think I don't like to party?'

'Did I say that?'

'Your face did it for you.'

Ryan knew nothing of her private life . . . yet. He hoped that might change the longer they worked together. Hoping there would be an opportunity for time off at some point, he was about to offer to take her to dinner when her mobile rang, causing him to hold off.

O'Neil stopped walking, fumbling her phone from her bag. Ryan glanced at the imposing Crown Court immediately across the road. On the opposite side of the junction, festive lights were hung around the Eye On The Tyne public house. All the bars and restaurants along the waterfront were gearing up for Christmas. When he glanced at his guv'nor, her glum expression gave away the caller's ID. He half-expected her to hurl the device over her shoulder into the inky river behind them. Instead, she moved closer so he could listen in.

She smelt good.

She lifted the phone to her ear. 'What can I do for you, sir?'

'Where the hell have you been?' Ford yelled. 'I've been trying to raise you.'

'I've been briefing Detective Sergeant Ryan.' O'Neil rolled her eyes. 'There's a lot to do.'

'There's even more now!' he barked. 'There's another video at HQ.'

'We've had this conversation already.'

'There are two. The first is Kenmore, the second is local to you.'

O'Neil and Ryan exchanged a worried look.

'Do you people never check the force-wide incident log?'

'Frequently,' O'Neil said. 'But it wouldn't do much good if this is what you're suggesting: a DVD from our patch we've not yet seen, potentially part of Operation Shadow. Whoever received it obviously had the good sense not to share it.'

'Pick it up, view it and let me know what gives.' The dialling tone signalled the end of the call.

The grey man was well out of order, although his rudeness hardly registered with O'Neil. She was more relieved than riled, pleased to be rid of him, if the truth were known. In her former job, she'd dealt with dickheads like him every day.

'Did you get all that?' she asked.

Ryan nodded. 'You want to view it at HQ or at our place?'

'Our place?' Her eyes sparkled in the moonlight, but not enough to hide her melancholy.

'You OK?' He found himself staring.

'Never better.' She was lying.

He'd touched a nerve.

They agreed that she'd walk up to Forth Banks, collect the package and rendezvous at 'their place' in half an hour. Ryan watched her go, then turned the other way, wondering what on earth had brought about her sadness.

An hour later, he put the phone down as she entered the flat. Nothing appeared to be bothering her now, though she didn't say why she'd taken so long and he didn't pry. She was the one with the questions.

'Any joy with the shoe?'

'It belongs to someone other than the judge,' Ryan said. 'Both housekeepers are in agreement that he only ever wore black.'

'Anything else?'

'His Cornish housekeeper, Morwenna Evans, sounded a bit sheepish on the phone. It turns out she gave investigators a description of a coat she thought Trevathan was wearing when he left the area—'

'She was mistaken?'

He nodded. 'She found it hanging in the boot room and was frightened to say. Doesn't matter now he's been found. I made a note of the discrepancy for future reference.'

Opening her handbag, O'Neil removed a carton of milk and a small evidence bag containing coffee grounds. She held them up, her expression a combination of guilt and playfulness. 'I rifled someone's tea fund. Don't suppose they'll miss it. I'll put the kettle on, shall I?'

'Bit risky for you, isn't it?'

'No, I've done it before.'

'I meant nicking their stuff.'

They were both grinning, and then Ryan feigned disapproval. 'Theft is something I should report to the police, guv. It would be a dereliction of duty not to do so.'

'I'd much rather you helped me drink the evidence.'

'My duplicity will cost you.'

'Will this do?' She handed over a package containing two individually wrapped DVDs, the ones Ford had been banging on about. She opened her desk drawer and took out the one from Brighton, stacking them one on top of the other. 'That's tonight's entertainment sorted.' Her eyes fixed on Ryan's computer screen – frozen on the North Shields crime scene – then shifted to the notepad lying open on his desk. 'Nice to see you haven't been wasting your time while I was out. *Love* the doodles. Very artistic! If that's supposed to be me, the hair's all wrong.'

Ryan checked the pad.

Next to a load of scribbled questions relating to the case – Voyeur? Photographer? Lured? Motive? – was a sketch of a devil woman complete with tail and trident. Chuckling under his breath, he turned to speak to her. O'Neil had already moved away.

While she was busy making coffee he marked the DVDs in chronological order and gave the theory she'd put forward in the pub the once-over, even though he was convinced that Spielberg was part of the problem and not someone who'd stumbled upon a crazed killer while stalking him. His train of thought was interrupted by the sound of cupboard doors opening and closing behind him as O'Neil searched for crockery and placed it on the marble counter top.

A few minutes later, she appeared by his side. 'You're washing up,' she said, handing him a mug. 'Despite a begging request, our controllers haven't stretched to a dishwasher.'

'There's always carry-out, guv.'

'Fine. You're buying.'

O'Neil opened the second drawer down, took out a folder and sat down, her boots immediately landing on his desk. Leaning back in her seat, she rested the file on her knee and put her specs on ready for viewing. Ryan suggested they start with Brighton, given that she'd already been there.

She agreed. 'Take a look at these first.'

She passed over the reports relating to that crime scene. It made sense to begin with one that had already been processed and that she'd had sight of physically. She waited while he skimmed through the various documents: some stills of the scene, information on forensic samples – blood, hair, fibres – it was all there. When he'd seen enough, he switched on the tape and let it run, pausing now and then so she could talk him through it.

'The location is a listed building,' she said. 'A derelict coastguard lookout Spielberg probably found on the net. The DVD was sent to Sussex Police HQ in Lewes. Hours later, they received a call with instructions where to look, same as ours. Forensics went in to do their thing. Blood was found to be human; so much of it had been spilled, there was little chance the victim could have survived.'

'What do we know about the screwdriver?'

'Heavy duty. Square shank. Flat head. Brand new. Could've been purchased specially. You don't want to hear this, but it's the kind you can buy in any DIY store. Problem is, these offences are so far apart geographically, it could have been bought anywhere in the UK and taken to the scene. The blood was tested, but there's no DNA to match with it, no unidentified bodies in the morgue with stab wounds, no hits on the PNC.'

'You're depressing me.'

'While I was there, I examined Sussex Police incident logs. A fairly prominent gay man had been reported missing by his partner the day after the video was recorded. Tierney, his name was. It was treated as low priority – grown man walks out, no hint of foul play – an everyday occurrence in Brighton, or anywhere else, I should imagine. As far as I know, he's not yet surfaced. Officers locally are following it up. The timing fits. The DVD came in the very next day.' She pointed at the screen. 'Let's take a look at Kenmore.'

Ryan took the Kenmore disk from its plastic casing, the original having been retained in evidence and dusted for prints by Police Scotland. It slid effortlessly into a slot in his computer, opened up and began to play. They watched in silence, the sound muted, neither detective making any comment. Like North Shields and Brighton, the scene was bloody with no body visible. It was hard to see what they were looking at. A small space with a curved stone staircase disappearing off to the right, exactly as described in the diagrams and sketches they had already had sight of.

'The lighting is poor on this one,' O'Neil said.

'That's the first thing that struck me too.' Ryan placed his hands together, the tips of his fingers resting on his lips, his thinking pose. 'At five past six on an October evening there'd be what, half an hour of light left?'

'If that.'

'The dimensions given suggest that it would be harder to illuminate such a tight space. Risky too. In the Scottish countryside it would be like a beacon in the darkness, drawing unwanted attention. The temple is situated on a country walk, a dog-walker's route, a favourite spot for anglers, poachers and foragers.'

O'Neil fixed on him. 'You've been there?'

'Years ago.'

'You never said.'

'You never asked. It's not important until we head up there. I remember that walk. Not the folly, funnily enough. It's distinctive in the photos, not something I'd have forgotten if I'd seen it.'

'Maybe you were on a different stretch of river.'

'No. I parked in Kenmore and walked from there.' Ryan paused, trying to remember, but he couldn't. Dragging his laptop towards him, he typed in www.geograph.org.uk. He entered 'Maxwell's Temple' and hit search. A photo of the temple popped up on screen. It had a grid reference attached: NN7746. He clicked on it. 'That's one mystery solved,' he said. 'The folly is on the north bank. I was on the south. I know that because I stumbled upon Taymouth Castle by accident.'

He searched for the castle and turned the laptop to face her.

'Oh God!' O'Neil said.

'Enchanting, isn't it? Queen Victoria's honeymoon choice. It was used as a hospital for Polish troops during the Second

World War. By the time I got there it was being turned into a golf complex with luxury apartments you can actually own. They'll sell too. I met a group of enthusiastic, well-heeled Yanks, all wanting their slice of Scottish history – and why not? Wish I could afford one. I'll show you when we go up.'

'Maybe we can stay there,' O'Neil said.

'Bring your best PJs – it's posh.'

'I can do posh!'

They grinned at each other.

Her mobile rang, killing the moment.

She took the call.

After a few seconds, she said: 'I'm going to have to call you back.' Dropping her head, avoiding eye contact, she listened for what seemed like a very long time. 'Yes, yes, understood . . . OK, call you soon.' She ended the call in a very different mood, her mind firmly on the job. 'Sorry, Ryan. Any thoughts on how Spielberg managed to get the judge to the folly or the other victims to locations of her choosing?'

'None, but I just had a thought. There's a pattern developing here. These crime scenes are all waterside locations: River Tay at Kenmore; the Brighton lookout, North Shields Fish Quay. At the very least, we should alert the Port of Tyne authority and River Police to be on their guard. Presumably Brighton coastguard have already been briefed, given the close proximity to the coast?'

'Yes, that was in place before I left.'

'Shall we?' Ryan held up the remaining DVD, the most recent offence, a location as yet unidentified – and still no call to point them in the right direction. They were shocked by what came next. Unlike the others, the scene was recognizable

– a residential property this time – a slight pause in viewpoint forcing them to dwell on the weapon of choice, a long-bladed knife glinting beneath the overhead light. Again, there was no victim in sight.

'She's been watching too many movies,' Ryan said.

'You took the words right out of my mouth.'

Something Ryan had seen prompted him to freeze the image. *Where there was detail, there was evidence.*

He took his time scanning the screen. An old tea chest doubled as a bedside table, various items on top: a digital radio-alarm clock, a notepad and pen, a landline telephone. Next to the unmade bed was a dining room chair. A dark shirt lay over the back of it. Ryan's eyes seized on the blue-and-white lanyard that hung beside it, a white, plastic credit-card-sized ID or access key attached.

'Could we be that lucky?' He zoomed in. 'Can you make out the writing?'

Pushing her specs up onto the bridge of her nose, O'Neil sat forward, peering closely at the screen. Because of the angle of the thing and the light reflecting off it, it was impossible to read.

'No,' she said. 'Can you go in further?'

Ryan's efforts only served to blur the image. Zooming out again, he moved on, hair pricking the back of his neck and arms. What was on camera was bad enough. It was what he couldn't see that scared him the most.

They replayed each disk, made notes independently on each run-through, then played them again, this time with the narrator's voiceover audible. When they'd finished, O'Neil put down her pen, took off her glasses and threw them on Ryan's desk.

'Are we any the wiser?' she asked.

'I think we are.' He turned to face her. 'She's staging the scenes, particularly the last one. She placed that knife where it would catch maximum light, no doubt about it. She certainly knows what buttons to press.'

'Yes, but why?' O'Neil looked at him. 'Staging usually occurs when an offender is trying to throw us off or redirect the investigation. She's doing the opposite. She's drawing our attention to it.'

Ryan agreed. 'It's like she has a compulsion to record the scene, not as it is, but how she wants it to be, rearranging things with artistic merit in mind. It might not be logical to us. We're dealing with a fruitcake. It probably makes perfect sense to her. Seriously, her view of the world is through a lens. If she doesn't like what she sees, she changes it.'

'Isn't that what we all do?'

'To a lesser extent, yes, but most of us aren't permitting some scumbag to get away with murder or conspiring with one. I appreciate that my observation doesn't take us anywhere, but I wouldn't be surprised if she was an art graduate or professional photographer with a sideline in snuff movie-making.'

'You think this is sexual?'

'I have no clue what it is yet. It's odd that they should choose a different setting altogether – and a lot more risky.'

'You think she's getting more confident?'

'I don't know. There's a slight tremor in her voice on this one. That could be because her target didn't come to her – she went to them. She walks up, knocks at the door. Bang. The victim is a goner.' Ryan angled his head one way and then the other, trying to ease the tension in his neck. Ford wanted answers – in relation to one victim in particular – more than that, he wanted them yesterday. That was unrealistic. There would be no quick fix here. Whoever was taunting them was on a mission and they weren't about to stop.

7

O'Neil disappeared into her bedroom. Seconds later, Ryan heard her muffled voice through the door. She was talking to someone on the landline. He wondered why the secrecy, what had brought about her sudden change of mood. They had agreed to share all intelligence and yet there were obviously things he wasn't party to, unless of course it was personal, in which case, why didn't she say so?

Along with her specs, her mobile was still lying on his desk. His eyes seized on it, his brain toying with the notion of checking the ID of the person who'd interrupted their conversation.

He glanced at the device again.

He couldn't do it.

Well, maybe a peek.

Keeping an eye on the door, he snatched it up. Accessing the calls list, he scrutinized the name at the top. *Hilary.* The display indicated that she'd rung from home.

Ryan felt terribly guilty.

Maybe O'Neil had got closer to Jack's widow than he was aware of. Perhaps taken over from him as the go-to person for advice and friendship. Who could blame her? Ryan had been crap as Jack's protector. The two women probably shared the same interests. That was a good thing. Something he should be grateful for. Still, O'Neil appeared on edge in the short time she was on the phone.

Why had she asked him how Hilary was if they were in touch?

Puzzling over it, he was about to put the mobile down when it rang in his hand. The caller was the controller who'd sent her the text when they were at the crime scene. In O'Neil's absence, Ryan took the call, a good way to explain, should he ever need to, why his paw prints were all over it.

'Stan, my guv'nor is tied up on the other line. Can I help?'

'You need to take this.' He kept it brief. 'It's her. I'm tracing the call.'

Ryan was already reaching for his digital recorder. Acting quickly, he switched it on and put the phone on speaker. The line clicked before the call went live. 'O'Neil's phone.'

'Who the hell are you?' The male voice took her completely by surprise. She'd specifically asked for O'Neil, the Senior Investigating Officer, the one in charge. It angered her to think that she wasn't being taken seriously. If only he knew that's what all this was about.

Why didn't they listen?

'More to the point,' Ryan said. 'Who are you?'

'Never mind that,' she said. 'I want to talk to O'Neil.'

'Tough,' he said. 'She has staff to take messages. That'll be me. Shall we start over? I'd hate to get off on the wrong foot. My name is DS Matthew Ryan, Ryan to my friends. I'm one of the good guys. Somehow I don't think we'd get along. Now it's your turn to be nice and share.'

*

Having heard her voice on four separate DVDs, Ryan would have known it anywhere. It had been in his head constantly, like a favourite music CD on repeat play, except her song wasn't one he fancied listening to. It was hard to place her age. Possibly mid thirties. She was educated though. He was sure of it.

'I don't think you heard me,' she said.

Ryan forced a laugh. 'You don't get to call the shots here, pet.'

'Listen, arsehole! I'm nobody's pet, least of all yours. O'Neil is obviously your boss. She's the one I speak to. Now put her on.'

'Not possible—'

'Why's that?'

'You've been demoted. She has more important cases. And here's the thing: we're not interested in crime scenes without bodies. My guv'nor and I like our scenes meaty – literally and figuratively speaking – cases we can get our teeth into. So why don't you tell me where we can find the other victims and we'll call it quits.'

This Ryan character cracked her up. She was torn. Either he was thick or he had guts. He reminded her of her father – of *her* – a person with strong opinions and no fear in voicing them.

'I'll do better than that,' she said.

'Go for it.'

A beat of time as she left him dangling. She was in control and well he knew it. She sensed the dipstick holding his breath, wondering if she'd abandon the call or stay on the line. Her stopwatch was registering less than three minutes. Perfect timing. 'I believe you need some sea air, Matthew: 21 High Spencer Street, Whitley Bay.'

The dialling tone seemed to draw a menacing line under the address. O'Neil emerged from her room just as Ryan was writing it down.

'Who was that?'

'That, guv, was our new best friend.'

'Did you get it on tape?'

Ryan held up his recorder, a big grin on his face.

'Great!' Flexing the fingers of her right hand, O'Neil gestured that he should hand it over. She took the device from him and turned away, listening carefully to the conversation.

Without sight of her face, Ryan sensed her fury.

She turned slowly, face set in a scowl, eyes wide.

She threw the recorder on his desk.

'Delete it!' she said.

'What?'

'You heard me.'

Ryan wavered, confused by her strop. 'It's evidence, guv.'

She waited for him to do it. 'Don't you look at me like I'm the one in the wrong here, Ryan. That "evidence" will end up in a courtroom one day. You might have talked to suspects like that in Special Branch. You *never* do it under my command. Is that clear?'

'If you say so.'

'I do, because it was entirely inappropriate. We need to maintain a professional approach. Anything offered in evidence needs to reflect that. We don't want you sounding like some gobshite on the phone. It's not cool. And don't you dare touch my phone again, *EVER!*'

Ryan held up his hands as if she were holding a gun. 'Guv, you weren't here.'

'I was in the next room—'

'On the phone to someone else!'

'You could've knocked. I'd have hung up.'

'I'll ask her to wait next time, shall I?'

O'Neil glared at him then walked away.

'Guv, I'm sorry!'

She rounded on him. 'Too bloody late!'

'So now I've had my hands slapped maybe you could tell me how you'd have handled it?'

'I'd have tried to engage with her, not put her back up—'

'Yeah, like that was going to get us anywhere—'

'It gets her talking to us! I have expertise as a hostage negotiator, Ryan. I'd have used those skills. She doesn't have a hostage – at least we hope not – but information is her hostage. She's holding the biggest hand. I would've talked to her in a way that would gain her trust. As long as we have dialogue, we have *something*.'

'Fine!'

'No, not fine! If Professional Standards got hold of that tape you'd be on a hiding to nothing. I know how their minds work, Ryan. They'd see it as entirely unacceptable – *and it was*. If you can't see that then perhaps we shouldn't be working together. Think on it. This conversation is over.'

8

Whitley Bay was around ten miles east of the city centre. Another coastal location. It took less than twenty minutes to reach their destination, a local authority flat in dire need of a paint job and a crew to fix the garden. At O'Neil's insistence, they were both wearing body armour. With a violent offender and possible accomplice on the rampage, she was taking no chances.

They could be walking into a trap.

She was quiet in the car, still pissed with him for mouthing off. Ryan wanted to apologize; tell her that, of course, he understood that he was out of line, that his judgement was under par, that he should have handled the call differently. Except, deep down, he didn't believe it. He was damned if he'd give Spielberg the power she craved. He decided to wait. He'd have to pick his moment to explain his actions. Now was not the time to wind her up.

O'Neil cut the ignition and was out of their new wheels before Ryan had undone his seat belt. She moved towards the front door like an athlete, her Kevlar vest making her hips appear even more petite than they were in reality. She inspected the front door. It was locked. No sign of a forced entry. Her nod was a sign that he should check the rear of the premises. He did a quick recce, investigating alternative access points, and returned shaking his head.

Wary of going in gung-ho, O'Neil took a moment to consider her options. She didn't ask his opinion and he didn't offer one. Having been put in his box, Ryan intended staying there until it was safe to come out – the sooner the better as far as he was concerned. They had argued before and it always left a bad taste in his mouth.

She banged on the front door.

No answer.

She hit it again.

No response.

She glanced in Ryan's direction. 'If I thought there was a body inside, a life to save, I'd have no hesitation.'

'We won't know until we get in there,' he said.

'True.' Another glance at the door. 'Kick it in.'

Ryan carried out her instructions with ease and went in first. 'Police! Is there anyone here? Hello? Anyone home?'

Silence.

Avoiding bloody footprints in the hallway, Ryan ventured further in, senses on alert. He checked out two rooms on either side of the hall and gave O'Neil the all clear on both. The interior of the flat was in much better condition than what they had seen on the way in. The place was tidy, a high level of cleanliness. If he were to hazard a guess, Ryan would've said it belonged to a woman. He was proved wrong when he opened a closet in the hallway and found what appeared to be a young man's clothing.

If not young, then someone very much down with the kids.

Halfway along the hallway O'Neil's mobile rang. She silenced it quickly, beckoning Ryan to retreat to the open front door while she took the call. 'Go ahead, Control.'

Her voice was almost a whisper.

'The property is registered to James Fraser,' the controller said. 'On the electoral roll at the same address for five years, give or take. Thirty-seven years old. No form. He holds a current shotgun certificate as well as a firearms licence. He's a member of the shooting club at Roker. Also listed on organ and blood donor registers. Occupation: nurse. That's it for now.'

'Find out where he works and if he's been in lately,' she said quietly. 'Silent response if you get any more intelligence, understood?'

'Yes, ma'am . . . you need backup?'

'No, I'm double-crewed. We'll handle it.'

She hung up and turned to Ryan, keeping her voice low. 'That puts a different spin on things. James Fraser, the guy who owns the flat, is into guns. We should wait for a firearms team.'

'I didn't hear you ask for one.'

'That's very observant of you.'

Ryan allowed himself a half-smile even though his guts were churning. O'Neil was a hands-on investigator. He could see she was in two minds: worried for their safety but wanting to burst through the door at the end of the hallway and save a life – if it wasn't already too late.

'Unarmed, you're an obvious target,' she said.

'Don't you mean *we*?' He swallowed hard, eyes fixed on the bedroom door. It seemed to move towards him the more he stared at it. A picture of his father, fatally wounded, flashed through his mind, dissolving as his focus shifted to the floor. 'Those footprints are heading out, not in, guv.'

'She's devious. This has to be your call.'

'Understood.' He was about to set off.

She blocked his way. 'Kevlar can only go so far, Ryan. If they aim for the head, you know the rest. If someone starts firing, get the hell out of there.' He tried to move. She had hold of his arm with a grip he'd have been proud of. Their eyes met briefly, a potent message passing from one to the other: stay safe. 'You saved my life. Don't you dare do anything reckless, I need you on my team.'

'I need me on your team too, guv. Does this mean I'm back in your good books?'

'Of course, you idiot, now concentrate.'

Ryan checked his arm. White fingernails were digging into his skin, so strong was O'Neil's desire to hold on to him. Finally, she loosened them and let go. He left her then, approaching the bedroom, heart pumping harder with every step, her warning echoing in his head. It was prudent to remind him that his flak jacket offered only so much protection. It would lessen the impact of a strike to the chest, not stop a headshot.

He felt guilty thinking it, but death was a price too high to pay, even for Queen and country. When his father died on a routine drugs bust, murdered by a knife-wielding heroin dealer, his mother's life was effectively over. Ryan was pleased he had no wife. No kids. Adrenalin streamed through his veins, his body's automatic response to danger.

He listened at the door.

Nothing.

'Mr Fraser? Police! We're concerned for your welfare. Coming in.'

Ryan put his foot through the door, ducking as it smashed

against the bedroom wall. Fortunately, he met neither threat nor attack. The similarity to the North Shields crime scene ended there. This time, what they had viewed onscreen wasn't the same as what they got in reality.

A male lay on the floor, green eyes permanently fixed to the ceiling. Gunshot wounds Ryan could cope with. Stabbings were his Achilles' heel. In his head, the victim suddenly morphed into his father, three deep puncture wounds to his chest, no chance of survival at the hands of a madman. Twenty-five years after the event, Ryan could almost hear a flick-knife leave its casing, plunged into his own flesh and blood with fatal consequences.

As the image continued to scroll through his head, he turned away before O'Neil noticed his reaction. Taking a pen from his pocket, he lifted the lanyard off the chair's backrest. He held it up, the better to see the organization it belonged to: Northumbria Healthcare NHS Foundation Trust.

He checked the image against the dead man.

'Hospital ID, guv. Meet James Fraser. Emergency Care Matron. Doesn't say which hospital.'

'He's the tenant,' O'Neil said.

Ryan crouched down beside the body, sickened by the death of this relatively young man. 'He put up quite a fight. There are defence wounds to the fingers and palms of both hands.'

He stood up.

O'Neil was more alive than Ryan had ever seen her. On autopilot, she put on gloves, retraced her steps, dropped the latch on the front door and got on the phone to Forensics while he went off to search the flat. Within a minute or two, he found what he was looking for: a 2mm steel cabinet fixed to the wall inside a large cupboard in the spare bedroom. Suitable for both shotguns and firearms, it was undamaged and open.

No weapons inside . . .

Ammunition either.

O'Neil wandered in, pocketing her mobile phone. 'Find anything?'

'And some.' He pointed at the cabinet. 'This is the biz, guv. Police approved and jemmy-proof, same as mine at home.'

'And mine.'

'You're firearms trained?'

Her eyes were blank. 'Don't sound so surprised.'

'How come I've never seen you on the firing range?'

'You're looking at a champion.' The statement was a deflection.

Ryan let it go. 'Why does that make me feel all warm and fuzzy?'

O'Neil laughed, the tension melting away, their angry exchange forgotten.

9

Ryan woke wondering what possible link there might be between a high-ranking Scottish judge and a Geordie nurse. Despite a long and taxing day yesterday, he slept badly, only falling into a deep sleep an hour before his alarm went off at six. It was odd, crashing at their office, sharing living quarters with a woman where the only agenda could ever be a professional one.

In the shower, his mind switched once again to the investigation, specifically the crime scenes. Spielberg had suddenly changed tack: using three derelict premises, removing the body; then a residential address, leaving the victim in situ, complete with ID?

Mind games.

O'Neil was up and at it. Cradling a cup of coffee, she scrutinized a map, stills of a crime scene they had yet to visit and other documentation lying on her desk. Leaning against the door jamb, Ryan watched her for a while, her face set in concentration.

He could tell there had been a development.

'Morning, Ryan.' She spoke without lifting her head, eyes pinned to a map. 'James Fraser works – or should I say worked – at Rake Lane Hospital. Beyond that, it's the usual story: highly regarded, brilliant member of staff, lovely lad, no enemies. No one I talked to has seen or heard of him since he left his department at the end of his last shift.'

'Which was?' Ryan crossed the threshold, closing his bedroom door quietly behind him.

'Sunday. He finished work at 6 a.m.' Saddened by the next task on their agenda, O'Neil checked her watch. 'We'll give his mother a bit more sleep, then she's our number one priority.'

Ryan nodded soberly. 'And then?'

'A lengthy drive, a long day ahead of us.' She tapped the map. 'What do you reckon: A1 or A68?'

'To Kenmore?'

'The post-mortem, the crime scene, the whole shebang.'

Ryan took his iPhone from his pocket, accessed his contacts, specifically the Kenmore Hotel where he'd stayed several years ago. Tapping the address placed a pin on a map and offered an ETA and alternative routes. 'It's six and two threes. Three hours fifty-eight minutes on the A1, four hours five on the A68.'

'You have a preference?'

'We'll get a whiff and a glimpse of the sea from the A1.' Ryan was happiest by water, as she seemed to be when they'd worked their last case. They had more than policing in common.

'That's the decision made then.' O'Neil pointed over his shoulder to the kitchen beyond. 'Coffee should still be warm.'

'Thanks. You want more?'

'Thought you'd never ask.' She held up her empty cup.

Ryan took it to the kitchen bench, poured a refill for her and one for him. Seconds later he returned, keen to know more about their drive north and what she had in mind to do when they got there. He dragged his chair closer to hers and sat down. Trying his level best to ignore the effect her perfume was having on his senses, he asked if the documentation for all four incidents was already on HOLMES.

'Yup, all here on the system. I want to do this right, Ryan. *We* are the lead team on this investigation now. So it's ears open and mouths shut when talking to detectives who've been involved thus far. If that changes down the line, I'll let you know.'

'We might miss local knowledge that way.'

'It's a chance I'm prepared to take. Many a case has failed on misinformation. We're not investigating colleagues here. Working in complaints has taught me that if you show your hand, they'll be queuing up to put their own spin on things. You know the score. Coppers can't stop themselves. Even the crap ones like to think they're Columbo. If you listen to their theories, it'll influence your thinking. What I need from you is a fresh pair of eyes. That way we start with a blank canvas, no preconceived ideas. We make our own minds up whether to accept or reject information that comes our way.'

'Sounds like a plan.'

'Good. Any questions?'

'Yeah, what did Price have to say last night?' The call had come in from the Chief Constable as they were about to retire. She'd waved him off to bed and he was curious to know if she had any update on Kenmore.

'Not much. There was enough blood at the scene to suggest a severed artery. I expect we'll have that confirmed this afternoon. First responders found the scene disturbed: paw prints in the blood, trace evidence of dog hair investigators matched with that found at the judge's home. The dog was found weeks later, spotted by a tenant on a neighbouring estate. The animal was hungry, a nervous wreck, but otherwise healthy. It's with Mrs Forbes until the family decide what to do with it.'

Ryan was relieved to hear it. 'They got nothing from house-to-house?'

O'Neil shook her head. 'The investigating team also spoke to anyone and everyone who happened upon the scene when it was being examined. It generated a lot of enquiries that took them nowhere. As you pointed out yesterday, Kenmore is a popular area at any time of year. Asking locals if they'd seen strangers hanging about was hopeless. Detectives working the case did everything they possibly could to find Trevathan. They combed the area, checked hospitals in a fifty-mile radius, dragged the river and sent divers down with zero results. His body found its way to the surface all by itself.'

'That's not a lot to show for two months' work,' Ryan said.

'Yeah, well, Police Scotland were in the driving seat then,' O'Neil said. 'Now it's our turn.'

10

Having broken a woman's heart, Ryan and O'Neil were on the road before nine. They didn't discuss Mrs Fraser's reaction to the death of her son: the frail body wracked with sobs, the sheer disbelief that she'd seen him for the last time beyond a clinical viewing room at the morgue. Shattered didn't come close to describing it. The woman was utterly devastated, her life in ruins, the damage irreparable.

Most coppers knew what it felt like to knock on the door and deliver a death message. Few knew what went on when the door closed again. Ryan did. He caught Mrs Fraser before she hit the deck, sat with her until the Family Liaison Officer arrived, tried to comfort her. Like all families bereaved by homicide, the woman was inconsolable. He couldn't tell her that he'd been there too. What possible good would it have done?

Losing a loved one to murder united no one.

Sensitive to his personal situation, O'Neil had offered to tell Mrs Fraser herself. He argued but she insisted, and when it was done they skirted a subject too painful for both of them. That didn't mean that fallen colleagues – Jack Fenwick and Ryan's father – weren't uppermost in their minds.

Avoidance strategies weren't always negative.

O'Neil had her foot to the floor, hell-bent on distancing

herself from the trauma of the past hour in the shortest time possible. As they left the city behind, her mobile rang, the call buying Ryan time to process what had gone on in the house.

'O'Neil.'

'Police Scotland, ma'am – DC Turner. My guv'nor asked me to call and let you know that Maxwell's Temple is bolted, secured and closed to visitors. The key is with police in Aberfeldy – the station that covers Perth and Kinross Highland.'

'Address?'

'Twenty-seven Kenmore Street, ma'am. PH15 2BL.'

'Hold on.' O'Neil repeated the address for Ryan's benefit. 'Can you let them know to expect me?'

'Will do, ma'am.'

'Appreciate it.' O'Neil gave an ETA and hung up.

She glanced at Ryan.

He punched the postcode into the satnav and saved it as a destination, keeping them on track for the morgue. 'I hope the scene provides some answers.'

'I can't see it, given the time lapse. There's no real urgency, but I'd like to get there before dark or we'll be kicking our heels until morning. Let's hope the post-mortem is quick.'

'Now we have Trevathan's body, do we get to find out what case he was about to try?'

'In a word, no.'

'Why not?'

'Delicate material. Price referred me on and I can't seem to get through to the Lord President—'

'He must have a clerk—'

'I meant emotionally, not physically. Transparency is crucial to our investigation but not if it undermines a case of greater magnitude. It's their default position, Ryan. You know how this works. As ridiculous as it sounds, they're not sharing. I tried telling them we're not the enemy. It made no difference. Don't concern yourself. I'm not about to let their lack of openness defeat us.'

They lapsed into funereal silence, caught up in thoughts of terrorism and a well-established tradition of secrecy from above. Working for Special Branch, Ryan was used to the Home Office putting the shutters up, remaining tight-lipped on matters to do with national security. This governmental conspiracy to keep them in the dark was ludicrous and un-necessary when they were on the same side.

Although he loved working with O'Neil, he wished his retired ex-colleague Grace Ellis was along for the ride. He'd like her take on the case; Newman's too, for that matter. Frank Newman was her husband, formerly MI5. If anyone could find out what the judge's trial was about, it would be him. They would both be green with envy if they knew what Ryan was working on.

O'Neil's hand covered a wide yawn. As she changed pedals to apply the brake she appeared to wince a little. Ryan sus-pected that her leg was playing her up. She'd been caught up in an explosion at the end of their last case and been lucky to get away with nothing worse than a broken ankle.

'You want me to drive?' he offered.

'Please. I'll pull over.'

'You missing Svendsen?'

She roared with laughter.

Their last outing had taken them to Norway, where they'd been chauffeured around by a detective called Knut Svendsen.

He'd taken a shine to O'Neil, acting like a lovesick teenager whenever he was around her. Ryan had ribbed him mercilessly over it. Svendsen wasn't put off – quite the opposite – the more Ryan made fun of him, the more O'Neil refused to play ball, the better he liked it. After the morning they'd put in, it was great to see her laugh.

'Do you ever hear from him?'

She glanced sideways. 'No! Why would I? I'm not in the habit of giving out my number to strange men.'

'Lack of information has never stopped any detective I've ever known . . . except maybe Maguire. That waste of space couldn't find a hooker in a brothel.' He was referring to her former bagman. 'Not that I should, y'know, mention you in the same sentence as a hooker.'

O'Neil chuckled. 'Stop digging that hole, Ryan. Now I've got you, Maguire doesn't seem so bad.'

Ryan put a hand over his heart. 'I'm crushed, guv.' And he was.

11

A couple of miles past Berwick-upon-Tweed, O'Neil indicated left and pulled into a lay-by. They got out to stretch their legs, the North Sea shimmering in the distance, the sun drawing a sparkly line across the surface. Ryan leaned against the car, feet and arms crossed, staring out to sea. Living within sight of water along the north Northumberland coast, he did his best thinking by the shoreline.

O'Neil turned to face him. 'I can see your mind working overtime,' she said. 'What's up?'

'I was wondering about victim association.'

'Between Trevathan and Fraser?'

'If there *is* any, it's passed me by. You?'

'Same. We'd better hope there is. If these are random killings, we're in trouble.'

'There are no obvious connections I can see—'

'Yeah, well I'm a firm believer in three degrees of separation, Ryan. You never know what we'll turn up when we cross-reference their backgrounds. Or, better still, when we find another victim.' With that depressing state of affairs occupying their thoughts, they got in the car and drove on.

As they crossed the Forth Road Bridge, Ryan glanced at his watch. 'Mind if I check in with Caroline? She has a big case on today: Teesside-based drugs ring – some heavy players too, not some Mickey Mouse firm. They're international and sophisticated, ten of them in the dock.'

O'Neil was impressed. 'Sounds like they're going down.'

'If my twin has anything to do with it, they definitely are. Open and shut,' she said. Caught in possession of cocaine and amphetamine with a street value of three million. Drugs squad have been carrying out surveillance for the best part of a year. Impossible to assess the true value of the drugs sold. At a rough estimate, they're responsible for smuggling in the region of thirty-eight million pounds' worth into the UK over the past few years.'

'You must be so proud of her.'

'To be perfectly honest, I wasn't keen on her going into criminal law – any more than she wanted me to join the police.'

'Why? Nothing seems to faze her.'

Ryan shrugged. 'Over-protective, I guess.'

'She's making a real name for herself with the CPS. You should be celebrating.'

'I am.' Ryan checked his watch, keen to make that call. 'I wasn't early enough to wish her luck this morning. The court will have adjourned for lunch now. Do you mind?'

'Not at all. It's sweet of you to consider her.'

'She wants me to drop the daily calls. Keeps telling me she's a grown-up.' Ryan pressed 1 on speed-dial: his twin's personal number went straight to voicemail.

'Hi, it's Caroline. Leave a message. I'll call you back.'

Exasperated, Ryan glanced at O'Neil. 'I'll try her work number.'

'She'll be fine, Ryan. It's natural for you to feel responsible for her.'

'Even though she'd rather I didn't?'

'Even then.'

Caroline had been the centre of Ryan's universe since they were kids, even more so since their mother's death. He'd called her daily when he could steal away from work, if only for a brief conversation. If he didn't care for her, who would?

'Does it scare you, her working a case like that?' O'Neil asked.

'Not today.' Nerves tugged at Ryan's gut when his sister failed to pick up. 'She's surrounded by a firearms team. They're taking no chances.'

Ryan didn't tell O'Neil that he'd almost declined his new job because it would take him away from home, removing a level of support for his twin, or that Caroline had insisted that he grab the opportunity and run with it. O'Neil admired his sister. She was impressed by her ability to study, to work, to have a normal life in spite of her blindness, if a little fearful that her disability left her exposed and vulnerable. Although he'd never voice it publicly, Ryan shared that concern.

If she were under attack, she'd never see it coming.

The ringing tone terminated, a chirpy message kicking in. 'You've reached the voicemail of Caroline Ryan. Sorry, I can't get to the phone right now. If you leave a number I'll call you.'

A beep signalled the arrival of an incoming call.

Ryan delivered his message in an upbeat tone to mask his anxiety. Caroline wanted him to concentrate on his job, not hers. 'Hi, it's me checking in. I have a call waiting. Hope it's going well. Ring you later.' He rang off, accepting the other call. By bizarre coincidence, it was Grace Ellis who came on the line. He was immediately suspicious. And so, it seemed, was O'Neil.

'Grace! I was just thinking about you. How's married life?'

'Oh y'know, we're aiming for a year minimum,' she said. 'Two if we're *really* lucky. Thought I'd ring and see what my protégé is up to.'

What had she heard?

'Oh, y'know,' Ryan mimicked her. 'Moseying along as usual.'

'You back with Roz yet?'

'No, I'm done with Roz, as well you know.' Ryan felt his cheeks warm up. With the phone on speaker, O'Neil was all ears. That said, his past love life was no one's business but his own. He tried to laugh it off before Grace got going. 'Actually, I'm done with women. Period. I'm now a confirmed bachelor, destined to live alone – unless you decide to give Newman the elbow, then I'm all yours.'

O'Neil was smiling.

'I should be so lucky,' Grace said. 'How's O'Neil?'

Ryan's heart nearly stopped. 'Why d'you ask?'

'Shootin' the breeze is all.'

The Americanism jarred with Ryan. Then he remembered where she'd been. 'Are you still Stateside?'

'Got back last week.'

'How was it?'

'The best, I *love* New York Siddy.'

'That is the most pathetic US accent I ever heard.'

She giggled. 'My talents lie elsewhere. Where are *you*?'

'Heading north.'

'Over the border? Got time to pop in?'

'Not this trip – much as I'd love to. Soon though, I promise.'

'So how *is* O'Neil?'

Ryan could feel his boss's interest in the conversation growing. 'As it happens, she's sitting next to me.' That was code for Grace to get off the line.

She didn't. 'How come?'

'We're working on something.'

'In Professional Standards?' she huffed. 'Have you lost your mind?'

'I've moved on,' O'Neil interrupted.

'Still listening at keyholes, eh?'

'Always.' O'Neil played it cool. 'Especially yours, Grace. Retirement doesn't mean you're immune from a knock on the door from my old team. It can happen day or night, without warning, when you're least expecting it. You be sure to watch your back, won't you?'

'I can sleep nights,' Grace said. 'Shame the same can't be—'

'How's Newman?' Ryan cut her off before she said something they might both regret. He still had a mind to use her, to use them both, just as soon as he had a chance to discuss staffing with O'Neil. It was obvious to him that this case required more than a core team of two.

'Frank is fine,' Grace said. 'We've been sailing and your name came up – both your names, as a matter of fact. You should join us, next trip. We're always looking for crew so we can sit back and enjoy the retirement view. Heading home now to put our feet up. You two keep up the good work. Your contribution to our pension pot is very much appreciated.' She cut the line, sending Ryan and O'Neil into fits of laughter. Grace Ellis was like a breath of sea air.

12

In view of the likelihood of criminal proceedings, the Procura-
tor Fiscal had been notified of Lord Trevathan's death the
minute his body was found floating in the Tay. He'd authorized
the immediate attendance of a forensic pathologist. The corpse
had since been transported to a morgue in Perth. Not far short
of their destination, O'Neil instructed him to ignore the satnav
and stay on the M90/A9. Cancelling his indicator, he pulled
out to overtake the car in front, the occupants of which were
having a heated domestic.

'That guy has a serious case of road rage,' she said. 'He's
going to kill them both.'

'Guv?' Ryan pointed at the slip road.

'No,' she said.

The A93 intersection sailed by.

'Where are we going?' Ryan asked.

'We're bypassing the morgue. I know Trevathan's home is
forty miles further on, but I'm more interested in his missing briefcase than watching him suffer the final indignity of
being dissected and gawped at by all and sundry after his
death. Pathologists will be in possession of forensics. They'll
have been made aware that they're dealing with a murder case
before they even open him up. We'll get their deliberations
soon enough.'

'You sure? Given Trevathan's status, I hardly think they'll hang around.'

'Even so, it'll take hours to process him. We'll be there and back before they're done.'

Ryan was also dying to get his hands on that briefcase. Dropping a gear, he took a bend at speed, accelerating out of it. O'Neil went quiet all of a sudden, seemingly no longer in a mood to talk. When he glanced at her, her whole body seemed to shudder involuntarily.

'You OK, guv?'

'I hate post-mortems at the best of times – more so when a victim has been immersed in water for months. There's nothing quite like the putrid stench of decomposing flesh to put you off your lunch. Let's stop and eat before our noses get a whiff, eh? I'm starving.'

'Yeah, let's,' Ryan said. 'No point spoiling a whole day.'

She glanced at him and then looked away, concentrating on the twisty road, the fields of green flashing by as they sped towards their destination. The drama of the landscape increased the further north they got. 'I'm sorry to be such a wimp. I bet this never happened when you were working with Jack.'

'Don't be daft. We're all affected by that stuff.'

Ryan wasn't keen on medical examinations either, but they came with the territory, the police force demanding more than officers were capable of sometimes. The last twenty-four hours had been particularly taxing: listening to Spielberg's chilling narration; attending that bloody lock-up; witnessing the puncture wounds on James Fraser's body; telling his mother that he'd been murdered by persons unknown without being able to offer an explanation as to why. A normal day at the office, but Ryan was beginning to feel punchy.

'I should've thanked you,' he said.

O'Neil glanced at him. 'For what?'

'Delivering the bad news to Mrs Fraser.'

'Now *you're* being daft. It was the least I could do. I know . . .' She paused, trying to find the words. 'I just know.'

Ryan was kicking himself. His reaction in Fraser's bedroom hadn't passed her by. He felt guilty now. It was rare that he let his guard down. But there were times when emotion took over, occasions when his professional and personal lives clashed in the worst way possible, when he was powerless to prevent a collision, even when he saw it coming.

'Don't worry about it,' O'Neil said. 'You have personal reasons to be affected by that stuff, Ryan. You need—'

'I *need* to get a grip, is what I need. I can't afford to show my bleeding heart every time I face a stabbing.' He was about to thank her, to tell her he'd get over it and that it wouldn't happen again, when she beat him to the draw.

'If I doubted your ability you wouldn't be on my team.' She saw his reservation. 'Ryan, you're not Superman. For crying out loud, give yourself a break.'

He dropped the subject.

Feeling his angst slipping away, he drove on without further comment, ignoring several opportunities to pull over. She didn't point out possible places to eat and neither did he. He'd lost his appetite. Trevathan's briefcase had taken precedence over everything else.

13

Lord Trevathan's home was approached by a private driveway, protected by a gate lodge and lined by magnificent Douglas firs. This was prime Scottish real estate – fifty acres of privacy bordering the banks of Loch Tay – an enchanting mansion house hidden away in a tranquil clearing, forested hills providing a dramatic backdrop.

Dating from the sixteenth century, it was a property steeped in history, owned by one family for generations. Such was the wow factor, O'Neil asked Ryan to stop the car halfway along the gravelled driveway so she could jump out to drink in the view. He remained in the vehicle, staring through the windscreen at the red sandstone house, exquisitely proportioned with mullioned windows and a rounded tower at either end. It was nice to see a piece of Scottish heritage still in private hands.

'Enchanting.' O'Neil pocketed her phone as she climbed in, not bothering to strap herself in on the private road. 'You like?'

'If it was on a beach, it would be perfect.' Ryan glanced at the mansion again. 'I'd rather have the remains of Dunstanburgh Castle.' He could see that historical monument from the tiny front garden of his coastal home. It sat on a remote Northumberland headland with an unparalleled view over the North Sea. Derelict or not, that was one property he wouldn't mind owning. The image faded from his mind, the mansion in full focus now. 'I wonder what will happen to this place. Trevathan is unmarried. There are no children to inherit his wealth.'

'He's a lawyer, Ryan. I'm sure he'll have made a will.'

'Yeah, but in whose favour?'

'That's an action waiting for attention right there. I'm pleased I'm not responsible for the death duty.'

'Maybe we should be looking at the taxman.' Ryan started the car and pulled away, heading for the house.

It was a relief to stretch their legs after four hours in the car. The air was cold and crisp, the sky clear and blue. Ryan would much rather have taken O'Neil for a walk down to the Loch or a wander through the woods, but he could feel her haste as she mounted the steps to the impressive front door, hobbling ever so slightly. She was keen to get inside and find that briefcase.

Catching up with her, he pressed the bell and heard it ring inside the house. Almost before he'd taken his hand away, Mrs Forbes, Trevathan's petite and smartly dressed housekeeper, opened the door. Her eyelids were red, her face haggard and lined beyond her forty-nine years.

'Mrs Forbes?' Ryan offered up ID. 'We spoke on the phone earlier. I'm DS Matthew Ryan.' He gestured towards his guv'nor. 'This is Detective Superintendent O'Neil. May we come in?'

The housekeeper ushered them inside as if they were under surveillance.

The entrance hall was extraordinary, with centuries-old stone flags on the floor, chocolate-coloured wood panelling adorning the walls, designed to impress visitors. At the same time, it was exceptionally warm and welcoming. At the top of an imposing staircase, life-sized portraits of three judges in ceremonial dress were displayed proudly, testament to the judge's formidable ancestry and legal credentials.

Pointing out which one was her former employer, Mrs Forbes lapsed into uncontrollable weeping.

Excusing herself, she turned and fled the hallway.

Almost immediately, a tall, sturdy man with a stony face arrived in her place. He introduced himself as Trevathan's gillie, explaining that he was also Mr Forbes. Apologizing for his wife's hysterics, he pointed through an open door, inviting them to wait in his master's study, then disappeared, presumably to comfort or chastise his wife, whose weeping echoed from the passage beyond.

O'Neil rolled her eyes at Ryan, eager to get on.

Two French doors overlooked the garden. O'Neil walked towards them, taking in herbaceous borders and the loch shimmering in the distance, hardly a ripple on the surface of the water. As she turned to face him, Ryan could see she was in awe of the place.

Her eyes settled on something over his shoulder. She pointed at the wall behind him. Ryan swung round to find a second painting of Trevathan hanging over a striking fireplace, this one much less formal. The judge was staring at them, a steely gaze under a green flat cap. Dressed in a tweed shooting jacket, breeks, woollen socks and sturdy black shoes, he was standing beside flowing water, a shotgun cocked over one arm, a gundog by his side.

'I wonder if that's the same dog he had with him when he died,' O'Neil said.

'It's a fine dog.'

'Looks like he's smiling.'

'They all do.'

Ryan knew dogs, Labrador Retrievers in particular. Caroline had owned a succession of guide dogs since she was a kid, each one remembered fondly and preserved in photographs she would never see. Ryan was eager to catch up with her. He hoped her case was going well.

A knock drew his attention.

The door swung open and Mrs Forbes entered, apologizing for her lack of self-control. Ryan invited her to sit. She perched awkwardly on the edge of an antique armchair as if she'd never sat down in the study in all the years she was in the judge's employ. The superintendent took a seat opposite, her DS standing directly behind her.

'Mrs Forbes, it's our understanding that Lord Trevathan left Cornwall early to collect a briefcase for an important trial,' O'Neil began.

'So I understand. I was on holiday.'

'We believe it may contain vital information that will aid the investigation into his death. Do you still have possession of it?'

A flash of panic crossed the housekeeper's face. The detectives had their answer before the woman opened her mouth.

O'Neil pushed her: 'Mrs Forbes?'

'No.' Her voice was croaky, hardly audible, as if her ability to speak was shutting down. 'It was collected,' was all she managed to say.

'By whom?'

'Someone from his chambers.'

'Someone?' O'Neil wanted specifics.

'They didn't give a name.'

'There was more than one person?'

'Two. One male, one female.'

'When was this?' Ryan asked.

'Shortly after His Lordship was reported missing. The day after his trial was supposed to start in Edinburgh.'

'I see.' O'Neil took over. 'Did they call ahead, or arrive unannounced?'

'The latter.' Mrs Forbes' eyebrows pinched together. 'I had an important appointment in Aberfeldy. I was leaving via the gate lodge when they drove in and asked me to hand the briefcase over as a matter of urgency. I asked them to come back later. They were very insistent.'

Ryan could see it happening. They wait outside until someone drives up and make their move as the gates open. No wonder Mrs Forbes was so nervous when he and O'Neil arrived.

'And you did what?' he asked.

Mrs Forbes looked up. 'I followed them to the house.'

'You let them in and handed it over, just like that?'

The housekeeper was nodding, her eyes misting over. 'I was running late.'

Ryan tried not to look stunned. 'I assume that with such important documents you asked to see some form of identification?'

Clearly not . . .

'Mrs Forbes, would you like me to call your husband?' O'Neil's soft voice masked her irritation. She was trying to put the woman at ease, despite the urge to shake the living daylights out of her for not checking the ID of those collecting the briefcase. 'I'm happy for him to join us if you'd like him here—'

'No! Please don't.' The woman wiped away her tears, an

expression of regret on her face. Fear even. Relations in the Forbes household were obviously strained.

Ryan drew up a chair and sat down. 'Would it be correct to say that you and Mr Forbes have had words over this?'

Nodding vigorously, Mrs Forbes tucked her tissue up her sleeve and then pulled it out again, twisting it around the forefinger of her left hand. 'After the police told my husband why the judge had returned to Scotland, Stuart went to look for the briefcase.'

'But you'd already handed it over?'

'Yes.' The housekeeper was stalling, her distress over Trevathan's demise morphing into guilt. She drew in a deep breath and let it out again before elaborating on her one-word reply. 'I told the polis that the Lord President had ordered the case notes to be returned to court, that he was going to pass them on to another judge.'

'That wasn't true?'

'Not strictly.' Mrs Forbes was growing more and more agitated. Her master was no longer able to rebuke her, but his assertive gaze bore down on her from the portrait above the fireplace. She looked at the floor, a subservient pose, as if he were present in the room, demanding an answer. Ryan and O'Neil exchanged a troubled glance. The woman was clearly embarrassed by her stupidity.

'Stuart was livid,' she told them. 'He said I'd be in a lot of trouble. Am I?'

'Let's not worry about that now,' Ryan said.

'How can I not? You're suggesting they're not who they said they were.'

He disregarded the statement. 'Do you know if police called his chambers to verify the identity of these people?'

'No, I'm sorry, I don't.' It was the first straight answer she'd given.

O'Neil's nod was Ryan's cue to get on the blower to Trevathan's clerk. He got up and left the room to investigate while O'Neil carried on questioning the anxious housekeeper, who was bending over backwards to apologize.

'I don't know what possessed me, Superintendent. You must think me irresponsible for handing over such important documents to a couple of strangers. I know Stuart does. By then we knew there was something dreadfully wrong, though neither of us ever dreamt it would end the way it did. I can't take it in.'

'It must be distressing for both of you.' O'Neil wasn't there to play nursemaid. She got back on track before the woman lost it again – she needed her calm and providing information. 'Of the couple who took it, which one handled the briefcase?'

'The man did.'

'Do you know what it contained?'

'No, ma'am.'

'I find it hard to believe that you offered it up without checking what was inside, Mrs Forbes. It could have contained personal items, could it not?'

'Yes, I suppose it could.'

O'Neil's eyes were like lasers. 'Did you look inside?'

'I didn't need to. The judge only has the one briefcase. I didn't think that there might be anything personal in it at the time.'

'Was it locked?'

'I told you, I didn't look inside.' Mrs Forbes was wringing her hands. 'Am I under suspicion?'

Ignoring the question, O'Neil took out her phone, tapped the recorder app and laid it on the table between them, an action that made the housekeeper even more petrified. 'This is a formality,' O'Neil explained. 'There's no need to be concerned. It'll save me from having to write down what you say. You'll have to make a formal statement in due course, but this is just for me. Is that OK with you?'

'I have nothing to hide.'

'I'm pleased to hear it.' O'Neil hoped Mrs Forbes was telling the truth. If she found out she wasn't, she'd have no hesitation in charging her with attempting to pervert the course of justice or wasting police time. 'I know it was a while ago, but I want you to think long and hard and describe these people for me – in as much detail as possible, please.'

Mrs Forbes shut her eyes, the better to picture her visitors.

Ryan slipped into the room behind her, an imperceptible shake of his head as he approached. He'd drawn a blank at the chambers.

The housekeeper opened her eyes at the sound of him entering, then switched her focus to O'Neil. 'The gentleman was a tall chap, thinner and taller than my husband, six two or thereabouts, the woman not much shorter, maybe five ten, eleven . . . Actually, a bit shorter, she was wearing high heels.' Mrs Forbes used her forefinger and thumb to indicate three inches. 'The man was dressed in a smart but ill-fitting suit. A dark suit, plain, I think. He was wearing glasses, steel-rimmed. His hair was neatly trimmed, almost black. Hers was too, come to think of it – and tied up. They were like peas in a pod. Irish-looking, if you know what I mean: dark hair, fair skin, blue eyes I think, or maybe green.'

Wow! Ryan thought. That was more description than he or O'Neil had anticipated or hoped for. 'Can you take a stab at age?'

'She was mid thirties, the man slightly younger.'

'Who did the talking?' he asked.

'She did.'

O'Neil backtracked. '*Was* she Irish?'

'English.' The woman was on a roll. It didn't last.

'Northern, southern?' O'Neil prompted her. 'It might help us.'

'I'm not good on accents. They weren't Scots, that's all I can tell you.'

'You said the man wore a suit,' Ryan said. 'Was the woman also smart?'

'Very. Her lipstick matched her coat. Cherry red. Film-star looks.' Ryan's eyes sent a message to O'Neil, the movie reference exciting them both. 'What exactly do you mean by "film-star looks?"'

'Glamorous, you know, like Lauren Bacall.' She apologised, acknowledging that the detectives were probably too young to remember her. 'Attractive and knows how to use it,' she added. 'Self-assured. Acted like she'd just walked off set.'

O'Neil didn't dwell on it. 'Handbag?'

'Not that I remember.'

'You said you followed their vehicle from the gatehouse. Can you describe it?'

'It was a Mercedes. Grey, I think.'

'Local registration?'

94

'I wouldn't know.'

'Who drove?'

'She did.'

'Would you recognize these people again?'

'Her, for certain. It would be hard not to. I'm not so sure about him.'

'That's all for now.' O'Neil stood. 'Thank you for talking to us and for giving such a detailed description. We may ask you to help us with an artist's impression after we've made some more enquiries.'

'Of course. I'm so sorry about the briefcase.'

O'Neil said nothing on the way out. She let Ryan take the wheel again. Next stop, Aberfeldy to pick up a key. She was impatient to move on to Maxwell's Temple. They would debrief on the way.

14

The air was so cold it caused Ryan and O'Neil's breath to condense as they exhaled, sending puffs of white clouds into the air as they walked along the riverside path heading for the folly. In crime scene photographs taken on Tuesday 8 October, the branches covering it were losing their leaves, the magnificent hexagonal structure covered by an autumnal umbrella, in shades of brown and gold. The door to the structure stood ajar. Now it was bolted shut with a heavy-duty padlock.

Ryan opened it up.

Taking a torch from his pocket, he shone it inside before entering. At ground level, the scene was preserved exactly as it had been found. So concerned were local police that something serious had taken place there, no attempt had been made to clean up the blood, now brown where it once was red.

The smell of urine hit Ryan's senses as he stepped through the door, the result of years of misuse, not from the attack that had taken place a couple of months ago. People had used the folly as a toilet stop even though there were the proper facilities not far away in Kenmore. If you needed a piss around here it seemed that even a temple would do.

Steps wound themselves round a central column, disappearing into a black hole. It was a tight climb. Ryan was pleased to emerge at the top where he could again breathe uncontaminated air. The viewing platform offered a great vantage point from which to view the fast-flowing water, the village and a stunning riverside walk in both directions.

They would have seen Trevathan coming a mile away.

Ryan called down to O'Neil. She was standing twenty metres away, her back to him, talking on her mobile in low whispers. By the time he reached ground level she was hanging up.

'Everything all right, guv?'

She swung round. 'Jesus, Ryan! You scared me.'

'Who were you expecting, Spielberg?'

'Don't joke.'

'Sorry if I spooked you.'

'You didn't. I'm perfectly OK,' she snapped. 'Why shouldn't I be?'

'No reason.' Again, Ryan got the distinct impression she was hiding something. He didn't share that thought. Instead, he pointed up at the viewing platform. 'No wonder they used a cherry picker to take their pictures. Like the report said, access is tight. It's impossible to move around in there without disturbing evidence.'

'I wouldn't worry about that now,' she reassured him. 'Only one CSI entered. She came down from the top to check that no one was mortally wounded inside. I spoke to her supervision. She's the best there is.'

'I hope you're right.' Ryan scratched his head with both hands, a grim expression on his face. 'Any evidence in there has been totally compromised. The folly is open to the elements from above. The place is full of debris: leaves, bird shit and things with eight legs. Feel free to check it out for yourself.'

'I'll take your word for it.' O'Neil gave an involuntary shudder. 'Hindsight is a wonderful thing, Ryan. And, for what it's worth, I agree with you, the place should have been covered over and sealed completely. There was no body though. The Crime Scene Manager made a judgement call.'

'Shame it was the wrong one.'

'Yeah, well, what's done is done. Lock it up. We best get going.'

Ryan secured the door to the temple. They retraced their steps along the riverbank, passing some pretty static and mobile homes, then walked across the seventeenth-century humpback Kenmore Bridge, the point at which the river met the loch. The light was fading as they reached the car.

'What now?' Ryan said.

'The PM for me,' O'Neil said. 'I want you on a train to Edinburgh.'

'From here?' He was horrified.

'No, I'll drop you in Perth.'

'I assume to visit Trevathan's chambers?'

'Correct.'

Ryan glanced at his watch. 'They'll be gone by the time I get there.'

'No they won't, I checked. Caroline isn't the only brief with a major drugs case on the go. Edinburgh has one too, and by all accounts it's not going well. So tonight it's all hands on deck, everyone staying late. The drive to Perth will take an hour or so. There's a direct train from there at 17.06 that gets in to Edinburgh Waverley at 18.21.'

'Waste of time, if you ask me. If they're that busy, they're unlikely to tell me anything—'

'Turn on your detective charm then.'

'On?'

'Use your initiative, Ryan. Trevathan's colleagues are up to their necks in a major prosecution. Distracted and under pressure, they might throw you a crumb to get rid of you. If you draw a blank there, book a nice hotel and hang around at the law courts tomorrow morning. You never know, you might get lucky. Staff love to gossip. Some will talk to anyone prepared to listen. Be receptive, you're good at that. I want to know if Trevathan's trial went ahead or was adjourned – and don't come back empty-handed.'

Ryan's attention strayed to the Kenmore Hotel across the river. 'Do I get to eat first?'

'Sorry, there's no time. You'll have to grab a sandwich and eat on the train. We need to get on top of this. Having gathered all the barristers together, listed the trial, warned and prepared God knows how many witnesses, I'm sure the Lord Advocate's office would've pursued the case, with or without him—'

'Except there's not a whisper of that anywhere.'

'I'm thinking it was or is being heard in secret, Ryan. These cases can go on for months.'

'A new judge would have to be briefed though, surely. That would take time—'

'They've had time. I reckon they would want to begin proceedings at the earliest opportunity. The new judge wouldn't necessarily be aware of pre-trial issues, so they'd have to read up on the case and hear the evidence when it was presented in court, same as the jury. Why else bother to retrieve that briefcase if they didn't need to use what was inside?' She stuck a hand out. 'Chuck us the keys?'

'I don't mind driving.'

'My ankle is fine now.'

Reluctantly, Ryan handed them over.

O'Neil pressed a button on her key fob. The lights flashed, unlocking the doors. They strapped themselves in and she drove off at speed, keen to reach Perth before rush hour. In his head, Ryan questioned her motivation to be rid of him. He couldn't help wondering what she had up her sleeve.

'I thought you said you hated post-mortems,' he said after a while.

'I do.'

'Then slow the hell down. You'll be attending your own if you put us off the road.'

'I want you on that train.'

'Why don't we swap?' he suggested. 'You go to Edinburgh and—'

'No.' O'Neil turned left. 'I have it covered.'

'I insist—'

'I said no, thanks, Ryan.' She shot him a dirty look. 'Besides, I have something else to do.'

So, he was right.

Ryan crossed his arms defensively over his chest, his focus on the winding road ahead. Ordinarily she took her time while driving, progressive but steady. Not this trip. Hell-bent on reaching their destination, she was pushing on – and some. She could handle a fast ride too. In spite of his comment a moment ago, he didn't feel the least bit anxious.

'Don't sulk,' she said. 'It doesn't suit you.'

'I'm not. That's not my style.'

'Nor mine to pull rank,' she said. 'We all need to face our

demons at some time or another. You faced yours last night. Now it's my turn.'

Bullshit!

Ryan knew she wasn't playing with a straight bat. Whatever she was hiding, whatever she had in mind to do, she wanted him out of her way while she did it.

15

The Perth teashop was tucked away in a side street off the beaten track. A doorbell signalled O'Neil's arrival as she entered. Grace Ellis and a male companion were waiting, the only customers on one side of the room. The man stood up as she approached.

Old school.

O'Neil liked that.

Used coffee mugs were on the table in front of them. O'Neil offered them a top-up. They declined, so she ordered tea for herself, pulled up a chair and sat down. There was a moment when no one spoke, a moment of uncertainty. The Detective Superintendent wasn't altogether sure she was doing the right thing. Now she was there, it was shit or bust.

'Thanks for coming,' she said. 'Retirement suits you, Grace.'

'You're welcome,' Grace said. 'You look rough, Eloise. You're working too hard.'

O'Neil grinned. Grace had always been a straight talker.

But much as she liked the woman, O'Neil had good reason to be cautious around Grace Ellis. When his old boss went missing, Ryan had defied O'Neil's warning to leave the investigation to Professional Standards. Despite being suspended from duty, he had managed to infiltrate her enquiry. Even now, she had no idea how he had pulled it off, only that he had. And she had a hunch that Grace, with her wealth of experience from a career in the Serious Incident Squad, had been heavily involved, if not the linchpin of the unofficial investigation. Not that she could prove anything, with Ryan refusing to rat on his co-conspirators.

'I was expecting to meet you alone,' O'Neil said. Grace had recently married an old flame Ryan referred to simply as Newman. O'Neil assumed this must be the bloke now sitting by her side. She shifted her gaze in his direction. 'We've not been formally introduced.' She stuck out a hand. 'Eloise O'Neil.'

'Frank Newman.' The handshake was solid. Dependable.

The tea arrived and they stopped talking.

O'Neil held Grace's gaze across the table. She was an amazing detective but belligerent at times, confrontational. And so it proved. At Jack's funeral, having had a bit too much to drink, she'd said some hurtful things about O'Neil's failure to listen to Ryan, suspending him when he could have assisted her investigation legitimately. Ryan had intervened, telling Grace in no uncertain terms to back off.

She was right though.

In her heart, O'Neil knew it. She should have listened to him, except she hadn't know him well enough to trust him. Only once he was exonerated had she been willing to pool intelligence, and the dynamics between them had gone from open hostility to a degree of trust that was rare in her experience.

That didn't mean he'd told her everything.

The waitress left them.

O'Neil fixed on the male. 'Mr Newman, no offence, but I'd like some privacy. Would you mind?'

Grace cracked up. 'You're kidding, right?'

'No, I'm deadly serious. I need help and you fit the bill.'

'So talk,' Grace said. 'Frank and I come as a pair these days.'

'Then we have nothing to say to one another.'

'I'm afraid it's non-negotiable.' Grace placed her hand over her husband's, giving him hard eyes as he pulled it away. She sighed, her focus on O'Neil. 'See what you've done now? Have a heart, will you? We're on honeymoon.' A dark cloud passed between the two women. Grace's radiance and sarcastic attitude fell away. 'Eloise, I'm so sorry. That was tactless.'

Newman had no clue what was going on, only that his wife had, metaphorically speaking, ripped a plaster from a raw wound leaving her ex-colleague in pain and was mortified by it. O'Neil could hardly breathe. She'd tried so hard to put the past behind her. Not normally vindictive, right now she wanted to leap over the table and rip off Grace's head. Instead, she threw in a verbal grenade.

'I know you were helping Ryan by monitoring HOLMES when Jack Fenwick went missing, Grace. In case you're in any doubt, that's enough to send you away for a very long time.'

The retired detective never flinched.

The best defence was always attack.

'Are you on something?' Grace pointed at O'Neil's now empty cup. 'That herbal tea must be hallucinogenic.'

The bravado didn't wash. O'Neil had charged enough coppers, retired and serving, to know when one was floundering. 'Just so you know, Ryan never said a word. I'm a detective too, Grace – a bloody good one – I worked it out all by myself. And you . . .' She switched her attention to Newman. 'Mysteriously,

I can't seem to find any information at all about you, Mr Newman. I wonder why that is.'

Not a flicker.

'I know you've been digging,' he said.

'Of course you do.' O'Neil crossed her arms, leaned into her chair, a bell tinkling as the only other customers got up and left the premises. 'I'm curious by nature. I dug and I dug, and yet I couldn't penetrate your backstory. I'm guessing I got a little too close.'

Newman remained silent. Whoever he was, he was well connected. Grace was expressionless, resisting the temptation to jump in – a first for her. Sensing her frustration, O'Neil stroked her bottom lip with her forefinger, buying herself time, eyes on Newman.

'Did your handler tip you off?'

He gave no answer.

No matter how hard she pushed his buttons, he was too experienced to admit or deny that he was part of any governmental undercover organization, be that MI5 (British Security Service) or MI6 (Military Intelligence). There was no doubt in her mind that he was a spook, if not now then in the recent past.

'Well, guess what?' She eyeballed him across the table. 'I had a knock at the door from your spook friends early one morning and suddenly the focus is on me. Unlike you, I am a real person with a real background. I'm sure you know everything there is to know about me, Mr Newman.'

'Not everything,' Grace said hurriedly.

O'Neil took that as a declaration that Grace hadn't told Newman about *her* private life. If that were true, it was something. She carried on, impatient to tackle the spook while she had the chance. 'Mr Newman, I don't know how, or even if, you got involved with Ryan's extracurricular activity during Jack-gate. I don't want to know, but I won't tolerate interference if Grace ever comes to work for me, now or in the future, is that clear?'

He said nothing.

O'Neil shifted her attention to his wife. 'Don't worry, Grace. I don't intend to pursue your husband any further. I know when I'm wasting my time. You're different. I'm not coming after you either, as it happens, not officially, because yours is the kind of deviousness I need on my team. It's a shame that I can't use Frank, but I'm sure you can appreciate why.'

Grace was noncommittal.

O'Neil could see that she was wavering, trying not to show it.

Time to push her buttons.

'If you're not remotely interested, feel free to walk away,' she said. 'Ryan will be none the wiser. He doesn't even know I'm here. I thought I'd give you first shout on an exciting opportunity to boost that pension of yours. A two-way transaction: taxpayers' cash in return for your expertise. I heard you were bored with retirement.'

Newman chanced his arm. 'Maybe if you told us what the case is about?'

'No can do,' O'Neil said.

Moving in closer, she linked hands, elbows on the table. It was like a game of blink first. Unfortunately, Newman was winning. She looked away, deliberating over whether she could trust him, wondering how much Ryan did, whose side he might take if he were there. O'Neil didn't doubt Newman's credentials, but he was an unknown quantity and that was enough to make her nervous. There was a fine line between the good and bad guys.

'And if I was prepared to work without Frank?' Grace asked.

'Then my door is open.'

'You know I'm discreet, Eloise. Tell me what you have in mind.' She shot a glance at Newman. 'Frank, cover your ears. You're making her nervous.'

'Nice try.' O'Neil laughed. 'I'm not questioning your discretion, but I'm not that green. You know how these negotiations work.'

Grace sent a silent message, one woman to another: *I didn't tell him.* Frustrated by the stalemate, she sighed loudly. 'When lives are at stake, I generally like to know what I'm getting into.'

O'Neil raised an eyebrow. 'Who said anything about lives at stake?'

'If they weren't,' Grace said, 'you wouldn't be knocking at my door. If they are, then I think you should reconsider inviting Frank along. Believe me when I say, he's no slouch. And just so we're clear, he's no flash in the pan or weekend shag either. We've known each other twenty-odd years. There's no one in the world, including Ryan, I trust more.'

'Not going to happen. You're either in or you're out, Grace. Take a few days – there's no hurry. Ryan and I have a lot of work to do. Think on it. You know how to get in touch.' O'Neil turned her attention to Newman. 'A pleasure meeting you, Mr Newman.'

Scooping up her phone, she threw a twenty-pound note on the table and walked out.

16

O'Neil was about to start the car when the passenger door opened and Newman climbed in. Grace got in the back. As the doors slammed shut, O'Neil met her gaze in the rear-view mirror. Grace had that hunger in her eyes that all coppers get when a case intrigues them to the point of obsession. If O'Neil was reading her right, she couldn't wait to get started.

Her relief was profound.

It hadn't taken long to work out that she needed a detective of Grace's calibre on board. As soon as she'd received Official-Sensitive documents from Ford, O'Neil had known she had a case on her hands. She'd scoured the personnel database for someone suitable, preferably a serving officer. On each run-through, she'd drawn a blank. The job was simply not as attractive as it once was. Detectives had been bailing in their droves, seeking employment in the private sector or taking their money to spend in retirement.

And who could blame them?

Still, as good a player as Newman might prove to be, he was surplus to her requirements for the time being. If that changed going forward, a phone call to Grace would locate him in an instant.

O'Neil turned her head towards him. 'You have something to say to me, Mr Newman?'

'You should be careful, Superintendent. Poking around in my background won't buy you any friends. And I think you're going to need some, if you don't mind me saying. I'm a very private person. Cautious, too. If someone asks about me, I tend to want to know why.'

'Fair's fair,' O'Neil said. 'And what did you find out?'

'You're working on classified material. Something to do with a certain judge?'

Eloise didn't respond.

'Does the name Leonard Maxwell ring any bells?' he continued. 'No? How about Lord Trevathan? Same guy. Different title. They fished him out of the Tay on Monday. It appears the poor man got out of his depth.' He paused. 'Still not convinced?'

He was very well informed.

O'Neil examined him closely. He was mid fifties with the physique of someone much younger: handsome, casually dressed, with ice-blue eyes capable of piercing metal.

'I'm listening,' she said.

'You have several linked incidents, a big cheese from the Home Office peering over your shoulder, and serious finances for a wide-ranging investigation with a modest crew. How am I doing?'

O'Neil held her nerve. If the situation hadn't been serious, she'd have broken into a round of applause. Intuition was a wonderful thing. Hers hadn't let her down yet. Newman *was* the genuine article. Knowledge like his was a gift for a unit like hers. The man sitting beside her had all the skills she needed to uncover the mystery surrounding Lord Trevathan.

'Oh, one thing I forgot,' he said. 'You have the clout to pick your own team, to engage people with talent and diplomacy. Whether or not you're prepared to admit it, to yourself or to Ryan, in my modest opinion you're going to need to do that sooner rather than later.'

'Sounds like me and him,' Grace chipped in.

O'Neil ignored the attempt at humour. This wasn't a game and well Grace knew it. The unit was a career-changing opportunity and O'Neil couldn't afford to put a foot wrong. 'If I need your advice, Mr Newman, I'll ask for it.' She pointed at the door. 'I'm busy now, so if you don't mind.'

Grace was visibly disappointed. 'You're making a mistake, Eloise.'

O'Neil's eyes flew to the rear-view. 'Don't you mean another one?' She still felt guilty about Jack Fenwick.

'You have a chance to redeem yourself,' Grace said. 'In fact, you've already made a start. Isn't that why you took Ryan on, to clear your conscience?'

O'Neil swivelled in her seat to face her. 'How dare you!'

Grace did right to back off.

O'Neil was livid.

Newman wasn't happy either.

'I'm sorry, Eloise.' Grace backpedalled quickly. 'I didn't put that very well. Your instincts are spot on. Ryan has moral integrity. He used the back stairs to find Jack because the suspension left him with no other choice. For what it's worth, he hated doing it. Most of all, he hated deceiving you.'

'Yes, and in doing so he put his career on the line.'

Grace's attitude softened. 'You could have pulled the plug – you had the chance. But you didn't. You've protected him because he's a good cop. He'll do the hard yards and then some. He's loyal and trustworthy, like Frank and me. If you let us in, we'll be behind you every step of the way.' She looked at Newman. 'Frank, tell her.'

Newman said nothing.

There were times when silence spoke the loudest.

This was one of them.

'OK, I'll tell her.' Grace eyeballed O'Neil. 'He knows stuff, Eloise. He has access we don't. Without him, I reckon you're screwed.'

'That was quite a speech.' O'Neil turned to face her. 'Now get out of my car, Grace. You too, Mr Newman.'

Neither of them moved.

'I said, get out!' O'Neil blew out a breath as the doors slammed shut. That encounter was worse than any post-mortem.

17

O'Neil was spitting bullets as she drove to the morgue. Her overreaction to the news that Grace and Newman knew as much about her enquiry as she did left her with few staffing alternatives. Initially, she'd called Grace to check out her availability and willingness to get involved because she was the best there was. She hadn't bargained on her being so clued up about the case. As for Newman, his access to classified information made him an asset she'd dearly love to have on her team.

And now she'd blown it.

The post-mortem was almost over when she arrived. There were two forensic pathologists finishing up, a senior examiner and a female assisting who appeared to be dissecting human tissue. Other samples: blood, hair, nails, gastric contents and liver had been already attended to, saving O'Neil's delicate disposition the horror of viewing the worst of it.

Perfect timing.

The body would have rapidly decomposed had it not been submerged in cold water. The medical examiners gave O'Neil no more or less than she expected. As usual in cases where an interval had occurred between fatality and discovery, they were only able to give an estimated time of death. The judge's demise had occurred some time ago.

What was left of his fingernails had long since turned black.

He had knife wounds to his chest, a deep gash to his neck that explained the severed artery, as well as slippage of skin and other post-mortem injuries associated with having been in the water for a prolonged period. Barring a handkerchief, there was nothing in his pockets, according to the lab technician who'd stripped the body and bagged the clothing.

The body was being examined with such care and respect by the pathologist and yet, in O'Neil's head, the remains on the table had ceased to be a person, let alone the brilliant advocate she knew they represented in life. Only Trevathan's spirit remained. Not in a biblical sense. She didn't believe in the afterlife. It was something intangible that tugged at her subconscious. Maybe just that he was in her thoughts. Respect for the siblings he'd left behind was enough to drive her on. Through her efforts, justice would prevail.

Another glance at the corpse.

Hideous disfigurement. The feeling of suffocation was strong now. She should have left it a little longer or, better still, sent Ryan in her place. Arguably, he may have succeeded where she'd failed to get Grace Ellis on board. Eloise was kicking herself. Why in hell's name did she always take the rocky road? As if her job wasn't hard enough.

The walls were closing in. She was struggling now, slating herself for a physical reaction she had no control over, clawing at the neck of her shirt, trying to get some air. Fortunately, her distress went unnoticed and didn't last long. Once over the nausea, she left the morgue. The pathology report would follow in due course. These things took time.

Having sat outside in the car for half an hour recovering, O'Neil realized she'd had nothing to eat all day. She considered and then immediately discounted the hospital canteen, regretting her decision to keep driving earlier in the day, passing up the opportunity for lunch with Ryan. The fact that she'd sent him to Edinburgh sat heavily with her now, as did her decision to leave him out of her negotiations, if she could call them that. She missed his company, his camaraderie. Worse than facing your demons was facing them alone.

His phone went to voicemail.

She sighed. 'It's Eloise. Call me when you can. I'm heading to Newcastle. When you're done there, get the train. I hope all's well your end.'

Ryan took the phone from his ear, pissed that he was being left to travel back alone and worried on two counts: that O'Neil's ankle wasn't up to such a long drive home and that she sounded so forlorn. The emphasis on the words 'your end' implied she was having a hard time at hers. That was tough. He'd tried saving her the misery of a post-mortem. She'd refused.

Her call.

Ryan hit speed-dial and got her message service: 'Eloise, it's me. Pick up if you're there.'

Nothing.

Hanging up, he ordered a pint and sunk half of it in one go. The boozer was the type of nondescript establishment he preferred, catering for a fairly lively crowd he was certain were coppers, on their feet, drinking and chatting at the bar. He was tuning in to their conversation when O'Neil returned his call, his phone vibrating in his trouser pocket.

*

'Sorry I missed you, I was on another call,' she said. 'I can hear background noise. Where are you?'

'Having a pint in the Oxford Bar. What can I say? I'm a Rebus fan.'

'You're not on your jollies, Ryan.' She spied a sign up ahead and slowed down. *Indecision, indecision.* She could drive home alone or head for Edinburgh.

'Nothing wrong with a bit of culture, guv.'

'How can you read that crap when you see it every day?'

'You must have a social life. I don't.'

'Yeah, right.'

Fuck's sake! O'Neil cursed herself. What was wrong with her today? She wasn't usually this flighty. She left the road at the next turn-off.

'What's up?' Ryan said. 'You sound down in the mouth.'

'I am. I hate to use the words "collateral damage" – no victim should be considered less important than another – but it looks like James Fraser was just that. I managed to get a number for his best mate, Wendy Rogers. She's also a nurse at Rake Lane Hospital.' A blue light appeared behind her. It was shifting too. O'Neil indicated left to let the driver know she'd seen him. 'Hang on,' she said. 'They're playing our song.'

None of the coppers at the bar looked up. The scream of a police siren was coming down the line, not from close by. 'You're getting pulled over?'

O'Neil laughed. 'No, Dad, I'm fine. Sticking to the speed limit and everything. Sorry for the distraction. Where was I?'

'Wendy Rogers.'

'Right. A helpful contact. She told me that Fraser was in the habit of running to and from the hospital. He worked a lot of night shifts. On a Sunday morning, he tended to run to his mum's where, depending on what he was planning to do later, he either had a kip and stayed for lunch before heading home, or ate breakfast with his mum, made an excuse and left.' She paused. 'If you think about it long enough, it'll come to you.'

Ryan made the connection almost immediately. Mrs Fraser lived in a flat behind Collingwood's Monument at Tynemouth, the town sandwiched between the victim's home in Whitley Bay and North Shields. 'Don't tell me, his favourite route was the North Shields Fish Quay?'

'Correct. He talked Wendy into a run after work one time, sharing the Sunday roast and pretending to be his girlfriend to shut his mother up. You saw how distraught Mrs Fraser was. She's a lonely woman, unable to cope as an empty nester. Since her husband died, she'd been banging on about James going home so she could take care of him. Taking Wendy along seemed to do the trick.'

'Did she describe the route they took?'

'She did. I can't yet confirm if it's the course they followed last Sunday but I don't believe in fairies, do you? If Fraser kept to his routine – I know I do – he almost certainly ran right past our crime scene.'

'So what, they're killing randomly now?'

'Maybe not.' O'Neil swore under her breath. 'Where the hell am I?'

'You're talking to yourself, guv. That's not a good sign. Are you lost?'

'Took a wrong turn. On track now.'

'You're suggesting Fraser saw something?'

'That's my best guess. His jogging gear and the time of day were a dead giveaway. Whoever killed him would realize that he was a local, not a tourist. They would figure out that he'd come forward when the case hit the press.' The implication was clear. 'They have other work to do, Ryan.'

'You know, you could be right. His mother saw him on Sunday—'

'For the last time,' O'Neil interrupted. 'If I remember rightly, she said he arrived early and left at around eleven a.m.'

'But I asked her if he seemed worried about anything. She said no.'

'Maybe he wasn't. Maybe their presence didn't register. His killers weren't to know that, were they? Or maybe Fraser didn't mention it to his mum for altruistic reasons. You saw her. She's a bundle of nerves. He might not have wanted to worry her. We need to speak to her again. That's best done face to face. The poor woman has been through enough.'

'I suppose they could have followed him to her house, seen her open the door and waited until he left again.'

'Yup. They follow him home to Whitley Bay three miles away and make sure he can't shop them to the law. On the information we have, it's the most likely scenario – unless you have other ideas?'

'None.' Ryan took a moment to get his thoughts in order. 'An unplanned murder makes sense of the tremor in Spielberg's voice. The fact that the body was left at the scene instead of being removed like Trevathan or the Brighton and North Shields victims.'

'Exactly. Talking of Brighton, there's no update there. Sussex police are on the lookout for a victim and will call me as and when there are developments. No news yet from the coast-guard. We need to get a handle on this investigation before it spirals out of control.'

Ryan put his phone in his pocket, O'Neil's words ringing in his ears. Resigned to spending the evening alone, he glanced at a discarded newspaper on the bar, a report into the deaths of four mountaineers in an avalanche in Glencoe, the total number who'd lost their lives in one season reaching fourteen; unprecedented high winds, sub-zero temperatures and extreme snowfall creating the perfect conditions for tragedy.

Depressing.

He turned the page.

O'Neil was dealing with a different kind of avalanche, one Ryan knew she'd struggle to cope with in a unit consisting of two. They needed help but it was far too early to tackle her on the subject. With the Lord Advocate, Scotland's Solicitor General and the Crown Agent baying for justice on Trevathan's behalf, she'd want to be seen to be keeping all the balls in the air, demonstrating progress before utilizing her authority to take on more staff. Her reputation was at stake. His too, now he came to think of it.

'You going to buy me a pint or ignore me?' The voice took him by surprise.

Ryan swung round.

O'Neil was standing right behind him, a glum expression on her face. 'My ankle's killing me, I'm dog-tired, starving and could use a drink. Couldn't be arsed to drive home. Are you happy to keep me company? I'm wearing a new scent. It's called Mortuary. I'm surprised they let me in here.'

Ryan couldn't tell her how pleased he was to see her. 'My shout, guv, what can I get you?'

O'Neil glanced at the optics behind the bar. 'Seeing as we're in Scotland, I'll have a wee dram of Jura Air.' She smiled at him. 'Second thoughts, let's live dangerously and make it a double. I need a good kip and we've a long day ahead of us tomorrow.'

18

They arrived at Parliament Square before nine, splitting up once inside the High Court so they could cover the building quickly and rendezvous in the car park at eleven, ready to return to Newcastle in good time. Ryan got there first. While he waited for O'Neil to surface, he tried Caroline again. They still hadn't made contact and he was starting to get worried.

This time he got through.

Ryan was hanging up as O'Neil walked out into the sunshine at a fast pace, head down, unaware that he was watching her. He'd enjoyed hanging out with her last night – more than he cared to admit – and when they parted for separate rooms he felt dismayed. She drove him mad and he strongly suspected that she knew it.

She came to a sudden stop.

Dropping her head on one side, she narrowed her eyes. 'You have good news?'

'Makes you say that?'

'You're grinning like a cat.'

'My mind had drifted elsewhere.' He couldn't tell her where. 'There is good news, but sadly nothing to do with our case. The jury in Caroline's trial returned guilty verdicts on all but one offender late yesterday afternoon. The judge adjourned, sending them back to Durham prison in no doubt that they were facing jail, with sentencing scheduled for ten this morning.'

'So that's where she was, out celebrating.'

'And she will be again. The trial judge just doled out eighty-one years between nine offenders. The public gallery was in uproar. Crown Prosecutors were commended for a job well done, as was the undercover drugs team – it'll be all over the papers tonight. Caroline is thrilled.'

'Result! I'm relieved, actually.'

'Sorry?'

'You checked your phone several times last night, I was beginning to think I was boring you.'

'You're a lot of things, Eloise. Boring isn't one of them.'

O'Neil flushed slightly and changed the subject. 'Do you have *any* news for us?'

Ryan shook his head. 'I tapped a few court officials: two clerks, a stenographer and an usher who had a lot more nous than I initially gave him credit for. They're under threat of prosecution if they breathe a word.'

'They told you that?'

'I overheard them talking, didn't I?' O'Neil fixed him with a stare; she wasn't buying it. Ryan grinned. 'OK, if you must know I left my phone on someone's desk. How was I to know the recorder was switched on? The clerks should've waited until I cleared the room before reacting to my visit. It's not nice to talk about people behind their backs. Besides, you asked me to use my initiative.'

'You bugged their office?'

'Inadvertently!' Ryan lifted his hand, inviting a high five.

O'Neil gave him one.

'I wasn't half as lucky,' she said. 'The police and press stone-walled me. They're being gagged too. The administration team were worse. They were so nervous they asked me to leave. Cheeky sods escorted me to the door. Do you see any point in hanging around?'

'None. It's a brick wall, guv.'

'Then we drop one ball and pick up another.' She threw him the car keys. 'It's your turn to drive.'

They arrived at their Newcastle base shortly after two p.m. The journey south had flown by, the conversation flowing, mainly about the case, in particular the silence surrounding Treva-than's trial. They had concluded, jointly and separately, that it probably involved the prosecution of suspected terrorists, the accused anonymized by false names or merely referred to by letters of the alphabet. Cloaked in such secrecy, a legal action involving national security would be difficult, if not impossi-ble, to penetrate. Anyone caught leaking information would be liable to prosecution for contempt of court, punishable by imprisonment.

O'Neil told Ryan she'd give the matter more thought before coming to a decision as to their next move. Then she steered the conversation to the North Shields crime scene and James Fraser's death. His post-mortem was scheduled for later.

This time, she agreed, he could go in her place.

'I want you to contact the Family Liaison Officer,' O'Neil said. 'Tell her what we suspect might have happened to Fraser. Be very clear: we need more information from his mother without alarming her. We don't tip her off that he may have seen something suspicious in North Shields or might've been followed. Ram that message home, Ryan.'

O'Neil handed him a list of questions she wanted answers to: *Did James have a key? Did he let himself into the house on Sunday or did Mrs Fraser open the door? Was anyone waiting for him when he left the house? Anyone in the street that she can recall?* Beneath the list, O'Neil had scrawled a further instruction: *On no account must Mrs Fraser be made aware that there's a possible link to an incident a couple of miles down the road.*

Ryan looked up from the note. 'I think this last one is a must. The poor soul has been through enough. Mind you, if she thinks about it hard enough, asking her if anyone was waiting outside when Fraser left will be like telling her he was being followed.'

'We can't help that, Ryan. We need to be clear on what happened. On second thoughts, meet with the liaison officer personally. I'd like you to see the whites of her eyes. If you don't think she's up to getting the information we require without compromising our investigation, do it yourself.'

'You think she's safe?'

'Mrs Fraser?'

Ryan nodded.

'I'm not sure. If there is any suggestion that she met James at the door, we must assume that those who killed him saw and can ID her. We can supply a panic alarm—'

'And say what?'

'We don't need to give the real reason. We could tell her it's basic procedure following a sudden and violent death, to ensure a quick response if she needs help, or just to put her mind at rest. Pass that on to the liaison officer. Depending what comes back, we'll return to it later.'

Ryan made the call, asking the liaison officer to meet him at a pub known to locals as The Corner House. Situated on the Coast Road, it was less than ten minutes from the city centre. He was there and back in under half an hour. 'Job done,' he said, chucking his car keys on his desk.

O'Neil raised her head. 'How was she?'

'Good as gold,' he reassured her. 'So what's next?'

'We need help and we need it now, so I'm bringing in someone we both know,' O'Neil said.

Her plan threw Ryan. 'Actually, I was hoping to talk to you about—'

'Too late. I've made my play. There are several scenes and limitless issues that need to be dealt with urgently. We can't do it alone.'

Ryan's stomach took a dive. He was angling for Grace and Newman and felt a little pissed off that O'Neil had settled on someone without consulting him. 'We're not doing it alone,' he said. 'We have incident rooms here at HQ, in Scotland and Sussex, dozens of detectives inputting data and waiting on actions. We delegate, surely.'

'Don't question me, Ryan.' O'Neil took off her specs and studied him. 'You haven't been to Brighton yet. We need to get down there and I want someone here on the ground to coordinate. This is, potentially, a quadruple murder case now. When the press get wind of the fact that the body found in the Tay is the second most senior judge in Scotland, they're going to join the Home Office in demanding answers. Unless you have a crystal ball, we have none to give them.'

The truth stung.

I'm bringing in someone we both know.

Ryan could think of only one male and one female serving officer they were both acquainted with. He was prepared to work with neither. The idea of operating alongside his ex-girl-friend, DC Roz Cornell, was enough to bring on a migraine. The alternative – DS Maguire, O'Neil's former bagman – was even worse.

The intercom buzzed, cutting off his objection before he had a chance to voice it. O'Neil glanced at the visual display on her desk, buzzing their visitor in at street level. She nodded towards the front door.

'That'll be her now.'

Her. Roz. Oh God!

Ryan wanted to work with *her* like he wanted a hole in the head.

'Are you going to let her in or sit there with your mouth open?'

Reluctantly, he got to his feet, eyes still on O'Neil. Her expression was steadfast, her mind made up. She was strong-willed and he admired that – *just not today*. He had no chance of influencing her decision. He had to try . . .

'Guv, this is a mistake I think we'll both regret.'

'If she's no good, I'll fire her.'

'I can't work with her.'

'Rubbish – you've done it before.'

'Guv—'

'May I remind you who's the boss around here?'

'I though you didn't pull rank.'

She made a face. 'I changed my mind.'

She was taking the piss. She hadn't and never would claim superiority. Like all work colleagues, they'd had their moments but, in the main, they rubbed along nicely.

'I thought we were a partnership – consulting on everything.'

'Get. The. Door.'

Ryan walked away, practising a welcome his heart didn't share as he moved towards the entrance, a black cloud over his head. As he buzzed to open the heavy iron door, he took a deep breath, determined to be nice.

The pair of sharp, expressive eyes on the other side didn't belong to the person he was expecting.

19

'You look like you've chewed a wasp.' Grace Ellis handed Ryan her coat and holdall as she exited the lift. 'I heard you needed an office manager. I'm relying on you to give me the low-down on this secret squirrel unit. Sounds like my kind of gig. Whose crazy-arsed scheme is it anyhow?' She looked happier than he'd ever seen her. Positively glowing. Unable to keep the grin off his face, Ryan gave her a big hug, holding on for longer than he meant to. 'Hey, mister!' She pushed him away. 'I'm spoken for.'

'Newman is one lucky bastard,' Ryan said. 'And you are a sight for sore eyes. What did you do with him?'

'He's unpacking.'

'Where are you staying?'

'Malmaison. Our room has a Millennium Bridge view. Slumming it,' she joked. 'I reckon we can handle that for a good cause. You know Frank, he's like you – only better looking – as long as he can see water, he's happy. Well, happy might be a bit of an exaggeration. Right now, he's sulking. Wants to know why he's not involved here too. We need to work on Eloise.'

'Work on me?' O'Neil had come to find them.

Grace blushed.

O'Neil stuck out a hand, the formality surprising Ryan. The two women weren't exactly friends, but they had been well

127

acquainted prior to Grace's retirement. There was an awkward moment as O'Neil set down demarcation lines with the woman Ryan's ex had referred to as the pit bull. The thought made him smile. O'Neil and Grace were polar opposites – he looked forward to the fireworks. His new guv'nor had chosen well.

Still counting his blessings that it was Grace and not Roz who'd walked through the door, he said to no one in particular, 'How come I wasn't consulted?'

Grace snapped her head round to face him. 'You saying I'm not good enough?'

'Take no notice, Grace. Staffing is my baby,' O'Neil said. 'Come in and make yourself comfortable. We have much to do.' She led the way into the apartment proper.

'Blimey!' Grace was staring at a bank of computers on the far wall. 'You want for nothing, do you?' She scanned the room. 'Except maybe a Christmas tree. We'll have to sort that out. I'm not working without one.'

O'Neil rolled her eyes. 'Priorities, Grace.'

'No one is more important than Baby Jesus.'

Ryan laughed.

O'Neil didn't. 'Our jobs are uploaded onto HOLMES: how they came in, how they were reported, where we're up to. Statements in the system have all been checked off. House-to-house needs updating. You must review it all, every scrap of information. In other words, you are now a one-woman incident room – the way you like it.'

'She's nailed you already,' Ryan said.

'You still need a tree!' Grace spoke over her shoulder as she walked away, unconcerned with O'Neil's agenda. She turned. 'And my other half? You need him too. He's a real star, if you ever fancy giving him a whirl. You might have to stand in line. He doesn't suffer fools, if you know what I mean—'

'Don't make me regret taking you on,' O'Neil said in return.

At the risk of annoying O'Neil, he jumped in: 'Guv, when we were searching for Jack, Newman was brilliant.'

'You don't say.'

'No, hear me out. Without him, there's a lot we would've missed. Frank has contacts we don't and he's prepared to use them. Fingers in pies is exactly what we need.'

'Don't you think I know that?' O'Neil said.

'So what's the problem?'

'Ryan, we're serving police officers. We need to do things by THE book, not HIS book. The two things are very different—'

'You're reading the wrong book,' Grace said loudly, forcing Ryan to stifle a grin. She was already at work, organizing a workstation behind them, moving bits of equipment out of her way, replacing them with her own stuff. He loved having her around.

'I've made my decision,' O'Neil said.

'The wrong one.' Grace turned, leaned against her new desk, arms crossed. 'If you don't use Frank, it might be a while before you crack this case. It wouldn't do to fail on your first outing.'

'Ryan, a word.' O'Neil was losing patience. They moved into the hallway. 'I hope she isn't going to keep on about him.'

'I can think of one way to stop her.'

'I know you have a lot of time for him—'

'That's a gross understatement,' Ryan interrupted. 'What would it take for me to convince you that he's a good idea?' O'Neil seemed to waver, so he pushed on. 'Meet with him. Talk to the guy. He doesn't say much and, to be perfectly honest, I don't know a lot about him. He's . . . How can I put this? An acquired taste. I didn't take to him straight off. He grew on me. He'll grow on you too.' He nodded back into the room they had just vacated. 'Grace trusts him implicitly.'

'They're married!'

'Agreed, but *I* trust him and you trust me. It's like a daisy chain of trust.' Ryan made a funny face. O'Neil didn't laugh. 'Listen, Newman was a spy when spies went out and did instead of sitting around on their arses staring at computer screens. Utilize him to your advantage – to ours, I mean. Believe me, you won't regret it.'

'He's dangerous—'

'But effective.'

'No, I can't risk it. The last thing I need is a maverick on my team.'

'You've met him?'

'Yesterday. And I didn't take to him.'

'Guv, Newman was the one who went out and made the connections when Grace and I were searching for Jack's killers. Say what you like about him, he has my vote.'

Just as he appeared to be getting his message across, O'Neil's phone rang. She checked the display and asked for some privacy, waiting until he walked away. Ryan swore under his breath. The opportunity was gone. After a minute or two, she was back in the room. Whatever the call was about, it was serious. She was pissed off and making no attempt at hiding it.

'We're getting a visitor,' she said.

Ryan was immediately on the defensive. 'I thought no one knew we were here.'

'Well, they do now.' O'Neil's eyes shot towards the door. 'Do the honours and meet our guest. Actually, don't bother, I'll do it myself.'

'If it's Ford you better keep him away from her.' Ryan threw a glance in Grace's direction. 'Somehow, I don't think they'll get along.'

'I heard that.' As O'Neil made a move, Grace pulled a scary face at Ryan.

'How old are you?' he said crossly.

She burst out laughing.

They heard the access door open and close, a heated exchange in low whispers between O'Neil and their visitor. When she returned to the room, Newman was in tow. He shook hands with Ryan, a friendly exchange between brothers in arms. Grace strode across the room, kissed her husband and over-egged her soft Geordie accent.

'Were you missing me, pet?'

Newman stepped away from her embrace, ice-blue eyes on O'Neil.

She scowled at him. 'I assume you followed her here.'

Grace bridled: 'What do you take me for?'

Newman's expression was unmoving. He was in work mode and nothing would deter him from what he'd come to say. 'What would your response be if I told you that your offenders began their antics in Copenhagen. The victim was the British Ambassador to Denmark. The woman you've been listening to sent a DVD there too.'

'Fuck!' Grace raised her hands in the air. 'Eloise, I didn't know this, I swear.'

The death of an ambassador, a person holding the most senior diplomatic rank, was about as serious as it could get.

'Hang on. That was in the papers,' Ryan frowned, 'but it happened months ago.'

'July twenty-eighth, to be precise,' Newman said. 'At least that's the date on the DVD, the same day he went missing.'

'Wasn't it reported as a robbery?' O'Neil said.

'It was.'

'What day of the week was that?'

'Sunday. Danish police were on it immediately. His body was found in an abandoned warehouse two days later.'

'Any witnesses?'

'One. A local woman. She'd seen a male and a female acting suspiciously near the Ambassador's official residence in Kastelsvej a couple of days before he went missing. She didn't raise the alarm at the time, but came forward when the case was reported in the press. The Foreign Secretary consulted at the highest level, imposing a news embargo on anything more than basic information.'

'Which makes Trevathan the second victim, not the first,' Ryan said. There was a deathly hush as the full impact of his statement sank in. He could see his guv'nor's brain working overtime. If she had any doubt that Newman was required, it was gone.

'OK, you're in,' she said. 'I seem to have been outvoted.'

'Yes!' Grace punched the air. 'Just don't go adding his name to the payroll.'

'I'm sure Eloise and I can come to an untraceable arrangement,' Newman said. 'As far as this unit goes, I'm the invisible man.' He eyeballed O'Neil, keen to get going, asking for the lowdown on the enquiry to date. She told the former spook and Grace to read up on the case and be ready for a full briefing by six o'clock. Her unit had doubled in just two days.

20

She sought to obliterate any light. Covering the windows of her living room with thick newspaper to conceal her whereabouts was the way to go, cancelling out any reflection that might give away her location, creating a proper darkroom. Placing a simple wooden chair facing the camera – one of few props – she set up the tripod, inviting her accomplice to sit so she could adjust both focus and lighting.

He grinned at the lens, begging her to let him do it. That was out of the question. SHE was to be the live subject of this transmission, not him. He was the grunt. She'd been forced to remind him, time and again, that she was the brains behind their operation, the driver of their mission.

She'd brook no argument.

He was sulking now, trying to convince her that it would be more menacing coming from a man. Idiot. Gender didn't come into it. He was a vicious little shit who took pleasure in hurting people but had absolutely no composure. No style. She would bring the shoot to life in a way that he could not. Her eye was trained to stage the beauty of the moment.

She peered through the lens.

Smoke from his cigarette danced with dust mites in the air, adding to the drama. Never before had she been this rapt. It wasn't perfect, but she'd get there if she persevered. As always, patience was key.

She took her time. The camera angle didn't please her. He was partially obscuring the message she'd carefully painted thick and black on a crisp white bed sheet, allowing time for it to dry before pinning it to the wall – the perfect backdrop.

Fail to plan, plan to fail. That was her mantra.

Modifications complete, she stepped back to observe her handiwork with her naked eye, then dimmed the lights a touch, adding just enough shadow to create a chilling atmosphere for her film debut. Already scripted and rehearsed, her message was more than a communiqué. It was a tribute to her people. She'd learned the words by heart and would deliver them with clarity and profound passion, as was fitting for such a just cause.

She wasn't in the business of churning out propaganda. She'd hate viewers to accuse her of that. There was nothing misleading in her message. No hype. This was truth. Her truth. They'd had their say; now it was her turn, an opportunity to redress the balance and set the record straight. It was high time they took her seriously.

She felt proud.

As the self-appointed leader of her group, it was her responsibility to make the world sit up and take notice. She relished the prospect of spelling out her motivation, knowing that in doing so she would strike fear into the hearts of her audience, remind them that there would be more deaths, that no one was safe. And when the chosen were all dead, she'd upload her masterpiece to her favourite channel and explain herself.

That was the plan.

Not until she was satisfied did she switch places with her accomplice so she could examine what she looked like, sitting in that chair. She wrapped the black scarf around her head and face until only her eyes were visible. She paused a moment to compose herself, then pressed the button on her remote control – a still for the album. Her grinning associate walked towards her, turning the camera round so she could see it. She nodded, her eyes sparkling with deep joy through slits in the material. The image was quality, almost poetic in its simplicity. She took a deep breath and began to speak.

21

O'Neil briefed Grace and Newman. Actions had already gone out to satellite incident rooms on the shoe and axe from the North Shields scene, the bloody footprints in Fraser's flat, the route he took to his mother's house, the DVDs generally. In light of Newman's bombshell, the enquiry into who stood to benefit from Trevathan's will was less important now, she told them.

The Superintendent focused on her newly recruited retired detective. 'Grace, if you think of more that should be done, we'll put it out – no names required – we are Gold Command on these jobs. Our enquiry will be closed to satellite rooms and I'll decide what we feed into HOLMES, what we leave out.'

'Ooh!' Grace feigned excitement. 'I do love a silent room.'

It was the name she'd coined for the covert command centre she, Ryan and Newman had set up in her house. Irked by the mention, Ryan eyed her closely, his message best summed up by the cliché: don't bite the hand that feeds you.

O'Neil let it go without comment. Inviting him to carry on, she took her mobile from her pocket and checked the display. Ryan was fairly certain she was bluffing. There was no call, no incoming text. His guv'nor was simply taking the opportunity to establish a hierarchy, drawing a line between official and unofficial personnel, as she'd done when Grace first entered the apartment.

'The Home Office, our bosses, are keeping us in the dark,' Ryan said. 'There'll be a reason why they're not sharing intelligence. Frank, do you have anything on Trevathan's trial?'

Newman shook his head. 'The case is sealed.'

'Can it be unsealed?' O'Neil asked.

'Nothing is watertight,' he said. 'Leave it with me.'

'We have no alternative,' Ryan grumbled. 'We're locked out—'

'Sounds familiar.' Grace couldn't help herself.

O'Neil peered over the top of her specs, warning her to be careful.

Newman moved quickly on. 'The more you dig, the more nervous the Home Office will become. If you get close, they'll want to monitor everything you do. You can count on them making life difficult.'

'He's right.' Ryan's focus was O'Neil. 'Guv, we need to set a protocol so every one of us is clear on what we're doing, why we're doing it and what we're going to reveal to those working on the ground.'

'Agreed,' O'Neil said. 'I'll talk to Ford.'

'Good luck with that,' Ryan scoffed.

O'Neil ignored him. Whether they liked it or not, the grey man would have to be updated from time to time. 'We'll operate as an intelligence cell, running our own closed enquiry. That way, any other interested parties won't see all – I stress *all* – of what we find out. If we want something from Ford, we'll need to give him something in return.'

'I agree,' Ryan said. 'Otherwise it'll look suspicious.'

O'Neil carried on. 'We can choose to use the HOLMES computer system however we like. Grace will oversee linked incidents, looking for any ambiguity. I'll decide whether to view only or update electronically. Grace, I need you on board because you have more incident room experience than the rest of us put together. You will action jobs to satellite rooms. Ryan and I can't do everything.'

'And when the case comes to court?' Grace asked.

'I intend full disclosure at the pre-trial review phase. I'll make the sitting judge aware of the cell, why we chose to operate that way, and I'll ask for certain information to be kept secret.'

'Including my involvement,' Newman said. 'Just so you know, I will protect my informants.'

He would too.

'Ryan and I had a chat about that earlier,' O'Neil said. 'Don't worry, Frank. I'll be sure to take that into account when deciding whether to feed the machine or keep information we discover to ourselves.'

'I've done it numerous times when MI5 were being awkward,' Ryan said.

'MI5 don't trust anyone.' Grace glanced at Newman. 'That's how Frank and I met. I was getting rather close to someone his old colleagues were trying to protect. He was sent to show me the error of my ways.'

'Not that it made any difference.' Newman's joke resulted in a sharp elbow to the ribs.

O'Neil eyeballed her new recruits. 'Let me recap. You are employed here, Grace – we are now a unit of three. Frank doesn't exist. The way I see it, we have three categories of job:

the ones we don't mind sharing; those that are suspect – we feed those into the system under the Gold Command banner; and finally the red-hot jobs that we, and *only* we, act upon.'

Ryan was nodding. 'That's standard procedure in anti-terrorist cases. It's the only way we ensure that information isn't leaked – to or by anyone.'

'An effective strategy,' Newman said. 'If it's MI5 you're up against, they'll put up walls if they think you're poking your noses into business that doesn't concern you. And they'll be watching you in case you uncover information they don't have.'

Ryan was torn. There were two sides to every argument. Undercover policing and MI5 were separate entities, both conducting important work, viewed as the good guys until the wheel came off, then public perception changed. When jobs went wrong, as they sometimes did, the press were up in arms demanding complete transparency. Unfortunately, that didn't protect people who put their lives on the line. If you wanted to infiltrate organized crime gangs, hard-core activist groups or terrorist cells – or, God forbid, your own government – rules sometimes went by the wayside. They all agreed that people working behind the scenes deserved anonymity.

Paradoxically, this wouldn't help their unit.

Ryan hoped that Newman might cut through the bureaucracy. A spook with the ability to hide in plain sight was the perfect man to take on those seeking to withhold the truth in the interests of national security. He might even get lucky and find himself a whistle-blower, prepared to speak out for the greater good. In doing so, they might be putting their own life at stake in the process. Newman wouldn't want his informants compromised.

Ryan summarized: 'Over and above the fact that two of our victims operated in the public eye, we have nothing of evidential value. The important thing – apart from the list of actions Eloise issued – is the mysterious couple who made off with Trevathan's briefcase. His chambers deny they were responsible for retrieving it. If that's true, they'll be doing their utmost to find it.'

22

O'Neil didn't believe that the briefcase was in the hands of the Home Office and no one disagreed with her. Grace guessed that it might be with MI5, but it didn't sound like it to Ryan. It wasn't their style to use super-sleek, shiny vehicles in pristine condition. They preferred toned-down cars, the better to blend in. There was nothing covert about the grey Mercedes the couple had been driving; Mrs Forbes remembered everything about it. She'd given a good description of the woman too: film-star looks, high heels, distinctive red coat. MI5 operatives were usually nondescript, regular height, regular everything, nothing about their appearance that your average punter would remember. They certainly didn't wear expensive gear that screamed at you. Unless, as Newman was quick to point out, that was the impression they were trying to give, in which case the opposite was true.

'We'll bear that in mind as we move forward,' O'Neil said. 'So what we have is two high-profile deaths, both male, one nurse we think happened on the crime scene at the wrong moment (James Fraser may have seen the offenders we're seeking), and two missing victims from crime scenes in Brighton and North Shields, the local one is female.' She glanced at Ryan. 'Any update from the Family Liaison Officer?'

'Not yet.'

'When we're done, call and ask for one. Mrs Fraser may need our protection. Potentially she's the only living UK witness.'

'Unless our offenders are the man and woman who took the briefcase, in which case Trevathan's housekeeper also needs protection,' said Ryan.

O'Neil took a deep breath, frustrated by a case that was growing in complexity. 'Our priority – and this is where you come in, Grace – is to establish links between the British Ambassador to Denmark . . .' She glanced at Newman. 'Help me out here, Frank. I don't recall his name.'

'Paul Dean,' he said.

'Thank you. Grace, everything you can dig up on him and Trevathan, quick as you can. Frank, you're on the trial Trevathan was due to preside over. Ryan and I will be feet on the ground. As I said before, I'll try a direct approach to Ford, but I'm not confident. He's been less than cooperative so far. We're not just being paranoid either. He's been found out for withholding information. That said, the trial might have nothing whatsoever to do with our investigation, but without more intelligence we have no way of determining possible connections between the victims and the trial.' O'Neil took a short breather, checking the briefing sheet she'd prepared earlier, then added: 'Frank, you're more informed than we are. Use your contacts in whatever way you can. And just so we're clear, I do not want to know how you come by information. Get me what you can and I'll square it my end. Anything you think is relevant, feed it to Grace. Grace, you do nothing with it until I say so.'

Ryan caught Grace's eye across the room. She was excited to be on board, couldn't wait to get stuck in. There were three or four legs of the enquiry, each one as important as the next. Her role was making witness and evidence connections, finding similarities, overseeing satellite rooms, acting as researcher, receiver and office manager all rolled into one. She'd love that. Nothing fired her jets like running a major incident room. Retirement really had disappointed her. Cut adrift from the police force, she'd struggled to find her way. Ryan suspected the same was true of Newman. There was only so much fishing and sailing you could do if you were born to investigate criminal activity.

Ryan couldn't imagine life beyond the end of his career. 'Some of Frank's intel may be politically charged,' he said. 'We can't share it, except with each other.'

'I feel like a spook already,' Grace said.

O'Neil flashed a worried look at Ryan. He threw her a reassuring smile in return. Even though their employers weren't playing it straight, it was difficult for her to accept that they might have to use underhand methods to get at the truth. Coming from Professional Standards, that kind of subterfuge didn't sit well with her.

Time to show solidarity.

Ryan eyeballed the newlyweds. 'Eloise and I are coppers,' he said. 'We have to be careful. If things go tits-up, you're not the ones whose necks will be on the line. Ford is a nasty piece of work. He wants answers. If he doesn't get them – or we go too far – he'll take great pleasure in relieving us of our warrant cards.'

'And he'll do the same if you don't go far enough,' Newman reminded him.

'We still have rules and regulations to consider.'

There was an awkward moment.

O'Neil took the pressure off Ryan. 'We'll have a briefing at the end of each day, if not here, then remotely. Any questions?'

Grace glanced at her own briefing sheet, all but one item ticked off. She held it up, a flicker of discord on her face. 'This mentions a voice-recognition expert.'

'Already in the system,' O'Neil said. 'I should have mentioned it.'

As sure as he was of his own date of birth, Ryan had known Grace would bring the matter up. She'd identified the single most important aspect of the case. Ordinarily, their job was about observation. Without sight of Spielberg, they were screwed. It was impossible to form impressions, let alone make judgements, without body language, posture and gestures to go on. Her voice might prove to be their not-so-silent witness. Technology had moved on apace in recent years. Computer programmes could ascertain far more than dialect from the way a person spoke. Clever software was used extensively to detect emotional stress, excitement or confusion in speech patterns, exposing benefit and insurance fraud around the world. It helped law enforcement and criminal intelligence agencies track down the conmen and women who wanted something for nothing.

The discussion was about to turn ugly.

Newman sensed it too.

Both men knew where Grace was heading.

'The woman taunting us is cold and calculating,' Grace said. 'You can't wait until she kills someone else before you get an opinion on this. We all think it's the same voice. You know as well as I do how long it will take to organize a full profile. We haven't the luxury of time. Ryan? We have someone trustworthy in mind, right?'

O'Neil was way ahead of her. 'That's not going to happen.'

'Why not?'

'Because it's highly irregular—'

'And I'm not?' Grace huffed. 'Cut the crap, Eloise. You have the opportunity to go to someone with an ear for these things. Ryan's twin is cheap, discreet and, more to the point, available. She's also been vetted by the CPS, who, in case you didn't know, employ her these days. What's not to like?' Grace was using her eyes to smile and beg at the same time. 'C'mon! Caroline is as good on voices as I've ever come across in thirty years' policing. It would be a mistake not to use her.'

'In your opinion,' O'Neil said.

She was calm but forceful. Still, Ryan felt the need to step in between the two women. Pushed too hard, O'Neil would never go for it. Grace wasn't helping. When she had something to say, diplomacy went out the window. There was no way she was backing down. Right now, she was searching his face, waiting for support, determined to get her point across.

The pit bull needed taming.

'Excuse her bluntness,' Ryan said. 'She's a civilian now with no respect for rank—'

'Doesn't mean her point is invalid,' Newman said.

'Thanks, pet.' Grinning, Grace popped a piece of cake into her mouth and spoke with it full. 'Eloise, I know you're a detective who, how can I put it . . .' She paused. 'Shall we say, prefers a more conventional approach.'

Ryan cut her off at the pass: 'I think what Grace is trying to say—'

'Er, excuse me! I can speak for myself. My suggestion may be unorthodox, but Eloise shouldn't rule it out for that reason alone. We all know that Caroline has an amazing ability to pick up on the finer details of speech and dialect, not to mention emotional undercurrent. So what if it's cutting corners? We need a break and we need it now.'

Ryan shifted his gaze to O'Neil, using her title this time in case she thought he was taking liberties. Even if Grace no longer appreciated rank, he did. 'Guv, you know it's not a bad idea. Caroline would be happy to lend a hand. She'll work for nothing and immediately. It makes sense, if only until the official report comes through.' He checked his watch. 'If you call her now, she might still be at the office.'

'She's a valuable asset,' Newman added.

'You've used her before?' O'Neil was no fool.

Grace put a hand to her chest, acting the innocent. O'Neil scanned them one by one, three pairs of shifty eyes staring at her. Taking a deep breath, she gave her consent. This unit was beginning to feel incestuous.

23

Ryan reassured O'Neil that Caroline's temporary assistance was a good move. Although a lawyer in her own right, his twin had extrasensory skills the CPS had identified and utilized to the full. Being blind, her hearing was so well developed she was able to pick up on tone, pitch, speed and cadence – the unique speech patterns we all possess – so much so, she was given the majority of pre-trial recordings to listen to in her role as a Crown prosecutor. In all but title, she was an expert in voice recognition.

Ryan's unscheduled appearance at her office further along the Tyne at St Ann's Quay raised no suspicions. He was a well-known face there, escorting his twin to dinner as often as his work allowed. Despite her curiosity and many questions as to where they were headed, he gave her no explanation, over and above the fact that she'd be among friends.

When Caroline realized it was O'Neil, Grace and Newman that Ryan was taking her to see, she couldn't have been happier. Greetings dispensed with, the newly formed unit kept their cards close, telling her very little about the investigation before she sat down with the DVDs, affording her the opportunity to make her own judgements and present an unbiased opinion. O'Neil explained that one further recording had been sent to the British Embassy in Denmark they hadn't yet received, but she'd put in a request for it.

The video copies Caroline would listen to were numbered V1–V4 chronologically in order that she could easily remember them. The originals were under lock and key (minus the one from Denmark), each one bearing an exhibit label with a unique reference number for easy identification, irrelevant for her purposes.

She began with V1 (Kenmore), listening for what seemed like an age to her audience, asking to break off here and there to replay parts of the soundtrack until she'd heard enough.

'Wow!' she said. 'She's a compelling subject. The pauses I find interesting. They're her way of underlining what she's trying to convey without having to repeat or qualify her statements. On the face of it, there's no vulnerability in her voice. There is awkwardness beneath the confident façade though, don't you think? An underlying tension there. A need for justification perhaps—'

Grace huffed. 'Not a psychopath then?'

'I'm not qualified to say and, with respect, neither are you. Impaired reality might be a better phrase.' Caroline turned her head towards the retired cop. 'I've never liked labels, Grace. They stigmatize people. Criminality doesn't always equal emotional disturbance.'

Newman smiled at his wife. 'Well, that's put you in your place.'

'Oh, c'mon!' Grace said. 'The woman is psychotic. Delusional. Mental illness, personality disorder – call it what you will – she's hardly the full shilling, is she? If she's not off her head in the medical sense, that makes her worse, not better in my book. Either way, she doesn't seem depressed about how much pain and suffering she causes, does she?'

O'Neil cut her off. 'Will you stop riding roughshod over this discussion, Grace. You insisted on Caroline's involvement, now let her speak. You were saying, Caroline.'

'Underneath what can only be described as callousness, this woman cares a great deal.'

'No!' Grace jumped in again. 'She's a monster and you're making her sound like Nanny McPhee!'

Caroline laughed.

They all did.

It was good that they still had a sense of humour.

On the tape, there was a moment when the narrator paused. In that split second, Ryan's twin heard something the rest of them did not. She'd cocked her head on one side, eyes closed, concentrating hard. 'There's background noise here. Could be rushing water. Was the scene isolated?'

Ryan was suddenly in Kenmore on the viewing platform of Maxwell's folly, a swollen river roaring beneath him, white and foaming where it bubbled over rocks. The sound of his twin asking to see the next video dissolved the image. Ejecting V1, he inserted V2 in its place, the Brighton DVD. He pressed play and waited for the voiceover to stop before pausing it for Caroline to offer an opinion.

She was concentrating hard, fully absorbed in her task. 'Is she working alone?'

O'Neil wanted to know why she had asked.

'The narrator has been very careful not to mention anyone else. It might be her way of protecting another person.'

Reminded of O'Neil's theory, Ryan interrupted. 'Based on

something our controller said, Eloise wondered if the woman might be a stalker. I'm not so sure. If this particular victim had been stalked I'm sure he'd have reported it. There would be evidence: gifts, phone calls, letters. There weren't any.'

'I was merely putting forward a suggestion that she might be a bunny-boiler stalking the killer and not the victims, if that makes any sense.'

'It doesn't,' Grace said.

'Why not?' Newman asked. 'Stalking is psychological warfare. Maybe she's starring in her own fantasy, removing bodies to protect the object of her desire or getting ready to blackmail him. There's a big difference between being at the scene and going in later. Videoing the kill would add shock value. The fact that we don't have that suggests she wasn't there when it took place, which explains why she recorded after the event, not during.'

'She wants to be bloody careful it doesn't backfire on her,' Grace said. 'I have to say, I'm with Ryan on this – it's too far of a stretch. She's complicit, in my humble opinion. Up to her neck in it.'

'The way I see it, there's either no connection or a strong connection between the two,' O'Neil said. 'And, in my defence, the suggestion was made prior to any knowledge of the Copenhagen murder. Spielberg might stalk someone here in the UK, but it would be impossible to follow a target abroad without prior knowledge of his movements. We can probably knock that theory on the head right now.'

'Spielberg?' Caroline was lost.

'The death messenger,' Grace said.

Ryan explained. 'Spielberg is what we're calling her until we find an ID. She's as proficient with a camera as she is with a knife. Now she has firearms, there will be no stopping her.'

O'Neil shook her head at Ryan, a warning not to give too much away. 'I should've made it clear from the outset that whatever is said in this apartment stays in the apartment.'

It didn't need saying.

A black look from Grace prompted O'Neil to apologize.

Ryan's attention gravitated to the computer. He'd uploaded V3, the screen paused on the North Shields lock-up. He was pleased that his twin couldn't see what the rest of them could. The bloody scene was enough to turn the most unflinching stomach to mush. As yet, there were no reports of a missing female. And no body had been found.

'If she has a partner,' Caroline said, 'and it sounds as if you believe she does, I reckon it's a male. There are very few murder cases where both offenders are female. We don't need the Office for National Statistics to tell us that. Assuming there is a he lurking in the background, it wouldn't surprise me if this woman regards herself as his protector.' Her hand found the head of her own guardian – her guide dog. Bob wagged his tail in appreciation as she offered more insight. 'For what it's worth, I don't think she's one half of a monstrous Hindley/ Brady type partnership. However unsavoury her motives to you and me, she believes she's righting wrongs. It wouldn't surprise me to learn that she cares deeply for her other half.'

'Lover?' Grace winked at Newman. 'They have a tendency to get under your skin.'

'Matt?' Caroline tipped her head on one side. 'Did I miss something?'

She alone called him that.

Ryan almost blushed. 'The newlyweds are making out,' he said.

O'Neil dropped her head. Not quick enough for him to miss the sorrowful expression on her face. What was that all about? When she looked up, he averted his eyes and went back to the screen. He'd sat through the footage several times. Nevertheless, listening to the voiceovers back-to-back validated his opinion that Spielberg had turned up the heat. The North Shields video was her most chilling of all, in his opinion.

God help them if she ever flipped out.

'I'm no profiler but I don't think he's a lover,' Caroline said. 'But I'd say that this woman would appear perfectly normal to anyone who comes across her. Can I listen to the next one?'

Inserting V4, Ryan pressed play, wondering if his twin would be able to identify the difference between videos recorded in industrial buildings and a residential property. Halfway through, she asked him to pause it. Instinctively, he knew she'd picked up on something.

'She sounds rushed in this one. Bordering on upset. Could that be right? I'm sensing anxiety – panic even – she's not comfortable. You've all had years of experience. You've listened to witnesses recount traumatic events. What do you think?'

Ryan levelled with her. 'We all thought she was less confident here. There's a fundamental variation in her speech.'

Caroline agreed. 'If I didn't know any better, I'd say it was another woman entirely. A killer – she's admitted as much – but it's as if this situation was a mistake, accidental even, never meant to happen.'

'Don't you mean incidental?' Grace's tone was hard. 'There is a difference.'

Caroline ignored the dig. 'All I'm saying is there's real malice in the first three, not so much with this one.'

'Spontaneous or scripted?' Ryan asked.

'She doesn't sound like she's reading on any of the tapes.'

'Doesn't sound like she has a conscience either.' Grace said. 'Have you noticed how she reinforces the fact that they deserved what they got. It's a disclaimer.'

'Extrovert or introvert?' O'Neil asked.

Caroline waggled her hand from side to side. 'That's a tricky one. It's like asking if she's a leader or follower. It's important to understand who might be the dominant partner. Without a second voice, I can't help you. What I will say is, she sounds socially persuasive, like she's someone who's listened to in life. A teacher, perhaps.'

'Or film director,' Ryan suggested.

'What makes you say that?'

'The scenes were staged.'

'Right,' Caroline said. 'Did anyone detect a hint of York-shire?'

Grace was on it immediately, accessing her computer, tapping buttons furiously, trying to establish whether there had been any mention of the county across the HOLMES database within Gold Command – Operation Shadow. She shook her head, a scowl almost. 'There's nothing on the system.'

'She's trying hard to disguise it,' Caroline said. 'It wouldn't surprise me if she's taken elocution lessons – it's definitely there.'

'You should see the faces on these three,' Ryan said. 'They're standing here with their mouths open.' He switched his attention to the others. 'She used to play Guess the Accent when she attended the School for the Blind as a kid. She even won prizes.'

Caroline blushed.

'That's some party trick,' Newman said.

'A qualified voice-recognition expert will narrow it down further,' O'Neil said. 'No offence to you, Caroline.'

'None taken. Identifying exactly where in Yorkshire won't be easy, even for an expert. There are many dialects within the county; pronunciation and sentence construction is beyond me, I'm afraid.'

'You're doing fine,' Grace said in her defence.

'Better than fine,' O'Neil added.

Ryan was grateful for the show of appreciation.

Newman threw in a question. 'Who took the call when Spielberg gave scene locations locally?'

'For the North Shields scene, or Fraser's house in Whitley Bay?' O'Neil asked.

'The latter.'

Ryan pointed at his chest, answering 'Me,' for Caroline's benefit.

'Did you tape it?' Newman asked.

'I did.' His eyes found O'Neil's.

She didn't flinch.

'Ryan?' Newman was waiting. 'Caroline needs to hear that too.'

'I'm sorry.' The lie came easy. 'For some reason it didn't record.'

'What reason?' Grace blurted out. 'I taught you better than that, mister.'

'You did, and I can only apologize. I must've pressed the wrong button.'

Caroline detected the misrepresentation and kept it to herself.

Ryan could've kissed her. 'It's late.' He grabbed his jacket off the back of his chair. 'I'll walk you out, Caroline.'

'No need, I'd better get going too,' Newman said. 'The sooner I get away, the sooner I'll return. I'll drop Caroline at the station.'

He kissed Grace goodbye and left the apartment holding Caroline's hand. Ryan hung his jacket back on the chair. O'Neil flashed him a thank you for covering for her ass. They had been rumbled but not, it seemed, by Grace and Newman. Saved from embarrassing questions, O'Neil's residual doubts over Ryan's twin faded away.

24

Trying to keep herself cheerful, Grace arrived at work at the crack of dawn, complete with a Christmas tree and fairy lights. After putting it in the window, she got stuck into her computer where she remained for the next four hours monitoring HOLMES. With Newman away, Ryan and O'Neil decided to hold off on their planned trip to Brighton. They had photographic and recorded evidence from Sussex Police, CSI and progress reports, enough to go on until the victim was found. When he was – *if* he was – they would visit the town and then fly from London direct to Copenhagen. It seemed the best way forward when they were spread so thinly.

There was no obvious connection between Ambassador Dean and Lord Trevathan, apart from the fact that they had high-end jobs, worked in the public eye and had both died from stab wounds close to water. In the Ambassador's case, one blow to the stomach, one to the heart, the second proving fatal. He would have died, if not instantly, then within a few minutes. Ryan was confident that if a link existed between the two men, Newman would find it in London.

Like most undercover work, spying on individuals was often mind-numbingly boring, long hours spent immobile, unable to take a piss or eat. It was a world away from any Bond movie Newman had ever seen.

Despite choosing to live on the east coast of Scotland, he loved London. He walked unhurriedly from King's Cross railway station, heading in a southerly direction towards the Houses of Parliament. As he passed the building, vehicles were being checked for explosives with an under-car device he knew was the best and most effective product currently on the market. Only then was the black-and-orange hydraulic barrier lifted.

Not far away, Thames House, the home of MI5, was similarly well protected: a security code trackpad and secure lift into the building, plate-glass anti-climb devices on all window-sills. No chances being taken. Four police bikes sped out of the building, double red lines marking the side street. The Double-tree Hotel was situated here. If Newman had time to stay over, he'd book in and ask for a room with a view of the Thorney Street entrance to Thames House where he could observe the comings and goings of those employed there. If he took a southeast corner room, he could hitch up a slow-drip camera, monitoring the building twenty-four hours a day. Even better, the building next door was going through major refurbishment.

It paid to have a plan B.

The Thorney Street entrance was open. Someone walked out as Newman was watching it, which meant anyone could walk in. However, if they tried, they would meet with tough opposition. The rear entrance was secure, even if it didn't seem so. A female was standing outside smoking, coat flapping in the wind. He noticed the familiar lanyard around her neck, turned inward to hide her identity. She was one of millions of workers in the city wearing them. Nothing unusual about her . . .

Except there was.

In his younger days, he might have tapped her for a light, started up a conversation, turned on the charm. That wouldn't be smart. Simpler to follow one of the young geeks, most of them employed in cyber-security, leaving on pushbikes; easy enough to scare one half to death and take what he wanted. But Newman didn't intend to do that either.

Agents of his generation never retired. It was important to keep spooks of his calibre in the loop, ready to be reactivated at a moment's notice. Consequently, he still had clearance. He could come and go as he pleased. That didn't help. He didn't want to be scanned in and out of MI5 or pass through the many security devices. He wanted no one to know he was sniffing around. Time to call in favours.

'Did you ever contact Ford for disclosure?' Ryan asked. 'We need information on Trevathan's trial.'

O'Neil stopped shuffling papers. 'I did. He told me it was a matter for the Secretary of State for Scotland.'

'And what did the Secretary say?'

'Well *his* underling, another junior minister who wouldn't tell me his name, passed me back to the Home Office. I eventually got to speak to a human, for what good it did. Come to think of it, human might be stretching it a bit.' Lifting her mobile from her desk, she accessed a voice recording and pressed play.

'*This is Detective Superintendent Eloise O'Neil. Could I ask who I'm speaking to?*'

'Lawson.'

'Mr Lawson, I'm investigating the death of the Lord Justice Clerk, Leonard Maxwell, Lord Trevathan.'

Silence.

Ryan rolled his eyes at O'Neil. Her rank and status within the police was meaningless to some Home Office employees. As far as they were concerned, she was a pleb in uniform, shit on their shoes. The 'Plebgate' scandal – an altercation between Government Chief Whip, Conservative MP Andrew Mitchell, and police – came as no surprise to officers who, day in day out risked their lives, whether on general patrol or within the Diplomatic Protection Unit guarding Downing Street. Evidence had been called into question on both sides. Whatever the truth of it, Mitchell resigned, his position untenable. A year later, the dispute raged on. There had been several arrests, including five police officers, the lengthy investigation criticized by the Director of Public Prosecutions. Ryan had no doubt that the axe would fall on those accused of misconduct in public office. The recording of O'Neil's prompt to Lawson cut into his thoughts.

'Are you still there, Mr Lawson?'

'Yes, ma'am, how can I help you with that?'

'I'd like some information on the trial His Lordship was set to conduct on Monday the fourteenth of October.'

'I have no information to give in that regard.'

'Did you recover a briefcase from His Lordship's residence on Tuesday the fifteenth of October?'

O'Neil paused. When he failed to respond, she pushed harder.

'I have a statement to that effect from his housekeeper, Mrs

Forbes. She claims that two unidentified people – one male, one female – collected the briefcase. She assumed, or was led to believe, that they were from his Edinburgh chambers. My enquiries have drawn a blank there.'

'We have no information to give you on that subject, ma'am.'

'You will appreciate the difficulty that presents.'

Ryan had to admire O'Neil's style. She had no qualms about challenging Lawson's authority.

'Sir, if you do have the briefcase then there will be no police time wasted trying to find it. If you don't, that leaves only two scenarios: either you know who has it, or you are as clueless as I am. Perhaps you could indicate which it is?'

'I have no information to give you at this time.'

'Then am I to assume that the briefcase is still missing and has been collected by person or persons unknown for unlawful means?'

'I have no information to give you at this time.'

'I wonder if it's just me you're not talking to, Mr Lawson.'

Silence.

Grace stopped what she was doing, swivelled her chair to face Ryan and O'Neil. If Lawson had been in the room, she'd have stuck the nut on him. O'Neil was showing impatience, on and off the recording.

'Mr Lawson?'

'Are you asking a question, ma'am? My apologies, I thought you were making a statement.'

O'Neil's frustration was almost palpable.

'Can you tell me perhaps how you'd like me to proceed? In case you're in any doubt, that is a question, sir. Shall I do so on the assumption that the briefcase has been taken by unauthorized

persons, or as though you or some other person in authority has it?'

'I'm sorry, ma'am, we have no information to give you at this time.'

O'Neil stopped the recording. 'The royal "we" was a mistake,' she said. 'He tripped up there.'

Ryan was nodding. Someone else had been listening in.

'Dodgy bastard . . .' Grace mumbled. 'That briefcase will be sitting on his desk in Whitehall. If he doesn't have it, I'll run naked across the Swing Bridge.'

'Please don't.' Ryan looked like he'd just sucked a lemon.

Suppressing a grin, O'Neil restarted the recording.

'Perhaps Mr Ford could answer for himself.'

'Nice one, guv,' said Ryan, while Grace signalled her approval with a fist pump.

There was a moment's silence on the tape, then Eloise continued:

'You have said repeatedly that you have no information to give me at this time. Does that mean that the matter is under review, that you may be able to release such information at a later date?'

'I have no information to give you at this time.'

'I'd like to thank you for being helpful, Mr Lawson. For your information, I'm going to proceed as if the briefcase is unlawfully missing and most probably in the hands of criminals. And, because you know how my unit is funded, sir, if you have information now that you are failing to disclose, please tell Mr Ford that I will recoup any wasted police time, energy, effort and money from your own department. Thank you very much.'

O'Neil stopped the recording. 'He thought he was home and

dry. He could not have been more wrong.' She grinned at the others, pressed the play arrow on her mobile phone.

'Before I go, I'd like some information about a British expatriate. Can you tell me if Ambassador Dean had received threats of any nature before he was murdered in Copenhagen?'

'Who told you that?'

It was Ford's voice, loud and clear.

'Sorry, sir. I'm losing you. Hello? Sir? Are you there?'

The dialling tone arrived when O'Neil cut him off.

'Ha!' Grace was out of her seat, hands pressed together, head bowed, no eye contact, as if paying homage to His Holiness the Dalai Lama. She raised her head. 'Oh, Special One, I am truly impressed.'

Ryan laughed.

O'Neil did too.

Such an evasive response and downright lack of cooperation from the powers that be was no more or less than they'd expected. For all that, it was no easier to take. O'Neil's nous and leadership had cemented a unit forced to plough on regardless. Her retired and serving detectives might well be in a temporary state of desperation, but she was confident that they were up to it. No conspiracy of silence would blow them off course.

25

The afternoon was a long hard slog, the hands of the clock winding themselves round to six before Ryan took a breather for anything more than a bathroom break. O'Neil was still head down in her work; the axe from the North Shields scene was clean and prints on the Coke can were useless – it had probably just been lobbed from a passing car. She took it in her stride, resigned to the fact that no one was going to hand her evidence on a plate. Grace was so swamped she'd had to insist that any requests to Gold Command must come in via email from here on. She simply didn't have time to field calls and do all O'Neil had asked of her.

Ryan was missing his former role: preventing terrorism, monitoring subversive organizations and disrupting organized crime. Back then he knew who the enemy was. From the dejected look on her face, O'Neil was probably feeling the same way. Her old job – investigating police wrongdoing – was preferable to fighting those who were supposed to be facilitating their enquiries.

What they wouldn't give for a level playing field.

Fountain Lake, Battersea Park, London. Newman was sat on a bench reading a newspaper. A figure approached, grey woollen coat, striped scarf, a nondescript man in his forties, earphones in place. He was holding the volume control, occasionally nodding as if talking to someone. In fact he was doing nothing of the kind.

He took a seat, making no attempt to greet Newman. 'What do you want, Frank?' he said.

Newman kept his eyes on the news. 'To locate a briefcase,' he said. 'It's in the hands of a Mercedes driver. Young. Attractive. Female. Male accomplice. One of yours, I suspect. She's getting in the way of an operation—'

'Whose?'

'Special unit operating out of Newcastle.'

'Nothing to do with us.'

'Shame. I need the lowdown on that too. You have work to do.'

'Like I said—'

'I'm in credit, Tom. Find out. There's a time and rendezvous point written on the page I'm reading. Memorize it.'

Tomkinson's eyes scanned left and right as if he was taking in the park's lake view. He stood up, took off slowly, heading back towards Chelsea Bridge.

Ryan's tired eyes met O'Neil's across their desks. They were exhausted, making negligible progress. At every turn, a brick wall presented itself, wrecking their theories, ruining their plans. There was no one to interrogate, no leads to follow up. They had nothing tangible to go on and little prospect of that state of affairs changing anytime soon. All they had were scores of unanswered questions. Their work base, nice though it was, was driving them nuts.

'Crime pattern analysis isn't going to help us,' O'Neil said.

'There are no signposts, just the bloody woman's voice baiting us. I know we haven't seen them all yet, but the crime scenes we've visited so far are clean. I'm beginning to think Ford wasn't so stupid after all in thinking that Spielberg robbed a blood bank and staged the killings to piss us off.'

'Except we have three bodies now,' Ryan reminded her.

'And nowt else.'

They lapsed into morose silence, hoping that Newman's informant activity might pay off. He hadn't yet called to update them.

Grace was getting restless.

O'Neil lifted her head. 'Did you contact the Family Liaison Officer?'

Ryan nodded. 'Mrs Fraser said James let himself in with a key.'

'So why didn't they kill him at his mother's place?'

'Good question.' Grace didn't turn around. 'His killers couldn't know he didn't live there.'

'I asked the very same question of the FLO,' Ryan said. 'She questioned Mrs Fraser again. Apparently she was in the kitchen when James arrived. She joined him in the living room for a hug almost immediately. You know what mums are like. There were no blinds or curtains up in that room. People living alone like to see foot traffic, don't they? In that respect, Mrs Fraser is no different. She didn't notice anyone hanging around outside but my guess is they saw her and decided to wait it out.'

'Lucky for her.'

'I'm fairly sure she's safe.'

'Are you, Ryan. *Really*?' Grace turned to glare at him. 'What if it was your mother? Would you be so certain then? There may be no suggestion that she saw the offenders, but they're not to know that, are they?'

She had a point.

Ryan switched his gaze to O'Neil. 'Mrs Fraser didn't go outside when James left the house, but if we're right, the offenders know where she lives. Because of that and the fact that Grace is giving me such a hard time, I'll organize a panic alarm immediately. The one thing we have is money. Let's spend it.'

'Fine,' O'Neil said. 'Give me a reminder in two weeks and we'll review it. In the meantime, I have high-profile victims in three countries with seemingly no connection whatsoever, a male and a female with film-star looks yet to be identified, and no missing persons reports that match our timeline, such as it is. Oh, I forgot, we have no forensic evidence either. The national database isn't much good unless you a) know what you're looking for, b) have a clue when it occurred, or c) you have evidence to compare it with.' They had zilch. 'Now can we get this fucking briefing underway?'

26

They had less than five minutes to prepare, by which time Ryan had gone walkabout to take a phone call. Grace had a fresh sparkle in her eye, a notebook flipped open on her knee, a signal that she was ready to feed back to the team. O'Neil's frustration was at boiling point. Using her hands as winders, she gestured for Ryan to end his conversation as soon as he could.

He hung up, put the phone in his pocket.

'Finally!' she asked. 'What have you got for me, Ryan?'

'You said we might get a lead from the shoe at North Shields. Well, it seems we're in luck. There are very few stockists of that particular brand.'

'Action that please.' O'Neil was talking to Grace.

'Shall I shove a brush up my arse and sweep the floor while I'm at it?'

'Thank your lucky stars you're an overseer,' O'Neil said. 'Or you'd be doing everything yourself.'

Winding her neck in, Grace scribbled a note, adding to the growing list of competing actions she intended to put out to the Northumbria incident room. 'Seeing as we're already on feet, let's stick with that a moment. There's an update on the bloody footprints from James Fraser's flat: confirmation that two people were there at the time he was killed, shoe sizes six and ten.'

'That's not much help,' O'Neil said. 'Those are both pretty standard.'

'Agreed. The impressions weren't that great either. They've gone off to the UK National Footwear Database. Let's hope we get a positive result on the tread patterns.'

'Can we agree not to rule out anyone who isn't a size six or ten?' Ryan said. 'I've known enquiries stall when detectives made assumptions they later found to be untrue.' When he was a rookie, his boss had written a load of possible suspects out because they didn't wear shoes of a particular size, only to find out the offender was wearing shoes two sizes too big.

O'Neil agreed not to discount anyone because of it.

Grace eyed the next item on her list. 'The toxicology report on Trevathan is in. It showed Propranolol beta blocker in his system.'

Ryan's interest plummeted. 'Is that all?'

'You were expecting cocaine?'

'I meant try harder. We're not impressed so far.'

'Show some patience,' Grace bit back. 'Did I say I was finished?'

'Get on with it then.'

'Our lads finally nailed James Fraser's movements after he left work on Sunday morning.' She beckoned them across to her computer, where she'd uploaded a local map with the jogging route already picked out. It had approximate start and finish times, pinpointing where he'd been seen by witnesses or captured on CCTV. 'He left Rake Lane Hospital after his night shift ended at six a.m. He took the A192 Preston Road North, was seen running east into Tynemouth Road here, then south onto Stephenson Street, zigzagging through Saville Street,

Bedford Street, eventually dropping down onto Liddell Street, Bell Street and Union Quay.'

'AKA the Fish Quay,' Ryan said.

Grace nodded. 'There are no fewer than six CCTV cameras and two receiver antennae along that stretch.'

'Fraser *was* clocked,' Ryan whispered under his breath. 'He ran past our crime scene?'

'Looks like it. Unfortunately, none of the cameras are trained on the lock-up, so we have some homework still to do. At around ten past eleven, he left his mother's house, ran up Pier Road past Tynemouth Priory, seen here and here by joggers he knew.' She was using her forefinger to indicate specific points on the map. 'Along Sea Banks and on past King Edwards Bay. A webcam caught him on Longsands Beach on his way home to High Spencer Street in Whitley Bay.'

'Good job!' O'Neil patted her on the shoulder.

'Not my doing,' she said.

'Well, pass on my thanks to the incident room,' O'Neil said. 'And after the briefing, get yourself away. You need a break. You're no use to me burnt out.'

Ryan eyed O'Neil as they retook their seats. A class act, she always gave credit where it was due and *always* valued her staff. She was no pushover when it came to sharing bad news either, dealing with the bereaved with sensitivity and patience. She never backed down if she thought she was right and yet was the first to admit when she was wrong. You knew where you were with her. Integrity, discretion and fair-mindedness were characteristics he valued above all else, traits she shared with his former boss Jack Fenwick.

'I'm not finished yet,' Grace said. 'The incident team are

cross-referencing CCTV footage to see if we can identify a vehicle that was on the Fish Quay in the early hours *and* in Whitley Bay between eleven ten and midday, which is the Home Office pathologist's best guess on time of death. Now for the really good news.'

'She always saves the best 'til last,' Ryan said.

O'Neil waited with bated breath.

'I got an email from a probationer whose beat is the Fish Quay,' Grace continued. 'He happens to share his duty patch with a young lass called Gloria. She was in a bit of a state and on the batter.' She looked at O'Neil. 'In case you are in any doubt – you being a posh girl – that doesn't mean she works in a fish shop, Eloise. It means she's on the game.'

'You should do stand-up.' O'Neil was enjoying the camaraderie.

'So,' Grace said, 'when the probationer enquired further, she told him she was picked up in the small hours of Sunday morning by a guy called Stevie – sorry, that's all I've got. Well not quite, I'm coming to that. Anyway, she was taken to a doss-house and dropped back at the Fish Quay around six-thirtyish.'

Grace paused deliberately, allowing the information to sink in. She could see her colleagues' minds working. It didn't take long for them to make the jump.

'She couldn't be more specific on timing?' There was hope in O'Neil's question.

''Fraid not. She was pretty tanked up.'

'Damn. She might've seen Fraser. He'd be arriving about then.'

'My thoughts exactly, but she did see something?' Grace raised a smile. 'After she got out of the car, Gloria went for a wander to beg a smoke from one of the other working girls. When she returned seconds later, she noticed that Stevie's vehicle was still parked where she got out. Suddenly he came tearing out of a lock-up across the road like he'd seen a ghost. He got in his vehicle and drove off at speed. The tosser almost ran her down.'

'He saw the body.' Ryan wasn't asking, he was telling. 'That explains the scuff marks the CSIs found near the entrance.'

'There is another scenario,' Grace suggested. 'He walked in on the murder taking place.'

O'Neil was shaking her head. 'He wouldn't be alive to tell the tale.'

'We don't know that he is.' Ryan eyeballed her. 'They would hardly kill Fraser and let Gloria's punter go—'

'Unless they couldn't catch him,' Grace said in support of O'Neil.

'If they came out after him, Gloria would surely have seen them. They wouldn't think twice about offing a prostitute, would they?' Ryan said. 'Especially if she'd had a skinful.'

'Which suggests her punter saw the body rather than the offence taking place.'

'What do we know about this guy?'

'He's a regular, a nasty piece of work, up one minute, down the next.' Grace lifted a hand. 'No pun intended. Gloria never knows what mood he'll turn up in but, he normally pays well, especially if he wants extras.' She grimaced. 'Don't ask, Ryan. Eloise won't want to hear it any more than I did. Anyway, Gloria was skint, so she took a chance and went with him, daft cow, even though a couple of weeks ago he broke her nose.' Grace took a breath. 'This is where it gets interesting. In return for her trouble, Gloria nicked his watch. That's what Saturday night was all about. He wanted his property back. After screwing her brains out, he searched her bag. Fortunately, she didn't have the watch on her. Unfortunately, he gave her another clout. The bastard says he'll be there every week until she returns the watch or repays the debt in other ways.'

'Then we'll be around Saturday night to lock him up,' Ryan said. 'Assuming we haven't already found him.'

'It gets better.' The detectives exchanged an excited look as Grace peered at the email on her computer screen. 'The watch has the initials SFW engraved on the rear of the casing with the inscription: *40 Today!* One very clever probationer has retained it in evidence, get this, "in case it comes in useful".'

'Ha! CID training coming up,' Ryan said. 'I assume there's an action out to trace Stevie boy?'

'What did Gloria do after that?' O'Neil interrupted. 'Sorry, Ryan, this is important.'

'She sat down on the pavement for a smoke.' Grace shifted her gaze from O'Neil to Ryan. 'And yes there's an action out.'

O'Neil wanted more. 'So no one came out of the lock-up after Stevie?'

'No, and we all know why, don't we?' Ryan said. 'The killers had more important things to do in Tynemouth. They had already gone to kill Fraser.'

His words hung in the air.

And still he wasn't done theorizing. 'They wait outside his mum's house until he leaves to go home. They kill him, but don't risk going back to the lock-up to move their first victim in daylight. The place is crawling with folks on a Sunday. People love walking along the Fish Quay, eating chips or calling in for a cuppa at the Old Low Light Café. I do it myself on a regular basis. They'd have to wait for a more appropriate time to get rid of the body. They dump it in the river, make their video and away they go.'

O'Neil cut him off. 'They wouldn't risk making the video at night, Ryan. Their lights would be visible from outside.'

'OK, maybe my timing is out.' Ryan thought for a moment. 'The counter on the North Shields DVD was running at 15:45 when I noticed it. What time was sunset on Sunday, fourish?'

Grace brought up the information. 'Nine minutes to, to be precise.'

'Guv, even on a good day most people would be away home by then. At this time of year it's bloody cold down on the Fish Quay when the sun goes down. I reckon they sneaked in unseen, made their video around the time recorded on the DVD, and dumped the victim soon after dark. Do we know if this Stevie character is local?'

Grace grinned. 'We even know what type of vehicle he drives. The incident team are doing a PNC trawl of that make and model. It won't take us long to trace this bloke.' Ryan and Grace high-fived. It was the best news they'd heard all day.

27

For once Grace did as she was asked without a fight and left straight after the briefing to go back to her hotel. It was getting on for eight thirty when Ryan let her out and watched her exit the lift on the ground floor. He felt guilty for having intruded on her first months of married life and suspected that O'Neil did too. She wouldn't have asked had she not been under pressure to prove her worth. She was desperate to engage the right calibre of help. Grace and Newman happened to fit the bill. The spook still hadn't surfaced. Ryan took that as a positive sign.

'She's good, isn't she,' O'Neil said when he walked into the room.

'The best there is.'

'You rate her. That's nice.'

'Not nice, she earned it. There's nothing she doesn't know about running a major incident room. She might be argumentative from time to time, but she's the salt of the earth. Grace would do anything – and I do mean *anything* – to protect those she cares about.' He sat down under O'Neil's scrutiny. There was a shot of whisky on the arm of his chair and one already half-empty in her hand, a half-bottle on the desk behind her. Lifting his glass, he sniffed the amber liquid. 'You'll be a friend for life for taking her on. It'll give her purpose.'

'She's newly married! Isn't that purpose enough?'

'You tell me, I've never been married.'

'Me either.'

There it was again, that same flash of sadness Ryan had seen on O'Neil's face yesterday. There were occasions when she looked like a torn soul. She hid it well, but now and again he caught a glimpse of the edge of an emotion he couldn't easily identify.

Ford wasn't the only one keeping secrets.

Ryan suspected that Eloise had been deeply hurt in the not too distant past. He'd been there too. He hadn't noticed her pain at first but, since he'd got to know her better, he'd recognized the signs. Whatever the story behind it – and there would be one – it was making her very unhappy.

'Ever considered what you might do after you've done your time?' he asked.

'You make it sound like a life sentence.'

He chuckled. 'Feels like it sometimes.'

'No, I've not given it a thought.'

'Well give it some now,' he encouraged her. 'What'll it be: sun, sea and sangria, or will you stick around in the cold, windy north? Personally, I'd rather stick pins in my eyes than live abroad.'

'Oh, I don't know. Right now I could handle the Bahamas for a month or two.' Kicking off her heels, O'Neil lifted her right leg and wiggled her toes, a dreamy expression on her face. 'I love the feeling of sand beneath my feet, the sun on my back, the sound of crashing waves. Sailing would be good. Grace and Frank appear healthy on it, don't they? Is small talk now your specialist subject?'

Ryan bridled, taken aback by the question. 'Just making conversation, guv.'

She apologized, an awkward moment.

He stood up, walked to the window and stood by the Christmas tree. He could never tire of the view from their base: the iconic bridges, the Sage, the River Tyne shimmering in the moonlight, like a rippling silver ribbon snaking its way to the North Sea. More often than not, the sight would calm him. This time, it didn't help.

What in God's name had made her act that way?

Ryan knew very little about her, only where she lived, though he'd never been invited round. Fair enough. Lots of coppers defended their personal space. In that respect, they were no different, except she'd turned up uninvited at his tiny cottage on the coast when he went into meltdown after Jack's death. She adored the sea view almost as much as he did.

He downed his whisky in one slug.

When he turned to face her, she stared at him. Inscrutable. Intense. As if a chasm had opened up between them. A minute ago they were having a perfectly amiable conversation. Now it was as if a switch had been flicked, all the warmth had gone out of her. If he had to put a word to it, he'd have described her as numb. He was tempted to ask her what had changed. They had built a rapport and had some fun. Had she backed off because they were now formally linked whereas before they were not? It was the only plausible explanation. Maybe she couldn't be his guv'nor and a close friend and confidante.

That must be it . . .

Shame.

'Am I boring you?' she said.

'Excuse me?'

'You're someplace else, DS Ryan. I'm not used to being ignored when I'm sharing a bottle of expensive Scotch. I thought we were off duty—'

'I thought we were on first-name terms.' He hadn't meant to sound so pissed off.

'Only when the others are here and we're pretending to like each other.'

He couldn't work out if she was being serious or having a laugh. 'And when they're not?'

'You can call me whatever you like.' She *was* teasing him, trying to backpedal on her cutting remark. It had altered the dynamic between them and she knew it. Lifting her glass, she threw him a wide smile. 'Join me in a top-up?'

'I'm good, thanks.'

She poured herself another and left the room.

Newman hadn't been waiting long when Tomkinson arrived – same drill, different park bench. The brief he'd been given hadn't taken long to process. Both men sat for a while without speaking.

'Are you concerned with the missing briefcase?' Newman asked.

'No.'

'You have it?'

'Five have it.' It was getting late. Tomkinson blew on his hands and rubbed them together, telling Newman that he'd started the alarms on all grey Mercedes at Thames House to see who turned up to switch them off.

'Good plan.'

'Works every time. Who wants a flat battery?'

'Who wants to know they've been made by a geriatric?'

'The simple methods are the best.'

Newman almost chuckled. 'Name?'

'Hill, Judith.' Tomkinson knew the name alone wouldn't cut it.

Newman clocked a digital stick in the empty sandwich box his ex-colleague would leave behind. 'What's your take on Trevathan's trial?'

'Never went ahead. His murder is unconnected. It was no assassination.'

'That's what I thought.'

'What about the special ops unit?'

'Classified.'

'That much I know.'

Tomkinson was succinct, as always. He'd done his home-work. While he spoke, Newman listened intently and without interruption, making notes on his fresh crossword puzzle. What Tomkinson had to say provided Frank with a challenge he didn't expect, one he knew would blow up in his face when he returned to base. As debts go, this one had been repaid in full.

O'Neil was back. She drank like Kalinda off *The Good Wife* although, in her case, the shots were tequila. There were other similarities. The in-house private investigator at Stern, Lock-hart, Gardner kept people at a distance. So did O'Neil. How far did the similarity to Kalinda extend? Had O'Neil come out of an abusive relationship too? Ryan chanced his arm. He daren't enquire directly. He tried another route, hoping she'd open up and tell him the truth.

'Is that making you feel better?'

'As it happens, yes.'

'No one said this job would be easy, guv.'

The comment threw her. 'It's not the job.'

Good start. 'Then why are you so down in the mouth? Having second thoughts?'

'About this?' She waved the hand holding the whisky, her forefinger pointing at their swish surroundings. 'Hell, no!'

Ryan almost choked on his words. 'Is it me?'

'No. I needed a colleague I could trust. You fit the bill perfectly. It's definitely not you, Ryan. Please don't think that—'

'What then? These eggshells are killing my feet.'

She wasn't smiling.

Ryan sighed. 'When you offered me this job, you said we'd have a lot of fun. I've had more fun sparring with that tosser Maguire.' His jovial reference to his predecessor, her second-in-command, drew no reaction. She was frustrating the hell out of him. He retreated to work once more. 'It's unlike you to be so negative. It's early days, guv. We'll get there if we push on.'

'I'm fine, Ryan. Just knackered.'

'You want to get out of here for a bit?'

'You trying to cheer me up?'

'Do you need cheering up?'

A shrug. 'Maybe.'

'Why don't we take a walk, get a bit of air. Always works for me. Where would you like to go?' he said. 'My shout.'

'Aren't you meeting Caroline?'

'She's at the Sage with Hilary.'

'Yes, I forgot. Sorry I spoiled your evening.'

'You didn't.' Ryan lied. She had, but not in the way she suggested. 'Caroline is staying over in town tonight. She always does if she's out late. Alnwick is a hike for her at the best of times. At night, it's impossible. I'm meeting them for a nightcap. I'll see Hilary into a taxi, walk Caroline to her hotel.'

'You're very considerate.'

'Cautious.'

'I meant where women are concerned. That's nice.'

'Careful, guv, that's twice you called me nice.'

'And twice you called me "guv" in the last few minutes.' She took a long, deep breath. 'Look, I was out of order before. Ignore me when I'm like that. It's not you, it's me.' She paused, cleared her throat. 'There's no need for formality, not when we're alone.'

Ryan's pulse quickened. 'Alone' suggested intimacy, attachment, something more than they had right now. He glanced at his watch. 'I've got time for one or two, if you have.'

Uncrossing her legs, O'Neil slipped her shoes back on and stood up, glancing at her own watch as she lifted her bag from the floor. In the blink of an eye, her expression changing from someone willing to make nice to someone in a state of sheer panic.

'Shit!' Her eyes met his. 'I don't believe this. I'm sorry, Ryan. I didn't realize it was so late. I have to go. Now.' She made for the door, then glanced back at him, a pang of conscience perhaps. 'Some other time?'

'Sure. No problem.'

'See you tomorrow.'

With that, she was gone.

More curious than miffed, he walked to the window and looked out. A moment later, she emerged on the pavement below, her flaming red hair whipping around in the breeze as she crossed the street to where a silver car sat waiting. She opened the door and jumped in. Really? A Porsche Carrera? Who knew she was so well connected? From this angle, it was impossible for him to see who was driving as the car moved off. The vehicle screamed affluence. Whoever owned it certainly wasn't afraid to show it off. Unable to compete, Ryan grabbed his leather jacket from the back of his chair, switched off the lights and left the apartment alone.

28

O'Neil got out of the car when the door was held open and heard the expensive clunk of a high-end vehicle as it closed behind her. She felt his arm slip round her shoulder, a slight pressure of his fingers as he gave her arm a squeeze and led her from his designated parking spot in the underground car park of his apartment block. It was a chilly evening.

They travelled up in silence.

The lift too was inaudible. Everything about the place was hushed, calming. It was somewhere she'd love to live if she could afford it. There had been a time when it might have been possible. That was history now, so far gone, she wondered if it had ever existed.

He stood back as she entered his apartment, displaying perfect manners, as always, helping her off with her coat, placing it on a hanger he took from the hallway closet. He seemed unaware of how it made her feel to be there. Eloise played along, giving the impression she was over it.

She wasn't.

Still raw from the separation, her heart felt fragile, as if it might shatter at any moment. No matter how much effort she put into hating him – and she did – it didn't cancel out the love or lessen her loss. It served only to increase her rage. At times the pain was unbearable. She felt hollow, as if someone had scooped out her guts and discarded them, leaving an empty shell behind. Anyone who could make another human being feel so utterly worthless didn't deserve success – much less happiness – and yet he had both. Eloise had tried hard to ignore articles about him in the newspapers. It was difficult when his face was staring out from the front page on a regular basis. He was headline news, a hotshot lawyer going places.

'Same again, Eloise?' Her host was holding a crystal decanter in his right hand. He'd smelled whisky on her breath when they kissed in the car. He was too polite to mention it directly.

She nodded. 'Thank you.'

Her eyes misted ever so slightly. It was hard being around him, and yet it was strangely comforting. Eloise wanted to sever contact; he'd insisted on keeping in touch, a sentiment driven by guilt, she imagined. His conscience simply wouldn't allow him to let her go completely, even though he knew it hurt her to see him, to remember what they once had: a close bond and plans for the future. In the end, she acquiesced, agonizing as it was, too spent to argue any longer. More than that: she'd accepted his help.

She dropped her gaze, self-hatred permeating her skin. She was no better than Gloria, a prostitute taking what was offered from a man more powerful than her, the only difference being that he didn't knock her around. On the contrary, he saw himself as her protector.

'Two fingers or three?' He invited her to sit.

She held up two fingers by way of an answer and sat down, watching as he poured the drinks. He handed her one, brushing the back of his free hand across her left cheek. A sympathetic gesture, a demonstration of the level of affection he still felt for her.

He sat down opposite, eyeing her with interest.

'How are you?'

She knew his concern for her welfare was genuine, but that didn't make it any easier to take.

Swallowing her grief, she replied: 'As well as can be expected – I believe that's the accepted phrase.' She looked away. 'Lovely tree.' She didn't intend to hang around. She'd stay long enough to hear what he had to say and then she'd leave. She'd run as fast as her legs would carry her to the sanctuary of her new office. She'd rather be with Ryan. She could tell he'd been gutted when she fled 'their place' earlier. He deserved better. She'd never tell him that he'd restored her faith in men, but she had every intention of taking him into her confidence.

When the time was right . . .

29

Saturday, 14 December, 7 a.m. Ryan had the news playing low on the radio. The world was mourning a symbol of peace. Following a memorial ceremony in Johannesburg earlier in the week, world leaders were making themselves ready for the state funeral of Nelson Mandela in his ancestral home of Qunu in South Africa's Eastern Cape province.

The entry alarm bleeped.

Ryan switched off the radio, expecting O'Neil to emerge. Instead he looked up to see Grace. Newman had made it home in the early hours of the morning, but she hadn't slept well. Stuff on her mind, she said. Ryan knew the feeling. Despite a couple of beers with Hilary and Caroline, he'd tossed and turned all night, wondering what was eating O'Neil, where she'd disappeared to in such a hurry and who with.

'You know what was keeping me awake?' Grace didn't wait for an answer as she dumped her bag and sat down. 'In every case, the DVDs arrived on a Tuesday and, in every case, the footage was filmed on a Sunday. I reckon she's a weekday worker with a sideline in knocking people off at weekends and enough cash to move around at will. Not that it takes us anywhere. Flights are ten a penny these days. We still have integration in this country. The EU is a free-for-all. Mind you, the result of the upcoming referendum might put paid to that.'

She shuddered at the thought. 'Sorry, I promised not to talk politics, so let's not go there. The point I'm trying and failing to make is that thousands of Brits fly into Copenhagen unchecked every week.' Her eyes strayed from her desk to O'Neil's bedroom door. 'Is Eloise still in her PJs?'

Ryan ignored the question. 'Where's Frank?'

'Expecting a call.' She was logging on. 'He'll be here.'

'He has news?' Ryan asked.

'Yes, but he never told me everything. You know what he's like. He hates to repeat himself. He'll feed back when we're all here and not before. I was hardly awake when he climbed into bed. He was spent, I know that much. I wanted to get an early start this morning. He wanted to eat. A first-class ticket and still no catering on the train last night. To say that he was unhappy would be a gross understatement.'

'That's poor service.'

'Piss-poor. The air was blue. I couldn't be arsed to cheer him up. I told him to get over it and left before breakfast. He'll be here, hopefully in a better mood and with something of value to contribute concerning Trevathan's trial. I've been thinking about that too. It must be a security issue. Why else would Ford impose such secrecy?'

'We'll know soon enough.'

'Did you know MI5 has doubled in size in the last fifteen years?' She made a show of looking over her shoulder checking for eavesdroppers. 'That's probably confidential. Keep it to yourself or I'll have to kill you. I'm under strict orders not to repeat anything Frank tells me – not that he tells me much.' She hardly stopped for breath. 'Can you believe it? There are over two and a half thousand staff engaged in counter-terrorism alone. If anyone is in any doubt that the UK is under threat from ISIS, they can think again.' For the first time since she'd come in and began spouting off, she looked at him, properly looked at him. 'You're such a cheerful soul this morning. What's up, Grumpy? You get out of bed the wrong side too?'

'I can't get a word in edgeways—'

'Conversational intercourse is good for the soul. You should try it sometime. While you're at it, try the other kind, you'd be far less bloody miserable.'

Ryan didn't laugh.

He was still thinking about what she'd said about ISIS. The country *was* under attack. It depressed him, more than he cared to admit, to her or anyone. Earlier in the year, the slaying of Fusilier Lee Rigby on a London street in broad daylight had shocked the nation. Because of his former role in Special Branch, Ryan knew jihadists were plotting many more acts of terrorism. Such threats were taken very seriously and he was under no illusion that worse was to come. MI5 worked closely with GCHQ, the National Crime Intelligence Service, the Serious and Organized Crime Agency and other law enforcement agencies. He could only conclude that their decision to work against his new unit on this occasion meant that there was a plot being hatched somewhere that was an even greater threat to national security than the murder of an ambassador and a high-ranking judge.

'Coffee's hot,' he said.

Grace was staring at O'Neil's bedroom door. 'If she has company, she's not making near enough noise.'

Ryan didn't laugh. 'She's not in. Went out last night. Never came back.'

'Party girl! Good for her.' Grace poured herself a brew and got to work.

So their guv'nor had a private life. It was none of Ryan's business. The fact that *he* wasn't Porsche man was probably for the best. It hadn't done him any good getting involved with a colleague – not that he was comparing Eloise to Roz Cornell. They were very different women.

He tried not to sulk.

He was pleased for O'Neil.

The hell he was.

Frank had given Grace the digital stick his London informant had left behind. By nine thirty, she'd uploaded the image of Judith Hill and sent it to Mrs Forbes. The housekeeper was on the phone in seconds. She'd taken one look at the photograph and confirmed that Hill was indeed the woman who'd collected the briefcase from Trevathan's home. This was unequivocal corroboration of the best kind.

'Great,' Ryan said. 'Though I doubt it's going to get the enquiry moving.'

'You said that with a lot less conviction than the news deserved. This is progress, another piece of the puzzle in place. Stop stressing. O'Neil will be here.'

Ryan looked away, unable to hide his disappointment that she still hadn't surfaced, an emotion that was eating away at his gut like a parasite. He couldn't make up his mind whether he was worried about Eloise or cross with her. She hadn't made contact to explain her delay.

It wasn't like her.

Pulling his mobile from his pocket, he was about to give her a call when Grace's phone began to vibrate on her desk. He breathed a sigh of relief as she answered, assuming that it might be O'Neil.

It wasn't.

'That must be *some* breakfast,' Grace said. There was a short pause as she listened. 'Apparently not . . . we're expecting her soon . . . um hmm . . . he is . . .' Ryan saw the look of intrigue before she could hide it. She smiled at him, eyes narrowing slightly. 'Yeah . . . OK, I'll ask him . . . I'm sure he can slip away. Yeah, yeah, see you later.'

She hung up.

'What's going on?' Ryan asked.

'Frank wants to see you.'

'Well, I'm sitting right here.'

'Out of the office,' she said.

'Did he say why?'

'No, but I'm sure he has a reason,' she said matter-of-factly. 'Can you make the Centurion at eleven o'clock?'

'If I must.'

'Great! That's what I told him.'

'I'll square it with the guv'nor,' he said.

Grace shook her head ever so slightly as they heard the entry alarm. Ryan understood it to mean that Newman had something to say he wasn't yet ready to share with O'Neil.

30

The Centurion used to be a first-class passenger lounge at the city's central railway station. It was now a busy public house. Newman was leaning against the bar, a pint in his hand and one on the counter lined up for Ryan. It wasn't the first time they had shared a drink here. Then and now, Ryan was nervous of going behind O'Neil's back.

The spook showed no emotion as Ryan joined him at the bar. He kept his voice low, his sole focus on what he'd come to say.

He never wasted words.

'Trevathan's trial was linked to terrorism. Three Muslim brothers: a conspiracy to blow up the Royal Naval Armaments Depot at Coulport.'

'There are easier targets,' Ryan said. RNAD Coulport was the storage and loading facility for UK nuclear warheads, part of the Trident programme. 'That place is locked down so tight they'd never get in without a private army. The intent alone will get them life.' He paused, gathering his thoughts. Civilians were at greater risk from radicalized Europeans now than ever before, including women and young boys prepared to die in order to destroy a way of life they disagreed with. Many were British. 'Aren't they a bit behind the times?'

'How d'you mean?'

'I thought they were getting ready to switch focus, attacking soft targets, rather than the police or military.'

'Correct,' Newman said. 'The mob due to stand trial in Scotland have been planning this for years.'

'MI5 had someone undercover?'

Newman nodded. 'A real pro. He's been monitoring subversives his whole career, surveilling this particular crew for almost three years, tapping their comms, infiltrating their cell, building a dossier so damning I'm told there's now a price on his head.'

'Jesus.'

'They won't kill him. They won't need to. Word is, they're well connected, with your lot in their pocket – not foot soldiers, either, but senior ranks. Suffice to say, they're ruthless bastards, capable of doing a job on him.'

'Any link to Ambassador Dean?'

'None. For that reason alone, I think we're coming at this from the wrong direction. The nature of the trial is skewing our thoughts. I'd bet my pension that our case is unrelated.'

'Well, if it's not terrorism, what's with the cloak and dagger, Frank?' Ryan glanced at other drinkers at the bar. 'And why here and not in front of O'Neil? I deceived her once before. I won't do it again. Things are different now. She's my guv'nor—'

'She's a lot more than that.' Customers were crowding the counter, close enough to listen in. Newman pointed to a free table. They made their way to it and sat down. Ryan felt tense. The spook's expression gave nothing away. 'We've both been trained to look beyond the obvious and cover all the angles. What I have to say isn't something you'll want to hear.'

'What does that mean?'

'This new unit—'

'What about it?'

'It was set up for a specific reason. I wanted to find out what it was, who'd originated it and why, who sanctioned this level of finance from the public purse . . .' Despite the urge to, Ryan didn't interrupt. He let Newman have his say. 'Ordinarily, it takes months to organize a unit like ours, and yet here we are with all the bells and whistles, including firearms. That's a big deal, as big as it gets. Whoever is behind it moved heaven and earth to make it happen. Not only that, they moved rapidly.'

'I thought you didn't want to be linked with us.'

'I don't—'

'So why are you poking your nose into stuff that doesn't concern you?'

'Before I delve into any case, be that terrorist plot, a secret trial or the Muslim brotherhood, I like to know what's behind me, who has my back, as well as who I'm up against.'

'You just said it wasn't terrorism.'

'And I stand by that. I still need the names of those I can approach, those I should avoid, or shall we say those who require handling differently. Targeting the right information is good housekeeping. It's the safest way for me *and* my informants.'

'Smoke and mirrors. Now get to the point.'

Newman stared at him.

Ryan held his gaze. 'There is a point, I take it?'

'Listen, I understand your scepticism, but you're in the big league now. The first killing took place in July on foreign soil, nothing whatsoever to do with us. Danish police were dealing. The DVD was in their possession, so they knew what was going down but, at our request, they reported Ambassador Dean's death as a stabbing, a random attack by a drug addict. Happens every day in cities the world over.'

'Then a few months later, another high-profile victim, a second DVD.'

A nod from Newman. 'Now our lot are worried. In fact, they're shitting themselves. Trevathan has friends in high places. They're calling for a special ops unit to investigate. They get their wish: the new unit is created. Money's no obstacle. This is top-level stuff. The only way to find out why and what's really going on is to find out who's pulling the strings.'

Ryan stroked the scar on his chin. 'Are you telling me Ford isn't running the show?'

'It would appear not.'

'So who is?'

'No idea.'

'You expect me to believe that, Frank? We're having our meeting in a pub.'

Newman stared him down and then levelled with him. 'I happened on something that you should know.'

'I'm listening.'

'The apartment we're using is O'Neil's.'

'What?' Ryan's disbelief was fake. Newman's revelation came as less of a surprise than it otherwise might have. The first time he'd met Eloise at 'their place' it occurred to him that she seemed right at home. He'd written the feeling off. She'd been in post a couple of weeks, had overseen the set-up, was more used to being there than he was – a matter he kept from Newman.

'It gets worse,' Newman added. 'It's not under any mortgage, neither was it bought with her own funds. Someone called Hilary Forsythe signed the cheque for the full amount. One payment of almost three-quarters of a mill.'

Ryan's mind raced back to the Quayside, specifically to the despondency O'Neil tried hard to conceal when he first coined the phrase 'our place'. Newman might have solved part of that mystery, but Ryan couldn't believe what he was hearing. 'Hang on,' he said. 'Rewind. You're telling me that the apartment is owned outright by O'Neil but was bankrolled by someone else?'

'It's her name on the deeds.'

The hair stood up like rods on Ryan's neck. He'd examined O'Neil's phone while she was mumbling to someone on the landline in her room. The name HILARY was displayed clearly in the viewing window as the last person to call her. He'd assumed it was Jack's widow; now he wasn't so sure. He could hear O'Neil yelling at him not to touch her phone ever again; pictured her flight from the apartment last night, getting into a Porsche Carrera. If only he'd seen and taken down the registration.

'You think she's on the other bus?' Newman asked.

'What? No! How the hell should I know – and what if she is?' O'Neil was an enigma. She rarely, if ever, talked about herself. It would explain why she was friendly but at the same time nervous in Ryan's company. She was wise to the vibes of the opposite sex. Maybe she wanted what he could never give her.

'Ryan, pay attention, we haven't got all day.'

'What?'

Newman was staring at him. 'Maybe Hilary Forsythe is

O'Neil's secret,' he was saying. 'You can read people, Ryan. You know as well as I do that she's hiding something. It's as plain as day.'

'Who fed you this crap?'

Newman supped his pint. 'You know better than to ask.'

'C'mon, it's a simple enough question.'

'I don't discuss informants and you know it. Suffice to say, I have the means to access certain information. If the price is right, anything can be bought—'

'You expect me to take your word for it? Just like that? You've gone beyond your brief, pal. O'Neil is our boss, a damned good one at that. She sent you to London for a specific reason, not to dig into her private life, so why are you?'

'The way I roll.' Newman's expression sent a clear message: like it or lump it, mate. 'I don't imagine you'll accept what I say wholesale. I do expect you to challenge her over it—'

'Oh yeah . . .' Ryan held up his hands as if the spook were pointing a gun. 'Do I look like a fool to you? You want to confront her on the subject of her sexuality, be my guest. Then close the door on your way out. She'll axe you in a heartbeat – and Grace too.'

'That's a chance we'll have to take.'

'Have you told Grace?'

'It's none of her business.'

'Nor yours.'

'But it is yours.' Newman paused. 'You know what Grace is like. If I tell her, she'll take the direct route, go straight to O'Neil and confront her. And maybe she'd be right to do so. Eloise is her guv'nor too.'

Ryan palmed his brow. If Newman didn't trust O'Neil, Ryan

sure as hell didn't trust him. He dropped his head, the name on the cheque Newman had mentioned repeating like an earworm in his head. He looked up. 'Hilary Forsythe rings a bell but, for the life of me, I can't remember where from.'

'It's a name on a cheque for the time being – I have feelers out.'

Ryan was no longer cagey, he was angry. 'You're not sure about this, are you? You doubt your own information—'

'No. What I gave you is confirmed. The only thing that doesn't add up is the timing. O'Neil has owned the apartment for over a year. That doesn't fit with why and when the unit was set up.'

'A year?' Ryan took a moment to think. Newman was correct: it didn't make sense. 'I can assure you that no one has lived there, Frank. The apartment was brand spanking new. So new I had to strip the plastic coating off the ceramic hob. It hadn't been used, none of it had. It was like walking into a show home. You're wise to hesitate. I'm certain O'Neil will enlighten you if you give her a chance.'

'You sure about that?' Newman eyeballed him. 'What do you know about her apart from what you see on the surface? She doesn't say much.'

'Neither do you.'

Newman didn't comment.

'You made my point, Frank. Get your facts straight before you shoot your mouth off about Eloise. Maybe the unit was going to be set up ages ago and was knocked on the head. You know what it's like: some boffin at Whitehall has a great idea, does half a job, then bins a project because rising costs have taken it over budget. It happens every day—'

'You don't believe that any more than I do. I'm sorry, I know you rate her. I do too, but a strong team is built on trust. There are shifting sands beneath our feet and that makes me uneasy. O'Neil was a thorn in our side when we were looking for Jack. And don't you think it's odd that we're operating out of a privately owned base?'

'Yes, but there'll be a perfectly reasonable explanation—'

'Like what?'

'Remember the laptops stolen from an office commandeered by John Stevens?' Stevens, a former Northumbria and Metropolitan police chief, had been heading up Operation Paget at the time, the investigation into the death of Diana, Princess of Wales. 'That was a security breach like no other.' He pointed at Newman's phone. 'Look it up. All hell broke out over it.'

'You're clutching at straws, mate.'

'Am I? Our lot said never again would they risk information of that magnitude falling into the wrong hands. It may have passed you by, but we've sold our empty stations and police houses. Fuck's sake! Until recently, Grace lived in one. There's very little real estate left to resurrect. If O'Neil wanted somewhere secure, I can think of no better place, whether she owned it or not.'

'That still doesn't explain her name on the deeds.'

He had a point.

Ryan was beginning to doubt himself.

Newman spotted it immediately. 'I'm sticking my neck out here. I think she may have been recruited by MI5. She's using you.'

Stranger things had happened. Theirs was a shadowy world

where such things were not unknown. Was O'Neil capable of such betrayal? It was a question Ryan presently had no answer for. He found himself nodding, his mind racing through the possibilities, unable to disagree or come up with a plausible excuse on O'Neil's behalf. If the intelligence gathered proved to be correct, the stress of keeping secrets went some way to explaining her strange behaviour.

'No,' Ryan shook his head. 'I don't buy it, Frank. If she *was* MI5, her name wouldn't be linked to this operation, much less appear on the deeds, not in a million years.' He spread his hands, a gesture of openness. 'She joked about being "*Eyes Only*". She'd hardly do that if she was, would she?'

'Maybe. Maybe not . . . People tend not to take you seriously if you throw in something absurd, even if it's the truth.'

Ryan was running out of ideas.

'Leave it with me,' Newman said. 'It shouldn't take long to trace Forsythe, assuming that's her real name.'

'Yeah, well you'd know all about identity theft, wouldn't you?'

Newman ignored the dig. 'We nail Forsythe, we're halfway to making our move on O'Neil.'

'You've been a spook too long, Frank. You need to re-join the real world.'

Without comment, Newman stood up and made his exit. Ryan didn't follow. Of all the scenarios that had gone through his head on the way to the pub, none compared to the bombshell the spook had delivered. Newman made O'Neil sound like the enemy.

Maybe that's what she was.

31

Having got his head into gear, Ryan was back at base within the hour. He took in a breath as he entered the apartment. O'Neil was nowhere to be seen. He felt relieved, unsure how he would face her with Newman's revelations ringing in his ears. Ryan felt guilty for the treachery and for ridiculing Newman without good cause. The spook was calling it as he saw it. Ryan owed him an apology and made his way across the room to voice it.

'I was out of order earlier,' he said quietly.

Newman waved away the act of contrition.

Grace looked up. 'Out of order?' Newman put a finger to his lips, alerting Ryan to the fact that O'Neil was in the apartment, his wife to the fact that she should let it go. When no explanation was forthcoming from either man, Grace rolled her eyes. 'Don't tell me you two have been fighting again!'

Ignoring his new bride, Newman spoke quickly, half his attention on the bathroom door, half on Ryan. 'We can make this easy,' he said. 'Next time we get an opportunity to examine O'Neil's phone we take it. If we can get a number for this woman, I can find out who she is instantly.'

'What woman?' Grace whispered.

Ryan acted as if she wasn't there. 'Not going to happen, Frank. O'Neil told me, in no uncertain terms, never to touch her phone and I promised I wouldn't.' He shook his head vigorously, a gesture that generated a scornful expression from the spook. 'I mean it, Frank. I won't snoop on her. Don't ask me to—'

'Fine! You get the prize for righteousness. Leave it with me.'

He was about to move away as O'Neil re-entered the room. 'Did I miss something?'

'Boys' talk,' Grace covered for them. 'I've heard more scintillating conversation at the crem.'

'We have time to mess around?' O'Neil eyed the two men warily. 'You ready to go to work now?'

Ryan and Newman were nodding like schoolboys caught smoking behind the bike sheds. With no clue as to what was going on between them, Grace got on with her work, content to wait it out until she had the opportunity to bone them about this mystery woman.

O'Neil was staring at Ryan. 'Was there something else?'

'No, guv.' In his ears, those two small words sounded very wrong. What he wanted to say was: *Whatever gave you that idea? Of course there's something else! By the way, is that your real name? Is the name Hilary Forsythe fictitious too? Who the hell are you, Eloise? What are you? And while we're at it, why have you been lying to me?*

'Can we have a word?' O'Neil took him into the hallway and shut the connecting door. 'Is this about running out on you last night?'

'What? No!'

'Are you sure? You seem pissed off.'

Ryan flushed up. 'You had other plans. It's no biggie.'

'We're cool?'

'We're cool.'

'Glad to hear it.'

Her smile could melt steel. Ryan fought the urge to meet her eyes. She'd see through him. How long could he keep up the pretence? He liked this woman – more than liked – and it bugged him to think that she wasn't who she said she was.

She's using you.

He could've decked Newman for saying that, but what if she was? What then? What if the new unit was a cover for something else? What if everything he thought he knew about her was a sham? Ryan hated to think he was that gullible. On the one hand, he was beginning to regret ever setting eyes on her. On the other, he'd do anything to prove Newman wrong.

'Ryan? Will you please tell me what the hell is wrong with you?'

Now he looked at her. 'I'm fine, guv.'

'I can see you're not.'

He offered no explanation.

How could he?

'Whatever it is, get your act together, and don't take all day,' O'Neil said. 'In view of our plans to stake out the lock-up this evening, I'd like to bring the briefing forward. Frank will take the lead. Since he's back from the capital, I must assume he has something to feed in—'

'He hasn't done it yet?'

'I had to pop out. He was here when I got back. Where were you?'

'Needed some air.'

'You *need* to focus.'

Ryan wondered if she'd followed him; if she'd seen him

meeting Newman out of the office – if she was testing him – if she was MI5. That was a lot of ifs. He couldn't shake that thought as she led him to the others, inviting Grace and Newman to leave their desks and sit with them.

The spook fed them what he'd already told Ryan about the terrorist trial, including the fact that he didn't think it was related to their case. During his delivery there was no sign of distrust of O'Neil. Frank was the consummate professional: psychologically sound, even-tempered, able to think on his feet. In short, he had reverted to type, his doubts about the unit and O'Neil safely filed away until he was ready to investigate further.

'Anything else?' O'Neil asked.

'Five have the briefcase.' It was a test O'Neil passed with flying colours. She didn't flinch, not a flicker. Newman hit her again, so quick she didn't even feel it. 'To be on the safe side, I've swept the apartment and checked all the comms. We're clean. All that remains is to examine mobile phones and we're good to go. I want to make sure that there are no tracking devices attached.'

'Good plan,' she said.

Ryan couldn't look at either of them. He felt like a shit, knowing what Newman was planning. When he chanced a cursory glance at O'Neil, she showed no concern, acting like she had nothing to hide. She had all the attributes of a spook. Ryan couldn't deny it.

32

Gloria was standing in her usual spot, pretending to ply her trade at the Borough Road–Clive Street junction, under strict instructions not to accept any work. O'Neil had taken care of her financially; so generously, in fact, the girl reckoned she could take a week off if she wanted.

Ryan wished she would.

He hated using Gloria as bait, even to catch the punter who'd beaten her up, wandering into a crime scene, leaving a shoe behind. That was the unit's thinking until they could prove otherwise. O'Neil hadn't been able to trace the punter by any other means. Officers were still checking the PNC for make of car. Likewise, they were trying to locate the jeweller who'd engraved his watch with the initials SFW.

So far: no bites.

Because of that, O'Neil had decided to lie in wait for him, nicking him the old-fashioned way. Her new recruits thought it was a good call. It was one she couldn't take credit for. Ryan had suggested it from the outset. There were times when there was no alternative to boots on the ground.

At the morning parade, local police had been briefed to stay clear – unless an emergency situation developed – giving the unit free reign to conduct enquiries in the vicinity in unmarked vehicles. The last thing they needed was a panda car arriving on the scene.

Despite the pouring rain, Ryan was willing Gloria's punter to attempt a pick-up. They had been waiting since nine p.m. It was almost eleven now. Prepared to sit it out till dawn if necessary, he was expecting a long wait. Assured by the Crime Scene Manager that he was finished with the lock-up, Ryan and Grace were hiding in there, waiting to pounce. They were on one side of Gloria, Newman on the other, O'Neil in a vehicle on higher ground in case Stevie made a run for it. Ryan pictured her alone in her car: alert, binoculars trained on the approach road, patience running out. Or maybe she was calling Hilary Forsythe, the woman who'd bought the apartment they were using as a base. Maybe the two of them were laughing at the thought of him freezing his balls off in a draughty lock-up, unconcerned with the operation he'd helped set up.

Grace shifted her position beside him, trying to get comfortable. She hadn't questioned him further on the subject. There could be only one explanation for that – she'd been told not to – Newman wanted to check his facts before they tackled him again. That was good news. Ryan was hoping he'd been given a bum steer, passed on uncorroborated information as truth, worrying them unnecessarily.

Hope was a far cry from belief.

Hanging on to that thought, Ryan felt his tension rise, eyes on Gloria. The rain was relentless, almost horizontal off the North Sea, no let-up in sight. The girl had no umbrella, a short-cropped leather jacket her only protection against the cold and wet. Half a dozen cars had stopped in the time she'd been there. They had each pulled to the kerb, windows wound down, leaving without completing a transaction, potential customers swearing at her before setting off again, getting the one-finger salute in return. She'd been told to act normal, as if she wasn't under surveillance, a role she was fulfilling beautifully.

O'Neil's voice came over the radio: 'What's your status, Unit One? Are you getting registration numbers from there?'

Ryan glanced at the CCTV rigged above his head, installed by the Technical Support Unit earlier that afternoon, a small hole punched in the glass to enable unrestricted line of sight, the camera lens trained on Gloria. 'Affirmative. I hope this punter shows.'

'Patience, Ryan . . .' Radio reception was poor. It crackled as O'Neil spoke again. 'Unit One, dark vehicle approaching from the east.'

Wiping condensation from the window to get a better view, Ryan pushed the transmit button on his radio, adrenalin surging through his veins. 'We have the eyeball, guv. Different make and model. It's not our target vehicle.' The car cruised by . . . and on past Gloria. 'Damn!' Ryan whispered under his breath. He was beginning to lose hope. 'That's a negative, guv.'

'Hold your position and stay alert. He may come on foot.'

Ryan relaxed again.

Grace shivered uncontrollably.

'You cold?' he asked.

'I'd be a damned sight finer sat in O'Neil's warm car.'

'Want my jacket? I'm toasty.'

'You can't be.'

He made a funny face. 'I have my thermals on.'

'You're such a wuss.'

'No, just practical.'

'Give *them* your coat then.' Grace pointed through the window. 'They'll catch their death out there in this rain. Can you believe the risks they take in order to make ends meet?' She was angry and didn't wait for an answer. 'Few make enough to get by, let alone have a decent life. Every one of them will have been attacked at some point or another. Fuck knows how many unreported rapes there are among them.' She shook her head, her focus on the road. 'Look at the girl on the left. She's barely a teenager.'

Ryan followed her gaze to a skinny waif-like figure shivering on the pavement. Years ago, she'd have been working in a vibrant fishing industry, engaged in the manufacture of traditional crafts or engineering locally, much of it long gone. Despite regeneration of the area, leisure and tourism had failed to fill the gap. With youth unemployment up and wages down, kids were struggling to survive.

At ten past midnight, Grace checked her watch, mumbling under her breath, shifted her weight from one foot to the other. 'I'm busting for a pee,' she said.

'Find a dark corner. I won't peek, I promise. And try not to break your neck.'

'Sorry, Ryan, needs must.'

Her pants were hardly down when Newman's voice cut in: 'Vehicle heading west.'

Grace swore. 'Tell the bastard I can't stop mid-stream—'

Newman's voice hit the airwaves. 'Repeat, Unit One. I didn't get that.'

Ryan grinned. 'That's received, Unit Two. Stand by.'

A vehicle pulled up as Grace joined Ryan at the window, adjusting her strides where she'd pulled them up quickly.

'Better?' he asked.

'Much.'

The two detectives held their collective breath as the guy inside the car wound his window down and spoke to Gloria through it, her hesitancy raising their antennae. Anticipating that Stevie might show up in a different vehicle, Ryan had primed the girl to light up and throw her cigarette towards her punter should the right one arrive. She was already smoking, the fag presently in her hand. When she didn't approach the car, the driver got out, walked round the vehicle and moved towards her in a threatening manner.

They had words.

When the conversation didn't go his way, the man grabbed Gloria by the arm, pulling her towards his car by her hair. She timed it perfectly, sparks flying off the end of her cigarette as it glanced off his vehicle.

'That's a Go, Go, Go!' Ryan said into his radio.

Nearest the door, Grace was out of the building first, sprinting like a gazelle across the road, as fit as someone half her age. Gloria glanced left as Newman ran towards her from the opposite direction. Spotting him, her punter made a run for it, hitting Grace so hard she fell and hit the wet tarmac, where she lay motionless in a puddle as Gloria's soggy cigarette floated by.

As Newman went to her aid, the running man glanced over his shoulder to see if he was being followed. It was a mistake. Ryan took him out, a rugby tackle that sent them both crashing to the ground. Ryan managed to grab hold of him, dragging him to his feet, cuffing him before he could make good his escape.

'Detective Sergeant Matthew Ryan, Northumbria Police. What's your name?'

'Why? I've done nowt wrong.'

'Name!'

'Steven Francis Watson.'

Ryan cautioned the suspect. 'Stand still! You're going no-where; I'm arresting you on suspicion of murder and assault. Consider yourself nicked.'

The impact of that statement made Watson stagger slightly. His eyes fled to the lock-up as if he understood why they were there. He was shitting himself as he raised his hands.

'No, look, I had nothing to do with what went on in there, I swear.'

O'Neil screamed to a halt in her vehicle. She got out, leaving the door wide open, her focus on Grace, who was being helped to her feet by Newman. 'Grace, are you OK? Do you need a medic?'

'No!' Grace rubbed her head, still dazed.

O'Neil nodded to Ryan. 'Get him in the car, I'll meet you at base.'

'No, wait!' the prisoner protested. 'I'll tell you everything.'

'You'll have ample opportunity to do that at the station,' Ryan said.

The man struggled to reach O'Neil as she turned away from him, elbowing Ryan in the process. 'Get the fuck off me!'

'Don't make this difficult,' Ryan gave a tug on the cuffs, inca-pacitating his prisoner.

'Ow!' he yelled. 'I'm sorry, I was scared.' His eyes shot to Grace. 'I'm sorry, I didn't mean to push you over.'

'Tell it to the judge, Mr Watson.' Grace was shivering violently and soaking wet. 'Get in the car! We're going for a drive.'

'I'll drive,' Newman said.

Grace gave him hard eyes, warning him to back off.

'Let Frank drive. You've had a bang on the head.' O'Neil threw the keys at Newman.

Grace caught them mid-air and climbed in the driver's seat, a face-off with her husband and O'Neil through the window. 'Relax,' she said. 'I've had worse cleaning my teeth.'

'Are you lot listening?' Watson yelled. 'I done nowt wrong.'

Ryan put a hand on his head, shoving him through the car door and into the rear seat. Content that Grace was OK to drive, Ryan conveyed a silent message to Newman – *I'll look after her* – and got in beside his prisoner, who continued to spill his guts on the short journey to the station.

'Hey!' he said. 'I assaulted Gloria. I admit it. I had nowt to do with the dead girl. You've got it all wrong, I swear.'

Grace floored the accelerator, heading for the local nick. Either she was keen to transfer their suspect into the custody of the Murder Investigation Team to be detained until formally interviewed, for as long as it took to check out his story, or she was trying to scare him to death. Unfortunately, or fortunately, depending on your point of view, the bottleless lowlife would cough all he knew before he even reached the cells.

Ryan winked at Grace through the rear-view mirror while using reverse psychology on the man sitting next to him, something Ryan remembered her teaching him: 'Ask a prisoner questions, they'll blank you; tell them to shut the fuck up, they'll do the exact opposite. Works every time.'

They shot along Union Quay, left onto Brewhouse Bank, another left onto Bird Street, Charlotte Street and right at the roundabout onto Stephenson Road. Grace didn't do slow. The speedo was climbing rapidly as they headed away from the coast. She wasn't saving the horses. She was screaming along, keen to dump the prisoner and then put Newman's mind at rest.

'I'm holding my hands up,' Watson whined. 'I was having fun with Gloria—'

'Save your breath,' Ryan said.

'There's no law against screwing prostitutes. It's what she does. She's a fucking tart. She'll shag anyone for money.'

'At the station!' Ryan said. 'Do us all a favour and keep it shut till we get there. The Murder Investigation Team will give you plenty of time to get it off your chest. They've got all night.' He considered a forearm smash. He wanted to tell the scumbag that Gloria had a name, that she was a vulnerable kid, that he was old enough to be her father. He'd assaulted her multiple times. He saw her as someone to be picked up and discarded at will, a hooker who deserved whatever he had in mind to dish out. What she deserved, in Ryan's opinion, was as much police protection as the next person.

He'd make sure she got it.

The prisoner was still snivelling as they arrived at the station, his bottle gone completely. 'Fuck's sake! I kicked her out where I picked her up. I needed a piss. I went into the lock-up, saw the girl lying there covered in blood and legged it. I didn't come forward for obvious reasons. I knew you bastards would try and pin it on me. You always do. It wasn't me, I swear!'

'Shut it!' Ryan repeated, tuning him out. No urine had been found in the lock-up. Thanks to Grace, there was now.

33

Ryan was invited to play second string on the interview. He agreed on the proviso that he could leave if called back to base. The Senior Investigating Officer from the Murder Investigation Team – a dynamic young woman of similar age to him – agreed that he could sit in and bail out if it became necessary. Despite the gravity of the offence for which he'd been arrested, Watson declined legal representation.

'You really ought to have a solicitor present,' Ryan warned.

'At this time of night? Do me a favour. I can't be doing with hanging in the cells until one rolls off his lass and tips up here. I told you, I've got a good job. There'll be no Legal Aid bollocks coming my way. Don't see why I should pay either, considering I've done nowt beyond slapping a hooker and drink driving. I'll put my hands up to that, no sweat. Just get on with it.'

'Suit yourself.'

The caution had hardly been administered, the digital recorder switched on, when the prisoner coughed to assaults on Gloria and Grace, as well as driving under the influence while disqualified, much to the surprise of the SIO. It was almost one a.m. She was tired. If her prisoner was intent on admissions that might end up on a charge sheet, who was she to complain? When he'd got the small matters out of the way, the idiot turned his attention to the substantive matter for which he'd been arrested: murder of a person unknown. He blurted out a plausible explanation for being at the scene and for the lack of urine on the floor.

'It was dark in there', he said. 'You've got to believe me. Don't tell me you've never been caught short. We've all done it, yeah?' He pleaded with Ryan. 'Tell her, man.' Met with silence, he switched his attention to the SIO. 'It's different for us, pet; full of beer, we can't hold on to it, know what I mean? I was busting for a slash and snagged my zip undoing my flies. I put my phone torch in my mouth while I tried to get it free. The fucking thing was stuck fast. It wouldn't budge. That's the God's honest truth. I was hopping around in there, trying not to piss myself, when I spotted the girl. Piss or no piss, I legged it. Ask Gloria. She'll alibi me.'

'Do you need an alibi?' The SIO let him stew a second. 'Mr Watson, if you weren't responsible for the state of that lock-up, who was? We know the victim was female. How do we know you didn't have her tied up in there, bound and gagged, waiting for you to give her what for?' She looked down at his antecedent history. 'You have previous for violence and for perverting the course of justice.' She raised her eyes. 'Whoever killed the woman you allege was lying dead on the floor removed the body afterwards. Was it you?'

'No! I swear – on my mother's life.'

'You have a mother?' Ryan scoffed.

He wanted to put Watson in his place, frighten him the way he'd terrified Gloria. He wanted to make out that even though he may not have seen the killers' faces, they sure as hell would have seen his and might be coming after him. Gloria had said he could have his fancy watch for the price of a nose job. Shouldn't cost him more than a few grand.

'Start talking,' Ryan said.

'I've not stopped talking. If I tell you what I know, can I go home?'

'And climb into bed with your missus?' the SIO said. 'You do have a wife, don't you?'

'And kids,' he admitted, eyes flitting between the two detectives, eventually landing on Ryan.

'It had better be good.' Ryan's expression was deadpan. 'You've been arrested on suspicion of murder.'

'Detective Sergeant Ryan has a point,' the SIO said. 'What else happened in the lock-up, Mr Watson?'

'Nothing, I swear.'

'Did you leave anything behind?'

He nodded. 'A shoe.'

'Left or right?'

'Left.' No hesitation.

'Can you describe it?'

'It was brown, a brogue.'

The SIO bent down to retrieve a plastic evidence bag she had concealed in a box on the floor. The brogue was clearly visible to the prisoner. 'Is this the one?' The suspect confirmed it was his. The SIO eyeballed him. 'I bet that took some explaining to the missus.'

'I know this looks bad for me. The girl was in there when I left. I swear, I had nothing to do with her death.' Watson began to weep. He was scared stiff, which was exactly where the detectives wanted him.

Time to close the gap.

Right on cue, the SIO put the suspect at ease. 'Assuming for one moment that you didn't murder anyone, it stands to reason someone else did—'

'Hallelujah! That's what I've been saying all long.'

Having put his mind at rest, the SIO unbalanced him, timing the killer blow perfectly. 'Unless your friends like knocking women around as much as you do. How do we know you weren't working in tandem with someone else, using Gloria as an alibi? I gather your assault on her was nasty. Not something she'll forget in a hurry. You made sure of that.'

Ryan liked her style.

'It wasn't like that.' Watson said, sweat pouring off him.

'What was it like? Who was in the lock-up with you?'

'No one! I saw no one!' He thumbed in Ryan's direction. 'That's what I was telling him on the way over here. He wouldn't fucking listen, would he? You can question me all night and you'll get the same answers. I promise you, I have nowt to hide.'

'Did you check if the girl was breathing?' Ryan asked.

'And leave my DNA on her? Yeah right, you think I'm a dummy?'

The SIO turned to Ryan, one eyebrow raised. 'Forensically aware . . . I like that.'

'Exactly what we're looking for.' Ryan cut off the prisoner's objections with another question. 'How near were you to her?'

'I dunno. Five, six feet, tops.'

'So you didn't touch the body in any way?'

'No, I told you.'

'Did you touch her clothing?'

'No! Why would I? You'd have to be some perv to do that. She was covered in blood. What do you take me for?'

'How about the walls of the lock-up ... did you touch them?'

Watson palmed his brow, a slight shake of the head. 'Not that I recall. I definitely didn't touch her, or her clothing, only the corrugated iron sheet when I first went in ... or maybe on the way out. I wasn't thinking, was I?'

'Well you'd better be now.' Ryan pushed a sheet of A4 towards him. 'I want you to draw a picture of the inside of that lock-up, the location of the corrugated sheeting, how you got in, where you stood and exactly what position the body was in ... and, if you can remember, where you left your shoe. Can you do that, Stevie? That would be really helpful.'

'No sweat, man.' Watson pulled the paper towards him and picked up a pen, visibly relaxing. He was now onside. The detectives had him and they knew it. What's more, so did he.

Ryan's phone vibrated in his pocket: *Newman*.

He stood. 'Sorry, ma'am – I have to take this.'

'Go ahead. I'll finish up here.' She announced his departure for the benefit of the tape before he was out of the door.

Wandering along the corridor, Ryan noticed Grace sitting in the next interview room to the one he'd just come out of. She was drinking a cup of tea, the faint smell of antiseptic hitting his senses as he walked in and sat down next to her. She'd seen the police surgeon – not of her own free will, he presumed – probably at the insistence of O'Neil.

Good call.

'It's me,' Newman's voice hit Ryan's ear. 'Can you speak?'

'Sure.' *Frank*, Ryan mimed. 'Grace is fine, by the way, thanks for asking.'

Grace rolled her eyes in a way that made him think that the

newlyweds had fallen out. He wondered if they had spoken to each other while he was interviewing Watson with the SIO or if they'd had words before Operation Gloria.

Newman ignored the dig. 'O'Neil would like you both to return to base ASAP. We're in business. Sussex Police have been on the blower. We have a recovery in Brighton. It's all hands on deck.'

Ryan could read people, even people like Newman. When he asked the spook what else was going on – because sure as hell something was – Newman ended the call abruptly. The detective sergeant sighed. That was a bad sign. If he were any judge, this day would not end well.

34

Grace was silent in the car on the short journey to their base. She didn't offer an explanation and Ryan didn't pry. He guessed that her uncharacteristic reserve had more to do with the bump on her head than with Newman. The man was a machine. When they arrived at the apartment, O'Neil was nowhere to be seen. Ryan knew instantly that the spook's call had been a ruse, that he and Grace had been summoned to base under false pretences. What's more, she didn't look surprised.

'Do we have a body in Brighton or don't we?' Ryan asked.

'We do,' Newman said. 'O'Neil nipped out to HQ.'

Ryan's focus switched from Frank to Grace. 'So what's with the pet lips?'

Grace's body language was confrontational. She had her arms crossed, her focus on her husband, her expression a mixture of uncertainty and unrest. Newman, on the other hand, was cool, ice-blue eyes giving nothing away – a man easily able to hide emotion.

A stand-off then . . .

'Will one of you let me in?' Ryan asked. 'We have work to do.'

'That's what I told him,' Grace said. 'Telling tales out of school is not on my agenda. We have more important things to deal with.'

Newman glared at his bride. 'Stop pissing about, Grace. The

fact that you won't tell me adds weight to what we already know.'

'It might not.'

'What the hell?' Ryan had no clue what they were arguing about.

'Grace knows stuff about O'Neil she's not prepared to divulge,' Newman said. 'Apparently, she's too principled, even though there are things going on that a) we don't fully understand and b) are being deliberately hidden by your guv'nor—'

'It's personal,' was all Grace would say in return.

'How do we know unless you share it?' Newman said.

Grace rounded on him. 'You'll have to take my word for it.'

They began arguing; not a silly squabble, really going for it. Ryan tried to interrupt before someone said something they might regret. When Newman wanted information, even from his wife, he was like a man possessed. He went after it with every weapon in his armoury – including putting the bite on the only woman he'd ever loved, knowing it would break her heart to get on the wrong side of him. He never raised his voice. He didn't have to. For every point she put forward, he had a counter-argument that made her think twice. Grace was losing the fight, if only she could see it.

'Let me be the judge of what you have on O'Neil,' Newman said. 'If it's not relevant, I'll back off—'

'Not on your life!' she snapped.

They were rowing so enthusiastically no one heard O'Neil enter the apartment. 'Jesus! I could hear you from outside,' she said. 'You want to have a domestic, do it on your own time.'

An awkward silence.

Three heads turned towards the voice.

No one spoke.

O'Neil's coat was dripping wet, her face flushed and weather-beaten. The dripping umbrella in her right hand created a puddle on the floor as she stood there gawping at them. A violent storm was moving in off the North Sea. Rain hammered on the windows, streaking down the glass in torrents, the rumbling of thunder a sign of impending doom.

'You all look very sheepish, I must say.' Her eyes scanned them one by one. 'Ryan? Are you going to tell me what's going on?'

Guilt rendered him speechless. His throat constricted, like a hand was applying firm pressure to his Adam's apple, cutting off his air supply. He should've gone to her from the outset, levelled with her, told her of Newman's suspicions. He owed her that much.

'Not a domestic then?' O'Neil addressed them all. 'Is anyone going to fill me in?'

The team eyed each other across the room, a deathly hush. O'Neil's focus was the two men, Grace's too. Her face was red and blotchy, anger eating her up. Ryan noticed his reflection in the blackened glass behind her. His shoulders were down. He had no bloody idea how he was going to repair the damage of what was to come.

'You bottleless shits!' Grace exploded. 'Well, if you won't come clean, I will. While he was in London, my other half was digging the dirt on you, Eloise.'

O'Neil shrugged, unconcerned. 'It's happened before.'

'I told him personal stuff is off limits.'

'Nothing is off limits,' Newman said. 'You all know how I operate.'

'What gems did you come up with this time, Frank?' O'Neil was looking directly at him.

'Before we discuss that, I want you to know that I was covering my back, nothing more. I like to check out all the players before I dive into a case. It was important to know who was blocking our investigation and why, where the balance of power was, who was really running the show.'

'That would be me, at this level anyway,' O'Neil said. 'I report to Ford. That should be enough, even for you, Frank.'

Newman didn't try to hide his scepticism.

O'Neil switched her focus to Ryan, almost a glare. 'I must say, I expected more support from my wing-man.'

'This is not his doing,' Newman said. 'He tried to talk me out of it.'

'Not hard enough.' There was spite in O'Neil's words.

'I'm not having that,' Newman said. 'Ryan insisted that you were the boss. If you told us to jump, we should ask how high. For what it's worth, he refused to involve himself and was very vocal on the subject. This is down to me, Eloise. I take full responsibility.'

'Do you now?' O'Neil was seething, trying not to show it. Her eyes shifted to her DS. 'So why the guilty expression, Ryan?'

He held her gaze. 'When Frank told me what he'd found out, I was angry, I admit it. I thought he'd overstepped his brief—'

'And now?'

'If you want the truth, I can see where he's coming from. He's the one in the firing line, guv.'

'Oh really? I thought that was me.'

'You can criticize him all you like. If I were in his shoes, I'd have done the same. He was fact-checking, nothing more.'

O'Neil was rooted to the spot, a pool of rainwater at her feet. She hadn't taken her coat off since entering the apartment. Finding herself betrayed by the very people she'd come to trust, the look on her face had gone from indignation to deeply offended to . . . wounded.

She might be down but she certainly wasn't out.

'Come on then,' she said. 'Let's have it.'

Newman began and didn't stop until he was done. He gave no details of how he'd come by the information and O'Neil didn't question him on it. She was a pro, aware that if she asked him a million times he'd stonewall her on the subject. Nevertheless, she was shaken by the sheer detail he had at his fingertips, not to mention the speed with which he'd obtained it.

Ryan took a step forward. He was about to offer to take O'Neil's coat and umbrella, but she moved away, her body rigid, as if he'd raised his hand to slap her. He was struggling to keep faith with either side. Newman's investigation was fully justified but O'Neil deserved respect and loyalty.

'Guv' – he couldn't bring himself to call her Eloise – 'you must see why Frank had to cover himself. That way he was in control. That's the rules of the game, otherwise he'd be in jeopardy.'

'This is not a game though, is it?' O'Neil stared at Grace. 'And you were happy to go along with this? You surprise me. I thought you had more integrity . . . I thought you *all* had more integrity.'

'She does,' Newman said in her defence. 'That's why we were arguing. She knew stuff she wasn't prepared to tell us.'

O'Neil's face was flushed. 'Then I apologize unreservedly.'

'Don't you dare apologize!' Grace's eyes were like saucers. She glanced at Ryan, her husband and then O'Neil, her voice barely a whisper. 'You're going to have to tell them, Eloise.'

'Tell us what?' Ryan asked.

'Do you not talk to Frank, Grace?' O'Neil clearly didn't believe that husband and wife hadn't already shared her secrets.

'About you? No! Why would I? Your personal life is private, same as mine. Frank isn't interested in gossip unless it involves national security. Never has been. It's not my place to divulge anything I know about you to him or vice versa.' She flicked her eyes to Ryan. 'Or him. Ask him, if you don't believe me. Ryan knew nothing of Frank until he found him in my house when we were looking for Jack, and yet I've known him for a quarter of a century. There are some things you keep to yourself.'

'Well, my hands are up,' O'Neil said. 'This *is* my apartment, but I can assure you that the person who bought it has absolutely nothing whatsoever to do with this investigation.'

Newman took the direct route. 'Who is she then?'

O'Neil hesitated. 'You mean Hilary?'

'It's a simple enough question,' he said. 'You told me Ford was digging, pressurizing you to reveal the names of your additional personnel. If he had to ask, then he's not in charge. He's obviously a front man for someone higher up the food chain.'

'I'm not prepared to go into it. If you're unhappy with that, feel free to ship out at any time. That goes for you too, Ryan. I've had about as much as I can take from all of you.'

Frank wasn't convinced.

Grace either.

The 'perfectly reasonable explanation' Ryan had told Newman to expect didn't materialize. A moment of sorrow as the team waited in absolute deadlock. Ryan sat down, put his head in his hands. They could have handled that better.

Should have.

'Tell them.' Grace was almost pleading.

'Go to hell! I have nothing to hide.' O'Neil walked into her room and slammed the door behind her, leaving them none the wiser.

35

Ryan stood up as O'Neil re-entered the living room minus her wet coat. She'd been gone five minutes, no more. He'd come to view her as a mate and hated to think that he was in any way responsible for her pain. He felt tainted by the accusations levelled at her, ashamed for having done so little to preserve their special relationship. It had been a while since they had been on opposing sides. He'd never imagined they would end up there again. It hurt him deeply that the woman who'd handpicked him as her second-in-command – when she had her pick of detectives countrywide – was probably now regretting that decision.

She was looking directly at him.

'We're booked on the 07.55 to King's Cross. You need to pack for a few days away from base.' She turned away, reaching for the door handle. His hopes rose as she hesitated. She stood for a moment, ramrod straight, with her back to her so-called team. Slowly she turned to face them. 'Frank, your informants aren't entirely wrong. Hilary Forsythe is very well connected and known to me, but not as some shadowy figure covertly running the show. That, if you don't mind me saying so, is bullshit.'

Newman remained silent.

'Whether you choose to believe it or not, it's true,' O'Neil insisted.

'You can see why Frank might think it,' Grace said.

Ryan could see O'Neil was wavering, less certain than she had been a moment ago. He wasn't sure if that made the situation better or worse. What the hell was going on? She'd admitted owning the apartment, so why not come right out and tell them the truth?

Faced with such opposition, she turned away and walked slowly to the window. Taking her phone from her pocket she punched in a number and lifted the device to her ear. Ryan peered enquiringly at Grace and Frank, then checked his watch: 02:12 – an odd time to make a call. Seconds later, O'Neil began to speak and didn't waste her breath on a greeting.

'Hilary, I want the truth,' she said. 'Are you heading up my new unit?' She turned to face the team, her back to the window. She'd been humiliated once and it was obvious to everyone present that it was happening again. Her face was flushed, her eyes wild with fury. 'Thank you for being honest . . . no, that was a bad call, for everyone concerned . . . yes, well you might have told me, I now have a mutiny on my hands . . . Of course they are!' She raised her voice. 'What the hell did you expect? That's as it may be, but I'm not sure I can carry on under those circumstances.'

Ryan tensed as Eloise turned her eyes on him, still listening to Forsythe.

'There's nothing *to* discuss,' she said. 'You'll have my resignation at the conclusion of this case. Goodnight, Hilary.' She hung up, took a long, deep breath. 'You'd better sit down.'

The team did as she asked.

'Well, where to start?' She rubbed at her temples, her expression a mixture of vulnerability and despair. 'It seems that my benefactor *is* in charge. As you just heard, that is news to me. By the way, Hilary is a man, not a woman, an eminent judge, formerly based in the south, recently retired. He purchased this flat as a wedding present.' She paused. 'He was to have been my father-in-law. Let's say, it didn't quite work out. Nevertheless, he still thinks the world of me. We've kept in touch and see each other frequently. Dinner dates. The theatre. He's a kind, generous man. I'm not screwing him, in case you're wondering.'

'We weren't,' Grace said quickly. 'And we don't, do we, guys?'

'The Porsche,' Ryan mumbled under his breath.

'What Porsche?' Grace and Newman said simultaneously.

'Doesn't matter.' Ryan said it in a way that they wouldn't ask again, a raft of feelings competing for his attention. He was sickened by the news that Eloise intended to quit.

'He means Hilary's car,' O'Neil said. 'He picked me up here yesterday. He sees it as his responsibility to keep an eye on me.' She dropped her head, then raised it again, pain etched on her face as she confronted her accusers, on the verge of disclosing her innermost secrets. Her voice was hardly a whisper. 'His son is Stephen Forsythe QC, the bastard who jilted me at the altar last Christmas Eve.'

O'Neil looked away, an attempt to deflect any sympathy coming her way. Ryan's stomach took a dive. No wonder Grace didn't want to share information this personal. Right now, she didn't know where to put herself. She was biting down so hard, trying not to lose control, her jaw was like a blade.

'I knew the wedding had been called off,' she said. 'Nothing more.'

'I tried to give the apartment back,' O'Neil added, 'but Hilary wouldn't take it. He told me to keep it as an investment if I didn't want to live in it. Wouldn't take no for an answer. I never moved in.'

'And who could blame you?' Grace was visibly upset now.

Ryan hadn't seen her so moved since her own wedding day. He didn't know what to say to O'Neil, what he might do to help her out of this. Her revelation explained everything: her unhappiness, her odd behaviour, the whole damned lot – and he'd done sod all to support her.

'I'm so very sorry, Eloise.' Grace took O'Neil's hand in hers. 'You don't need to say any more.'

'I think I do.' O'Neil tried for a smile but it failed to show up. 'Turns out Stephen screws anything in a skirt, the shorter the better. If he hadn't moved away from the area, I might have seen him on the Fish Quay earlier this evening. Young Gloria would have been right up his street.'

Grace laughed and then cried.

When O'Neil's bottom lip quivered, Grace squeezed her hand and left the apartment without another word, giving Newman a dirty look as she passed him on the way out. The spook tripped over his apology, then followed his wife, leaving Ryan to clear up in their wake. He stood there for a moment, unable to tell Eloise how very sorry he was that she'd been forced into such an invidious position.

'Guv—'

'Don't!' She walked away.

For a while, he stood there – ineffectual – staring at her bedroom door, willing her to walk back through it so they could talk, all night if necessary, so he could make it right. It remained firmly closed. No sound from within. There was no way back from this.

36

There was something delicious about killing on a Sunday, traditionally a day of worship for believers, a day of rest for those with more sense. However people chose to spend it, church, family get-together, pub roast or lazy day in the garden, these were not activities on her agenda. She had more important things in mind. There were scores to settle and she wasn't done yet.

None of her victims had been that hard to overcome. The chosen rarely looked over their shoulder, even though they had every reason to. Take this one across the road, talking to the big fella with the dodgy moustache. He looked as if he hadn't a care in the world. Well, think again, Mr Robin Charlton. Your worst nightmares are about to come true.

It was such a thrill, watching him. She liked this part. In fact she enjoyed the anticipation almost as much as the kill.

She was becoming quite the voyeur.

Meticulous research. That's what she was about. Since her mission began, she'd learned much and with each step she'd grown in confidence. More relaxed now than ever before, she'd established that most busy professionals went about their business blinkered to the world around them, preoccupied, eyes on mobiles, attention focused on other things.

The initial execution had been challenging, of course, but not because she was new to it. She'd ended a life once before – a very long time ago – an event she could never have predicted. It was of no consequence now. She was wiser and therefore better equipped to meet new challenges. The only downside had been that the executions weren't being reported in the press. That wouldn't do. She'd have to think of a way to make them sit up and take notice.

Ooh! Boy Wonder was on the move.

She was facing the other way, watching his reflection in the window of a bookshop, the perfect place to linger and browse. She turned, nodding to her accomplice to follow, while she kept her distance on her side of the road. It was important to get to know the area before they made their move – Copenhagen had taught her that. Foreign landscape. Identifiable victim. Unfamiliar logistics. Escape routes were complicated, high on her priority list, nothing she couldn't handle, once she'd done a little homework.

Then as now, a quick stroll around Google sorted her out. In the end, the Ambassador had been dispensed with swiftly and efficiently. Still, a foray abroad and out of her comfort zone had acted as a stark reminder to take it slow.

As she kept pace with her target she remembered the heart-stopping moment when the wheel almost came off. The date was etched on her memory: Friday, 26 July. She'd been watching the embassy when a security detail appeared, heading in her direction – a situation she found as exhilarating as it was alarming. Not so her accomplice. His bottle went completely. Daft sod had actually looked at her, a terrified expression under his peaked cap. How many times had she drilled it into him: *No eye contact. Act like a tourist. Take photos. Pretend you're on the phone. Whatever you do, keep your distance.* If he did it again, she'd have a decision to make. It would leave her short-handed, but she could ill afford to carry someone who wasn't pulling their weight. She wouldn't think twice about ending their association. *Period.*

As things turned out, the threat failed to materialize. The security patrol moved away, apparently unconcerned about two strangers lurking in the vicinity. From then on she was more careful. With patience came a lucky break, a change of security staff alleviating her problem, lessening the chances of being clocked in close proximity to the perimeter fence.

Some things were just meant to be.

Two days later, her target walked out of the building into bright sunshine, not a care in the world. The diminutive figure was instantly recognizable from images she'd found online. The Internet really was an offender's best friend. He was a handsome man with greying hair, a touch overweight, gait on the sluggish side, his attire more casual than she'd expected, given his lofty title and status within the Danish community. With the confidence of a statesman, he nodded to the officer on the gate, donning a pair of sunglasses, a relaxed pose. Swiping his access card, he stepped out onto the pavement, leaving behind the safety of the embassy.

No bodyguard.

No shit!

A tingle of excitement ran down her back. Boy Wonder had stopped at a pedestrian crossing. She raised her camera to her face, loving the sound of the shutter as she captured his image. Like the diplomat, this target didn't have a fucking clue that his demise was imminent.

She grinned at the irony.

As an ambassador, Dean had enjoyed the protection of the Vienna Convention. Even if his wrongdoing was brought to light, he'd have been exempt from capital punishment. Well, she'd got around that. But then, she never had been a slave to convention.

She'd waited until they'd left the crowds behind before giving the nod. The grunt had taken out his weapon and pressed it against the diplomat's ribs. He'd thrown an arm round Dean's shoulder, making out they were old friends larking around, as he guided him up a side street to the kill site. Dean's gob had been going the whole time, trying to talk his way out of trouble.

Didn't do him any good, mind. The street was empty, only her and her cohort around to hear him.

Dean had fallen silent when they stopped walking, a look of terror on his face as she gestured to the abandoned building.

Inside, the stench of piss was nauseating.

He'd backed away from her, pleading with the two of them to let him go. Stumbling in the dark interior, he'd fallen on the concrete floor, the breath forced from his lungs as he hit the deck hard. When he'd scrambled to his feet, she'd been expecting him to turn and run, a futile attempt to get away, but instead he stood his ground. He was scared, not stupid. There was only one exit and it was behind her.

After a split-second's hesitation, the grunt moved in, an upward thrust finding its target with devastating effect, causing a deep puncture wound to the gut. Looking on from her ringside seat, she felt neither pity nor remorse.

The diplomat's knees buckled. He fell to the filthy floor clutching his stomach, thick dark liquid oozing through his fingers as he tried to stem the blood, blind panic on his face.

A feeling of euphoria swept through her, then as now. This was how she'd imagined Dean would end his days, a world away from the privileged life he'd led. After twenty years of being indulged at the British taxpayers' expense, wined and dined by royalty, earning the kind of salary she could only dream of, he'd finally got what was coming to him.

With his left hand pressed against the stab wound, he'd reached back with his right hand and tugged his wallet from his pocket, offering it to her, a final plea to let him live.

She'd kicked it away.

'No amount of money will save you,' she'd told him. 'You're going to have to pay with your life for the wrong you have done. You took it upon yourself to condemn someone else to an early grave. Now it's your turn.'

She'd never forget his expression. He'd looked incredulous, as if to say: if not robbery, then what? Why me? A moment later, the light left his eyes, massive blood loss causing him to fade in and out of consciousness. He was fighting hypovolemic shock, his condition already life-threatening. She asked him what it felt like. A sick joke – literal and metaphorical – seemed appropriate, a hint of why he'd been selected.

When she explained her reasoning, he made out that he didn't know what she was talking about. Liar. His breath was ragged by then, his voice almost inaudible. A cough squeezed more blood through slimy fingers.

'I don't understand,' he said.

'Well, understand this. Every action has a reaction. It's like a game of consequences.'

A nod was all it took. The grunt went in hard, delivering a fatal blow to the heart.

She smiled now at the memory. Dean was her first and therefore most special achievement, with many more planned, which made 28 July a date to cherish and to celebrate. Her premiere had gone like clockwork. A wrap. No retakes required. Red carpet coming right up.

She'd left him lying there, secure in the knowledge that no one was likely to find him until they had made good their escape. Just to make sure that he was found, she'd popped the DVD into the post before boarding the flight to London.

Oh yes, Sundays were special. And by next Sunday she'd be ready to rain down retribution on Boy Wonder.

37

O'Neil made coffee as usual, showing no signs of lingering bad feeling, making no mention of the events of last night. Ryan, on the other hand, felt utterly drained by the altercation. Unable to trust himself to bring the matter up without upsetting her, he remained silent.

Grace and Newman arrived early, sheepish both of them. It was a show of solidarity that Ryan appreciated wholeheartedly.

O'Neil invited them to sit.

'I want to clear the air,' she said. 'In future, I expect openness and transparency from all of you. If you have anything to say about this unit, the way it is run and by whom, you come to me. You do not discuss it with each other. Is that clear?'

'Crystal,' Ryan said.

Grace and Newman nodded agreement.

'Good. The other thing we talked about in the early hours concerning me is over. I won't discuss it again with anyone.' She stressed the word *anyone*, leaving Ryan in no doubt that the subject was closed even to him – especially to him. 'I trust you to keep it to yourselves. Now, has anyone got anything to say vis-à-vis their future in this unit?'

She scanned Grace, Newman and Ryan in turn.

Ryan spoke first: 'I'm in if you are, guv.'

'Me too,' Grace said. 'If you're thinking of resigning, forget it.'

Newman said nothing, though it was clear he was going nowhere.

O'Neil dropped her gaze, a mixture of sorrow and joy almost moving her to tears. The rest of them waited with bated breath. It had shocked Ryan when she'd told Forsythe that she planned to quit. He guessed she'd lain awake all night, tossing and turning, maybe even having a quiet weep. He'd not heard her, just sensed tension through the walls. She wasn't the only one unable to sleep.

'For now, you're stuck with me,' she said, glancing at her watch. 'Grace, Frank, do what you do best. Ryan, you and I need to get going.' She stood, pulled on her coat, collected a small suitcase from beside her bedroom door and made for the exit.

Sunday trains were notoriously unreliable. Fortunately, theirs was on time. Overnight, Ryan had prayed that there would be no delays. There was only so much small talk a person could stomach after a cards-on-the-table type conversation, more so if it was personal. O'Neil had hardly said a word as they walked to the railway station and he'd decided to let her be.

She bought three newspapers and read them for the major-ity of the journey south. Unless shutting her eyes was an avoidance tactic, she'd slept the rest of the way.

Sussex Murder Investigation Team gave Ryan and O'Neil every assistance from the minute they arrived at their HQ in Lewes: organizing a car, a room in which to work, complete with a HOLMES computer so they could access information as and when it arrived. The victim had been formally identified as Michael Tierney, the gay man who'd gone missing the day before the DVD arrived.

'DS Vikki Carter, ma'am. I've been appointed as your liaison officer.'

'Nice to see you again, Vikki.' O'Neil flashed her best smile. 'Recently promoted?'

'Yes, ma'am.'

'Thought so. Well done.' O'Neil thumbed left. 'This is DS Matthew Ryan.'

Smiling, her wing-man stuck out a hand out. 'Ryan.'

Vikki gave a firm handshake. 'Good to meet you, Ryan.' She was beaming because a big cheese from another force had remembered her name and the fact that she was a DC when last they met.

'OK to use your locker room?' O'Neil asked. 'I need to freshen up.'

'Of course. It's that way . . .' Vikki pointed over O'Neil's shoulder. 'First door on your left.'

'I remember. Are we in the same office as before?'

'Yes, ma'am.'

'Get Ryan settled. I'll check in with your SIO and catch up with you.'

Vikki walked Ryan to his temporary Sussex base. She was covering for someone on maternity leave, hoping to prove herself and earn a permanent position on the Murder Investigation Team. She confided all this to Ryan on the way down the corridor, joking that the last time she'd spoken to anyone of O'Neil's rank it had been a technical superintendent who worked for a shipping company in London.

O'Neil glanced at the clock on the wall as she entered five minutes later. It was getting on for 2.30 p.m. No pub lunch for her, or anyone else. 'Thanks for staying on to talk to us, Vikki. Your guv'nor has been called out to another incident, unrelated thankfully, so you're in the chair. What do we know about Michael Tierney?'

'He's a hotshot stockbroker. Forty-seven. Works in the capital from an office in Canary Wharf. Commutes daily. Shares a frontline penthouse here in Brighton with his civil partner, Robert Parker, a cosmetic dentist. Tierney's not local, ma'am. He hails from Norwich, went to school all over the place – his father was in the military. The victim ended up in Cambridge where he gained a first-class honours in maths.'

Ryan smiled at O'Neil. She'd asked for and been fed updates by her opposite number since Tierney was reported missing, putting him in the frame as the Brighton victim. Much of this information she knew already. Still, she allowed Vikki to trot it out. Encouraging junior staff, rather than stamping all over their big moment, was testament to her leadership.

Vikki stopped talking.

'You've done your homework,' O'Neil said. 'And before Tierney shot up in the world?'

'He taught at a posh boarding school.'

'This school . . .' O'Neil sat up straight. 'It's not in Yorkshire by any chance?'

Vikki's right eyebrow arched as she gave a nod. 'He taught mathematics there. Actually, he was a pupil there too. Sent there as a kid when his father was posted overseas. How did you know, ma'am, if you don't mind me asking?'

'It wasn't a guess.'

Attagirl!

Ryan was delighted to see O'Neil in control, last night's conversation consigned to the back of her mind for now – but not his. He'd decided on the train to carry on working as if nothing had happened. What else could he do? Problem was, a gulf had opened up between them, a gap he found impossible to bridge. Off the agenda for now, O'Neil's exposé would return, if not today, then next week, next month when – *if* – she decided to take him into her confidence.

'I emailed Gold Command to let them know that everything has been uploaded to HOLMES,' Vikki said.

'Excellent. Anything else?'

'No, I think that's it.'

'OK, find out exactly how much Robert Parker has been told about his partner's death and report back before you go off duty.'

'Will do.' Vikki turned to go. As she reached the door, she glanced back at O'Neil. 'Would there be anything else, ma'am?'

'Any chance of a coffee? I've got a splitting head.'

'You need a painkiller?'

'So long as it's laced with caffeine and comes in a cup.'

'Gotcha.' The detective pulled a face. 'Can't vouch for how good it'll be. I'll organize some and have it brought in.' Vikki left the room.

'I don't like the sound of that,' O'Neil said.

'The coffee?'

'The boarding school. Anywhere that houses children worries me.'

Ryan's joke had been ignored. Ordinarily, O'Neil would've laughed. Still in the doghouse, he turned his attention to the case. If, as Vikki suggested, details of the school had been uploaded to HOLMES, Grace would already have begun the process of checking whether Ambassador Dean and Lord Trevathan had attended the same school as Michael Tierney, tracking down any connections between the three.

He half expected the phone to ring.

O'Neil had read his mind. 'You need to call Grace. Trevathan was sixty, Ambassador Dean fifty-six, Tierney forty-seven. Maybe this boarding school in Yorkshire is something they have in common. Churning out the next generation of high-fliers is what public schools do, isn't it? I want information on any police investigations at that school going back sixty years, involving full-time boarders and day pupils, computerized or hard copy records. If there's any suggestion of abuse or neglect, I want it found.'

Ryan checked his mobile phone. 'She's already on it, guv.'

'Call her. I want full details on any local authority or church involvement: doctors, social workers and other professional visitors. Tell her to check out social media, online communities for former pupils, reunion websites – any bloody thing that might be relevant.'

'That's a hard ask.'

'Frank can help. He's good at digging the dirt.'

Before Ryan could respond – he ached for the opportunity to apologize properly for last night – someone knocked on the door.

Seeing his wounded expression, O'Neil backpedalled quickly. 'Ryan, I'm sorry. That was uncalled for. Don't you worry about Grace, she can delegate most of it to satellite rooms.'

Another knock.

O'Neil raised her voice. 'Come!'

A civilian entered with coffee on a tray. As he went to set it down, a plate of chocolate digestives slid towards O'Neil, tipped over the edge onto the table in front of her. She didn't make a fuss, just swept the broken biscuits back onto the plate. Blushing, the lad made himself scarce. He shut the door behind him and they settled down to work.

While O'Neil made some calls, Ryan logged on to HOLMES. The digital file on Tierney was quite thin but being updated by indexers in real time. It was important to understand how the initial information had come in to Sussex Police, who to, and the exact timing. He'd been over this with O'Neil but wanted to reacquaint himself with it in case anything had been missed in the telling.

The DVD had arrived at HQ, addressed to Chief Constable Martin Richards, on Tuesday, 12 October. The time-stamp showed the video as having been recorded in the early hours of Sunday, 10 October. There were statements to be read, reports from the Crime Scene Manager and the Underwater Search Unit to digest. The fact that Tierney's body had been found in the water off the Brighton coast made life difficult for everyone. Fire and water were the elements that best destroyed evidence, seawater more so than freshwater, as had been the case in Scotland.

Ryan clicked on photographs taken at the scene. No surprise there because he'd viewed the DVD, except the stills afforded him the time to pause a while and concentrate his mind on this offence instead of lumping it together with the rest. Murder scenes tended to merge that way when the circumstances and

MO were similar, especially where there was no body to dif-
ferentiate one from another.

The clock on the wall ticked loudly, competing with the
silence.

No contest.

Guilt settled on Ryan like a heavy weight. He hated conflict
within the ranks. To him, the enemy should be outside the
unit, not within. It ate away at him that O'Neil hadn't spoken a
word since the coffee was delivered. He glanced across the
desk. She was scribbling notes on a pad, only the top of her
head visible. This time yesterday they were friends. He hoped
they would be again.

There were a couple of knocks at the door.

O'Neil allowed Ryan to handle them: a short update from
the Family Liaison Officer supporting Tierney's long-term
partner, Robert Parker; more information from Vikki on
exactly what Parker had been told: that the victim's death was
not accidental and that a post-mortem would reveal more.
Parker told detectives that Tierney had gone out to spend the
evening of Saturday, 9 October with friends. Acting on that
information, detectives had established that he was last seen
walking away from the dinner party at around two in the
morning. They were still investigating how he'd got from there
to the abandoned coastguard lookout where he'd been stabbed
to death – information they had kept from Parker.

Without lifting her head, O'Neil put a hand out. Picking up
her mug, she took a sip of coffee, grimacing when she discovered it was stone cold. Ryan glanced at the clock. It had been
almost two hours since refreshments had arrived. He was
about to offer to fetch more when she looked up. His eyes flew

back to the screen, a wide shot of the room in which Tierney had been killed.

In his head, Ryan pictured CSIs in white suits documenting every drop of blood. There would have been little need for the application of Bluestar, the luminol-based chemical agent British forensic scientists used to irradiate traces of the liquid that kept us all alive, pure or diluted. No attempt had been made to wash it away here.

Because the crime scene had been linked to others elsewhere, Sussex Police had been exceptionally thorough. No expense had been spared. Bloodstain pattern analysis experts had reconstructed the crime scene to determine from what angle the victim was attacked, with what type of weapon – a narrow blade in this case. The injuries matched the screwdriver left at the scene. Forensic scientists had concluded that Tierney had been standing when the first blow was struck. An arc of blood on the floor led investigators to conclude that he'd turned and moved away from his attacker in an effort to escape, whereupon he'd been struck again, presumably in the back. A grid had been drawn, tagged and numbered, to enable scientists to establish, as close as they were able, how many blows had hit their target. The number was in double figures.

38

They left Sussex HQ in the pool car they had been loaned. Keying Tierney's home address into the satnav gave them a journey time of half an hour, an ETA of approximately five o'clock. O'Neil insisted on driving. On the way, Ryan updated her on the latest information fed into HOLMES, including the detail that Tierney's head had become detached from his body – unsurprising, given the time it had been in the sea – saving his partner the distress of identification at the morgue.

'Every cloud,' O'Neil said.

Ryan opened his mouth to speak and then closed it again when his phone rang. He checked the display. 'I'd better take this. It's Cath Masters, the SIO who interviewed Watson last night.'

Ryan could see O'Neil's frustration. Their job was about shifting priorities. No sooner were they making headway with one line of enquiry than they were forced to veer off in a different direction entirely. The ability to keep all the balls in the air was the difference between a good copper and a bad one, especially when conducting a multiple murder investigation. Information was gold. It didn't come in neat packages, delivered when most convenient to detectives. It came in thick and fast, at all times of the day and night, interrupting trains of thought – but that was also what made the job exciting: the constant challenge.

'Put it on speaker,' O'Neil said.

Ryan did as she asked, letting Masters know that O'Neil would be party to the conversation. While the two women greeted one another, Ryan wondered if their professional acquaintance extended to friendship, if Masters had knowledge of O'Neil's disastrous relationship with a moronic QC. There was no time for niceties, let alone sympathies, during a case this big.

'You have something for us?' O'Neil asked.

'Remember Watson said he owned a nightclub? It was a complete fabrication. He manages the joint. Nevertheless, the job is such that he's able to slip away for extra-marital activity with a string of hookers whenever he chooses and still keep it from his missus.'

Ryan tried not to look at O'Neil. He was struggling to understand how her ex could have left her at the altar on Christmas Eve, preferring the company of working girls. Forsythe was obviously the type who lived by the old saying: why buy a book when you can join the library? There were many of those in the job; dickheads, every one of them. Wouldn't know a good thing if it was presented to them gift-wrapped.

Masters was still talking: 'His story about being spooked in the lock-up checks out. Gloria made a formal statement to that effect. He can't have been in there more than twenty seconds, just enough time to get his zip down – or not, in his case. The shoe is definitely his. We have the other one now to prove it.'

'Good job, Cath.' O'Neil took a breath. 'Can you call the

National Footwear Database for me and let them know to cancel the action.'

'Already taken care of. There's no flies on your girl, Grace Ellis. Life in the old dog yet, eh?'

'Careful.' Ryan reminded her that walls had ears.

Masters chuckled. 'I'll deny I ever said it.'

O'Neil almost cracked a smile. 'You and Grace obviously know each other.'

'We've met once or twice. She's a formidable woman.'

'That's one way of putting it,' O'Neil said.

'Quite a reputation too.'

'In a good way,' Ryan chipped in.

Masters agreed. 'There's no one better at running a Murder Incident Room. You chose well.'

O'Neil changed the subject. 'We were fairly certain Watson was telling the truth. Sounds like he's cooperating—'

'After Ryan put the frighteners on.' Masters laughed. 'You've got yourself a player there, Eloise. If you get sick of him, sling him over, there's always a vacancy on my team for someone like him.'

That could happen sooner than you know, Ryan thought. Unable to face O'Neil, his eyes found the footwell. He spoke without raising them. 'How did Watson get on with the sketch?'

'He drew it well. Pretty accurate representation too, I reckon, bearing in mind that it would've been dark in there. He pinpointed exactly where he saw the body. Coincides with blood found at the scene. According to him, the lass was on her front, face down. I pressed him on age but he wasn't sure. Youngish, he said. Didn't think she was that old anyway. Adult female, certainly, somewhere between late teens and mid thirties. That's a guesstimate, based on what she was wearing. Arrogant shit reckons he knows women. Nearly stuck my fingers down my throat when he came out with that one.'

O'Neil kept her focus on the road, avoiding Ryan's sideways glance. He wanted to stand up for his gender; tell her that not all men were as obnoxious as Watson or her philandering QC. Instead, he let her mope, concentrating his efforts on Masters.

'Did he mention any features, facial or otherwise?' he asked.

'No, we lucked out there. Her hair was covering her face. Blonde, he thinks. Hard to tell in the poor lighting and with all the blood. Clothing pretty nondescript but intact: dark knee-length coat and a bag he described as bright yellow. Fluorescent, like an old-fashioned satchel, a distinctive black tag on the strap with a foreign name. I passed it to Grace. Like all good MIR managers she passed it back, asked my team to source bags of that kind. They came up with one manufactured by Proenza Schouler.'

'Never heard of it,' O'Neil said.

'Or me,' Masters said. 'Turns out it's high-end designer kit, a cool twelve hundred – sterling, not euros – which would suggest your female victim is loaded. Put it this way, we're talking Harvey Nicks, not TK Maxx. There are cheaper imitations on the market . . .'

Ryan heard a tapping sound, fingers striking a keyboard.

Masters was checking her computer.

'The Cambridge Satchel Company is one,' she said. 'Retails at a couple of hundred pounds, but it's neither fluorescent or foreign . . .'

That may be so but O'Neil and Ryan exchanged a glance.

Two mentions of the county town of Cambridge may or may not be significant. A snippet of information they would file away for later.

'Did you show the bags to Watson?' Ryan asked.

'Yeah, well, images of them. He seems to think the one your victim was wearing was identical to the more expensive brand. He may be an arse, a lying cheating arse, but he's a cracking witness. He swears the Schouler label is the one he saw. My team haven't found any others that fit the bill.'

'It might not be hers,' Ryan said. 'Could've been stolen and chucked in the lock-up by anyone.'

'No,' Masters said. 'It wasn't by the girl, it was *on* the girl. I'll email the drawing to Eloise. The sketch is pretty impressive. The strap was across her body, left shoulder to right thigh.'

'So probably right-handed.'

'That would be my guess.'

An email pinged into O'Neil's phone. She nodded to Ryan to pick it up. He accessed the sketch and turned it round to show her.

'Got it, thanks.' O'Neil pulled into a parking spot and cut the engine. 'Listen, we've got to go. Ryan and I are up against it here. Am I right in thinking that Watson just chose the wrong toilet spot?'

'I'd put money on it,' Master said.

'You may as well charge him with assault – assuming Gloria wants to press ahead – and bail him.'

'What about Grace?'

O'Neil looked at Ryan: his call.

'Forget it,' he said. 'She's old school. First, she hates filling out forms. Second, she'll find a way to bust his balls that doesn't involve a courtroom. We might even use the gobshite to our advantage further down the line. He squeals like a snout. May as well treat him like one.'

Masters laughed.

'I agree,' O'Neil said. 'Do me a favour, Cath. Let the bastard sweat a while before you let him go.'

'My diary is full,' she said. 'I'll be tied up for the rest of the day. Sadly, Watson will have to wait.'

O'Neil thanked her.

Echoing that sentiment, Ryan hung up.

They sat for a moment, mulling over the call. The body was there at around six thirty on the morning of Sunday, 8 December, removed sometime afterwards. Sunrise was seven fifty-three. Such a small window, but Ryan figured that while Spielberg kept an eye on the jogger, James Fraser, her partner in crime nipped back to dispose of the girl they had left in the lock-up. If Grace hadn't already come to the same conclusion, she soon would. He pictured frantic activity at base. She'd be organizing search teams, advising divers that there may be a distinctive bag, either on the riverbank or floating out to sea. Though they hadn't yet recovered a body, the unit at least had something to aim for now.

In the meantime, O'Neil and Ryan had an appointment with Robert Parker.

39

'Michael Tierney's civil partner could be key to this case.'
O'Neil pulled her collar up and quickened her step as they
walked a short way along Brighton seafront. It was bitterly
cold. 'If, as Vikki suggests, Robert Parker is a professional man,
articulate and discreet, maybe we need to take a chance here.
Shoot me down if you think I'm wrong but, if he's been with
Michael for thirty-plus years, he probably knows him better
than his mother, had she been alive.' She stopped walking as
they reached the building, five storeys of Regency splendour.

'This is it,' she said.

Ryan whistled. 'Very nice.'

'Yeah. Until we get in there.'

He knew what she meant. When it came to the families of
homicide victims, there was no such thing as a typical reaction
to the death of a loved one. Right now, his guv'nor was weigh-
ing up the pros and cons, making judgements based on what
they had gleaned from the FLO. Could Parker be trusted with
sensitive material relating to their case?

O'Neil's strategy for handling the interview made Ryan
nervous.

Sensing his hesitation, she made no move towards the
entrance. It was important to convince him before they went
in. 'Ambassador Dean had no significant other in his life, male

or female. Newman said his wife passed away two years ago. Trevathan never married. Neither of them had children. It's not been possible to interview anyone closer than a hysterical housekeeper to the judge. We need to push on now. Parker is how we do it.'

Ryan scanned the building, wondering if Tierney's partner was watching them from above, dreading the intrusion, savouring the last few moments before they shared information he didn't really want to hear. The words ignorance and bliss loomed large in Ryan's mind. Parker's world had already come crashing down. They were about to dump more misery on him.

'Ryan?'

He turned to face her.

'Do you agree?'

'Sorry, I thought you were telling, not asking, guv. Sharing sensitive information with a man we've never met before is risky.'

'It's a risk we must take if we're to break through the logjam. For the first time in this enquiry, we'll be able to get close to someone who knew the victim exceptionally well. Of course we must be sensitive to his feelings. Parker just lost his soulmate, but it's shit or bust, in my opinion. I believe he may be able to help us.'

'How d'you want to play it?'

'I'll lead. You follow up. He is, by all accounts, an intelligent man, but an extremely emotional one. I'm hoping that now he's had time to get over the initial shock, he'll be able to talk and listen. We'll know soon enough if we can share information with him. If we aren't of the same mind when we get in there, give me the nod and I'll back off.'

It was a good call, one Ryan was happy with.

The FLO had given him the access code to the apartment block. They took the lift to the penthouse and rang the bell. Behind gold-rimmed specs, Parker's eyes were tired and red. He'd made the effort to shave and was dressed in casual but well-tailored clothes. Mentally he was in bad shape, visibly tortured by loss, unable to comprehend how his future might pan out without Michael in it. Ryan had been hoping he'd be able to hold it together in the face of losing his long-term partner. Seeing him in the flesh, he wasn't so sure. And O'Neil's tactics wouldn't stand a chance if he wasn't up to it.

They were shown into an apartment much like their own office: under-floor heating, panoramic views out to sea, no chance that the wind whipping off the English Channel could penetrate the triple glazing. Beautifully furnished in muted shades of grey, it had set the couple back a cool two million, according to records Vikki had shared with them. Apparently, Parker was a wealthy man in his own right.

'I'm very sorry for your loss,' O'Neil began. He offered her a seat and she took it, waiting for him to settle on the sofa opposite before continuing. 'You will have been made aware that DS Ryan and I are from Northumbria Police. Because of this, I'm sure you've gathered already that the incident involving your partner is not an isolated one.'

'I did wonder,' Parker said.

'Do you mind if I call you Robert?'

He shook his head, composing himself.

As O'Neil put the man at ease, Ryan's attention drifted to an open door: it led to a mini gymnasium, complete with treadmill, exercise bike and weightlifting bench. A Camelbak hydration system was tucked neatly in one corner, some red Nike wrist weights like the ones he had at home lying on the floor beside it. After a few minutes, during a lull in the conversation, O'Neil caught Ryan's eye. He gave the briefest of nods, a gesture that she should go for it. Parker was holding his own.

It was time to take that chance.

O'Neil ran with it. 'Robert, I need your help. I'm going to divulge details to you that would normally remain confidential. Before I do that, I need an assurance that what I tell you will go no further than this room: not to friends, press – and this might sound very strange to you – but I'd rather you didn't discuss it with local detectives either.'

'You have my word, Superintendent.'

'We're investigating a number of incidents, in the UK and abroad, that we believe are linked. You are the *only* person we are able to talk to who knows one of the victims intimately. Let me be very clear: if this information gets out, it may hamper our investigation. I want to bring those responsible for Michael's death to justice. I'm sure you do too, before anyone else gets hurt.'

'I understand,' he said.

'I gather you've been told that Michael's body was recovered from the water and that the circumstances surrounding his death are suspicious, is that correct? Forgive me for asking but it pays not to presume these things.'

Parker gave a resigned nod. He knew what was coming and was steeling himself for it, just as Ryan was bracing himself for the distress of visiting yet another crime scene, the coastguard lookout where Tierney had been killed. Not that he expected it to take them any further after the first-rate job local police had done on it. O'Neil had been given a tour of the site by the Crime Scene Manager on her first trip to East Sussex. She was confident that they had covered all the bases. That was good enough for him.

She gave Parker a moment to compose himself before diving in again: 'We have forensic evidence that Michael was abducted, taken to a place not far from here and stabbed to death, his body disposed of at sea some time afterwards. The person or persons responsible were forensically aware. Nothing we have found matches any information on our database.'

Ryan expected Parker to get upset, but he remained in control in the face of such distressing facts. O'Neil was handling him gently, drip-feeding information, not wanting to rush him, sensitive to the fact that he could crumble at any moment, terminate the interview and ask them to leave.

'I understand that Robert went out alone the night he disappeared.'

'Yes. We'd been invited to dinner at a friend's house, but I didn't feel up to it. I had a dreadful cold.'

'What time did he leave here?'

'Around eight, maybe a few minutes after. When he didn't return home, I assumed he'd stayed over. We often do if it's a late night. When I called him next morning, he didn't pick up. I tried the house and was told he'd left in the early hours.'

'Would he have walked or taken a taxi?'

'Walked, it's not that far.'

'Could you write down the route?'

'I have done. Detectives locally are tracking his movements.'

'Good.' O'Neil continued with her plan. 'I'm going to give you a few names. I'd like you to tell me whether you've ever heard them before or if, to your knowledge, they meant anything to Michael.' She began with Lord Trevathan's given name: 'Leonard Maxwell . . .' Parker shook his head. 'OK, does the name Trevathan mean anything to you?' Same response. 'Paul Dean?'

'Are they all dead?' He looked horrified.

'Those are the names of two of the victims.'

'Three names, two victims?' Even in his present mental state, Parker had spotted the anomaly. 'I assume one is an alias?'

'Of sorts,' she said. 'You've heard of neither?'

Parker's jaw tightened as he shook his head. 'Are they gay men?'

It was an obvious deduction.

O'Neil was unable to give a definitive answer. Grace had checked the incidents of hate crimes on grounds of sexual orientation in the Brighton area. They were on the rise. Sussex Police were proactively encouraging victims to come forward and report such matters. It was the only way to get a clear picture of the problem and formulate an appropriate response.

'Not to our knowledge,' Ryan said. 'You've had problems?'

A glare almost from Parker. 'Not all people who live in Brighton tolerate queers.'

'Anything specific?' O'Neil asked.

'No.' A tear emerged from Parker's left eye and ran down his cheek. He brushed it away. 'It's the first thing I thought of when Michael went missing. He never mentioned any of those names to me. Believe me, I'd have remembered.' He hesitated. A guilty look. 'I used to get insanely jealous if he talked about other men. Stupid I know, given the length of time we've been together. I very much regret that now. Michael used to get so angry with me over it.'

Ryan thought about his own twinge of jealousy on Friday night. Seeing O'Neil get into that Porsche had brought on a sudden ache to be the person driving her away. She'd fled the apartment so hastily that he'd assumed – wrongly, as it turned out – that the owner of the car was a lover. The emotion was irrational. He shook it off, his eyes locking on to a computer on a nearby desk.

'Robert, is that your laptop or Michael's?'

'It's Michael's.'

'Do you happen to know the password?'

'Yes.' Parker got up, wandered over to the desk to retrieve it. He opened it up and logged on, handing it to Ryan. 'Keep it,' he said. 'I'll write the password down.'

Ryan waited for him to do that before asking: 'Did Michael have a mobile on him, do you know?'

'Of course.'

'It wasn't recovered with his body.'

'He was a busy man,' Parker said. 'He never went anywhere without it.'

'I assumed that would be the case.' If it *was* in the sea, Ryan had little hope that it would be found. Shame. It would contain a lot of personal stuff. 'Was Michael in the habit of backing up his information?'

Parker pointed at the laptop. 'It'll all be there.'

O'Neil was relieved to hear it. 'You may not be aware of everything in Michael's life,' she said, 'but I'd like to talk to you about the school where he taught in Yorkshire. Were you together then?'

'Yes.'

'I believe he went there as a child when his father was work-ing overseas.'

'That's right.'

'A happy experience?'

'I can't imagine he'd have returned to work there otherwise.'

It was fair comment.

Ryan was in to the contacts on Michael's laptop, business and personal, and was scanning the names. Unable to find references to any of the victims, he searched for Denmark, Kenmore, Newcastle and Tyneside generally. There were three hits in Copenhagen: a female banker, Agnete Møller; some-one listed only as Rolv Jakobsen; and Pål Friis, whose contact details included landline, mobile and a private address. The latter two were male, the Danish versions of Rolf and Paul.

'Excuse me for interrupting, guv.' Ryan shifted his gaze to Parker. 'I see that Michael had business contacts in Copenha-gen but did he have any friends there? There's a name and address here: Pål Friis?'

'We met while on holiday in Greece several years ago and kept in touch. He pops down here when he's in London. He's a cultural historian – straight, in case you were wondering.'

'I wasn't,' Ryan said.

'Any idea who Graham Hunter is? His address is listed as South Tyneside.'

Parker frowned, shook his head. 'A business acquaintance, I assume.'

Writing names in his notebook to pass on to Grace, Ryan got on with his search. Parker was asking what Tierney's former school had to do with anything. O'Neil told him the truth: in investigating Michael's death, it was important to understand his life . . .

'We need to build on what we already know about him. That includes his past: the school where he taught, previous jobs, clubs he was involved with as a younger man. An antecedent history will help us to work out what, if anything, connects him to the other victims. Anything you can think of, however trivial it may seem, we'd like to know about.'

'I'll give it some thought.' Parker added: 'We've been together since university.'

'That's a very long time.' Her sad tone of voice made Ryan look up.

Parker was losing it. 'We were to have been married on March twenty-ninth. Michael and I campaigned for legislation to make that possible. He chose the first available date. Said he'd waited long enough. He was *so* excited . . .' Parker struggled to finish what he'd started. 'He had such plans. Can you believe it? After three decades of soliciting votes for equality, we nearly made it.' He dropped his head in his hands and wept. Ryan fucking hated his job sometimes.

40

Heathrow was packed as always, travellers anxious to get away on time, last call for the 08.55 British Airways flight to Copenhagen just announced. Ryan and O'Neil made it with seconds to spare before the gates closed, an accident on the airport approach road having delayed their arrival. In the end they'd had to abandon their taxi and run the rest of the way.

Prior to that mad dash, Ryan had called Grace and asked her to look into the names he'd found on Michael Tierney's laptop, and if possible arrange for them to meet with the three Copenhagen-based individuals. The response had just arrived in his inbox.

'Anything interesting?' O'Neil was trying to read over his shoulder.

'Agnete Møller is presently in London, Rolv Jakobsen in Switzerland. They're business acquaintances, not close associates or friends. Neither has seen or heard from Tierney recently. Both are out of the frame for his death. They were in the US at the time – on Wall Street, to be precise. Nice work if you can get it.'

'They're alibiing each other? How convenient.'

'That was my first thought. Grace has been on to the FBI and confirmed they were in the country. The good news is Pål Friis is available to talk to us this afternoon.'

'Time?'

'Three o'clock.'

'Anything else?'

'Graham Hunter has been located, an address in Westoe Village—'

'Near South Shields?'

Ryan pulled a face, a roll of the eyes almost. 'Yeah, I know – a ferry ride away from North Shields. Could we be that lucky?' O'Neil didn't give a reply and Ryan didn't wait for one. 'Newman is on it as we speak. If I know Frank, he'll turn up unannounced—'

'Without ID?'

'He'll think of something.'

Her stare could penetrate metal. 'Is that it?'

'No, Grace has been busy. The CCTV cross-reference you ordered has come back positive. One vehicle – a VW Golf GTi – seen on North Shields Fish Quay in the early hours of Sunday *and* in Whitley Bay around midday. Spot on for James Fraser's time of death—'

'Trashed?'

He nodded. 'Burnt-out and abandoned on an industrial estate in Byker. It was there on Monday when staff opened up and reported to the local nick. No bloody use to us whatsoever. It had been half-inched from someone's drive a few streets away.'

'Might be a coincidence. Thieving kids—'

'Either way, there's zero likelihood of IDing the offenders. Both occupants in the car were wearing headgear.'

*

As the plane began to pull off its stand, O'Neil's mood was as leaden as the sky overhead. She remained like that for much of the journey, freezing Ryan out to the point that he didn't feel he could converse with her. He knew she'd come round eventually but suspected he might have a long wait. He couldn't help thinking of their last plane trip together. The investigation into Jack's death had taken them to Norway, and despite the fact they'd started out on opposite sides, with Ryan suspended and O'Neil heading an investigation into Jack's alleged misconduct, they'd established a camaraderie that was sadly missing now.

Ryan put his head back and shut his eyes. That last outing hadn't been all work. As he drifted off to sleep he could almost smell the sea. Her red hair wafted in the breeze as they shared a drink on the *brygge* in Tønsberg, yacht rigging slapping against masts as crafts bobbed up and down in choppy water, seabirds swooping in search of food, pecking at the boardwalk where hours before fishing vessels had tied up. O'Neil was happy then . . . and so was he.

They touched down in Denmark's capital just after eleven, a traffic detail picking them up, transporting them to the city's headquarters swiftly with the aid of blues and twos. With a plan to stay over for one night only, they had a full schedule ahead of them: a briefing with Danish detectives; visits to the embassy and crime scene; an interview with a key witness – the *only* witness as far as they could tell – and a meeting with Pål Friis.

With a reputation for excellent international cooperation through Interpol – and with Europol in the Hague – Danish police had been quick to respond to O'Neil's request for information, first through their liaison officer in London and later with the Efterforskningsenheden, the Danish equivalent of British CID. The branch responsible for murder investigation, the Drabsafdelingen, had put her in touch with the senior investigating officer dealing with Ambassador Paul Dean's murder, Politikommisær Liisa Ølgaard.

It was agreed that they would meet at Copenhagen Police HQ located on Polititorvet, southwest of the city centre. It was unlike any headquarters either Northumbria detective had ever visited, a piece of architecture to behold: neoclassical, triangular in shape, four storeys high with a circular central courtyard close to Copenhagen's *Havn*.

Ølgaard was no Sarah Lund, the fictional detective who'd shot to fame in the internationally successful and incomparable Danish TV crime series, *The Killing*. In place of the Faroese jumper and jeans the screen character was known for, Ølgaard wore a no-nonsense pair of strides and a crisp pink shirt, sleeves rolled up ready for business. She was very approachable, if a little reserved – and tiny. Ryan had the feeling that their joint case was every bit as complex as the storylines and plot-twists Lund had to cope with.

'Because of Dean's diplomatic status, our Security and Intelligence Service were brought in as soon as the DVD arrived at the embassy.' Ølgaard uploaded photographs onto a smart screen on the wall. 'As you can see, the scene was an abandoned building, not that far from the Ambassador's residence, but an unlikely spot for him to visit willingly. There must have been some coercion going on.'

'I understand you reported it as a robbery,' O'Neil said.

'At the request of your government, yes. Our investigators knew it wasn't a straightforward robbery case, though the ambassador's wallet was not on the body. His secretary is adamant that he had it with him when he left. She saw him pick it up along with his telephone before he left the embassy that day. We found his phone but not the wallet. Either the offender took it or someone else picked it up.'

'No attempt to use his credit cards since?' Ryan asked.

'None.' Ølgaard paused. 'They probably took the cash and dumped the rest. Our Security and Intelligence Service were recalled to the case when British Intelligence informed us of a possible link with a second death in the UK.'

The Brits exchanged a look.

'You're very well informed,' O'Neil said.

'They have reason to keep me sweet.' Before Ryan could query that odd comment, Ølgaard picked up the baton. 'I've been told that a senior member of your judiciary was the second victim. That he was due to try members of a terror cell operating across European borders and planning an attack on your country. This is of great concern to us. We must all be vigilant.'

'Indeed we must,' O'Neil said. 'May we go to the embassy before we visit the crime scene?'

'Of course, not that it will take you anywhere,' Ølgaard said. 'I have a car waiting.'

Ryan and O'Neil sat in the back, wondering what Ølgaard meant by the British government keeping her sweet. Sounded like an information exchange. She sat up front next to a female traffic officer whose driving style reminded Ryan of Grace. One speed. No dawdling. They left HQ heading south-east on

Polititorvet until they reached a crossroads, then right into Bernstoffsgade, right again into Vester Farimagsgade, passing two large parks in quick succession.

It took less than fifteen minutes to reach the embassy.

The red stucco building was surrounded by iron railings and flanked by smart apartment blocks; a trio of flags – British, Danish and European – flapping in the breeze outside. The main gate opened as the traffic car approached. It was obvious that they were expected.

Ølgaard was very efficient.

A keen sense of direction – confirmed by a quick Google search – confirmed Ryan's belief that they had merely skirted the harbour and were now a lot closer to the open sea. He could smell it in the air as he got out of the car. It made him instantly homesick.

Dean's replacement greeted the group in person as they entered the building. For a diplomat, she was relatively young, around Ryan's age. She examined them with sharp, intelligent eyes, a half-smile all she could summon due to the solemnity of the occasion.

'Welcome,' she said. 'I'm Ambassador Dean's replacement, Ruth Calvert. I'm only sorry your visit here is under such tragic circumstances. Please, Nora will take your coats, then we can adjourn to the library.'

Formalities dispensed with, they moved through an adjoining door and all sat down. Ryan and O'Neil went through the motions, paying their respects to the Ambassador's predecessor. Half an hour later, they left on foot, following the path he'd taken on that fateful day, their driver agreeing to go by road and meet them at the crime scene.

'We checked the hospitals as soon as Ambassador Dean was reported missing,' Ølgaard said as they walked. 'At first we thought he'd been involved in some kind of accident. Naturally, because of his diplomatic status, we reported the matter to the Foreign Office immediately.'

'You knew him well?' Ryan asked.

'Not well, but we'd met a couple of times. I'm so sorry we didn't take better care of him.'

'Not your fault.' O'Neil didn't dwell on it. 'The judge you mentioned – his body was removed from the crime scene. This is pure speculation but we think the offenders left the Ambassador in situ because they were unfamiliar with their surroundings and therefore loath to dispose of his body elsewhere – though the harbour is nearby.'

The comment confused Ølgaard.

'Most of our crime scenes are close to water: sea, river, loch,' O'Neil explained. 'Perhaps a lack of transport hampered them here.'

'Or they were disturbed and left in a hurry.'

'That's probably the case.'

'I find it curious that they changed their modus operandi after the first killing.' Ølgaard's eyes scanned the warehouse and came to rest on her British counterparts. 'Your countryman, Mr Dean, was a gentle man, very popular among Danish people. His disappearance was scandalous, his death in our country shameful. It shocked us all, not just the police here in Copenhagen but the wider community of Denmark.' She flicked her eyes to the stinking warehouse. 'This is no place to find the end.'

41

O'Neil thanked Ølgaard for her cooperation, asking to see the witness Anja Pedersen next. The car took them back to HQ. Anja was brought to the interview room within minutes of their arrival, a skinny figure, thirty-five years old with bright blue eyes and hair to match. She was casually dressed, a canvas satchel slung over her shoulder, reminding Ryan of the yellow one he hoped Northumbria underwater search units were currently trying to find in the waters of the Fish Quay.

Ølgaard spoke to Pedersen in Danish. '*De må gerne sidde ned.*'

Pedersen took off her coat to reveal a stripy mauve dress underneath, accepting the seat offered. Having been told by Ølgaard that the witness had been waiting a while, O'Neil thanked her for her patience before the interview got under way. The young woman shrugged, held up a novel by Icelandic author Yrsa Sigurðardóttir, an English edition: *I Remember You*. She spoke softly, unhurriedly. 'I'm a librarian by profession, happiest with time on my hands and a book in my lap.'

O'Neil smiled at the others.

Conscious of their appointment with Pål Friis, Ryan began: 'You made a statement to police that you saw a couple in Kastelsvej, near the British Embassy, before Ambassador Dean was murdered.' He took in her nod. 'You may be the only person

267

able to describe them for us, so we'd like as detailed a description as you're able to give. At this stage, we're anxious to trace
and eliminate them. They may or may not be guilty of any
crime.'

'Guilty is exactly how I'd describe them.' Pedersen spoke
with conviction.

Ølgaard said something in her native tongue. '*Hvorfor
virkede de mistænkelige?*' She looked at Ryan. 'I asked her what
stood out about them.' O'Neil had asked Ryan to lead the
interview – she didn't say why, just that this was one job they
wouldn't share – but she agreed that the Dane should chip in if
she could hurry the interview along in any way.

'Anja?' Ryan prompted. 'May I call you that?'

'That is my name.'

He loved the bluntness of Scandi women.

The librarian relaxed into her chair, in no obvious hurry,
eyes fixed on a point over Ryan's shoulder as if she might find
inspiration there. 'The man was around my age,' she said. 'He
was wearing a grey shirt with a white stripe, open at the neck.
He had dark patches under his arms even though the day was
cool, a foreign rucksack on his back. It had a logo I couldn't
read. I was too far away.' She paused. 'He wasn't Danish. Neither of them were. I thought at the time they might be British.
Don't ask me why. Their clothes, I suppose. You can tell a lot
from what a person is wearing.'

'*Hvid?*' Ølgaard said.

'White, yes.'

'Both of them?' Ryan asked.

'Yes.'

'You told Politikommisær Ølgaard that something about the man wasn't quite right.'

'For sure. He was odd. It was the shifty expression on his face, the fact that he was sweating so much and was the only one in the street with no destination, no focus, if you know what I mean. He smoked a lot. He was . . . how do you say it?' She paused, looking to Ølgaard for assistance.

'Loitering?' Ølgaard said.

'Yes, exactly.'

Ryan moved her along. 'Please continue . . .'

'It was the way he held his phone, not reading from it, I don't mean that, but not like a tourist taking pictures either. The more I observed him, the more certain I became that he was a character not to be trusted.'

'Did something happen to make you think that?'

'Two men appeared through the front door of the embassy. Security, I think, smartly dressed, though not in uniform. They took a good look at him and then walked away.' This was news to Ryan, O'Neil and Ølgaard too. Pedersen was in full flow. 'When you work in a library you see all kinds. You quickly learn to observe the weird ones. Some are lonely, others disturbed. I'm in charge. I have to know the difference. The nervous ones display strange behaviour like the man I saw in the street. Her too. When they saw the security patrol, they became agitated and turned away. The man dropped his head, using his phone as cover.'

'What time was this?' Ryan asked.

'Three o'clock or thereabouts, maybe a few minutes after – a Friday afternoon. It occurred to me that embassy guards were being lazy, that questioning the couple might delay an early finish for the weekend. I'm sure you have the same type in your country.'

'*Fortalte De mine kollegaer det?*' Ølgaard interrupted. Her words needed no translation. Her tone was enough of a hint that she was royally pissed off. The Dane turned to Ryan and O'Neil. 'This is the first I've heard of the two security guards from the embassy. She never mentioned them before. I would have questioned them earlier, had I known.'

'The detective I spoke to never asked me.' Anja said in English. She didn't flinch when Ølgaard got up and left the room, practically taking the door off its hinges as she yanked it open. The librarian rolled her eyes. 'I guess someone is in serious trouble.'

Ryan suspected that the security detail – if that's what it was – had seen the couple from inside the building and were now keeping shtum because they should have investigated. They would want nothing to do with a foreign national going missing on their watch, especially one as important as the British ambassador they were employed to protect. He made a mental note to follow it up. With any luck – they were certainly due some – there would be CCTV to verify Pedersen's account.

'What made you link the two events?' Ryan asked.

'The Ambassador's death was reported on TV and in the newspaper. It reminded me of the suspicious couple I'd seen just days before.' Her eyes had grown dark. 'I feel very guilty now. Maybe if I'd challenged them.'

'Given what we suspect, that would've been unwise.'

'I could've approached the patrol.'

Ryan reassured her. 'You weren't to know what was going to happen.'

'Lisbeth Salander would've done something.'

Reference to the fictitious character of Swedish author Stieg Larsson threw Ryan. He was suddenly on the back foot, wondering if the librarian was herself a bit of a fruitcake, overly influenced by the books she read. It was just as well Ølgaard had left the room.

O'Neil was getting restless and was, Ryan suspected, similarly astonished by Pedersen's lapse into a fabricated universe during a police interview. Checking her watch, O'Neil chanced a brief glance at Ryan, a gesture, if one were needed, to push on.

'What was the woman like?' he asked. 'More or less anxious than him?'

'Much less.' There was no hesitation. 'She was keeping her distance from him, but they were definitely together. There was no doubt in my mind. They were . . .' She linked hands tightly to demonstrate her point. 'More than close if you know what I mean. I'm not sure how to describe it.'

'Man and wife?'

'I don't think so.' Pedersen screwed up her face. 'More like brother and sister.'

'What gave you that impression?'

Ølgaard was back, her mood no better for her trip outside.

'She was protective of him, not the other way round,' Anja said. 'Looking out for him, if you know what I mean. She was acting oddly too, sketching on a notepad when there wasn't anything interesting in the street to draw.'

That artistic bent again.

Photographer or sketch artist, Ryan was certain that the woman Pedersen was describing was half of the couple he was after, the woman O'Neil had nicknamed Spielberg. Her voice echoed in his head now, snippets of their brief telephone conversation and the chilling dialogue from the DVDs she'd sent. If Pedersen's account could be believed – and that was currently under review – Spielberg was the driving force, not her male accomplice, just as Caroline had suspected when she fed back her thoughts on the DVDs.

Ryan focused on the witness. 'Can you give a good description of either of them?'

'Not him.' She struggled for the right words, lapsing into her mother tongue, her attention on her countrywoman. '*Han havde en hat på, der skyggede for hans ansigt.*'

Ølgaard responded in the same way. '*Hvilken slags hat var det?*'

'*Amerikansk, den slags man har på til baseball.*'

'His face was in shade.' Ølgaard translated. 'He was wearing a baseball cap.'

'Yeah, we gathered that.' Ryan turned to Pedersen. 'Is there anything about him you haven't already mentioned to me or Politikommisær Ølgaard?'

'He needed something to eat.'

'Excuse me?' Ryan didn't understand.

Ølgaard was about to ask for clarification when Pedersen spoke up. 'I'm not a doctor, but my sister is painfully thin. She has a disease—'

'Anorexia?'

'Yes, the man with the phone looked like her.'

'And the woman?'

'She was older, more confident – definitely in control – attractive too . . . with hair like your boss.'

Ryan glanced at O'Neil. Pedersen's description of this couple was strikingly similar to the one given by Trevathan's house-keeper – a thin man; a glamorous woman – but the two who took the briefcase had since been ruled out as MI5 operatives. It was important not to confuse the couples. The librarian was their sole eyewitness.

'She had red hair?' Ølgaard asked. 'Are you sure?'

The librarian nodded. 'From a bottle.'

It didn't surprise anyone that the woman they were discuss-ing might change her appearance to hide her identity. Whilst thin men could bulk up and make themselves fat, it didn't work the other way round. The male they were seeking was thin, emaciated. Such knowledge was gold. A heated argument in the corridor interrupted the conversation. Ølgaard's doing, if her smug expression was anything to go by. Pedersen became anxious. Ryan had to raise his voice above the din, telling her not to concern herself. They ended the discussion there. They were short of time and keen to get to Pål Friis.

42

When Grace had set up the meeting with Friis, the historian requested an outside rendezvous. Working at the Danish and International Art Museum, he said he spent too much time inside. Having experienced several hours in a tin tube at thirty thousand feet, Ryan knew the feeling and was more than happy to accommodate him.

The Renaissance-style King's Garden was truly special, one of the world's oldest parks dating from the 1600s. Ryan and O'Neil entered the grounds through the main gate, walking in silence towards the meeting point, bare trees offering no refuge from a biting wind. O'Neil seemed not to notice the chill. She was gloved up, a thick scarf wrapped around her neck, a long grey padded coat and knee-length boots, perfect for December.

Ryan's short leather jacket offered less protection. Despite the fact that they were shoved deep down in his pockets, he could feel his hands slowly turning blue. He checked his watch. They were early, so he took out his phone and called Caroline. It was a mistake to do so in O'Neil's presence. His twin knew instantly that he was unhappy and jumped in, ignoring his enquiry about her own state of health.

'Matt? What's wrong?'

'Nothing.' Ryan dropped his voice to a whisper. 'That I can talk about now anyway.'

'Doesn't sound like nothing.'

'It's been a long couple of days. You know how much I love flying. I'm knackered, that's all.'

'You've been knackered, before . . . and I'm not stupid.'

Ryan didn't respond. He pulled up sharply, allowing his guv'nor to walk on alone. She'd clocked his unease and was getting curious. Caroline's voice hit his ear again. 'Is O'Neil with you?'

'Affirmative.'

'Tell me you haven't fallen out with her.' A lengthy silence was all the answer she needed. 'Oh, Matt, what have you done? She likes you!'

'And I like her. Stuff happens.'

'When will you be home? We'll talk about it then.'

'Not sure,' he said. 'Tomorrow, maybe Wednesday, depends how much we have on. I need to get home for some clothes. The ones I have on will walk to the laundry of their own free will if I don't change them soon. I packed light, as usual. I'll call by if I can get away. Assuming you'll be there?'

Caroline confirmed that she would. She worked from home three days a week. The Crown Prosecution Service was good like that. It mattered not where she worked, so long as she put the hours in. Ryan ached to share O'Neil's tragic past with his twin. To ask her advice as to how, or even if, he should attempt to raise the subject when his guv'nor was adamant that it was off limits. He decided to keep it to himself. He couldn't bring himself to betray her trust a second time.

Ordinarily blessed with good judgement, particularly where women were concerned, he'd attempted to talk to O'Neil umpteen times, only to bottle out at the last minute. No matter how hard he tried, he hadn't been able to conjure up words that were good enough. No opener he practised seemed suitable . . . no direct apology adequate.

Up ahead, O'Neil's step faltered. Over her shoulder, she caught Ryan's eye. She tilted her head, indicating the Rosenborg Palace, the agreed meeting place with Pål Friis, unable to hide her delight at the sight of the building before them, even though she was still pissed off with him. Her smile was an act. Ryan decided he'd had enough. Friis was running late. *Now* was the time to tackle her. He could wait no longer.

'Gotta go,' he said into the phone.

'Whatever it is, don't do anything rash.'

'It's a bit late for that. Take care, I'll call you as soon as I can.' He hung up, pocketing the phone as he caught up with O'Neil.

'You done?' she asked.

He nodded.

'Everything OK?'

'Depends on whether you mean at home or here.' He held her gaze. 'Guv, are we cool, you and I?'

There was a moment when neither of them spoke, a split second during which Ryan felt her armour crack, a brief spark of reconciliation. Then, as quickly as it arrived, it was gone, her attention taken by someone behind him calling out her name.

'Detective Superintendent O'Neil?' Pål Friis proffered a hand as he approached, moving like a cheetah across a manicured lawn on long, thin legs. O'Neil shook hands with him, her colour rising ever so slightly. She glanced apologetically at Ryan as the historian introduced himself, their unfinished business on hold . . . for now.

'Please,' Friis swept a hand towards a park bench. 'Shall we sit in this magnificent park?'

Nothing he was able to tell them was of any interest. He could only confirm the circumstances in which he'd met and kept in touch with Michael Tierney and Robert Parker. Ryan tuned him out, unable to shake free of the revolving image in his head, the light fading from O'Neil's eyes the night before last as she explained that she'd been jilted by Stephen Forsythe QC, a man she'd loved and wanted to share her life with. Ryan couldn't conceive of the anger and embarrassment she must've felt as she fled the church – her plans shattered like broken glass, leaving her exposed and alone with nowhere to hide . . . Assuming she'd made it over the threshold.

The temperature in the park seemed to plummet as the sun fell behind the trees. Ryan pulled his collar up, a futile attempt to keep warm. He chanced a glance in O'Neil's direction, watching her mouth move as she talked, every single word delivered with clarity in the most sensitive way possible. Her expression was grave but sympathetic.

Friis was dumbstruck, unable to take it in.

Wiping his face with his hand, he stood up, eyes scanning the surrounding shrubbery. Minutes ago, he'd proudly shown them off. Suddenly, they had lost their appeal. It would be dark soon. There might be danger lurking in the shadows here.

He swung round.

'Murdered?' His voice broke as he tried to express his disbelief. 'Surely not! Michael was the most peaceful man I ever met. He wouldn't hurt a soul. Ohmigod! Poor Robert. Have you spoken to him?'

O'Neil nodded. 'I'm sorry for your loss.'

Ryan would like a quid for every time he'd heard that phrase.

'Was it a fight?' Friis asked.

'No, not a fight.'

O'Neil remained seated, an invitation for the historian to retake his seat while he processed the awful news. Words of comfort to the bereaved Dane faded from Ryan's hearing. His mind swung wildly from the past to the present and back again. He pictured Eloise, not as she was now, wrapped up against the cold, but in a flowing wedding dress, the delicate contours of a happy face hidden by a simple veil, exhilarated by the occasion, surrounded by friends and family. He wondered if she'd been prevented from entering the church while enquiries were made of the bridegroom. Or had she realized that something was wrong and gone inside, her professional persona taking over, fearing an accident of some kind?

It had happened before in the rush to get to church.

A million scenarios passed through Ryan's head. It was driving him mad, not knowing. He intended to find out more as soon as he was able through discreet enquiries. It wasn't a matter of idle curiosity; his relationship with O'Neil was at stake. It would remain in limbo until he understood what had happened. Only then could he devise a way to get through to her and repair the damage.

He'd quizzed Grace on the phone. She'd hadn't been able to help much. She had retired in 2010, a full two years before O'Neil was due to marry. She was in Hong Kong working as a Foreign Office courier when she'd heard via text, a bit of salacious gossip passed on by an ex-colleague in a moment of boredom – and only that the wedding was off. It was a whirl-wind romance apparently.

Ryan could hear Grace's voice in his head . . .

'I assumed she'd come to her senses and bailed at the last minute.'

'You knew who the groom was—'

'Ryan, get real! I can't remember the names of the men *I* slept with last Tuesday.'

He'd laughed. 'I know you like to live in the moment but you're a newlywed.'

'Hey! Married or single, I intend to live till I die.' She stopped pulling his leg. 'You know what these things are like, Ryan. By the time I returned to the UK, Eloise's lucky escape was old news. I heard she was happy and back at work.'

Only one of those statements was true. Ryan knew that now. How much effort must it have taken to keep up the pretence of normality? Then again, what other choice did O'Neil have? If she'd folded, not only would Stephen Forsythe have won, he'd have stripped her naked, taking away the one thing of value she had left: her career.

Devastating as it must have been, O'Neil wasn't the type to wallow in self-pity. It took a woman with real strength of character to pick herself up and carry on as if nothing had happened. Ryan had heard nothing on the grapevine. Not a whisper. If there had been any police guests at her wedding, they loved her enough not to breathe a word. In an organiza-tion riddled with rumour and speculation, that spoke volumes. It was then that Ryan made his decision to offer her a shoulder, should she want one, and to hell with the consequences. Not to make that play was unthinkable. He would do it as soon as the opportunity presented itself. He couldn't bear not to. He'd rather ship out.

43

Grace had booked them into the Marriott on Kalvebod Brygge, a fifteen-minute taxi ride from the airport. Ryan wondered if the waterside location was deliberate or coincidental, whether O'Neil had chosen it herself. Probably not, he decided. He couldn't see her cosying up for a nightcap this trip, forgiving him anytime soon for questioning her over Hilary Forsythe, or reneging on her decision to keep her private life a closely guarded secret from those who didn't already know – those that didn't need to.

The drink Ryan offered was declined, so he said goodnight and took the elevator to his fourth-floor room. With nothing better to do than mope around, and no dinner on the cards, he raided the mini-bar. Opening a beer and a packet of nuts, he sat down near the window. The view of the city's picturesque harbour was even better in the dark than he imagined it might be in the daytime.

The hands on his watch clicked on, minute after painful minute, each one seeming to take an hour to move. He considered ringing Caroline, but didn't want to tie up the phone in case O'Neil changed her mind about that drink. When she didn't get in touch, he became increasingly restless. Twice he picked up his phone to call and have it out with her, but each time he bottled it.

He would . . .

Just not now.

Flicking TV channels bored him rigid. He switched off the set in favour of his iPad. The act of keying the name into Google made his guts heave. The YouTube clip was a close-up. Stephen Forsythe was a handsome man. Impeccably dressed. Classy – on the outside at least – steely eyes, velvet voice, the kind it would be hard to argue with, in or out of a courtroom.

Ryan wasn't fooled.

During his career he'd been cross-examined by a succession of guys like Forsythe. Beneath a self-assured delivery on legal precedent, an arrogant shit lurked, hamming it up in front of a captive audience. He'd go down well with Spielberg. Ending the clip, Ryan threw the device on the bed, put on his running kit and made his way downstairs to hit the gym.

Ignoring the free weights, he took to a running machine. His efforts were rewarded. Within minutes, his negativity faded away, the release of endorphins producing a feeling of euphoria. He felt cleansed, regenerated, pumped up and pre-pared for anything. He was about to terminate his run when he recognized a face through the mirrored wall in front of him.

O'Neil looked around, didn't see him, or pretended not to.

Dumping her bag on the floor, she completed a few stretches and fired up a treadmill of her own. Her warm-up routine graduated to a gentle jog, red hair turning dark at the base of her neck as it became soaked in sweat.

Ryan stayed put, hoping to catch her when she'd finished, maybe chance a second invitation to the bar; 10k later he was still waiting, still running . . . bloody exhausted. With no more energy left, he slowed, cut the power and stepped from the machine. Throwing a towel round his neck, he ambled in her direction, trying to make out that his legs weren't ready to collapse. This time she acknowledged him. She had no other choice.

'Blimey!' She whipped her safety cord out of the machine's console, ending her workout. 'You really went for it.'

She didn't know the half.

Ryan had been running for a full hour, beating his personal best by miles. He could feel muscles he didn't even know he had. Before he could answer – he had no energy left for speech – O'Neil was in work mode, banging on about the case, not a bit out of breath.

'I was thinking about Pedersen. She might have one foot on Fantasy Island, but her powers of observation seemed pretty impressive to me – she'd registered our suspects' clothes, their body language, their attempt to conceal the fact they were together. I'm inclined to believe her, aren't you?' Ryan could only manage a nod in response. 'If we ever nick anyone, she'll make an excellent witness. There's no doubt in her mind that the couple she observed were not Danes. You *can* ID foreigners from what they're wearing. The unfamiliar rucksack, the odd behaviour, the fact that the two turned away when they saw the security guards, it all fits. These are the offenders we're hunting, Ryan. This is our big breakthrough.'

'Guv, I hear you. Can we celebrate in the bar? I'm choking for a drink.'

'Sure. I'll grab a shower and see you in there.'

Fifteen minutes later, O'Neil walked into the Pier 5 bar in a tracksuit, hair still wet, skin glowing, eyes alert as she walked towards Ryan. She was smiling, but nonetheless he felt slightly nervous of her renewed sociability. He summoned a waiter and they ordered a light supper: pink grapefruit and Caesar salad for her, Jacobsen Weissbier and club sandwich for him.

As they finished eating, her mobile rang. Checking the display, she got up and left the table without telling him who it was. She was away so long, he wondered if she was ever going to return and was relieved when she reappeared and sat down, picking up her drink.

'Problem?' he asked.

'Nothing for you to worry about.'

'I thought you said no more secrets.'

'I did, didn't I?' She levelled with him. 'Hilary was contacted by the Home Office and asked to explain himself. Ford's been whingeing that I haven't fed back on progress, picked up his messages or returned his calls.'

'Like you've had the time.'

'That's what I told Hilary.' She caught Ryan's eye over the top of her glass. 'I owe you one, Ryan. Using Newman was a good call. He's our secret weapon.'

'Yeah, but for how long?'

'We're cool. The power play between MI5 and MI6 doesn't bother me. The counter-terrorism unit are understandably nervous about details of the trial getting out. I can see their point of view – none of us want terrorists loose on our streets. That was their only interest in Trevathan's murder and our investigation—'

'They seem pretty interested in where we're getting our information. What did Hilary tell Ford?'

'Not to underestimate me. He's my number one fan.' O'Neil

didn't smile. 'No names, no pack-drill – that's how we were set up and how we'll continue to operate if Hilary gets his way. Believe me, he's no pushover.'

'I like him already.'

'He's a good man. A decent man.'

Ryan could see she was on the edge of going further. When she didn't do so, he made it easy for her. 'MI5 and/or Hilary must know there's someone else on our team.'

'But not who it is. I threw Hilary a bone. He doesn't hold the monopoly on secrets. Officially, our unit consists of three. Two are sitting at this table. The other one is the inimitable Grace Ellis, retired cop and ex-colleague he knows I have a lot of time for.'

'They swallowed it?'

She waggled her right hand. 'Ford did ask Hilary to think again.'

'The grey man's not altogether stupid then.'

'Hilary can't disclose what he doesn't know.' O'Neil ran a hand through her hair and let it fall into place, a victorious expression on her face. 'There are some things I like to keep from him. I'm not talking about his son's sexual proclivities either.'

'So, no need to warn Frank?'

O'Neil shook her head. 'Newman, I'm not worried about. As he's demonstrated already, he's more than capable of watching his own back.'

'And ours.' Ryan pointed at her empty glass. 'You ready for something stronger?'

'You think I need it?'

'I think I might.' Ryan hoped she wasn't going to turn weird again. He couldn't handle that. They lapsed into silence. For the first time since he'd entered the bar, he became aware of music playing gently in the background. A P!nk track: 'Just Give Me a Reason'. O'Neil was staring at him. Maybe she was going to flip. 'Did I say something wrong?'

'You didn't *say* anything.' She hesitated. 'Ryan, you have something unrelated to the case on your mind. It's getting in the way and I don't like it.'

Was she hinting that *he* should now bring up her split from Forsythe Jnr? Ryan was confused. She'd made it clear that she didn't want to talk about being dumped on her arse. He bought himself time by attracting the attention of a passing waiter. He ordered a pint, she chose gin and tonic with ice and cucumber.

O'Neil waited until the drinks arrived before continuing. 'Well? Are you going to spit it out?'

'The beer? No, it's good.' The joke fell flat.

Ryan put his glass down on the table, not knowing where to begin. She could never have married in secret. Regulations demanded that serving officers disclose a change in circumstances, so there would have been those in the know and those in the dark. Ryan was now somewhere in between: aware of what had happened, forbidden to discuss it. He was done with her avoidance tactics and felt compelled to say something.

Shit or bust, mate . . .

'Guv, what's been said can never be unsaid. I'll take a hike if you want, but sooner or later you'll have to talk to me. Although none of it is strictly my business, I can't walk around like nothing's happened. It's unfair of you to ask me to. I don't have a problem with knowing. Clearly you do.' He never took his eyes off her. 'It's like you said – "something is getting in the way" – but not from my side. You're the one who closed the door.'

Her glare could have knocked him over.

'You want to know how I feel, is that what you're saying?'

He gave it to her straight. 'I don't want you to talk about what happened if it upsets you. I just need to understand where your head is if we're going to work together. More than that, I want the real you, not the one preoccupied with what Grace, Frank and I know about your personal life. Personally, I'd like to punch Forsythe's lights out for what he did to you. But in the long run I reckon he did you a favour: you're better off without him, Eloise.'

O'Neil held his gaze. 'It's hard for me to talk about.'

'I know. What I don't understand is what you ever saw in him. He's a sleazebag.'

O'Neil panicked. 'You've talked to him?'

'No, of course not. I didn't need to. For those who care to look, the preening arse is all over YouTube.' He held out his mobile. 'Check it out if you don't believe me.' She didn't take it. 'You know what else? Forsythe was everything I suspected he might be. It beggars belief how you could be taken in by such a nob.'

O'Neil laughed, but despite her efforts to shrug it off, she obviously wasn't anywhere close to being over it. The subject was as raw today as last Christmas Eve. He should've spotted it long before now.

'Do you still love him?'

'No!'

That was all Ryan wanted to hear.

A stab of pain pierced his chest. Finding out that she'd been jilted had affected him more than he cared to admit. State-ments as well as questions spilled out of his mouth in quick succession. He simply couldn't help himself. 'Callous bastard. Why didn't the selfish prick have the guts to tell you sooner? What was it he found so threatening – your intellect, your independence?'

'Who knows? He spars with women like me across a court-room every day. Maybe he required a more subservient female to bolster his ego and open her legs at his command.'

'He never explained why?'

'I never gave him the opportunity.'

'Did he even try?'

'Not so much as a whisper.'

'You had no inkling?'

'None . . .' O'Neil choked on her words but her eyes were dry. 'Over dinner the night before he said I was the best thing that ever happened to him. He gave me a Cartier necklace to wear on our wedding day and we toasted our life together. "Just the two of us," he said. He wanted my exclusive attention before he had to share me with friends and family. I was well and truly conned.'

'Stop, Eloise—'

'No, I want to tell you.' There was the hint of a wry smile forming. 'One lucky Oxfam shopper may be wearing a Cartier without even realizing. Stephen would be a bit cross if he knew.'

'He's a fool.'

'Makes two of us. I was heading for a car crash and didn't see it coming . . . can you imagine how that made me feel?' Her mobile rang a second time. It was an unwelcome intrusion, cutting their conversation dead, breaking the connection they were so close to making.

Ryan hated being contactable 24/7.

'It's Grace, I'd better take it.' O'Neil pressed to receive the call and listened for a full half-minute, a frown developing. 'OK . . . yes, there's a reason for that.' There was a long pause during which her eyes found his, her intense expression implying news of some sort. Not the good kind, if Ryan was reading her correctly. 'I'll explain when we return to base . . . yes, he's with me now. I'll tell him, thanks for letting me know.' A flash of temper. 'I said so, didn't I? Don't question my authority, Grace. We'll discuss it when I get there.' Another pause. Eloise climbed down. 'Yes, I will. You too.' She hung up. 'We've had contact from Spielberg.'

'Another scene?'

'I don't know. She won't talk to anyone but you.'

44

Despite a severe weather warning set to cause travel disruption, their flight left Copenhagen on schedule, touching down at Newcastle International at five minutes to two, local time. Newman was waiting in the short-stay car park, leaning against his car. He'd driven out to collect them, leaving Grace holding the fort. Concerned that she'd been working too hard, he'd begged her to ease up. She'd refused. Marriage or no marriage, there was no taming the pit bull.

Ryan promised to have a word.

'Good luck with that,' was all Newman said in reply. He seemed preoccupied.

Ryan glanced in the rear-view, catching O'Neil's eye. 'Working too hard' was a euphemism for something far more serious. They both knew what it was and had discussed it on the flight. O'Neil would deal with it during their debrief later. She expected fireworks and had voiced the unsettling notion that another DVD was about to drop in their laps.

With a feeling of foreboding, Ryan waited for the right moment to approach Grace. After her words with O'Neil on the phone the night before, the retired detective was keen to clear the air and brief them on developments, hinting that there was much to discuss. Ryan could tell she was itching to get started. He wished he felt the same but the atmosphere in the room gave him a sense of foreboding.

'Miss me?' he whispered.

Grace shot him a dirty look. 'No.'

'Not even a smidge?'

'You missed your chance, mate. I'm taken.' Grace always hid behind humour when she was mad about something. Avoiding eye contact, she glanced across the room, her focus on Newman. He'd just sat down at a computer terminal and was logging on. Notwithstanding her present tetchy mood, Ryan could tell that she was smitten, impossibly in love with the spook and upset that they had argued.

'How's it working out with Frank?'

'What's with the small talk?' Grace turned, a scowl on her face. 'If you must know, it was nice to have him to myself for a day or two. We stayed over last night and I screwed his brains out on your bed. Hope you don't mind.' The smile on her lips never made it to her eyes. 'Thought I'd better tell you before the boss asks how your laundry made it to the washer on its own.'

The comment reminded Ryan of his conversation with Caroline. When he'd called to tell her he wouldn't be able to pay her a visit, she'd volunteered to drop by with a change of clothes for him. He glanced at his watch, hoping she'd arrive before Spielberg made contact. He needed her take on the call.

Grace was daydreaming again, her focus back on Newman. Ryan envied their relationship. Solid as a rock, it had stood the test of time, despite long periods of heartbreak and separation.

'Feel free to use the bed anytime,' he said. 'How could I object? You're practically on honeymoon.'

'We'll always be on honeymoon.' She softened, her words laced with regret. 'We have years to make up for. I only wish we hadn't wasted so much time.'

'Be grateful, Grace. It might never have happened.'

'I'm still pinching myself that it has.' She flicked hard eyes towards O'Neil, who was standing on the far side of the room, engaged on the phone, uptight and on edge. Whoever she was talking to, it wasn't going well. Grace was almost tapping her foot in frustration. 'Is the boss still giving you the cold shoulder?'

'No. We're cool.'

She raised a disbelieving eyebrow. 'Chilly is how I'd describe your relationship when you left for Brighton. She's hardly said a word to me since you flew in, Newman either for that matter. Any idea what that might be about?' Grace twisted the knife. 'Anyone would think you two had something to hide. Are there any guilty secrets you're dying to share?'

'Quit fishing,' Ryan said. 'And stop talking in riddles. If you have something to say, say it. Eloise and I are good.'

'Have it your own way,' she whispered through gritted teeth. 'Well, she was fine before you two talked last night.'

'Is that right? Well, rest assured, I'm not finished with either of you yet.'

Their mumbling caused Newman to swing round and face them. 'If you guys have nothing better to do, I'm ready to talk shop.' He glanced in O'Neil's direction as she hung up the phone, a face like thunder. 'I think we should discuss Spielberg's demands before she calls again. For what it's worth, I'm against indulging her, though I'm open to arguments as always. What do you reckon, Ryan?'

'About what?' O'Neil arrived in the nick of time.

Grace's mood was belligerent, no more or less than O'Neil had told Ryan to expect on their return to the UK. Suspicious of Spielberg's request to talk exclusively to him, Grace had made a few arsey comments on the phone. From the combative expression on her face, she was ready to let fly.

Ryan waited for her to kick off.

Atypically, she held back.

There was only one certainty in play. Any action that Grace was planning would include an opinion she'd had all night to formulate. Before she had time to voice it, O'Neil took the initiative. A small team relied on cohesion. Aware that their unit was crumbling around their ears, she'd decided to lay all her cards on the table and take the heat out of the row that was brewing. The unit wasn't ready for another falling out.

'But first a confession,' she said.

'What did I tell you?' Grace barked at Newman. He showed no emotion and she turned her wrath on Ryan. 'So, Spielberg wants to talk to you. How come she knows you by name? Since when did we start sharing personal details with suspects? Since *when* did we start lying to one another?'

'That's a lot of questions,' Ryan said.

'And they require answers.'

'Which you might get if I had the faintest idea what the hell you're on about?'

'I'm not finished, Ryan. You said your device didn't record last time you spoke to Spielberg, or words to that effect. You know what? You couldn't lie straight in bed. Pressed the wrong button, my arse! I knew that was bullshit the minute it came out of your mouth. You're better than that—'

'Are you finished?' Ryan already knew the answer.

'Not even close!'

'Grace, knock it off!' Newman said. 'Let him speak.'

'No, I'm sick of the deceit. Either we're a team or we're not.'

'She has a point, Frank.' O'Neil kept her shoulders straight and took a deep breath, getting ready to come clean. 'Grace has every right to be angry. Ryan did record that conversation and the device wasn't broken. That was a lie. He was covering my back. He destroyed the recording on my instruction.'

'What?' Grace stuck her forefinger in her ear and wiggled it around. 'I must be hearing things? I could've sworn you said you'd binned vital evidence.'

'It's called loyalty,' O'Neil said.

Grace snorted. 'Are you mad?'

'I had my reasons,' O'Neil bit back. 'Ryan was flippant with Spielberg on the phone. Unprofessional. This unit will stand or fall by its reputation. I made a judgement call. The recording wasn't something we could enter in evidence, so I told him to get rid—'

'Good work, Eloise!' The pit bull was in full-on attack mode. 'That has got to be *the* worst decision you have *ever* made. As a Professional Standards veteran, you of all people should've known better. What the hell were you thinking?'

'It was my decision to make.' O'Neil was incensed, even though she knew Grace was in the right; it was not only a bad choice, it was the wrong choice. Still, she fought back, unwilling to let Grace have it all her own way. 'Grace, let me give you a piece of advice. In future, if you want to question my authority, you do it without an audience—'

'Tell it to the judge—'

'Guv?' Ryan wanted the yelling to end.

O'Neil bit his head off. 'What now?'

He opened his drawer, took out the recorder and threw it on the desk. 'I didn't "lose" the evidence. What would be the point? The Control Room was trying to trace the call. They'll have recorded it too.' He put a hand up, fending off attack. 'I was in the wrong to wind Spielberg up. I'm not proud of it. I called it how I saw it and I'll take my chances when the case goes to trial. She's not the type to respond to officialdom. I thought that a more casual attitude might keep her on the line.'

'At last,' Grace said. 'Someone with sense!'

Ryan shot her a look: *be careful.*

'Can I say something?' Newman was the only one calm enough to take the temperature down. 'Let's consider all the angles here. No trial judge will criticize Ryan's approach if he got the right result. We're dealing with a serial offender here. If Spielberg wants to speak to him – and only him – he obviously made a connection, however negative. The very fact that she's no longer willing to talk to Eloise would suggest that he touched her in some way. We should use that to our advantage, run with it and see where it takes us. Ryan has a way with women.' He looked at Grace. 'He's even talked sense into you on occasion.' Newman winked at her and then eyed the others. 'Believe me, that's not easy.'

Grace laughed and then apologized to everyone for losing her rag.

O'Neil didn't hold it against her. They'd had their say and so had Ryan. It cleared the air and her fragmented team was beginning to repair itself. Just as well. They didn't know it yet but Hilary Forsythe was due to arrive at any moment.

'This is your call,' she told Ryan. 'If you're happy with Frank's suggestion, when Spielberg makes contact, I'm out, you're in.'

'On one condition,' he said. 'If she can get here on time, I want Caroline in on this. You've seen how good she is. She'll home in on emotions we might miss.' When there were no dissenters, he consented to take the next call.

Talking to a serial killer was quite a responsibility. He hoped he could pull it off.

45

O'Neil took a deep breath as she opened the door. Hilary Forsythe stepped forward, embracing her gently, a kiss on each cheek, the usual pat on the back as he held her for a moment longer than she was comfortable with. She pulled away, trying not to show how edgy she felt around him. It was the same every time he was near, the ghost of her past weakening her resolve to move on and leave behind the part of her life he belonged to.

'How are you?' That was always his first question.

'Fine.' The lie was her stock reply. 'Is this meeting really necessary?'

'I think so. Eloise, I worry about you. Not in a professional sense – I know you can do this job standing on your head. I meant—'

'I know what you meant.' She swept a hand out. 'Please, come and meet the team.'

Like his offspring, Forsythe was tall and fit, a classy dresser with impeccable taste in clothes, a tanned complexion and flawless manners. Unlike his son, he loved her dearly and the sentiment was genuine. In spite of how he made her feel, O'Neil was fond of him too. She took his coat and led him into the lounge area that doubled as her incident room, a feeling of trepidation eating away at her gut.

*

Ryan and Grace stood up as they entered.

'Ryan, it's a pleasure to meet you.' Hilary extended a hand. The handshake was solid. 'I knew your father. He was a good man, a dedicated policeman. You look exactly like him. Am I right in thinking that your twin works for the Crown Prosecution Service these days?'

'Yes, sir.'

'It pleases me that the two of you followed his fine example. The criminal justice system needs people like you.'

Ryan felt his heart swell with pride. 'Thank you, sir.'

Forsythe took in every detail: the state-of-the-art equipment; the piles of paperwork; the murder wall with details of known victims and one female as yet unidentified.

He raised his voice. 'Mr Newman, you can come out now.'

Three pairs of eyes met across the room.

So much for keeping Newman's involvement a secret.

A bedroom door opened and Newman appeared, eyes fixed on Forsythe. The fact that he'd been rumbled didn't appear to bother him. The former judge was as well connected as he was. Anticipating that his cover might already have been blown, he'd voiced his concern when O'Neil warned the team that he was dropping by.

Forsythe invited them all to sit.

'I think it's time we set the record straight, about me, this base and, more importantly, Eloise's appointment as operational head of this unit.' He sat down too, hitching his trousers at the knee, his shoes buffed to perfection. 'I gather you've discovered facts and drawn conclusions that may have challenged her authority. Had I known of Frank's link to Grace when this unit was created, I might have covered my tracks better. I can assure you that Eloise had no knowledge of my involvement until last Saturday. I was alerted by MI5 as long ago as December 2012 that those due to stand trial in Scotland on terrorism charges – the defendants in Lord Trevathan's case – had cross-border links with Northumberland.'

'That's news to me,' Ryan said. 'Did you investigate?'

Forsythe nodded.

'With respect, sir, I was employed at Special Branch then. At no time were we made aware of such a threat.'

'No one was, though it was significant, deemed a code red by MI5. A splinter group of terrorists, highly organized, were believed to be planning a sophisticated attack on Otterburn army base. A decision was made at the highest level to keep the circle of those in the know to an absolute minimum. As it turned out, the Northumberland link did not exist. MI5 and antiterrorist officers deployed here were stood down.'

Ryan was happy with the explanation.

'The inception of this unit coincided with my retirement,' Forsythe added. 'The idea had been on the table for a while. These are difficult times. Due to governmental cuts, all forces are strapped for cash. Few of them want to get involved in protracted enquiries that swallow up ever-decreasing budgets.'

'So you reinvented the wheel?' Ryan said.

'As you say. The outcome was an elite but scaled down National Crime Unit – one with teeth. You are the select few and, because of prior involvement and local knowledge, I was the obvious choice to oversee the unit, just as Eloise was the obvious choice to manage it. You could accuse me of nepotism, and I wouldn't blame you if you did. Despite the fact that no marriage took place, she is my de facto daughter-in-law. But let me tell you this: she has the experience and intelligence to investigate these very serious matters. Her integrity is indisputable. You will find no finer officer to lead you.'

'Hear! Hear!' Grace whispered under her breath.

'No one disputes that,' Ryan said in support.

Newman agreed.

O'Neil wanted them to stop.

She didn't get her way.

'I decided not to disclose my involvement for personal reasons. I know how difficult it is for Eloise to be around me, under any circumstances. Suffice to say, I remind her of a difficult time in her life. I suspect she'd have turned down the job if she'd known.'

Eloise felt her heart break a little more. Grateful that this wonderful man hadn't mentioned his son by name, she kept her head down. This was so painful for her. Aware of that, Forsythe drew attention away from her. Sadly, her thoughts were louder than his voice. His consideration for others was what had drawn her to him from the start; she'd loved him since the moment they were introduced over dinner at his house. He was the father she'd never had . . .

The only one she wanted.

'Are we out on our ear when this case is over?' Grace was asking.

'Staffing is a matter for Eloise. The unit will continue under her command with Ryan as a permanent fixture. I will hold no more than a watching brief over it. I agreed to take it on for reasons I just outlined. Ford is merely a go-between. To quote Eloise, "He wouldn't know an investigation if he tripped over one."'

'I might have put it differently,' Grace said.

'Frank, you showed good judgement investigating the unit,' Forsythe said. 'It flagged up a weakness. Rest assured that the information you uncovered is no longer available – *to anyone*. Neither has your security been compromised. You'll have to take my word for that.' He switched focus. 'Ryan, it was no surprise that Eloise took you on. We discussed you briefly after Jack Fenwick's death. You obviously made quite an impression on her. You and Grace have my condolences. I understand you were both close to Fenwick.'

'Thank you, sir,' Ryan and Grace said in unison.

'Grace, you are a perfect choice,' Forsythe continued. 'You have a notable track-record and formidable reputation.'

'With respect, that makes me sound like a bolshie cow.'

'If the cap fits,' O'Neil said.

The others laughed.

Grace never held her tongue if she had something to say. Chief Constable or cleaner, she made no allowances. Forsythe smiled at her, the confident smile of a man with knowledge she didn't have.

'Have we met before, sir? You seem familiar.'

'Back when you were a newly promoted detective sergeant – and proud of it, as I recall – I was a solicitor with a local firm. You declined my dinner invitation.'

'Did I? Sorry . . .' She didn't have a clue. 'There were so many invitations. I rarely remember those who got away and wish I could forget some of those who didn't.'

They all burst out laughing.

'I believe you had designs elsewhere.' Forsythe tipped his head towards the spook, who was rolling his eyes at the others.

'You're a lucky man, Frank. I had no idea you would feature in Eloise's plans. Welcome. She's an exceptional judge of character.'

'I have a question,' Grace was keen to move on.

'Ask it.'

'Why risk using this apartment as a base?'

'That I can't answer.' Forsythe looked at O'Neil, inviting comment.

In turn, O'Neil looked at Grace. 'That's ironic, coming from you!'

Ryan grinned. His guv'nor was back in control. Grace was almost blushing, a first for her. Clearly, Forsythe had no idea what was going on. He knew nothing of the shadow investigation they'd run from Grace's living room after Jack went missing.

'She has previous convictions for it,' O'Neil said. That's all the explanation he was getting.

'And you haven't answered my question,' Grace said.

'There was nothing sinister in it,' O'Neil said. 'Ford left me to source accommodation. He stipulated a location with no connection to force headquarters, but in close proximity. He didn't tell me why, only that he needed the unit up and running without delay. At the time I wondered why the rush, why he was so nervous. The only case I was aware of was the one in Brighton; I knew nothing of Lord Trevathan's disappearance or the links to Ambassador Dean's murder. I assumed that both the case and the sourcing of accommodation were tests, that Ford was evaluating my performance. He'd set such a tight deadline. This place was the only real option. It was standing empty, perfectly situated, easily made secure. Simple as that.'

She paused. 'On reflection, it was a mistake on two counts: first, it couldn't be accounted for on the budget; second, given its history, I hadn't realized the negative effect working here would have on me.'

'It's easy to be wise after the event,' Forsythe defended her. 'I happen to think it's a perfect choice.'

'We can live with it, if you can,' Newman told her.

Ryan was nodding in agreement.

'I don't buy it,' Grace said. 'Forgive me for being cynical, but it's clear Ford hated you from the get-go. Why would he allow you to use your flat if he wanted to oust you?'

'He didn't ask who it belonged to. Why would he?'

'And you didn't tell him?'

'Not at the time.'

'Let me guess,' Grace said. 'Your decision has come back to bite you.'

O'Neil nodded. 'It was only ever intended as a stopgap until this investigation was resolved. I made no financial gain, but Ford got wind of it. The man's a self-serving slug. He had someone check the finance code. Let's say we had a long conversation. He didn't force me out, so I assume it's a keepy-back, a stick to beat me with in the future.'

'Leave him to me.' Forsythe was studying her closely. '*Are* you OK with it?'

'Yes, I'm fine . . . I am!' she insisted. 'I've moved on, Hilary, and so must you. I don't need babysitting, by any of you.' She looked away, unable to face his gaze or that of Ryan. Despite pushing them away, she counted herself lucky to have these two men in her life.

Ryan quickly changed the subject, deflecting attention away

from her to Forsythe. 'Why were we not told about the first two murders at the outset?'

'That was not my doing,' he said. 'I assumed that Ford would share all the information he had been provided with. In withholding it, he acted without my authority. I can assure you it won't happen again.' He glanced at his watch. It was gone five. 'I have to go. Are there any other questions or comments?'

'I'm going to need more finances,' O'Neil said.

'And you will have them.' Forsythe took in each team member in turn. 'If any of you are reconsidering your position within this unit, please speak now.'

There were no takers.

Grace and Newman were going nowhere. O'Neil stood up, began busying herself with items on her desk, an avoidance tactic she knew was unlikely to fool anyone, least of all Forsythe. She didn't want to be the one to show him out. Ryan got up, thanked Forsythe for putting the record straight and showed him to the door.

In the hallway, the two men shook hands again.

'You take good care of her.' Forsythe said it as a father would, heaping yet more responsibility on a DS already under pressure to prove his worth. Ryan gave his word.

46

Ryan closed the door, his desire to protect O'Neil stronger than ever. At least now everything was out in the open, they could all move on. Caroline's effervescent personality lifted morale the minute she stepped through the door. Bob sat down beside her in the living room, his wagging tail a physical demonstration that he was happy to be among friends and off duty. Explaining why her attendance was so important, Ryan gave her a space to work in and left her to get on with it.

O'Neil began the briefing at six o'clock sharp, keen to show leadership and not dwell on the past. 'The British Embassy in Copenhagen have supplied CCTV footage from the Friday before Ambassador Dean was murdered. Anja Pedersen's two suspicious characters are on it. She was spot on in her description, although the images aren't great. They match none we have on the database. Politikommisær Liisa Ølgaard acted quickly, questioning the security detail Pedersen claims walked off without challenging the suspects. I'm afraid she drew a blank. Unwilling to incriminate themselves, they aren't coughing.' She turned to Ryan. 'Talking of cameras, is there any update on the model Spielberg is using?'

'Not yet,' he said.

'Nothing on her accent either?' Grace volunteered without a

prompt. 'The voice-recognition bods are taking their time. It's as well we have Caroline here for when Spielberg rings.'

O'Neil glanced across the room. Caroline had her earphones in, listening to the audiotape of Ryan's last conversation with Spielberg. She was paying them no attention. 'Chase these enquiries when we're done, Grace. Frank, what about the local contact we found in Tierney's address book?'

'Graham Hunter is a businessman, or should I say was—'

'Dead?' she asked.

'As good as. He still owns a home in South Tyneside but no longer lives there, nor is he working in the field of corporate finance any longer. His employer let him go last year when he became too ill to continue – it was a generous handshake, by all accounts. Hunter and his missus won't ever have to worry about money again. Which is just as well because Mrs H has her own medical problems that made it impossible for her to care for him at home. Hunter moved into St Oswald's six months ago.'

'There's no place better,' O'Neil said.

Ryan wondered how she knew. St Oswald's was a hospice for palliative care.

Newman's voice pulled him in another direction. 'Mrs H showed me photographs. Hunter is hanging on by his fingernails.'

'I take it you checked his admission record?' The question had come from Grace.

Newman gave her a pointed look. His reluctance to dignify her question with an answer was proof in itself that Hunter wasn't their guy.

'Sussex Police are investigating the rest of Tierney's friends and associates,' O'Neil said. 'Most of his contacts are London-based or living abroad, many of them in Asia. Hunter was the exception, which raises the question: why? Is he different in some way?'

'Are you kidding?' Grace said. 'When do we northerners get a look in where high finance is concerned? We're much too busy collecting coal off the beach and wearing flat caps.' At every opportunity she was vocal on the subject of the north–south divide.

O'Neil cut her off before she could climb on her soapbox. 'Will HOLMES automatically throw out any direct hits, Grace?'

'No.' There was nothing she didn't know about the major incident computer system she'd helped set up. 'But all indexers are trained to cross-reference names as a matter of course. They'll do that at the input stage. Every person has a unique reference number in case two people have the same name. It happens more often than you might think.'

'Have there been any duplicates?'

'No merged records so far.'

'Let's move on then.' O'Neil shifted her attention. 'Ryan? You wanted to talk about victims?'

'Yes. Discounting James Fraser, the three victims whose bodies we have recovered are high-achievers: all male, influential, middle-aged. A definite cluster.' Heads were nodding. 'The missing victim from North Shields is different – and not because she's female. It's her age. She's a lot younger than the men, in Watson's opinion—'

'Ah, the Word, according to Stevie Watson. We all know what a tosser he is.' Grace hadn't forgiven Gloria's punter for knocking her to the ground and was waiting to make his life difficult. Ridiculing him verbally would do for now. In time, she'd show him up in other ways. He could count on it.

Ryan ignored the interruption. '*If she's a lot younger than the men, it stands to reason that the killers' link to her is more recent. She could be the key to unlock this investigation. For what it's worth, I think we should concentrate our efforts on her.*'

'When we have an ID, we'll do that,' O'Neil said. 'In the meantime, unless you know something I don't, may I remind you that we've not established a geographical link between any of the victims, nor have we identified a school or university as the common denominator—'

'That's precisely my point,' Ryan said. 'The fact that the victims aren't of the same age means we're not searching for a class of '88 or anything like that. Maybe these are hate crimes.'

'Go on.' O'Neil was interested.

'Tierney is in a close relationship now. Trevathan never married. We've almost certainly ruled James Fraser out, but he lived alone. He's a young trendy male. Am I making links where there are none?'

'You're a straight man making gay men look bad,' Grace said.

'That's unfair,' O'Neil said.

'I agree,' Newman said. 'You're well out of order.'

'OK. You're right . . .' Grace climbed down. 'For once.'

'Apology accepted,' Ryan said.

'I didn't . . . oh, funny guy.' Grace pulled a face. 'I'm splitting my sides here.'

'Children, can we please get on?' O'Neil said. 'Look, we're all feeling frustrated, but I need your heads up and your minds on the job. There's been enough in-fighting and time-wasting. We need to stand together now. There *will* be a link. We just need to find it. Please, one of you, give me something to go on. Ryan?'

'The fact that our male victims didn't attend the same school or university doesn't mean that they aren't connected by an experience they might have shared at separate boarding schools. Maybe an interschool sports club or study group, some other extracurricular activity—'

'Is that a euphemism for something more sinister?' Grace asked, his words having piqued her interest. 'Are you suggesting a paedophile ring?'

'I'm just putting it on the table. What does everyone else think?' He turned to face O'Neil. 'Guv, you said yourself that anywhere that houses children worries you. Let's examine that in more detail.'

'I know what I said, but if there was abuse at the boarding school where Tierney was a pupil, it's not been reported. He'd hardly go there to teach if he'd been abused—'

'Unless he's a victim turned abuser,' Grace said. 'There are plenty around. Where better to find your prey than in a job that brings you face to face with vulnerable youngsters? I'm with Ryan on this. It's worthy of further investigation. The victim-to-victimizer cycle is too big of an issue to ignore.'

'Whether or not it's proven?' Newman said.

Grace challenged him. 'What the hell does that mean?'

'I'm just making a point. That theory has been open to interpretation for years.'

'I'm not suggesting that all abused children turn into abusers, just that Tierney might have. In light of Operation Yewtree, we can't ignore it.' Grace was alluding to a Metropolitan Police initiative to investigate a string of historical sex abuse allegations against high-profile figures, many of whom had continued their activities for decades. Some offences had been reported and not properly investigated, regardless of credible complaints based on reliable evidence. Historical abuse was the hottest issue around. It had dominated headlines for months.

'I have to agree,' Ryan said.

'I do too,' O'Neil said. 'But let's debate the victim-turned-abuser issue on our own time and stick to the facts. All we currently have is confirmation that Tierney once worked at a boarding school he attended as a child. Of itself, it means nothing, but Trevathan and Dean were also schooled away from home. All three men held high-end jobs – all with connections to the capital – which may or may not have put them in touch with one another. Given that they are all now dead, and their killer is telling us they all deserved to be so, we have to be open-minded to the possibility that they were sex offenders with no form.'

'We're going round in circles,' Grace said. 'You said there were no reports of abuse at the school.'

'With respect,' Ryan corrected her, 'she actually said we can't find any. Doesn't mean there are none. Allegations of this nature might not have reached local authorities or the police. They could easily have been suppressed, or worse, destroyed to protect the school's reputation. You know as well as I do that it's happened before. If there *was* abuse and Spielberg knows about it . . .' He let the implication hang in the air for a second.

'She's on a short fuse. We all know how long justice takes in this country. Maybe she and her accomplice aren't prepared to wait that long—'

'You're suggesting she's twatting them before they ever get to court?' Grace palmed her brow. 'Great! All we need is an avenging angel who's off her trolley.'

'No,' Ryan said. 'The woman I spoke to is perfectly sane. She knows exactly what she's doing and why she's doing it.'

Newman had been quiet for ages. 'I agree with Ryan. She might not be an abuse victim herself. Perhaps she knows people who are. If she sees herself as some kind of protector, she could be doling out vigilante justice without the victims' knowledge or consent – or even with it.'

'I would too, if I could get away with it,' Grace said. 'Some of the sexual predators on the Yewtree list have the fucking OBE!' Her eyes found Newman's. 'You and I gave the best part of our lives in the service of our country taking shite like that off the street. Our names were never on any New Year's honours list. These people make me puke. I hope they rot in hell!'

Ryan cut in. 'Trevathan was the Lord President of the Court of Sessions. His birth name was Leonard Maxwell. He changed it when he was appointed to the post. I wonder if any of the other victims did the same.'

'No, I already checked,' Grace said. 'There are no aliases and no name changes.'

'What's bugging you, Ryan?' O'Neil was the one asking.

'This hypothesis works only to a point. Where does our missing female with the yellow satchel fit in?'

'You think women can't abuse?' Grace scoffed. 'Think again.'

'Of course not. Watson called her a "lass" though, didn't he? If these are historical abuse cases, our theory doesn't stack up.'

'We only have Watson's word for it,' Grace said. 'What? I'm just saying!'

Ryan grinned at O'Neil. 'My new bestie says he's a bloody good witness.'

'He's talking about Cath Masters,' O'Neil explained. 'Cheeky bugger's already tried to poach him.'

'I hope you told her "hands off",' Grace said.

'I didn't, but I'm hoping to convince him to stay.'

Grace looked at Ryan. 'I wasn't aware you knew Cath.'

'I didn't, until she interviewed Watson for us. If she's inclined to believe him, then so am I. I don't see *her* as a push-over.' He laughed. 'No pun intended.' When Grace got up and walked away with no explanation, his jaw dropped. 'What the hell did I say?'

Seconds later she re-entered from the hallway with her coat on.

O'Neil was astounded. 'Grace? Where on earth do you think you're going? We're in the middle of a briefing.'

'Nowhere. And I shouldn't have to do this to a team so experienced—'

'Do what?' Ryan asked.

'Age is relative to the person giving the description. I don't deny that the yellow satchel is significant. Of course it is. Designer kit might indicate wealth. It *might* even point to a woman of prominence or, on the other end of the spectrum, a shoplifter. It certainly doesn't mean she's young. In fact, I'll stick my neck out here and say Watson knows shit! Bear with me . . .' Slinging her shoulder bag over her head – left shoulder to right thigh – Grace laid face down on the floor. She was wearing jeans, high-heeled boots and a three-quarter-length red coat. She covered her face with her hair. Unit members had already worked out what she was doing. It was quite a demonstration. Caroline's guide dog laid down beside her, snuggled into her body and licked her face as he'd been trained to do.

Ryan and O'Neil roared with laughter.

Even Newman was amused. 'Suddenly I'm married to a thirty-year-old,' he said.

'Lucky you!' Ryan's focus was still on the floor. 'You're such a drama queen, Grace. Get up!'

O'Neil tried unsuccessfully to keep her face straight and call the team to order. She couldn't do it. Two phones rang, one after the other, ending the joviality. As Grace scrambled to her feet to answer the landline, O'Neil went for her pocket, her smile melting away as she checked the display. She held the device out to Ryan. 'Operation Shadow,' she said. And then for Caroline's benefit. 'That's the code for Spielberg I gave to Control.'

Ryan pressed to answer. He was all ears.

47

The senior controller came on the line. It threw Ryan off balance to the point that he didn't catch the first sentence. '. . . a priority greater than the call you were expecting,' he explained. 'He ordered me to abandon the call and put him through immediately.'

'Rewind, Stan. Who did?'

'Ford. He came through on the priority line. Our mapping technology doesn't extend beyond the force area, so I couldn't instantly verify his ID. I had to call the number we have for the Home Office and be put through. He's legit and wouldn't take no for an answer. When I argued, he threatened me with blue forms.'

Ryan raised his eyes to the ceiling. 'Blue forms' was a term used for disciplinary action within the force. 'He conned you, mate. He hasn't got the balls, never mind the authority, with or without an SW1 address.'

All heads turned in Ryan's direction, including Grace's. She could see something was going down and couldn't wait to get off the phone and find out what it was. O'Neil was already second-guessing that Ford had something to do with it.

Seeing her interest, Ryan muted the mobile and filled her in.

'Put the phone on speaker.' She waited for him to do so and

then spoke. 'This is O'Neil. Are you out of your mind? Explain yourself.'

'I had a call to make, ma'am. With respect, my job was on the line, not yours. "A matter of life and death" – those were Ford's exact words.'

'Is our caller holding?'

'No, when I asked her to wait, she rang off.'

'Damn it, Stan!' O'Neil locked eyes with Ryan, worried that Spielberg might have been frightened off – for good. 'Could you not have diverted her to another line?'

'The trace was set up on your phone, guv.'

'Then why the hell didn't you put Ford through on the other phone?'

'I tried, it's engaged.'

O'Neil's attention shot across the room. Grace was just hanging up. O'Neil swore under her breath and counted to ten. Stan was still trying to justify his actions . . .

'I was about to try Ryan's mobile. That's when I lost your caller. The delay must've spooked her.'

'OK . . . put Ford through . . . on the *landline*. DS Ryan will take over. We're just going to have to hope she rings back.'

'I'm sorry, ma'am. I did try.'

The line clicked.

'Finally!' Ford said. 'Have you seen the news, Superintendent? The shit has well and truly hit the fan.'

'It has now.' Ryan was livid.

'Where's O'Neil?' Ford barked.

O'Neil was shaking her head. She didn't want to speak to him under any circumstances. The moron had probably thwarted the most important call of the case to date. The success of enquiries hinged on establishing connections with key witnesses and prime suspects. He'd blown their best chance.

Ryan lied: 'My guv'nor is incommunicado at present.'

'Where is she?'

'I'm not at liberty to say.'

'Switch on your TV then.'

Ryan did as he was asked. The BBC newscaster Huw Edwards appeared on screen, a breaking news story: 'It would appear that Ambassador Dean's murder in Copenhagen is linked to three in England and one in Scotland. This disturbing and highly confidential information we believe was leaked by someone operating within the British Embassy in Denmark . . .'

'And we all know who it was, don't we?' Grace said.

Ryan held a finger to his lips.

Too late.

Ford had overheard. 'I thought you said O'Neil wasn't there—'

'That was Grace Ellis. Don't pretend you don't know who she is, because I know for a fact you do.'

Ford hesitated for a split second.

O'Neil seemed torn between snatching the phone up and giving the jobsworth what he deserved and allowing Ryan to handle the grey man without her assistance.

'We know who'll be responsible for the breach,' Ryan said. 'It'll be one of two security guards—'

'Yes,' Ford interrupted. 'Ølgaard told me. They're being spoken to. That means sacked, in case you're in any doubt. The fact that they failed us is inconsequential. There's a media frenzy going on and you need to stamp on it or, believe me, heads will roll here too.'

'Maybe if you'd been upfront with us from the outset we wouldn't be in this mess. If anyone is joining the dole queue, it won't be one of us. I've pulled some strokes in my time, but you, Mr Ford, have taken it to another level. The lack of communication from your lot in London is staggering. You've demonstrated nothing but incompetence. You're worried about the press? You should be more concerned with saving your own neck.'

'Of course I'm worried about the press!' Ford barked. 'And so should you be. Very soon the British tabloids will be all over this, interviewing anyone they can lay their hands on. You'd better make sure they don't—'

'Can I stop you there? The press isn't a priority. I'm chasing a very dangerous individual while you're standing idle with your thumb up your arse. Deal with them yourself. Overriding that call wasn't only bad judgement, it may very well have cost lives.'

'I'm not pandering to the whim of a serial killer—'

'And you're happy with that decision, are you? We're wise to you, *Mister* Ford. We know you'd happily shaft us in order to step onto the next rung of the ladder. Well, it's not happening. And I'll tell you why, shall I? All calls into the Control Room are recorded for action and/or further investigation. When my guv'nor gets her hands on a copy of the incident log, it's you who'll be heading for the door.'

'You can't talk to me like that. I'll have your warrant card!'

'Have a nice day, sir.' Ryan cut the call, eyes on his boss. 'Can you believe that moron?'

O'Neil dropped her head in her hands.

48

Three days had passed without a peep out of her. Ryan checked the time on the menu bar of his computer screen: 8:05 p.m., Friday, 20 December – day eleven of the enquiry for them, the last working day of the year for many. In less than an hour's time, they would have yet another briefing. He eyed O'Neil across his desk. She had the phone wedged in the crook of her neck and was scribbling furiously on a notepad, trying her best to remain positive, deflecting press enquiries and Ford's continued interference. She'd told Forsythe that if he didn't get him off her back, she was out. Ryan knew she didn't mean it. All the same, it was painful to listen to.

An email pinged into his inbox, forwarded from Technical Support in-house. It had originated at Ne46 Technology, a third-party analysis firm with premises in the Tyne Valley, a company specializing in video production technologies and sector trends, historical and contemporary.

Nice to see that someone was still working.

Ryan's mood plummeted as he read the opening line of the document:

It is not possible to establish the brand of camera used
from the sample DVD beyond stating that, whilst it is not
the most up-to-date, the videos received were definitely

shot on an HDCAM recorder capable of digital
cinematography. This is available to both keen amateurs
and seasoned professionals.

Beyond that, the written report stated the obvious: the camera
was handheld, an aesthetic choice; a technique often chosen by
film-makers for time-saving purposes, the device being
quicker to set up. The writer pointed out an alternative scenario, that it was a method used by some cinematographers to
add realism. Well, it had certainly done that, Ryan thought as
he continued reading, becoming more and more impressed
with the content the further down the page he got.

'This is fascinating,' he said.

Grace looked up. 'What is?'

He read out the parts of significance. 'If we ever find Spielberg, I'll let you know how accurate it is. How are you faring
with Tierney's boarding school?'

'You want the truth?' She downed tools, picking up a mug of
cold coffee. 'I'm getting ready to shoot myself.'

'The school is refusing to cooperate?'

'On the contrary, the headmaster handed over everything.
But we've not found a single shred of evidence pointing to
abuse, despite extensive and wide-ranging interviews with current and ex-teachers. Ditto pupils. Local officers found nothing
on Tierney – not a whisper of anything untoward – and there
are no links to either Dean or Trevathan. No one involved with
that boarding school, either when Tierney taught or was a pupil
there, has a bad word to say about it or him. It was a happy
school. By all accounts, it still is. I just got off the phone with

an ex-detective superintendent from West Yorkshire. He speaks so highly of it, I'm inclined to believe we have it wrong.'

'That doesn't fill me with pride,' Ryan said. 'Given that the abuse angle was largely my idea.'

'Largely?' Grace peered at him over the top of her specs, flicking her eyes in the direction of Newman. 'Even *he* looks glum. That doesn't happen often. See what you've done. I reckon it's time to dump this line of enquiry and move on.'

'Yes!' O'Neil punched the air, her outburst taking them by surprise. She put down the phone. 'Guys, we have a major break-through. A yellow satchel has been found at the Tide Wrack, exactly as Watson described it, even down to the bloody make. Sorry, Grace, whatever you might think of him personally, he nailed this for us.'

'Is the Tide Wrack a boozer?' Newman asked.

'No,' Grace said. 'It's the point on the shore at Whitley Bay where only the highest tides reach, where all the loose material is washed up: dead fish, sea creatures, driftwood, items lost at sea. Ecologically, it's an important source of food for migrating birds and other species.'

'Hold the science lesson,' O'Neil said. 'If the victim is the owner of that bag, we have ID: Laura Stone – an award-winning TV documentary maker.'

Ryan's reaction was instantaneous. *Did Laura know Spielberg?*

O'Neil was still talking. 'Laura is another high-flier, a recognizable figure in her field of expertise, a budding Lucy Walker, if you will.'

A deep furrow appeared on Grace's forehead. 'Who's she when she's at home?'

'She directed *Waste Land*,' Ryan said. 'You know the one. About the garbage pickers in Rio.'

'Bet it was rubbish,' Grace said, making him laugh.

O'Neil was too stoked to join in with the hilarity and keen to give them more. 'Laura was nominated for the British Academy Television Award for Best Single Documentary in 2012. I'm making enquiries regarding content. In the meantime, our priority is finding her body. Tidal experts are calculating where she might be, assuming she's also in the sea. Underwater search teams will take their lead from them.'

'Is she local?' Ryan asked.

'She was. Her parents now live in the Ardèche, which might explain why she's not been reported missing. When her body is found – *if* it's found – French police will deal on our behalf. That's one less problem for us to worry about.' O'Neil paused. 'Save the black looks, Ryan. I know it's not ideal but we have no choice. We're spread too thinly as it is.'

'It's not that,' he said.

'What then?'

'I was wondering if Laura knew Spielberg, or if Spielberg had a hand in the making of that documentary?' Four pairs of eyes met across the room. 'Worth checking out?'

'Absolutely.' Newman turned to face O'Neil. 'You said Laura was a nominee. Did she win?'

'You're thinking bad loser?' Ryan said.

'Just a thought.' Newman pressed O'Neil. 'Did she win?'

'No, and I'll bear that theory in mind. Laura was up against the big guns. A BBC Panorama documentary took the award: Terry Pratchett, *Choosing To Die*.'

'I listened to that,' Caroline said. 'It was sensitively done.'

'Yeah well, Dignitas or no Dignitas, I don't fancy ending my days on a Swiss Industrial Estate with people I've never met before,' Grace said. 'When I've had enough, I want to die at home drinking gin and smoking Gauloises. You listening, Frank? I'm relying on you to make that happen.'

'Done,' Newman said.

Ryan wasn't interested in their opinions on assisted dying. His mind was buzzing. 'How old was Laura?'

O'Neil said: 'Thirty-two.'

'Then you have my apologies for the drama class,' Grace said. 'I still think Watson is a dickhead. I take it Laura now has priority status?'

O'Neil was nodding. 'If any of you have outstanding actions that relate directly or indirectly to the abuse angle and Tierney's school – unless there's some other link in addition – put them in for referral. Grace, filter that down to incident rooms so they're not wasting their time. Not only does Laura Stone stand out from other victims in terms of gender and age, she has links with film-making. From day one, we've had reason to believe that our killer does too. That means an entirely new direction, starting now.' There were no arguments.

49

O'Neil put her phone on the dash as the countryside flashed by. They were travelling so fast it was merely a smudge of green on either side of their vehicle. 'I thought you'd like to know that you are no longer answerable, in any way, shape or form, to the grey man,' she said, a glint of mischief in her eye. 'The term Hilary used was "surplus to requirements".'

'Because he got in the way of us talking to our suspect?'

'That didn't help his case. Forsythe knew he was making life difficult for us and had a quiet word with Newman. I gather emails were intercepted. In Ford's opinion, we are a couple of mug punters unfit for our current posts. He was currying favour with other junior ministers to back his point of view and have us removed from the unit with immediate effect. It backfired.'

'That is good news.'

She glanced sideways. 'I want to thank you, Ryan. Frank is as good as you said he was. I don't know how long he intends making himself available to us, but he's an asset I'd hate to lose. Grace too, even though her methods are somewhat unconventional.' The grin slid off her face. 'When Ford realizes he's out, he'll make a song and dance of it. He's not a happy man.'

'If he was caught red-handed, he has no grounds for complaint.'

'That won't stop him. But with Hilary out in the open, there's no need for a middleman. Still, watch your back.'

At 14.32, the satnav indicated that they should leave the main road. Following instructions, Ryan brought the vehicle to a halt three miles further on. He got out of the car, happy to stretch his legs, smiling at O'Neil across the roof of their vehicle as she climbed out too. Her focus was the 'home' of the person they had come to see, a seventy-foot narrowboat moored close to Shifford Lock on the River Thames in Oxfordshire – a quintessentially English sight if ever they had seen one.

'What I wouldn't give for life in the slow lane,' she said.

'Nah . . . you'd be bored in no time.'

'I'd cope . . . it's a beautiful spot.'

'Yeah. I've passed by this way before.' He thumbed in a northwesterly direction. 'Fifteen miles that way.'

'Careful, Ryan – that statement links you to a crime scene in Scotland *and* one here.'

'I was hoping you wouldn't notice.' Ryan walked round the car to join her. Balling his hands into fists, he turned them over and held them out ready to be cuffed. 'Guilty, ma'am.'

'Don't tempt me. An arrest would make me look good. I could do with some positive strokes. It feels like forever since any came my way. We only just got started and already I need time off.' She scanned the river. 'This place would fit the bill.'

'There's a lovely village not far away: Bourton-on-the-Water. It was the name that attracted me. If we have time—'

'We don't,' she said.

'You're no fun.' Ryan pressed his key fob, locking the doors.

It was misty and even colder on the Thames Path than it had been in King's Garden, Copenhagen, a climate that penetrated your clothing and pierced your bones. This time he'd come dressed for it: thick socks; sturdy shoes; a Shetland sweater he'd picked up in Lerwick last time he was there, an overcoat for added warmth.

The vessel in the water was painted British racing green, edged in gold. It floated in perfect harmony with its surroundings, smoke drifting from a stainless steel chimney above the cabin roof. On board, evergreen plants adorned the forward deck. Next to them, two sit-up-and-beg bicycles with worn leather seats leaned against the cabin, shopping baskets front and rear, the only way to transport provisions from the nearest town without a vehicle. There were no cars parked close to the riverside. Londoner, Ryan assumed.

Stood to reason . . .

Pointless having a car in the capital.

His eyes drifted over the craft. They came to rest on bold script across the aft where a professional signwriter had picked out the name LAURE in engravers' typeface. The French spelling of Laura – like Captain Berthaud, the main character of the TV series *Spiral* – hit him like a brick. It made him wonder if the producer who owned the vessel had a penchant for a documentary maker of the same name and/or crime – not necessarily fiction.

He looked at O'Neil.

'I noticed,' she whispered. 'Let's get in there.'

An attractive woman appeared on the stern deck through a wooden door, a concerned expression on her face. This was, without doubt, Gemma Clark, Laura Stone's producer. Having googled her before he left, Ryan confirmed her identification to O'Neil with a nod.

Clark beckoned them aboard.

Stepping onto the navigation deck, Ryan extended a hand to O'Neil. She ignored it, boarding without his help, disappearing with their host down steep steps into her living quarters. Ducking his head, Ryan followed them into what was essentially a contemporary studio, more generous than he expected, equipped with every modern convenience to facilitate comfortable living.

Clark turned to face them.

Ryan's wish to hear her voice outweighed the pull of the vessel's stunning interior, but he was unable to engage with her because O'Neil had already begun the introductions.

'I'm Detective Superintendent Eloise O'Neil, Northumbria Police,' she said. 'This is Detective Sergeant Matthew Ryan. I understand that you and Laura Stone were very close.'

Clark nodded.

Ryan wondered how close.

The producer had already been informed that personal items belonging to Laura had been found – her bag and ID – and yet she seemed unmoved by the gravity of the situation, not a flicker of upset now or in the recent past. He found that odd. Unsettling.

Clark swept a hand out, offering the detectives a seat. And still she hadn't spoken. O'Neil sat down, Ryan likewise, eyes fixed on their host. She was slight in build, around five eight, soft-featured – pretty rather than attractive. Made up, she'd be stunning.

Film-star looks?

Ryan shook himself. He wasn't thinking straight. They now knew that Mrs Forbes had been describing the MI5 agent who'd collected the briefcase. He had to draw a line under that and concentrate on the evidence from the one and only eye-witness currently in the pot, Anja Pedersen. Responding to Ryan's stare, Clark turned away, put the kettle on the stove and then swung round to face them, resting against the counter while she waited for it to boil.

'Sorry, you must think me very rude,' she said. 'Would you like tea or something stronger? You've had a long drive.'

Her accent was Irish.

What the fuck?

Lines were blurring again.

Ryan fought to separate them.

'Was she Irish?' was a question he'd asked Mrs Forbes. He'd got a negative response but was now beginning to question Newman's source. Could the couple who took the briefcase be their suspects after all? MI5 had lied to them before, if not directly, then by keeping them in the dark.

Images of hot women and skinny men scrolled through Ryan's head, along with Yorkshire and Irish accents, causing him to doubt himself. Complex enquiries made you question everything. For all he knew, Clark could be a failed actress turned producer – skilled in the art of subterfuge – able to pull off any number of personas and dialects without difficulty. Alarm bells were ringing loudly. She didn't sound like Spiel-berg. He was taking no chances. She sure as hell possessed some of her attributes.

With that disturbing idea running through his head, he was uneasy sitting with his back to the door. He'd been trained never to allow that to happen. In the confines of the narrow cabin, there was little alternative. The door behind O'Neil was as much of a threat. Ryan felt his heartbeat quicken, senses on alert, survival techniques forming in his mind. It paid to be ready should things kick off. Heavy clothes and the heat from the wood-burning stove weren't the only things making him sweat. A creak on deck was like a stab between the shoulder blades.

They had company.

O'Neil didn't react. Either she hadn't heard the noise or she was hiding the fact that she had. Ryan hadn't seen the need to be tooled up. Now he wasn't so sure. Their secure mobile firearms box was in the car, yards away, bolted to the chassis. A lot of good it would do them there.

As Clark moved towards the whistling kettle, he got there first. 'Let me do that for you.' Allowing her near boiling water was not going to happen. Now on his feet, he'd taken charge of the situation, regained the upper hand. 'Superintendent O'Neil would like to ask you some questions. We don't wish to spoil your evening or take up too much of your time.'

Clark held his gaze, her face flushed from standing so close to the stove.

Or was it something else?

Another creak on deck.

This time O'Neil heard it.

'Is there someone else on board?' she asked.

'I have a friend staying over.' The producer sounded genuine. 'I thought you'd like some space. I didn't think you'd want an audience while you were asking your questions.'

'Ryan, will you ask the lady or gentleman to join us while I make tea? Ms Clark, would you like to sit down?'

Satisfied that O'Neil had the measure of their host, Ryan

mounted the stairs, lifting a heavy-duty torch from the deck as he exited the hatch should he need a weapon with which to beat off an attacker. The smell of cannabis was strong. A man around thirty years of age was sitting quietly on a basket chair, wrapped up against the cold, feet resting on an upturned box. He was scanning the horizon.

He looked innocent enough.

Ryan took no chances.

'Sir, I'm Detective Sergeant Ryan, Northumbria Police.' Surreptitiously, he put the torch down. 'Could you come inside please?'

The man stood up, scooping a bag of weed and a wrap of loose tobacco from the table beside his chair. Arrogantly, he tore off the roach end, flicking the live bit into the water. Satisfied that the rest was out, he slipped what remained of the flattened cigarette into his pocket, seemingly unconcerned that he was in possession of illegal drugs or that Ryan was a copper.

'Before you start, it's medicinal.' He offered no further explanation.

'You want to give it up,' Ryan said. 'It's doing you no good.'

The man's eyes were vacant. He made no comment as he pushed past, descending the steps as he'd been asked to. He took off his coat and scarf as he entered the warm cabin below, revealing the leanest frame Ryan had ever seen on a living man. Clark waited until they were all seated before taking care of the introductions.

'This is Mo Mitchell.' She smiled at her guest. 'He knows about Laura's disappearance.'

'We're very concerned for her safety,' O'Neil said.

'So I understand,' Mitchell said.

Ryan was studying him closely. He was around five ten, gaunt, much like the bloke their Danish witness had described. Ryan was trying not to get too excited. It was important not to jump to conclusions this early in proceedings. Still . . . his eyes were drawn to tobacco-stained fingers.

A heavy smoker, Pedersen had said.

'We're interested in Laura Stone's documentary.' Ryan was facing Clark now. 'We understand that it was extremely successful and shortlisted for a prestigious award. It would help us if we had some idea of content.'

'You could have called. I'd have saved you a long journey.'

'It's no bother,' Ryan said. 'We wanted to meet you in person.'

Clark put down her cup, a flash of irritation. 'It was an amazing biopic, albeit ill-timed.'

'Ill-timed?' O'Neil asked. 'In what way?'

'She was up against a film exploring the right to die, Superintendent. Laura's film was about the right not to live. Put in context, the two are very different—'

O'Neil narrowed her eyes. 'The right not to live?'

'On her travels, Laura struck up a relationship with a woman with a progressive and life-limiting genetic disease knowingly passed on by her mother. Rebecca Swift, was her name. Rebecca has strong views . . . no, that's an understatement, she felt fervently that it was selfish of parents to put their own desire to bear children above the fact that such offspring would be born with a death sentence hanging over their heads. She was an amazing subject. It was a great documentary, controversial in the way they have to be to get shortlisted.'

'Our BBC contact told us the film was viewed the world over.'

'To critical acclaim,' Clark said. 'The reviews were astonishing. Any other year, Laura would've won the accolade hands down.'

'Is she dead?' The question was blunt, but not unexpected. It had come from Mitchell. 'We're not children.'

'We don't know is the honest answer,' Ryan said.

'But you suspect it?'

'Let's not jump the gun, eh?' Ryan was keen to keep them talking. 'We have many lines of enquiry. For starters, we'd like the names of everyone who took part in the making of that film, from the chief exec right down to the tea lady.'

'There weren't that many,' Clark said.

'Then it shouldn't take long.'

'Apart from Rebecca, three other sufferers took part – Josephine Nichol, Sandie Knox, Martin Schofield – each one fascinating in their own right.'

'Is Sandie male or female?' Ryan asked.

'Female. And, if you are looking for suspects, you can strike her off your list. She's since passed away. I have contact details for Jo, Martin and Rebecca on my laptop if you'd like me to print them off.'

'That would be helpful,' O'Neil said. 'What about crew?'

'I was the exec producer,' Clark said. 'The producer was a very dear friend, Art Malik. Not the actor, just named after him. A guy called Tony Gillespie produced the music—'

'Who took care of cinematography?' Ryan couldn't help himself.

'Dan Spencer. We call him Frank, after the BBC sitcom character.' Clark grinned. 'People usually laugh at that one.'

'Do they?' O'Neil wasn't in a laughing mood. 'Anyone else?'

'Adam Jang edited for us.'

'Chinese descent?'

'African.'

'Black?' Ryan put up a hand in apology. 'It matters in this instance.'

'Yes, black.'

Mitchell's eyelids were heavy. He was almost gone.

Ryan invited Clark to carry on. 'Mo was our sound mixer and we had a sound recordist – Monty. Sorry, I mean Sophia Montgomery.'

'Is that a complete list?'

'Apart from our in-house technical production team.' Clark reached for her laptop. Accessing a file with the full list of cast and crew, she tapped the keyboard and a small printer began spewing out the document. She handed it to Ryan. 'I hope you find Laura.' It was the first show of concern from her.

Mitchell's eyes were shut. Apparently a man less troubled and lacking a guilty conscience.

Ignoring him, Ryan scanned the page. The listed technical production personnel added four names to those Clark had already given. He looked up. 'Your in-house team—'

'What about them?'

'They're all male?'

Clark grimaced. 'I work in television, DS Ryan. You will find a disproportionate number of white males across the board. Women are still struggling for equality in my profession. Diversity and cultural identity are aims and objectives yet to be realized. It's no different from the legal profession, publishing or politics. I'm sure the same could be said in your own organization. I take it you're after a female?'

'With a distinctive voice.'

'Irish?'

Good question. 'Accents can be changed.'

'Well, there's another one off your list. You can rule out Monty. She doesn't talk.'

'What do you mean, she doesn't talk?'

'She's mute.'

'From birth?' O'Neil enquired.

Ryan could tell his guv'nor didn't like what she was asking, let alone what they were both thinking.

Clark seemed to have drifted away.

O'Neil was forced to give her a verbal nudge. 'Ms Clark? Sophia Montgomery . . . has she been mute since birth?'

'Since she was a kid, I think.' She almost shrugged. 'I don't really know. She's freelance. We come across each other from time to time. Not that often. Mo recommended her when we were putting the documentary team together. To be honest, I never thought to ask. I'm not one to pry. You'll have to ask her yourself. I was under the impression that it was caused by some traumatic event in her past—'

'It was.' Mitchell had woken up. 'She lost her mother at a young age – eleven or twelve, I think, maybe earlier. The trauma triggered her condition. She doesn't talk about it. No pun intended.'

'You know her well?' Ryan asked.

'As well as anyone, I suppose. She's an amazing talent. A great colleague, an award winner in her own right.' He leaned forward, propping his head up with his right hand, elbow on his knee. 'I'm sorry, it's been a long day. I can hardly keep my eyes open.'

Ryan ignored the sob story. 'Did she get along with Laura?'

'We all get on,' Clark said. 'You have to in our profession, otherwise the magic doesn't work. You're not seriously suggesting that she might be responsible?'

Ryan sidestepped the question. 'And you two . . . you seem very close.'

Maybe too close . . .

Formidable woman . . .

Skinny guy living in her shadow.

Clark's hackles were up and it showed. 'You came here to get information, which I have supplied. I didn't have to talk to you and neither did he but, given your curiosity, Mo is my best friend. We're spending Christmas together, not that it's any business of yours.'

'You've worked together often?'

'Hundreds of times. Why do you ask?'

'No reason.'

'I think we'll leave it there.' O'Neil stood up. 'Thanks for your time.'

Following her lead, Ryan got up too. This pair worried him and not only because they bore a marked likeness to the couple seen outside the British Embassy in Copenhagen.

He must talk to Pedersen.

Ending the exchange, leaving Clark and Mitchell wrong-footed was a shrewd move. At the very least, they required further investigation. Receiving O'Neil's nod to move off, Ryan pulled his mobile from his pocket as he followed her to the car. He was busting to get started.

50

When Grace came on the line, Ryan asked her to put on her Gold Command hat and delegate. 'The guv'nor wants round-the-clock surveillance on the houseboat, starting now, including covert images if the observation team can get them.' He explained the reasoning behind his request. 'Clark had company, a man called Mitchell. There are enough similarities between the two of them and the description given by Pedersen to make us nervous: IC1 male, IC1 female. Height and build is accurate. They're close too. Friends, allegedly. All circumstantial, of course, but the best fit so far.'

'Sounds promising.'

'It's more than that. The guv'nor thinks so too. If they move from that narrowboat, put a tail on them. We can't afford to lose them.' He rattled off the names of everyone Clark had given him. 'Pass the information out to satellite rooms. Eloise wants everyone traced and interviewed. Today, Grace. Make sure they understand the urgency. We want personal descriptive forms on everyone by morning. If you have to drag these people out of their beds in order to get them, do it. To interview everyone properly and verify stories could take weeks. This way we can probably eliminate many of them on sight. You'll be dealing with the Met in most cases. The film industry is London-centric. Its workforce won't stray much further than the commuter belt. Tap your contacts at Broadcasting House. They should be able to supply images of any crew who've worked for them in recent years, freelancers included. They're security conscious. No one gets in without a pass.'

'You can say that again. Easier to access the Bank of England vault than get in there.'

'We can probably rule out Malik as a suspect straight away,' Ryan said. 'He's Pakistani. Adam Jang too – he's black. Oh, and Sophia Montgomery is mute.'

'How convenient—'

'We've already been there, Grace.'

'And we'll return to it,' she said.

'Of course. Make it clear to the Met that they still need to interview everyone, regardless of colour or disability for what they know about Laura. We want to know who saw her last and in what capacity.'

'Tell the boss I'm on it.'

'I heard that,' O'Neil said.

Grace dropped her voice. 'She has ears like Dumbo.'

'I heard that too,' she said.

Ryan stifled a grin as O'Neil pulled her ears away from her head, making him laugh. He pressed a button on the phone. 'Careful what you say from now on, Dumbo is now on speaker.'

Grace chuckled. 'Thanks for the tip-off.'

Even though he couldn't see her, Ryan could tell that she was grinning, already on the starting blocks for the next leg of the enquiry. He could hear keys tapping at the other end. She was a multi-tasker in the true sense of the word. It came as no surprise that retirement hadn't fired her jets. Grateful for the opportunity O'Neil had offered her, she'd slipped seamlessly into her former role as a murder detective. Ryan had no doubt that she was cross-checking the HOLMES database to see if it contained any of the names he'd given her.

Second nature.

'I have one pair of hands,' she said. 'Two, if you count Frank. Eloise, what's the order of play for me?'

'I want a copy of the documentary broadcast or digital link to it as soon as you can get hold of it. It's not on the iPlayer, I already checked. I also want a TIE action on Clark and Mitchell and an address for Rebecca Swift. I'll tackle her myself. She was the focus of the documentary. That would suggest she was probably the closest to Laura. I want to know as much about her disease as she does by morning and confirmation of when and how Sandie Knox died. A death certificate would be perfect.'

'You really think Clark is a candidate for Spielberg?'

'We'll know soon enough,' Ryan said. 'If she is our target, she'll either attempt a run for it or sit tight and hope to ride out the storm.'

'You don't like her.' It was a statement, not a question.

'She's shifty.'

'Are you two heading home for Christmas?'

Ryan checked in with O'Neil for confirmation.

She shook her head. 'I want to see the whites of Monty's eyes. Put her down to me too, Grace. I have an address. I'll stick Ryan on the train.'

'No chance!' he said. 'I'm stopping.'

'I don't need a minder.'

'Never said you did.'

O'Neil let it go.

*

Sophia Montgomery's home was north of the capital, close to the M1 corridor, a two-hour commute to the City of London. It took Ryan and O'Neil twice as long as it should have to reach the outskirts of Bletchley where she lived, partly due to rush hour traffic, the annual migration of people wanting to get home for the holidays, but mostly because the weather was doing its best to curtail their journey. Severe storms had disrupted the rail network, taking down trees, causing minor structural damage. Huge floods had knocked out the power to thousands of homes causing chaos for the emergency services.

'Pull over,' O'Neil said suddenly.

'Guv? We're not there yet.'

'This'll do.' She was pointing to a pub off the main road, not the most salubrious Ryan had ever seen. He didn't argue, just turned into the busy car park and coasted to a stop. The navigation system showed the road they had left as the A421, a few miles short of their mark. The pub reminded Ryan of one in Gateshead, a bit rough and ready, not the type of establishment he expected to see around here. O'Neil must be desperate.

'In need of a comfort break?' He thumbed out the rain-lashed window and pulled a face. 'Don't think you'll find one in there somehow.'

'I need a pee, a drink and a moment to think through how I'm going to approach a woman who allegedly can't speak.' She opened the door, soaking herself instantly. 'C'mon, shift yourself.' Pulling her coat over her head, she ran towards the pub's entrance.

The bar was noisy, heaving with people in party mood and other weary travellers sheltering from the horizontal rain. Leaving Ryan to buy the drinks, O'Neil sloped off in the direction of the ladies' room. By the time he'd paid, she'd taken a seat near the door, away from the crowded bar and other customers. She wanted a lot of things. Company wasn't one of them.

He joined her, a glass in each hand. 'If you were hoping for a decent gin, you'll be sadly disappointed.'

'What is it?' She sniffed the clear liquid.

'Gordon's,' he said.

'Classy.'

'Show some gratitude. It's the only type they stock. After our long drive, I was hoping you'd take the wheel and swap it for my Coke.' She didn't bite. 'Fair enough. How is the ankle holding up?'

'A bit stiff on occasions – worse when I don't move it.'

'Well, now you have, are you going to tell me what's bothering you?'

'It's nothing!' She sipped her gin, screwed up her face. 'This is horrible.'

'Didn't sound like nothing in the car.'

'It's everything. The time of year . . . the fact that I've been cross-examined by my team . . . you and me. But mostly what's bugging me is this bloody enquiry. I'm beginning to wish we were investigating terrorism after all. This case is about a voice, Ryan. A fucking voice, and it's getting to me.'

'Can you be more specific?' He laughed.

O'Neil's face was blank. 'I'm sorry. I'm a bit nervous of approaching Sophia Montgomery. She's probably every bit as lovely as Mitchell said she was, but when Clark said she was mute, something exploded in my head. I couldn't shake the idea that if you never spoke – except on a DVD – you'd never get caught. There would be no voice comparison, *nothing* to implicate you—'

'Sounds logical.'

'Yeah, but now I'm wondering if I jumped too quickly.' O'Neil pulled so hard on her drink only ice cubes were left in the tumbler. 'Look, I can handle this on my own. You should go home and spend the holidays with Caroline. You've been amazing, all of you. You've worked round the clock on this case and I'm truly grateful.'

'It's what we get paid for.'

Eloise was pushing him away. Ryan hated the idea that, for her, Christmas had been marred by an unfortunate past. A loss, any loss, at this time of year would bring sadness rather than joy. From now on, while everyone around her was celebrating, O'Neil would probably be contemplating how different life could have been, had she chosen the right partner rather than the wrong one.

'What's really eating you?' Ryan said.

'I'm worried that my copper's instinct may be wrong on this occasion.'

'In what respect?'

O'Neil didn't answer.

'C'mon, there must be a reason. You're not usually this—'

'This what?' It was almost a snarl.

'I was going to say in two minds, ambivalent, indecisive. Feel free to pick your own adjective—'

She bristled. 'So now I'm unsure of myself as well as unfit to lead?'

'I never said that—'

'It's what you meant.' She met his gaze defiantly.

'Is it personal? If not, talk to me. Eloise, I'm not a fucking mind reader.'

O'Neil stared at him for a second, in two minds. 'My god-daughter has selective mutism. Taken out of context, the word "selective" is misleading. The condition is often seen as a choice. Please believe me when I tell you that it's not. The girl I'm talking about was perfectly fine at home until she started school. The minute she walked into a classroom, bang! She closed down, became anxious. It got worse. Now she's the same in a shop or in any other social situation. She knows how to talk but blocks communication because it's simply too stressful.'

'That must be very difficult for her family.'

'They're tearing their hair out.'

'Not easy for you either.'

'No. I've witnessed her go from a happy, smiley kid to an isolated teenager in a world of silence. She has no job, no relationships and no prospect of any. Kids like that are not shy any more than their mutism is deliberate.' O'Neil was on edge, trying her best to give the opposite impression. 'It's an anxiety disorder like no other. I'd hate to add to it if Montgomery turns out to be a sufferer. I should talk to some of her colleagues before I go piling in upsetting her.'

'It would be a missed opportunity not to see her when we're this close.'

'Would you mind if I sleep on it?'

'Here?' Ryan glanced at the shabby interior of the bar, shoulders dropping, facial expression glum. Much as he'd like a night in with O'Neil, he'd rather eat worms than spend it in such squalid surroundings.

O'Neil laughed. 'You should see your face.'

'What can I say? You're choosy about your gin. I'm a hotel snob.'

'Drink up. We'll find somewhere nicer.'

51

They found a half-decent hotel on the outskirts of Bletchley. At check-in, they booked a table for dinner at eight o'clock and went to their rooms to freshen up. Ryan took a quick shower, calling Caroline and Frank before he went downstairs. O'Neil was already at the bar, another gin in front of her, this one more palatable 'and in a clean glass', she told him.

When they had finished eating, O'Neil pushed her plate away and topped up their wine. 'I've come to a decision. I want you to raise an action with Grace. Before we tackle Sophia Montgomery, I'd like her neighbours spoken to, friends, associates, anyone who might have come into contact with her.'

'Already taken care of. I called Frank earlier, asked him to fast-track it for me.'

O'Neil put down her wine. 'You didn't think to run it by me first?'

'You've got enough on your plate. I figured you were right to be cautious. Tackling Montgomery without all the facts to hand was a bad idea. I could see how bothered you were by her condition. I thought it might put your mind at rest if you had some additional background before you made an approach. Armed with that you can make an informed decision whether or not to see her. Newman is lightning fast. He has contacts we don't. You OK with that?'

O'Neil dabbed her mouth with a serviette. 'Of course, thank you. John Maguire never looked after me the way you do.' She smiled at him. 'I warn you, I could get used to it.'

Ryan was too busy soaking up the compliment to respond.

'Something else on your mind?' she asked.

'As it happens . . .' He lifted the empty wine bottle, catching the eye of a passing waiter. He was stalling, undaunted by the fact that she knew it. What was really on his mind had no place in professional dialogue. Fortunately he had something else to feed her that would cover his growing infatuation. He ordered more wine and turned to face her. 'Did I ever tell you I do my best thinking in the shower?'

'I don't think so.' Her eyes sparkled when she grinned.

'It's true. Ordinarily, I keep my showering habits to myself but—'

'You came up with something?'

'I hope it's relevant.'

'Tell me.'

'Between shampoos, I went back to basics. A prior association between victim and offender has to exist. It's not in your face, I grant you, but it will be there – we just haven't found it yet. I kept coming back to the fact that we have three middle-aged men and one youngish female—'

'You mentioned that already.' O'Neil was disappointed to be going over old ground. 'We agreed as a team to concentrate on Laura, her being, in all probability, the most recent contact with Spielberg and/or her accomplice.'

'Yes, and that still holds true. To some extent, Laura was high profile too. That wasn't always the case, for any of them. Directly or indirectly they must've encountered their killer prior to their deaths. Whilst it's not glaringly obvious, it occurred to me that they all had similar-ish backgrounds.'

'You've lost me.'

Ryan leaned forward, elbows on the table, hands cradled under his chin. 'Consider the evidence we've gathered so far. Satellite teams have given us nothing tangible. On the face of it, that sounds grim, but then it occurred to me that during their journey to the top all four victims held positions that, at a stretch, you could lump together in one category.'

'"At a stretch" doesn't fill me with confidence, Ryan.'

'Hear me out. In each of the DVDs, Spielberg made it absolutely clear that her victims deserved what she was dishing out. We've known from the outset that the motive was revenge, but not what for. We've ruled out international terrorism and discounted child abuse, but that's the way things turn out sometimes. I'm now suggesting an alternative. The *only* thing I've come up with that is common to all four is that they are, or should I say were, people you tell things to. Dean used to be a youth worker; Trevathan a solicitor; Tierney a teacher; Laura Stone a journalist. I think Spielberg and her accomplice are killing people who either refused to listen or failed to take action on a matter close to their hearts. I have no idea how, but the more I think about it, the more convinced I am that Laura's documentary is the key that will open doors for us.'

'You think a life-limiting disease was the trigger?'

'I think so.'

'But Laura was raising awareness on an important issue. Why would they kill her for it?'

'I never said I had all the answers. We won't know until we view the footage. I suppose it depends on how balanced the piece was. Whether or not Laura showed both sides of the argument to the satisfaction of everyone in the same way Terry Pratchett did in his. We know nothing about her beyond the fact that she's probably floating in the North Sea. Maybe she had a moral conscience. Maybe she was pro-life, no matter the circumstances, and someone took exception to her interpretation of the information she'd been entrusted with. What if she came down on one side of the argument—'

'The *wrong* side?'

'Precisely.'

O'Neil picked up her wine, taking a moment to consider the premise. 'You know, that's not as daft as it sounds.'

'It would also explain why she didn't win the award,' Ryan said. 'As the subject of her documentary, Rebecca Swift is the person we need to talk to urgently, not Sophia Montgomery. Clark said the film was well reviewed. You know as well as I do that everyone is a critic these days. I'll bet not all of them came down in Laura's favour.'

They had homework to do, starting with the documentary.

52

Aware that they would be up half the night, they took the rest of their wine up to O'Neil's room on the fourth floor, put a Do Not Disturb sign on the door, and set her computer on the desk. Wasting no time, Eloise logged on, opening up the digital link Grace had forwarded from the production company who held the rights to the documentary.

As they settled down to watch the film, the atmosphere was both grim and hopeful: grim on account of the film's hard-hitting and deeply distressing content; hopeful because, the more they watched, the more convinced they became that they were making headway. O'Neil reckoned they could wrap the case up. She'd said as much.

Ryan reckoned it was the wine talking.

'I hope that wishful thinking rubs off,' he said.

'You think I'm being unrealistic?'

'No, but we're not even close to Spielberg's identity.'

'So prove me right, Ryan. Make me look good.'

She did look good.

He studied her for a moment. She was sitting on her bed, wine glass in her left hand, pen in the other, a notepad on her knee. Her eyes were fixed to the screen, long legs and bare feet tucked up beneath her. Despite the pressure she was under to solve Operation Shadow, she was more relaxed than she'd been in a long while. Ryan was feet away, sitting on the only available chair, closer to the desk. He couldn't deny it: the intimacy of a darkened hotel bedroom was a big turn-on.

If only she'd been over Forsythe.

'DS Ryan, may I remind you that you're supposed to be watching.' She'd spoken without making eye contact, a smile playing round her lips. She was teasing him for acting like a teenager. Ryan shifted his eyes back to the screen. It was great to have her back.

They dissected every moment of the footage and, on second viewing, took notes, as they had with Spielberg's own efforts at film-making. Rebecca Swift was, without doubt, the star of the show, a compelling character with the courage of her convictions, an honest, gutsy woman with strong views she was determined to put across. Undaunted by the camera, she made a fascinating subject. Not quite as beguiling as the redhead on the bed, but Ryan couldn't have everything.

'Laura must've been immensely grateful for Rebecca's poise,' he said. 'Without it, this documentary wouldn't have worked, on any level. I warmed to Knox and Schofield. Didn't care much for Jo Nichol though, did you? Not a particularly likeable character. Bit of a chip on her shoulder, if you ask me.'

'Understandable, I suppose.'

'Why? Her condition is less severe than the others. You wouldn't think so, for all the whining she did—'

'That's harsh, Ryan. She's probably scared witless. People cope with illness differently. Imagine if that was you. In fact, it's so depressing, I could do with another drink. Want one?'

'Thought you'd never ask.'

As the credits rolled, O'Neil removed her specs, scrambling

across the bed to grab the wine bottle, tutting when she found it empty. She got up, pulled open the mini-bar and peered inside. 'There's not much choice. You want a beer or something stronger?'

Ryan checked his watch: quarter to one. 'Scotch if you have it. Neat.'

'Think I'll join you.' She poured them both one, threw the empty miniatures in the trash and climbed back on the bed. 'I'll be honest, Ryan. I've never heard of this disease, have you?'

'Genetic genealogy was never my strong point, especially at this time in the morning.'

They were grateful that medical experts had explained the complexities of the disease – otherwise it would have been lost on them. Named after the German professor who'd identified it, Sauer's Syndrome involved DNA inherited from the auto-somal chromosomes, a dominant genetic condition predisposing those affected to aggressive and multiple cancers, affecting all parts of the body from an early age. In layman's terms, it was a complicated gene mutation, causing catastrophic knock-on effects in those unfortunate enough to receive it from a parent. Dodgy DNA in capital letters.

Ryan took his shot glass from O'Neil. 'Clark was spot on in her opinion of the documentary. It was unsettling and some-what bleak, but thought-provoking nevertheless. It's a credit to Laura, a quality production. Perfectly balanced too, didn't you think?'

'Which rules out the idea that she was killed for taking sides.'

'I wonder if, faced with similar circumstances, I'd hate my parents as much as Rebecca Swift does hers.'

'It's hard to be objective when you're healthy.'

'Healthy might be pushing it.' Ryan yawned, eyes watering as he covered a gaping mouth. 'Rebecca was amazing though, wasn't she? Such composure. No tears or tantrums, anger or melodrama, just plain hard facts. My kind of woman.'

'But not the one Pedersen saw in Copenhagen.'

'No. She's too small – too old.'

'Not old,' O'Neil countered. 'Laura referred to her as mid thirties.'

Ryan bristled. 'I thought she said mid forties.'

'Then you should've been paying more attention.'

'You sure?'

'Positive. You heard what your eyes were telling you.'

'I stand corrected,' Ryan said. 'She looks much older, not particularly ill, but those vacant eyes . . .'

'Haunting, weren't they?' O'Neil met his gaze. 'What was it she said? "I'm dying from the inside out and my mother made it happen." I'm with her on that score. Why anyone who knew they had a high chance of passing on such a devastating disease would have a child beats me.'

Ryan didn't answer. Didn't argue either.

53

A call came in to Ryan's mobile as he was finishing his breakfast. In spite of his best efforts, Newman hadn't completed his background check on Montgomery. People were proving difficult to track down, many of them disappearing for Christmas. Grace was similarly stumped, liaison with the Met proving more troublesome than she'd anticipated.

'Bad timing,' Ryan said. 'Don't worry about it. You think you'll be done by noon?'

'Hope so,' Newman said.

'And Grace?'

'If all goes to plan.'

'Perfect. Rather than sit around and wait, Eloise and I will pay Rebecca Swift a visit. We had a long chat last night – I won't go into it now, but suffice to say, we need to do that as a matter of urgency. She's in St Albans, less than an hour from here. When we're done, we'll commandeer an office at the nearest nick and call you at midday.'

'Works for us.'

'Any problems, give me a shout. By the way, can you and Grace try to watch the documentary before we speak?'

'Consider it done.' Newman rang off.

*

Ryan and O'Neil encountered biblical rain on the journey south. It was close to ten thirty before they reached their destination, a studio flat in Upper Marlborough Road, not far from the city centre; one of five contained within a recent conversion. Rebecca Swift lived on the second floor at the front of the house.

Before mounting communal stairs, O'Neil paused to admire black-and-white Victorian tiles in the hallway, retained by a savvy builder. 'I'd love these in my house,' she said. 'So many original features are ripped out these days. Why do people do that?'

'No taste, I guess. What's the plan when we get in there?'

'I'll take the lead. You take notes. Rebecca trusted Laura with her innermost secrets, a medical and ethical dilemma she cares deeply about, enough to want to share it with the world. I want to gauge the strength of their relationship. I'm sure she's not our girl, but keep your eyes open for anything odd.'

On the floor above, O'Neil knocked on the door.

It was opened almost immediately, surprising them both, not because of the tenant's apparent fleetness of foot, but because of the acute change in Rebecca's appearance. Healthwise, she was in a worse condition than she had been when she appeared in the documentary. She'd lost a lot of weight and had a pasty complexion and hollow cheeks. Logical, Ryan supposed. The film had gone on general release in July 2011 – almost two and a half years ago – which was a very long time in the life of a patient riddled with a disease that had no cure.

Rebecca's cold and bony hand shook when she offered it to each of them. She stepped aside to let them pass into the studio and closed the door quietly behind them. The space was cramped but tidy with hardwood flooring, a large south-facing sash window overlooking the main road. There were no seasonal decorations. The absence of even one Christmas card made Ryan's heart ache. There would be no celebration here this year, or ever, he suspected.

Rebecca gestured towards a compact dining table positioned in the bay, an empty coffee cup on the surface. She'd been watching from the window, reading while she waited for them to arrive. A copy of the *Guardian* lay abandoned on the table-top with a picture of a distraught Nigella Lawson on the front page. To the left of the photograph, a headline shouted: *GCHQ spied on charities and EU allies* – a story about British and US intelligence agencies having a comprehensive list of surveillance targets.

Nothing new.

Ryan's eyes drifted to a minute kitchen area, more especially to the open cupboard door above the bench. On the shelves were boxes of prescription drugs and pill bottles of every shape and size, enough morphine to fell an army. He wondered how often Rebecca Swift had contemplated suicide. She caught his eye, an accusing look that made him feel like a spy of the very worst kind.

'Shocking, isn't it?' She shut the cupboard door, pointing at the dining table with her walking stick. 'Please, if you've seen enough, take a seat.' There were only two chairs at the table and no sign of any more in the room.

'You two sit,' Ryan said. 'I'd rather stand.'

'How very gallant,' Rebecca said. 'Would you like something to drink? You've come a long way.'

Both detectives declined.

O'Neil sat down, introducing herself. Ryan had already called ahead to make sure it was a convenient time to visit. Rebecca knew only that they were Northumbria Police officers, not the reason for their visit, or why it was vitally important that they speak to her on this, the first day of the Christmas holidays.

O'Neil cut to the chase. 'Rebecca, I'm sorry to have to tell you this, but I'm investigating the disappearance of Laura Stone.' Swift showed no emotion, so O'Neil carried on. 'We wanted to tell you in person rather than give you distressing news over the phone. From our attendance here you'll have worked out that we have grave concerns for her safety. Have you had any contact with her recently?'

'Why would I?'

'She made a film about you.'

'And I've not seen her since. We knew each other. We weren't that close.'

'I understand the two of you met while on holiday?'

'Yes, she was kind to me. Very understanding.' She looked out of the window and then back at the detectives. 'That was before I realized that she had an ulterior motive for keeping in touch.'

'You didn't have to agree to her demands,' O'Neil said.

Rebecca pouted. 'You don't know Laura. She has a way about her.'

'You felt you couldn't refuse?'

'She didn't coerce me, Superintendent.'

'That's good to know. Did you meet here, in this flat?'

'Initially, yes. Is this about the documentary?'

'We think so. You two seemed to have quite a rapport on

screen. We watched it last night and found it moving and very brave.' Ryan was nodding his agreement with O'Neil. 'We have no idea how, but we believe her disappearance is connected in some way to the making of this film. We wouldn't be here if we didn't feel pretty sure about that. We're hoping you might be able to help us with our enquiries.'

Rebecca had drifted off.

'Rebecca? Are you OK to carry on?'

'Yes.' She rubbed at her forehead as if the action would generate more energy from within. 'Sorry, I sleep a lot. I get exhausted if I don't get my rest. It's very frustrating.'

'I'm sorry,' O'Neil said. 'We won't keep you long.'

'What do you want to know?'

'I'll be honest with you, neither of us had heard of your condition before we viewed the documentary last night. Am I right in thinking that you agreed to go public to raise the profile of the disease?'

'To make people aware, yes. That was the objective.'

'Then you achieved it. Did you know the other sufferers who took part: Jo Nichol, Martin Schofield and Sandie Knox?'

'Not beforehand.' Rebecca lifted her chin, her face set in a scowl. 'Sandie's the lucky one. She died already.'

'Yes, we know.'

Ryan was fighting the urge to give the woman a hug. He couldn't imagine what it must feel like to wish your life away or, in her case, wish you'd never been born. He still couldn't see how this documentary could have led to the death of Laura Stone. He wanted to ask a question but O'Neil was on a roll . . . Then Rebecca cut in:

'Why would you think I'd know the others?' she asked.

'There are less than a thousand cases of Sauer's worldwide. Fewer than a hundred in the UK. Laura had a lot of trouble finding people, I know that much. It's not like the PNC.' Reference to the Police National Computer system threw O'Neil, but Rebecca didn't stop for breath. 'You can't trawl a medical database and come up with a list of names. And before you ask, when I was fit to work, I was a civilian indexer in a murder investigation room just like the one you're running. Laura is dead, isn't she?'

'We don't know the answer to that question,' O'Neil said. 'Did you help Laura with her research?'

'I did much of it for her. I wasn't so ill then but registered disabled, so not working. I'm not surprised you hadn't heard of it. Not many people know about the disease. Laura put an advert in a national newspaper to attract others with the same diagnosis. She only had four hits.'

'Four?'

'That's what she said.'

'And yet she only used three.'

Rebecca shrugged. 'Maybe the fourth was too ill.'

Or maybe there was another reason, Ryan thought, but didn't say. Surely Laura hadn't been murdered for leaving someone out of her documentary? There must be another explanation that linked her to the murders of Dean, Trevathan and Tierney, something that hadn't yet clicked into place.

O'Neil passed Rebecca a list of names. 'According to the executive producer, this is a full list of cast and crew. Can you identify which ones you personally came into contact with?' She handed over a pen.

'Or any that might be missing?' Ryan added.

O'Neil nodded her thanks.

'Most of these were on set at one time or another.' Rebecca ticked off names and gave the list back to O'Neil. Barring Gillespie, Laura's music composer, every crew member's name had a tick against it. It had been immensely useful talking to her. On day twelve of the enquiry, they were finally making headway.

O'Neil wrote something on a sheet of paper and then lifted her pen. 'I'll be straight with you, Rebecca. We're very much in the dark. What I'm about to share with you is highly confidential. I'd like you to keep it that way. Can you do that? Laura's life might depend on it.'

'Of course.'

'We're convinced that other people have died as a result of that documentary, at home and abroad.' O'Neil handed her a second list. 'I'd like you to examine the names I've written here and tell me if you recognize any of them. Take your time, there's no rush.'

Rebecca stared at the sheet of paper, making no comment before passing it back. 'Is Dean the guy who's been in the news lately? I watch a lot of telly these days. His murder has been on a news loop for days. I've never heard of the rest.'

'They're all dead.' O'Neil said. 'Except, in their case, they're not happy about it and neither are their families.'

Rebecca flushed slightly.

Ryan was shocked. That was quite a dig.

O'Neil received his non-verbal warning shot. 'I'm sorry if that sounded harsh.'

'No need to apologize,' Rebecca said. 'You make a fair point.'

'You care, Rebecca. The documentary is evidence of that. DS

Ryan and I now know *how* these people died. If we don't find out *why* they died, their relatives will spend the rest of their lives trying to make sense of it.'

'I understand, but please don't judge me, Superintendent. It's a nightmare living with this disease. I had no children of my own because I wouldn't wish the condition on my worst enemy. Before Laura approached me, I didn't know anyone else affected, only those I met online.'

'Online?' It was out of Ryan's mouth in a flash.

'A support group, if you could call that. I don't go on it much now. It depresses me.'

'Can you write down the name of it?'

'I can do better than that.' Rebecca got up.

Ryan followed as she moved towards a laptop lying on her bed. Pulling it towards her, she staggered slightly, losing her footing. He caught her before she landed on the floor. She didn't say anything – falling was obviously a frequent occurrence – and neither did he. She sat down, logged on and tapped a few keys.

'Sorry, my hands don't always obey my thoughts.'

'Want me to do it?' Ryan said.

'No, I'm fine.'

The website in question arrived on screen. Ryan read over her shoulder, taking down the URL, noting that there were 354 members listed on the right-hand side of the home screen, as well as links to similar sites and medical blogs. He met O'Neil's gaze from across the room. Flicking his head towards the door was enough of a prompt for her to thank their host and go. Their interviewee was tired now.

'Thanks.' Ryan stood up. 'We'll let you know if we find Laura. Are you going to be OK?'

'No, I'm not.' Rebecca stared at him with an intensity that made him realize how inappropriate the question was, however well intentioned. 'Laura was an amazing woman,' she said. 'Very sensitive and caring. I liked her a lot. I hope you find her safe and well.'

As Ryan shook hands with her at the door, Pedersen's voice entered his head: *I'm not a doctor but my sister is painfully thin. She has a disease . . . the man with the phone looked like her.* Pedersen had been talking about the suspect she'd seen loitering in Kastelsvej, near the British Embassy in Denmark. Rebecca also had that appearance and, suddenly, Ryan understood. It was a light-bulb moment. Spielberg's accomplice – whoever he was – was a sufferer too.

54

At twelve o'clock on the dot, O'Neil FaceTimed Grace and Frank from St Albans police station, having made considerable progress. They had viewed the documentary and were up to speed on its focus.

It was time for a remote briefing.

O'Neil kicked the meeting off. 'Rebecca Swift was very helpful to us. She told us that Laura Stone had no knowledge of Sauer's Syndrome before the two met. It was only after Rebecca agreed to take part in the documentary that Laura began her research, advertising in a national newspaper for sufferers willing to talk about their experience.'

'How many takers were there?' Grace asked.

'That's where it gets interesting. Rebecca is adamant that four, not three, people got in touch. Grace, you need to talk to every member of her film crew again to see if any of them know who was left out and why. Now we have their contact details, that shouldn't be too difficult. Ryan thinks that Spielberg's sidekick may have been that person. There's a fifty per cent chance of inheriting the disease. If her accomplice is her brother, the likelihood is that Spielberg has that same devastating DNA marker. If it turns out one of them was that reject, it would not only link them to Laura but provide a motive for killing her.'

'A weak motive is still a motive,' Grace said.

Even though they weren't in the same room, Ryan could see and feel how excited Grace was. Unconsciously she'd taken hold of Newman's hand and given it a squeeze.

'Although she doesn't use it now,' Ryan said, 'Rebecca used to frequent an online chat room, a support group for sufferers. It was the only connection she had with other Sauer's patients prior to meeting up with Laura. It's a hard ask, given your workload, but we need more on that—'

'If you require IT help,' O'Neil cut in, 'just ask.'

'I'll start combing the site for mentions of Dean, Trevathan and Tierney,' Grace said.

'Good. What's the state of play up there? How's the surveillance of Clark and Mitchell going?'

'Fine. They're bunkered down for Christmas.'

'Wish I was,' Ryan said under his breath. 'Any news on Sandie Knox?'

Grace nodded. 'She died on January seventh of this year. I have a copy of her death certificate on file.'

'Cause of death?' O'Neil again.

'Carcinomatosis. The certifying doctor cited Sauer's as the primary cause of death. Before Frank and I viewed the documentary, we'd never heard of it. Leaving Clark and Mitchell aside for one minute, we're after suspects who loosely fit Pedersen's description, yes?'

'Correct,' O'Neil said. 'Except now we know that Rebecca Swift isn't our target.'

'I've also ruled out all the in-house technicians,' Grace said. 'Two of them are Asian, one weighs sixteen stone, the other is fifty-two years old. Clark's description of Jang and Malik was correct, so by my calculation that leaves only two females who are around the age and physical characteristics we're interested in: one of the film's subjects, Jo Nichol, and Sophia Montgomery, film crew. I'm still checking on them.'

'And males?'

'There are three in the mix: Martin Schofield – another sufferer who appeared in the documentary; Laura's music man, Tony Gillespie; and the cinematographer, Dan (Frank) Spencer.'

'Some are alibied?'

'Right.' Grace gave their names. 'Of the three men, Schofield is unwell, currently under psychiatric assessment in a secure hospital having twice attempted suicide. By all accounts, he's a wreck, incapable of carrying out the kind of frenzied attack our victims suffered.'

'What about Gillespie?'

'He has a short-term visa to work on a co-production in South Africa. He's been out of the country for the last six months and has stamps on his passport to prove it. He was abroad for all four deaths.'

'Spencer?' Ryan asked.

'Like the women, he's proving difficult to pin down. You'll have to leave it with me.'

'How did you get on with the background check on Sophia Montgomery?' O'Neil asked.

'Grab a brew,' Grace said. 'It's a long story, but I'm sure Frank will make it brief.'

'I'll try,' Newman said. 'Montgomery's mutism arrived suddenly, brought on by the death of her mother in an accident when Sophia was ten years old. No one has heard her utter a word since. Met police asked every member of the documentary crew about this, apart from Spencer, who they haven't yet been able to locate. In every case, they were given the same answer: she doesn't speak. I was told the same thing when I spoke to her former employer, her schoolteachers, social workers and speech therapists this morning. She stopped communicating through language, scraped through school and never went to university. She gets work where she can and lives alone. Lack of speech would suggest she's not our girl—'

'And the band played "Believe It If You Like",' Grace said.

'It's well documented,' Newman added.

'So is the bible – and we all know that's a fabrication.' Grace wasn't smiling. 'No speech equals no voice comparison. Very convenient.'

'That was my initial reaction too,' O'Neil said. 'Frank, you're not happy with her, are you?' For once Newman's facial expression had given him away. There was more coming . . .

'A coroner ruled her mother's death as accidental. She fell over a cliff – two hundred feet. Sophia was with her at the time, as was her younger brother, Mark. He was eight when it happened. They were staying in a holiday rental nearby.' The implication was clear to everyone.

Silence reigned.

'Where was the cliff?' O'Neil asked finally.

'Filey.'

Newman's answer was like a bombshell going off in their heads, the Yorkshire link they had been waiting so patiently for. Before Ryan had the chance to say anything, there was a sudden kerfuffle at the other end of the line. A dog barked. He assumed it was Bob. A worrying thought. The Labrador only ever did that to attract attention.

He had Ryan's.

'Frank? What's going on?'

Newman turned his head away from the screen. A wince. 'You OK?'

Ryan didn't hear a reply. 'Grace?'

Grace grimaced. 'Caroline fell over a chair.'

'My fault,' Newman admitted. 'I moved it. I'm so sorry, I never thought.' He disappeared off screen.

Caroline called out to Ryan. 'Matt, don't fret, I'm fine!' Quieter now: 'Frank, I'm fine. Please don't fuss. I got excited when I heard you say Filey. Should've had more sense than to break into a sprint when I'm not at home.'

She was laughing.

So was Newman as he sat down again – a sign that all was well.

Ryan relaxed.

His twin was used to order. Sighted people didn't always think to keep it that way. Fortunately, she'd learned to bounce over the years. Bob's complaint was for Newman, not because his handler was badly hurt. If Ryan knew the spook, he wouldn't make the same mistake twice. Frank adored Caroline almost as much as he did.

'There were no witnesses,' Newman continued. 'No one to say whether Montgomery's mother fell or was pushed.' His words sent a chill through everyone. 'Mark ran off to get help. Sophia was found on the coastal path, close to the edge, weeping. An orphan in shock who, from that point on, had nothing to say to investigators or anyone she came into contact with.'

365

'Except to her brother, perhaps.' Grace's tone was hard. 'Anyone else think her muteness was a result of her own bloody actions?'

O'Neil almost shuddered at the thought.

'Thought so,' Grace said. 'We should lock her up now and put the thumbscrews on. This has her name all over it.'

'No,' O'Neil said. 'When we go for her, *if* it's her, it has to count. Let's give Sophia Montgomery the benefit of the doubt.'

'Again?' Grace huffed. 'How lucky can one suspect get?'

Ryan gave her a look that said: *Thanks very much. I texted O'Neil's reluctance to see her in confidence.* Eloise was at the wrong angle to see the power of the eye contact passing from St Albans to their Newcastle base. Newman not so. The spook was seething, trying not to show it.

'What height is she?' Ryan asked.

Grace checked her computer. 'Five eight. Why?'

'Then she fits the profile.'

'We have a profile?' Newman and O'Neil said together.

Only Grace knew what Ryan was on about. 'Technicians were able to nail the height of the person we're looking for from DVD footage,' she said. 'It's fascinating what they can do nowadays. I bloody love technology.'

O'Neil turned towards him. 'Why didn't I know about this?'

'You were tied up, guv. Grace and I had it covered.'

She let it go.

'I agree with Eloise,' Ryan said. 'We *will* interview Montgomery, but unless we can get her to talk, we need to incriminate her. There's no point charging in there with nothing on which to base our claims. We show patience, pick away at her story, assuming she has one. Of itself, her height isn't enough. If it turns out that she's our girl, we may fare better tackling her brother. He's the weak link. Pedersen said he looked ill, not that they both did. She also said the woman was in charge, or words to that effect. That gives us leverage.

'Makes perfect sense to me,' O'Neil said. 'Grace, you can start by contacting the coroner's officer. I'd like the report on her mother's death on my desk when I get back.' Her mobile rang, an unwelcome intrusion. 'Damn it! It's Control, I'd better take this.'

Her voice faded from Ryan's head, his thoughts still on a ten-year-old peering over the edge of a precipice where her mother had been standing moments before. He imagined the scene from Sophia's point of view, her mother seeming to float, almost in slow motion, down and down, until she hit the ground with a sudden thud, organs rupturing, bones splintering, dead eyes staring back at her.

Trying to calculate the length of time it would take to fall that distance, Ryan concluded that it would be long enough to know what was coming. Ample time to ask the question: why? Had Sophia witnessed the fall, seen her mother lying motionless below or being washed out to sea? They would probably never know, but the image would stay with Ryan for days.

More than one of the victims had ended up in water.

55

The troubled expression on O'Neil's face brought Ryan up short.
He assumed her thoughts were also on Montgomery. That she
too was mulling over Newman's intelligence, keen to hang up
the phone and move on with matters hot off the press. He was
wrong. She muted the call and held out to him.

'It's Spielberg . . . for you.'

Crunch time.

Ryan glanced at the iPad on the desk in front of him. For a
split second, Grace stared at him before grabbing her phone off
the desk at their Newcastle base. He knew exactly what she was
about to do.

Grace was on to the surveillance team at lightning speed. 'This
is Gold Command. Do you have the eyeball on the targets?'

'Affirmative.'

'What are they doing now?' There was a short pause. Grace
could see Ryan staring at her through the screen as he pressed
a button on O'Neil's mobile. He seemed hesitant to take the
call. She glanced at Newman. 'What the hell is he waiting for?'

Frank ignored her. He had earphones in, effectively muting
the iPad so they couldn't be heard, while taking the opportunity to listen in to events happening in St Albans.

*

'This is DS Matthew Ryan. Welcome back.'

'Finally.' Spielberg sounded pissed off. 'I was beginning to think that you weren't speaking to me.'

'Funny lady,' Ryan said. 'Shame you're not as patient. I'm sorry I couldn't talk to you last time. Someone important was on the line. You could have waited, instead you hung up on me.'

The team had decided he should use the same acerbic tone with her, exactly as before. Clearly, he'd made a connection. Why else would she call? Ryan was finding it hard to shake the image that played out in his head a moment ago. He was conversing with a killer – *that was a given* – but was it the voice of Sophia Montgomery? A child murderer was hard to get your head round . . . even for a cop.

'Foxtrot 3 has the eyeball – both targets fishing off the narrowboat. They're chatting, Gold. Photographic evidence on way to you.'

'Keep filming,' Grace said. 'I want continuous timed evidence until I say otherwise. Is either target near a mobile or landline?'

'Negative on the landline.' He paused. 'It's hard to tell from here whether either of them has a mobile.'

'Make an approach. I want both targets in conversation with a Foxtrot ASAP.'

'Stand by.'

The surveillance leader spoke into his radio, a shutter repeatedly going off over his left shoulder. 'Foxtrot 3, break cover. Engage targets overtly. I repeat, engage targets overtly. I want confirmation that neither Clark nor Mitchell is on the phone. Keep talking until I ask you to disengage.'

'Affirmative.'

Within seconds, Foxtrot 3 appeared on the tow path in a drenched waterproof and muddy boots, trundling along as if he'd been walking for miles. The surveillance commander grinned. 'Gold, Foxtrot 3 now in position. Target 1 giving him a light. Target 2 appears to be participating in friendly banter. Camera still rolling. Over.'

Spielberg had made no comment. Ryan was still baiting her. 'I'd have rung if you'd left your number. Are you going to give me a name this time? You know mine. It's common courtesy to reciprocate.'

'Nice try, Ryan.'

'I didn't mean your own, silly. Make one up. Everyone needs a handle. Even you.'

There was a pause. 'You can call me Marge.'

'As in Simpson?' Ryan forced a laugh. 'C'mon! You can do better than that. She has a beehive hairstyle. I hear yours is much more glamorous. What colour is it this week?' She made no reply.

'Caught much?' Foxtrot 3 was leaning against the houseboat talking to Clark.

She smiled. 'Just a tiddler. My guest has done rather better.'

Foxtrot 3 took a long drag of his cigarette. 'I used to fish.'

'Oh yeah,' Mitchell was obviously bored stiff.

'You'd rather be in the Big Smoke, eh?' The surveillance

officer smiled. 'Don't blame you. There's not a lot else to do but fish around here.'

Ryan forced himself on. 'Not playing? OK. Maybe Marge does suit you. She's from a dysfunctional family, a gambler too, you have that in common, I suppose.'

'Call me what the fuck you like.'

Aggressive. 'How about Spielberg?'

The line was cut.

'Gold to surveillance commander. Your team can stand down. Targets no longer relevant. I repeat, targets no longer relevant. Good job!'

'That's received, Gold. We'll send you the evidence when we return to base.'

Having seen Ryan put down the phone, Newman gave him a round of applause and high-fived Grace. 'Result!' he said.

O'Neil glowered at the screen. 'This is not a game show, Frank.'

Newman turned to face her. 'You can't have it both ways, Eloise. We all agreed that Ryan should deal with her as he saw fit. What he did was well worth a punt. It's the first time we've had the opportunity and angle with which to provoke a response, and we got it. He handled it perfectly because now she knows we're on to her.'

'That's exactly my point. She might leg it.'

'Oh, c'mon!' Grace said. 'She's shown her hand and lost control.'

'Except we don't know for sure who she is,' O'Neil was saying.

'We have a pretty good idea, thanks to Ryan. Cutting that call validates our belief that the case is somehow connected to cinematography. What's more, Spielberg knows we know and she won't like it.' Grace eyeballed her former DS. 'You did good, Ryan. We had sod all before. Now we're coasting. I'm proud of you, even if Eloise isn't. Clark and Mitchell are in the clear. They were under close observation throughout your call.'

That information alone was cause for celebration.

56

In the past few hours, suspicion had shifted seismically from Clark and Mitchell to Nichol and A.N. Other. The big money was now firmly on the Montgomery pair. Knowing how close he was to Caroline had Ryan wondering about the existence of criminally minded siblings. It was rare to find such a combination prepared to collaborate in the ultimate crime.

Not unprecedented though . . .

Ryan recalled a book by John Pearson – *The Cult of Violence: The Untold Story of the Krays* – in which they were described as having worked together, almost telepathically, as if they were one. A shocking thought. If it turned out that Spielberg was Montgomery, her brother Mark under her control, might they be the exception that proved the rule?

'Ryan?' O'Neil was staring at him.

'Sorry, I was in London's East End in the fifties.'

'Doing what?'

'Thinking about the Kray twins.'

'I see the parallel.' O'Neil said. 'Rather more troubling is the fact that there is an alternative pair we must eliminate from our enquiries: female Sauer's patient Jo Nichol and male cinematographer Dan Spencer – who we still haven't traced. You've been quietly concerned about him, I know you have. I have too. I think it's time to check them out.'

'No point trying Spencer,' Grace said. 'Met police spoke to his neighbours. He's gone for Christmas. They have no idea where or for how long.'

'Bugger,' O'Neil said. 'Do me a favour, will you? Ask Caroline to compare Nichol's voice to Spielberg's. They don't sound remotely the same to me, but I'd like her opinion on it.' She glanced at her watch, then at Ryan. 'Fancy getting wet?'

They left Hertfordshire's thunderous skies en route to Middlesex. Nichol's house – an ex-local authority semi-detached – was less than half an hour away. A fifteen-mile journey to Enfield, the right side of the city of London as far as Ryan was concerned. Anywhere north of Soho would do. They arrived in time to see Jo Nichol run down her garden path in the pouring rain, straight into a waiting taxi. Immediately, it pulled out of its spot and sped off into heavy traffic.

'What do you reckon?' Ryan set off after them. 'Want me to pull it over?'

'No, She's in a helluva hurry. I'd like to see why.'

They followed at a safe distance, giving two-car cover so as not to draw unwanted attention, a skill Ryan had down to a fine art from his training in Special Branch. A while later, the taxi indicated left, turning off onto a road called The Ridgeway into the main entrance of Chase Farm Hospital. The cab observed the 15 mph limit through the one-way system. Ryan cruised by as it pulled into a car park close to the Oncology and Haematology Department, an external building away from the Highlands Wing, a sign for which proclaimed: ALL WARDS.

Once out of site, Ryan brought the car to an abrupt halt.

'Go!' he said.

O'Neil jumped out, continuing her journey on foot.

Ryan drove on a bit further, pulling up on double yellow lines. With no police sign to put in the window, he abandoned the car and sprinted along the road after her. If he copped a parking ticket, he'd send it to Ford just to take the piss. O'Neil had come to a stop. She was facing away from him, sheltering from the rain under a tree, taking pictures. He was at the wrong angle to see what was so interesting. And then he saw that Nichol had company. An IC1 male was giving her a hug.

'The skinny guy,' he said. 'Isn't he one of the staffers we saw on the BBC website?'

'Meet Dan (Frank) Spencer.' O'Neil turned to face him. 'I'm no slacker when it comes to identifying suspects. I didn't get to my rank for making the tea.' She grinned widely, exhilarated by her find. 'Wait until he pays the driver and do your stuff, Ryan. I'll take care of Ms Nichol.'

'You want me to tackle him alone?' Ryan laughed.

She laughed too. He could blow the suspect over. 'Feel free to shout for help if he gives you any trouble. I'm a black belt, remember.'

Ryan held up ID as they approached the couple. 'Sir, DS Ryan, Northumbria Police. Would you come with me please?'

Spencer hadn't seen them coming. Consequently, he'd not been ready with a plan of any kind. It was as plain as day that he was the cinematographer they had been looking for. He didn't deny it.

Ryan took him to the car, O'Neil staying with Nichol while she kept her outpatients appointment. The hospital was part of the

NHS, affiliated to the Royal Free London NHS Foundation Trust. She'd received all her treatment there. When she removed her cloche hat, the effects of chemotherapy were all too obvious. O'Neil wondered why there was no mention of it on her personal descriptive form. The only explanation could be that she was wearing a good wig.

Independently, the couple stressed that they had nothing to hide. They were friends, nothing more, neither one had been hiding from the police intentionally. O'Neil felt better about them when Grace emailed to say that Caroline had compared the voices of Nichol and Spielberg. In her opinion, they were not one and the same. Calling in a favour from an independent analyst confirmed that view unequivocally.

Fairly sure that Nichol and Spencer wouldn't take them any further, Ryan drove on to Bletchley. Sophia Montgomery didn't answer the door. There were no lights on inside the ground-floor flat. O'Neil pointed to the side gate. He walked through it, using his police-issue torch to illuminate the kitchen. No sign of life. No dishes in the sink. Nothing to suggest anyone would be cooking there anytime soon.

A noise from behind startled him.

He tensed.

Swung round.

The garden was in darkness. The shed door stood open, shifting one way, then the other, in the wind. Within seconds, Ryan was in the North Shields lock-up, the floor covered in human blood, an axe glinting on the floor, then in James Fraser's flat staring into a firearms cabinet with no weapons inside.

He killed the torch.

Turning his body side on, making himself less of an obvious target, his right hand found the grip of his Glock. Easing it from its shoulder holster, he released the safety catch. The use of firearms was strictly controlled. Ryan was trained and authorized to use his weapon but felt no less vulnerable.

Another noise.

Again behind him . . .

Fear crept over his shoulder and up his neck, making his hair stand on end. Turning slowly, he peered into the darkness. A hooded figure stood metres away, backlit by a streetlight. Driving rain in Ryan's face made it difficult to see the person advancing towards him . . .

Someone bigger than him.

The Glock felt heavy in his hand. Images of his father's coffin draped in a Union Jack flashed through his mind. His ten-year-old self was scared, unable to imagine life from that point on. That feeling multiplied as the figure took a step forward, ever closer. A rustle in the hedge startled him. Right now, being a live coward seemed preferable to a dead hero. Flanked front and rear, he made the call: he wouldn't hesitate to shoot.

'Damn it! I'm covered in muck.' O'Neil switched on her phone torch, aiming it at him. She was holding a coat over her head, making her look enormous. 'What are you doing? You look like you've seen a ghost.'

Ryan relaxed his grip on his firearm. 'Give us a moment, guv.'

He swore under his breath, one eye still on that swinging shed door. Having made his weapon safe, he re-holstered it before switching his flashlight on. He checked the outbuilding, kicking the door shut, angry with himself for having cowered in the face of a perceived danger, letting his imagination run riot. Quickly, he forgave himself. Fronting up to an early death did things to people. O'Neil was a copper. She'd understand.

'Nothing there,' he said.

'Who were you expecting, the Bogey Man?'

Ryan relaxed. She hadn't seen him draw his weapon.

'C'mon, we're wasting our time here. I'll get the Met lads to check again later. My fault. I should've taken your advice yesterday. We may as well head home.' O'Neil had a point. If Montgomery had gone for Christmas, they could be there for days.

They escaped widespread flooding by the skin of their teeth. Vast swathes of southern England were affected by it. Dorset, Hampshire, Surrey and Kent were practically under water, many homeowners facing the prospect of Christmas without power. It was a nightmare journey in the dark; three hundred miles that should have taken nearly five hours turning into seven and half.

For much of the way, Ryan was quiet in the car, concentrating on the road, livid at having missed Montgomery. Newman's report on her had shaken him. For the second time that day, his ten-year-old self appeared. It was hard to conceive of someone that age being capable of murder, let alone Montgomery having the capacity to remain silent for twenty-plus years afterwards. That was dedication of the worst kind, an ominous notion that he found unnerving. O'Neil felt a heavy burden to build a solid case. She wanted hard facts before they showed their hand. Supposition simply wouldn't do.

It was almost midnight when they finally limped over the Swing Bridge across the Tyne into Newcastle. Fortunately, the city had fared better than most weather-wise. Escaping the worst of a predicted storm, the Quayside was wet but definitely open for business, a festive atmosphere the order of the day in the run-up to Christmas, like any Saturday night in the Toon.

Geordies rarely needed an excuse to party.

O'Neil was asleep when Ryan parked the car, so peaceful he didn't want to wake her. In the end, he had to. A kind word, a gentle touch. She opened sleepy eyes, yawned, stretching her arms above her head, seemingly unconcerned with where she was or even how she'd got there. Clearly, nothing had registered. Resting against the headrest, her eyes closed again, her lips parting as she fell into a deep sleep.

Grace, Newman and Caroline were long gone when they let themselves in. There was supper on a tray, an open bottle of Scotch and a note that had come via the Coroner's Office:

Gwenda Jane Montgomery – mother of Sophia and Mark
– also had Sauer's.
  Grace x

Right this moment Ryan couldn't care less. Exhausted, he fell into bed.

57

Shortly after 6 a.m. No Sunday lie in. No mission today. She wasn't ready for the Boy Wonder. She turned over in bed, snuggled down, pulling the duvet around her. Even if she had been organized, she'd slept badly and was physically exhausted. Unusual. A restless night had been filled with nightmarish landscapes. She'd been lost in a strange city, a recurring theme lately. Then she'd found herself padlocked inside a creepy red building, rats chewing at her feet. She'd woken gasping for air, hair plastered to her face with sweat. The rats she assumed were the pigs.

She wondered what rat number two was up to.

Ryan was a clever bastard. She figured that his desire for justice matched hers to kill and to keep on killing. Her mind flashed back to their phone conversation, his derisory tone. Somehow, he hadn't seemed to grasp the seriousness of the situation. He wasn't thick and yet the first time they had spoken he'd failed to mention Copenhagen, even though there had been press coverage – online and in print – in the UK and in Denmark.

Not good.

She turned over onto her back, placing her hands behind her head, eyes fixed on a hairline crack in the ceiling she hadn't noticed before. Fractures were appearing in her plans too. She craved headline status but journalists had been bought, initially making out that Dean was robbed with no mention of her video in the press. No speculation over the diplomat's actual demise; the judge either for that matter. A blanket ban, she supposed, sanctioned by someone in authority. O'Neil probably. That really wouldn't do for someone coveting exposure.

Fuck her . . .

Fuck 'em all.

But then things took a positive turn: a leak by someone at the British Embassy had raised her profile. She thought the truth was finally going to break – the press were all over it for days – and yet now all they could talk about was the fucking weather.

It was a mistake speaking to O'Neil's bagman. From the get-go Ryan had been trying to get the upper hand. She'd enjoyed his banter at first but then he'd failed to take her seriously, left her hanging on the line, shown her no respect whatsoever. He'd trampled all over her right to be heard, just like the fuckers she was killing. Like a metaphor for her life falling apart, the crack above her head seemed to grow wider the more she stared at it.

She should've stayed on the line yesterday and fronted up to Ryan. He might think she'd fallen into his trap, but she'd cut the call for good reason. Losing her rag with someone who thought she was dumb was risky. She might say something she'd regret, exposing herself to identification, handing him exactly what he was after, and she wasn't having that. Instead, she'd taken her anger out on the one person she knew hadn't the guts to stand up to her, let alone fight back. So what if Ryan had tricked her into showing her hand? She'd just have to try that bit harder to impress him.

Introducing him to the grunt would do it.

She grinned, a plan forming in her head. Ryan needed a lesson in who was boss. She was the game changer, not DS-fucking-Ryan. By the time she was done, he'd regret taking the moral high ground. She'd make sure he understood the rules as well as her motivation.

Who was the victim here anyway?

Not the dead ones. Those losers were in the wrong, not her. But if Ryan wanted confrontation, he'd come to the right person. She'd keep going until chaos reigned. Then maybe he'd understand who was really in charge and why her personal safety was less important than her assignments. She was going to hell anyway. What did she care how she got there?

58

'I have news!' Grace said as she walked through the door and took off her sodden overcoat, Newman following close behind. There were no special greetings to Ryan and O'Neil in spite of their marathon journey north and late arrival, no let-up for unit staff, no allowances. 'I just spoke to Art Malik,' Grace said. 'He knows why Laura didn't take the fourth respondent to the newspaper ad. And what's more . . .' A grin spread across her face as she let the sentence hang.

'He has ID?' Ryan asked.

'He does indeed. It *was* Mark Montgomery.'

They high-fived.

No wonder she was buzzing.

'Laura told Malik that Montgomery was an agitating bastard she couldn't afford to have on set. In short, she denied him a platform, ignored him because he was unpleasant and aggressive.' Grace bowed graciously, like a ballerina. 'You lot can thank me later.'

'Wait a minute!' Ryan said. 'Laura worked with Sophia. Did she not know that Mark was her brother?'

Grace was shaking her head. 'That was the first question I asked. As a relation of film crew, he'd most probably be ineligible to apply. He'd hardly disclose it, would he?'

'I want him picked up,' O'Neil said. 'Get hold of his medical records, soon as you can – his sister's too.' She beamed at Ryan. 'This is great news.' By process of elimination, they could rule out Nichol and Spencer, leaving themselves with just one pair to concentrate on.

The rest of the day was long and drawn out with no news of Mark Montgomery's arrest and no sign of Sophia at her Bletchley home. O'Neil ordered satellite teams to carry out house-to-house, the result of all enquiries for immediate input into HOLMES. Minutes turned to hours, the afternoon dragging itself slowly and laboriously into early evening.

After the high of identifying the prime suspects, morale had plummeted to a low point. Not so their work rate; everyone, including O'Neil, was focused on the chat room. There was undoubtedly reasonable cause to bring the Montgomery siblings in for questioning. Evidence was mounting, unit staff could all feel it, but first it was vital to establish connections between victims and perpetrators. And thus far they'd drawn a blank on that score.

Thames Valley Police excelled at keeping in touch. They would continue a watching brief in Buckinghamshire but, with sixty-five millimetres of rainfall resulting in local flooding, they had their hands full. There'd been no sign of Mark or Sophia Montgomery.

Ryan suspected they had gone to ground.

Grace Ellis took off her reading specs, rubbing at tired eyes, unhappy with the way things were going. 'Support networks usually offer comfort,' she said. 'Not this one. The members are nothing more than a bunch of morbid weirdos. Some of these posts are hateful. They may all be living with the nightmare of

Sauer's, but this type of remote contact is a breeding ground for trouble.'

Ryan was thinking the very same thing as he trawled the site for clues. The interruption was a good excuse to take a break. He got up, made them all a drink, delivering it to their desks. There was no break for Grace. Her eyes never left her desk. He lingered a moment, his focus on the rain-lashed window beyond her. It was still tanking down.

He wandered away and sat down beside Caroline and Bob. 'You OK, Matt?' His twin sensed his presence.

'I've had better days.' The fact that she knew it was him sitting there blew his mind. Time and again, whether he was just out of the shower or back from a run, she never mistook him for someone else. He ruffled Bob's coat and got a tail wag in return. 'Then again, I've had a lot worse.'

'You'll get there.' Caroline went quiet for a moment. 'Do you think the victims were murdered because they knew something the killer wanted to protect, or because of something they were told and didn't act upon?'

'The latter,' he said. 'Montgomery has taken revenge. She feels wronged in some way. The victims were all in positions of trust: youth worker, solicitor, teacher, all people who offered guidance to others.'

'You think it may have got them killed?'

'It's the only thing we've come up with that connects them.'

Having overheard the conversation, O'Neil swung her chair round to face them, coffee in hand, eyes on Ryan. 'If we knew her motivation, it would help.'

'Youth worker.' It came out like a murmur. Newman hadn't joined the conversation, he was talking to himself, his focus on his computer screen, as theirs had been a moment ago. He'd hit on something.

'Frank?' O'Neil was all ears. 'What have you found?'

'Not what, who.'

'Who?' Grace nudged him.

'There's a Paul Dean mentioned here. Ex-youth leader.'

'Must've been uploaded recently,' Grace said. 'It wasn't there this morning, I checked.'

The HOLMES system was like a big sponge that was continually updated by staff around the country. Regular checks threw up different information. A few hours could turn an enquiry on its head.

Newman had done well to find this gem.

He pushed his chair away from the desk. 'There's an amazing thread in this forum. Come and see for yourself.'

Grace was first out of her chair. The rest of the team – minus Caroline – weren't far behind. Huddling around to get a closer look, they saw that Newman's screen was open on a chat stream, more specifically a long and venomous conversation between someone calling himself *Shdwman* and another person whose chat room handle was *dude1980*.

Neither had a public profile.

'*Shdwman* is angry,' Newman said. 'He's talking about his mum, tearing Dean to shreds; *dude1980* is egging him on. It goes on forever. This is just the end of it.'

Shdwman: He told her it was God's will. FFS!
dude1980: dick
Shdwman: Why the fuck didn't she get rid?
dude1980: she should have – not his life, was it?

Shdwman: It's no life, man.

dude1980: sorry . . . cant help u

Shdwman: I'm fucked.

dude1980: you have me bro

Shdwman: Not enough

dude1980: dont give up. this wanker will suffer

Shdwman: If you're going to swear, learn to spell.

dude1980: he'll get his

Shdwman: Not how it works.

dude1980: depends

Shdwman: He's split man. Google him. He's a big shot now.

dude1980: so am I

Shdwman: Fuck off loser.

Re-energized, Grace turned to the others. 'This is gold, Frank. "He'll get his" sounds like a definite threat to me. The timing is right too. The chat is dated January tenth of this year, six months before Dean met his death. We need Technical Support to track this IP address and extract any contact between these two, either before or after.'

'Sophia is not dude1980,' Newman said.

'No, Mark is.' Grace pointed at the chat handle. 'The numbers coincide with his birth year. If it had been her, it would have been dude1978.' She faked a frown. 'Why do people do that? I'd rather keep mine to myself: dude1959 doesn't have the same ring somehow.'

Ryan laughed.

'It all makes sense now.' Four pairs of eyes were on him. 'Shdwman is talking about abortion. Like Rebecca Swift, he wishes he'd never been born. If Montgomery is of the same mind and Dean took the opposite view, it may have got him killed. No wonder Rebecca left the site. She's a good person.' He pointed at Newman's screen. 'She wouldn't want to be associated with this crap. She chose a legitimate route to highlight her plight via the documentary. Locked out of the limelight, Mark Montgomery didn't. He turned violent with the help of someone we already think is a killer: his sister.'

'Psychopathic siblings has a certain ring to it,' Grace said. 'You think they're standing up for the unborn?' She made a face. 'Such twisted logic. Moral crusaders are the worst kind. The theory hands justification to Sophia, explains why she killed her mother.'

'We have no proof of that,' O'Neil reminded her. 'And no prospect of any without a confession. Forgive my cynicism, but I hardly think she's the type to cough.'

'Then we work on her brother,' Newman said.

O'Neil glanced his way. 'If we can find him.'

'That shouldn't be too difficult,' Ryan said. 'He lacked the nous to hide his birth year. Can you see him covering his ass, concealing his audit trail? I can't. If Laura's assessment of him was correct, and I'm inclined to believe it was, he's so angry he can't hold it together. That means he'll have made and will continue to make mistakes. Technical support might get lucky.'

'Sophia made mistakes too,' Grace said. 'Not throwing her brother over the cliff, for one. If he's an eyewitness, her freedom depends on his silence, and that's not a nice place to be.'

Ryan nodded. 'We need to find him and quickly.'

O'Neil gave Grace permission to set the ball rolling for an arrest. As the team settled into their work, Ryan wondered if Sophia's mother had taken the pair on holiday to break the news that they may – almost certainly would – develop Sauer's, become ill and die before their time. Had she slipped it into the conversation on that clifftop walk without anticipating the strength of their rage? Had they, separately or together, given her a shove?

There was no better place to do it.

An idea occurred to Ryan.

Logging on to his own computer, he brought up the contact details for Michael Tierney's partner and dialled the number. 'Robert, it's DS Matthew Ryan. How are you holding up?'

'Trying to move on. Thanks for asking.'

'I can only imagine how tough that is.' Ryan meant it. The guy was broken. 'You said you'd give some thought to Michael's antecedent history. I wondered if you'd had a chance to do that and, if you have, if you found anything that might be of use to us.'

O'Neil held up a thumb, validating Ryan's call.

Although much better than when they broke the news of Tierney's death, Parker still sounded shaky on the phone. 'I discussed everything I knew with the Family Liaison Officer here in Brighton.'

'When was this?'

'A few days after your visit.'

'Not to worry. It's probably on the system already.'

'There wasn't much there,' Parker said. 'As I told you, Michael had no enemies, Detective. The odd homophobe, but we're used to that. Is there something specific you're after?' The dentist was intuitive. 'I was hoping you'd made progress with your enquiry. I want you to catch Michael's killer and put him away. I can't bear to think of him wrecking someone else's life.'

'Me either.'

Parker didn't reply.

Ryan suspected he was weeping. 'There is one thing . . .' He paused, searching for appropriate words. 'When Michael was teaching, did he ever mention anything to you about Sauer's disease?'

Parker cleared his throat. 'No, why should he?'

'It's a line of enquiry we're following.'

'What has a cancer diagnosis got to do with his death?'

Ryan was surprised that Parker knew of the disease but then remembered that he was a dentist. 'We're not sure, is the truth of it. We're currently investigating a support group linked to the illness. This is highly confidential – so please don't repeat it – we've found reference to one of the other victims on a chat-room site. I was wondering if Michael might have had any contact with the group, or with someone who either had or might go on to develop the disease during the time he was teaching.'

'Oh my God!'

'Robert? Are you OK?'

'Tell me it's not her?'

'*Her*?' Ryan held his breath.

Parker didn't answer immediately.

O'Neil took in Ryan's tension from across the room. He put the phone on speaker. Responding to the stress he'd put on the word 'her', Grace, Newman and Caroline also turned to face him.

After a few seconds, Parker's shaky voice filled the room . . .

'The kid he spoke to—'

'I'm sorry, can you explain? I'm not following.'

'Michael came home very upset one evening. This was years ago. He'd received a distressing telephone call from a young woman—'

'One of his pupils?'

'No. Teaching was his day job. He did a couple of night's voluntary work on a suicide prevention line, an organization similar to Samaritans. He found it rewarding, except for this one night. The girl poured her heart out him, threatened to throw herself in front of a London Underground tube. She was deeply distressed. Inconsolable. So was he when he got home. They were all disturbing cases, but this one really shook him up. He resigned over it.'

'Robert, this is very important. Did he meet with her?'

'No, why would he?'

'Are you sure?'

'Yes, of course! She was a kid. He was a teacher. Michael was soft but ambitious, even then. He'd never jeopardize his career under any circumstances. If I remember correctly, he referred her on to a professional counsellor, someone at Social Services. There should be a record of it somewhere.'

'Any idea which one?'

'No, sorry.' There was a moment of silence. 'It makes no sense that she would harm him if he was trying to help though, does it?'

'Not to us, no. Do you recall if he rang or wrote to Social Services?'

'If I know Michael, he'd have emailed the referral, if only to cover himself. On second thoughts, I can't see there being a record of it now. It was ages ago, early nineties.'

'Nineties? Are you absolutely sure?'

'It was 1993, in fact. We went on holiday a week later. Sri Lanka. I thought it would do him good to get away. If you like, I'll check his old computers. I've got nothing better to do this Christmas.'

Ryan felt sorry for him.

'You still have them?'

'Michael ran a thriving business, Detective. His equipment formed part of his company's tangible assets. He never threw them away in case of an HMRC investigation. I begged him to dispose of them before the ceiling collapsed. Like marriage, we never got round to it. He's got stacks of equipment in the loft. I'll hunt it out and get back to you, assuming I can make it work and if I find anything.'

Frank, Grace, Caroline and Eloise were still processing the information when Ryan put down the phone. 'How's your maths?' he asked.

O'Neil was puzzled.

'Montgomery is thirty-five. If it turns out that she was the person Tierney spoke to in 1993, she was talking when she was fifteen years old. That's five years after she allegedly went mute.'

No one spoke.

59

Feeling like a kid on Christmas morning, Ryan woke with the realization that it was a day of immense significance – except that this was the eve rather than the big day itself. There were no presents to open. No turkey to baste. It was time to be watchful around O'Neil. He wondered how she'd cope with what would've been the anniversary of her marriage to Stephen Forsythe.

She'd been for an early walk, was fresh and alert when he found her at the kitchen bench, buttering a piece of toast. They ate breakfast in silence before the others arrived, a simple meal: toast, fruit and strong black coffee. She kept her head down, scouring the morning newspapers, her inability to make eye contact a hint of her mood.

'You're staring again.' She didn't lift her head.

'Was I? I'm sorry, I didn't mean to.'

'Ryan, yesterday was a mare. I want everyone to knock off at midday. I managed to book Grace and Frank dinner at their hotel to sweeten the blow, a thank you present for all their hard work. I can't release them entirely. Even if I could, travel to Scotland is impossible.' She tapped the newspaper. 'Gale force winds and gusts of ninety-five miles per hour aren't ideal driving conditions. You should take Caroline home when she

393

arrives. There's nothing doing here. If it all kicks off and I need you, I'll be in touch.'

'If it's all the same to you, I'll stay.' Murder Incident Rooms didn't close down for Christmas and well she knew it. If she intended to work through the holidays, then so did he.

'I could order you to leave.'

'That would be harsh.'

'I was joking.' Her smile faded. 'What's up?'

'Nothing.' He lied.

'Something is.'

He looked away, his turn to avoid an issue that was bothering him. He'd been dreading Christmas for weeks, long before he learned that it had unfortunate associations for her too. The closer it got, the worse he had felt. When a certain invitation arrived, it knocked him sideways.

'Ryan? Talk to me?'

'It's Hilary.'

'Fenwick?' The question was rhetorical. She knew he didn't mean Forsythe. They had talked about Hilary Fenwick only yesterday. Still blaming himself for Jack's death, Ryan looked out for Hilary and her children, the youngest of whom was his god-daughter. He was struggling with the prospect of seeing the family over Christmas.

'I can't face seeing her tonight.'

'You have to, Ryan. Little Lucy will be heartbroken if you don't go. Robbie and Jess too.'

'I will call in. Just not for long. I'll drop Caroline off and stick around for a bit. She's staying over and will spend the day with them tomorrow, so there's no need for me to knock off early. Her Christmas is sorted and I have no other plans. They won't miss me.'

'That's bollocks, Ryan, and you know it. Hilary adores you.'

He met her penetrating gaze. 'You don't want me around. I don't want them around. Cowardly of me, I know, but I can't and won't try to fill the gaping hole Jack left behind. It's not possible, even if I wanted to. Eloise, I'm not Santa Claus. I can't magic up happiness or bring him back any more than you can.'

She bristled at the reference to the man she'd been engaged to.

Ryan was past caring.

'You have to let it go, Ryan.'

'We both do.' He never took his eyes off her.

The chemistry he was certain they had lost had come flooding back over the past few days. Little by little, he'd felt it return. They weren't out of the woods yet, but they were heading in the right direction. There was no way he was leaving her to mope, this afternoon or this evening. There wasn't a hope in hell of that happening.

'Maybe you could spare the time to come and hold my hand?' He put on his best begging face. 'Figuratively speaking, I mean. We could grab a bite to eat later. Nothing special. I'll stand you a bag of your favourite nuts and a Babycham.'

The magic disappeared from her eyes.

The knock-back stung before she had chance to voice it.

'I'd love to, but—'

'You have plans. That's cool. Some other time?'

She didn't answer.

'Is it Forsythe?' He raised a hand, fending off a response. 'Sorry, none of my business, I'll butt out.'

She hesitated long enough for him to wonder why. What

might she have been doing at this time last year: champagne breakfast, early hairdo, spa? He imagined her celebrating her last morning of freedom as a single woman, blissfully unaware of what would happen to her later in the day. Hilary Forsythe would have been joyful too, getting ready to receive her into his family. His benevolent words arrived in Ryan's head . . .

You take good care of her.

She yielded. 'How did you know?'

'It wasn't hard to work out. He loves you dearly. You're not the only one affected by what happened a year ago, Eloise. You need to give the guy a break.' She dropped her head, resumed reading her newspaper, shutting him out for the rest of the morning.

'This is BBC Radio Newcastle. Breaking news at midday. In Devon, the flooded River Lemon claimed the life of a forty-six-year-old man who died trying to rescue a dog. Witnesses say the man was swept away shortly before noon after gale-force winds and persistent rain battered the southwest of the country. Despite the efforts of Devon and Cornwall Police, the man bystanders hailed a hero could not be resuscitated. The animal survived . . .'

Ryan noticed Caroline stroking Bob's head. He killed the radio, cutting off the distressing report and logged on to his computer. Within a few minutes, he was engrossed in the Sauer's chat room. It wasn't long before he stumbled across something that caught his interest. He didn't say anything but, responding to his preoccupation, O'Neil raised her head.

'Ryan? Have you found something?'

'Not sure.' He scrolled down the page. 'This chat stream

makes interesting reading. Someone who calls herself *broken-kiss* – assuming that's a female – claims her father went to see a brief in order to stop his wife from having a second child. The lawyer who took the case failed to secure a court order.'

'Any names mentioned?'

'No. She refers to a "him", so it's definitely a male. More importantly, she's talking to *dude1980*.'

'Keep checking.'

Caroline used Ryan's room to get ready to go out. O'Neil was dressing for dinner too. When her bedroom door opened, out of habit Ryan stood up. She looked amazing in a fitted black dress, killer heels, a string of tiny pearls and a pair of exquisite drop earrings to match. It was the style of a bygone era, reminiscent of a lead character in a fifties movie. She was glamour personified but, in spite of the effort she'd made, she didn't appear happy.

Ryan's bedroom door opened and Caroline entered the living room.

'Wow! You two are really going for it.' He felt more comfortable lumping them together in one compliment. It gave him a good excuse to stare. Caroline's hair was up and she looked lovely, if more Bohemian in style. Like O'Neil, she was fully made up. Ryan had never understood how she managed that. He couldn't brush his teeth without a mirror.

O'Neil checked her watch, slipped her phone into a silver clutch bag.

'You need to leave that here, guv. Just in case.' He hadn't given Spielberg his number. If she phoned, it would be on Eloise's device.

'Yes, I better had.'

Ryan held up his mobile. 'Want to take mine?'

'No, Forsythe has several and you have his number. I'll be fine.' She took the mobile out of her bag but hung on to it. 'Let me call Hilary and the kids quickly. I'd like to wish them a Happy Christmas before I go.'

As she made the call, Ryan walked to the window, feeling like a shit for passing on the opportunity to stay over with Jack's family. Outside of the job, Hilary Fenwick was his best friend. She hadn't complained – she knew he was working – although she was very disappointed.

Down on the street below, Forsythe's Porsche cruised towards the building. Several floors above, Ryan heard the throaty roar of the Carrera's engine as it changed gear, entering the underground car park. There was no way Forsythe's dinner guest would take her chances in the rain.

Moments later, the doorbell rang.

Ryan swung round.

O'Neil hung up as he walked towards her. Panic rose in her eyes – a plea almost – she didn't want to go. Not tonight. As she offered him her mobile, their hands touched briefly, a moment charged with electricity. Her scent was divine. This close, he could see how very beautiful she was. What must she have looked like in a wedding dress? For the first time in his life, Ryan felt jealous of another man.

The doorbell again.

Ryan shook hands with Forsythe as he let him in.

As the two men walked into the living room, O'Neil's mobile rang in Ryan's hand. She almost lunged forward to take it from him, grateful for the excuse to answer. Any justification to delay her dinner date was welcome. Much as she loved Hilary Forsythe – Ryan had no doubt that she did – this was one engagement she could well do without.

She raised her eyes from the screen.

'Operation Shadow,' she said.

Caroline promised to keep quiet and wished her twin the best of luck. Forsythe nodded for him to take the call. Taking the phone from Eloise, a deep breath in at the same time, Ryan put the phone on speaker so they could listen in. It was THE most important call he'd ever take.

'Marge, thanks for ringing! And on Christmas Eve! And there was me thinking we'd fallen out.'

'Whatever gave you that idea?' Her voice was noticeably weaker.

'You have a habit of cutting me off. That's not polite.'

'Something came up.'

'Like what?'

'Nowt important.'

There was a noise in the background. Caroline had her head on one side, concentrating. When she made no attempt to draw Ryan's attention, her brother took it as a cue to continue. She hadn't nailed the sound.

'Do you have company?' Ryan asked.

'Do you?'

Clever.

'C'mon, you can tell me. Did someone come in? Was it Santa? You must've been extra good for him to call this early.' Ryan listened carefully, one eye on Eloise. Her panic was gone. Spielberg was her Get Out of Jail Free card. Forsythe may as well cancel their dinner reservation. 'Is he with you now?' he asked. 'Is that why you can't talk?'

'No, I'm alone.' Her voice broke.

'C'mon, it's Christmas. Why so down in the mouth? You should be out celebrating.' When she didn't answer, Ryan carried on: 'Anyone would think you were party to our intelligence.'

'What's that supposed to mean?'

'We have an eyewitness, Marge.'

'Bully for you.'

'You were seen outside the British Embassy in Copenhagen. You think you turned away when the security guards came? There were other people watching you. The person who saw you will do well on the witness stand. She thought you had a close personal relationship with the man you were with. I think that man is very important to you. Is it your brother, Mark?'

In the silence that followed, Caroline immediately became animated. She tugged at Ryan's sleeve, causing him to face her, used her index fingers to draw tears on her face. Ryan squeezed her hand as a thank you. He changed tack. It was time to stop being flippant.

He might have an in here.

'Are you still there, Sophia?' It was the first time he'd called her by her real name, personalizing their relationship. She didn't reject it. Maybe her work was done and she didn't care. Maybe she was finally getting ready to do everyone a favour and end it all. If Robert Parker was correct, she'd threatened to do it once before. 'Has something upset you? C'mon, spit it out. You can talk to me. Nothing is ever as bad as it seems. I can help.'

She cleared her throat. 'Sod off, I'm fine.'

Caroline shook her head. Sophia was lying. The others didn't need her to tell them that. If Montgomery was getting upset, there was a reason for it. It signalled a definite chink in her armour that Ryan might capitalize on. He tried again.

'Clearly you need to talk, Sophia. If you have a problem let's discuss it.' No response. 'Something is bothering you – I think I know what it is.' Still nothing. Ryan glanced at his watch. Montgomery would ring off before the call could be traced. Time to let her know that his luck finding a witness in Denmark wasn't all he had.

Turn the screw.

'You lied to us, Sophie. You told us, time and again, that your victims deserved what you doled out. That wasn't true though, was it? The guy you killed in Whitley Bay didn't do anything to you, did he? He was an innocent bystander. Is that what's upsetting you, the fact that you've killed a man who wasn't part of your plan? I *know* he wasn't part of your plan. I worked that out already. You did it because he saw you, because he could ID you, isn't that the truth of it?'

O'Neil and Forsythe were nodding encouragement. Interview technique was not about giving suspects information that would benefit them in any way, rather to prove that detectives hunting them were closing in and to provoke a reaction from cavalier offenders like Montgomery. Up to now, Ryan had kept communication flowing, but he was running out of time.

'The guy you killed was a nurse, a person universally liked, someone who'd spent his adult life in the service of others. I can appreciate how bad that makes you feel. Who did it, Sophia? Was it you or Mark?' She didn't admit or deny anything. To Ryan, the dialling tone was like his case flat-lining.

Montgomery was gone.

'Good job, son,' Forsythe said. 'I'd say you came out on top there.'

Ryan didn't feel worthy of praise. Unaware of his discontent, or possibly ignoring it, Forsythe turned to face his twin. 'And you, my dear, must be Caroline. I've heard so much about you from so many barristers. All good, I hasten to add. My colleagues at the bar aren't known for giving compliments unless they're justified. I knew your father. He was a good man, a credit to his uniform.'

'Thank you, sir.'

O'Neil studied Ryan. 'Why the face? You did well.'

'I did nowt.' He scowled. 'She never even said why she called.'

'I have a view on that,' Caroline said.

'Go for it! I can do with all the help I can get.'

'She was like Ice Woman on the tapes and didn't flinch when you were goading her about the nurse, even though it must have appalled her to discover that Fraser was a medic if, as you suspect, her brother has the disease. Sophia won't cry easily. Her tears would suggest that she's upset about something far more serious than killing someone who got in her way, perhaps something personal or, dare I say, monumental.'

Ølgaard's voice arrived in Ryan's head: *anorexia?*

Then Pedersen's: *Yes, the man with the phone looked like her.*

Ryan's eyes widened. 'What if it's both monumental and medical?'

'What do you mean?' O'Neil asked.

'At one of the briefings last week we discussed how long justice takes in this country, right?' He glanced at Forsythe.

'No offence, sir . . . I put forward the idea that our offenders weren't prepared to wait for the judicial process, that they were impatient vigilantes wreaking revenge. What if *one* of them physically couldn't wait? If Mark Montgomery is deteriorating rapidly, that would explain why his sister is upset.'

'Or maybe Sophia is ill herself now,' Caroline said. 'We all develop diseases at different rates, don't we? Some people live with cancer for years, others fade away immediately after diagnosis. Her personality would suggest that she'd belong to the former category. You said yourself, she's fighting those who wronged her.'

'Ryan, you and I have work to do,' O'Neil said. As Gold Commander with a depleted team, she was going nowhere. Forsythe took it well. The case was ultimately her responsibility. Ryan was already raising an action – a nationwide trawl of hospital admission departments – in an effort to trace either sibling. O'Neil removed her earrings, kicked off her heels and sat down.

60

With Forsythe's help, the search warrant was secured within hours. He flew Ryan and O'Neil to Bletchley in a private jet he'd hired to take him south on Christmas Day. Clearly, O'Neil was not the only one pleased to avoid an encounter with the past. Unsurprisingly, father and son hadn't seen eye to eye this year. The truth of it was, they never would again.

Both target properties had escaped the flooding. The detectives searched Mark Montgomery's flat first, local crime scene investigators in tow. Apart from a worn pair of size ten shoes, they found nothing startling there: an untidy mess, a lot of drugs – prescription and illegal – no family memorabilia to speak of, a computer wire but no computer, a sorry excuse for a home all round. The CSIs would do a job on the place, lifting samples for comparison with DNA found at crime scenes.

Maybe they'd get lucky.

Ryan and O'Neil were ferried between addresses by Thames Valley police on empty wet streets. The wind had gone but the rain was relentless. There would be no white Christmas for any British kids. No sledging or rides on new bikes. No roller-skating and scuffed knees.

Ryan's mobile rang as they pulled up outside Sophia Montgomery's place. The house was in darkness. No need to rush in there. He checked the screen, grinned at O'Neil.

'Grace?' Eloise already knew the answer.

'The one and only.' Ryan pressed to receive the call. 'Merry Christmas, missus. I wasn't expecting to hear from you today.'

'Liar.'

'I'm serious. Please pass on my regards to Frank.'

'And ours to you too, Matthew.'

'Hey, cut it out! The Sunday name is reserved for Caroline and well you know it. If you're not tucked up in bed with a movie, eating chocolate, what are you guys up to?'

'You're at work. We're at work. Caroline is with us now. She had a great night last night, a super morning with the kids. They all said to tell you they loved their presents. Lucy made you a card. It's so sweet. And we have a special visitor here at base.'

'What?' Ryan was horrified.

'Don't panic,' she said. 'With no transport to take him anywhere, Hilary joined us. He brought goodies. It's quite a party. We're drinking good champagne and eating luxury mince pies. Tell Eloise she has a full backup team.'

'Sounds like fun.' He glanced across the rear seat. 'They're in the office.'

'So I gathered.'

'I have two presents for Dumbo.' Grace didn't stop for breath. 'Not from me, I hasten to add. She knows I'm not that generous. These are special delivery, from Santa.'

O'Neil shuffled closer to Ryan, enjoying the chat.

Grace was on top form.

'Careful what you say,' Ryan warned. 'Someone we both know is listening.'

O'Neil played along. 'Can we have our present now?'

'Only if you've been good.'

'I have, get on with it.'

'Mark Montgomery's symptoms came on two years ago. I'm in possession of his medical records and on first-name terms with his GP.' She chuckled. 'I think he fancies me. The good doctor described Montgomery as unpredictable but resourceful, with a list of ailments as long as your arm. He was in a very bad way. It's a wonder he ever managed to carry out those attacks.'

'When I pick him up, I'll be sure to ask him.'

'Too late,' Grace said. 'That's your other present. Someone we know just registered his death.'

'On Christmas Day?'

'Yesterday. Sophia Montgomery rang the GP late last night to let him know, hours after she spoke to you. You're such a hard bastard, Ryan. She was very upset. You obviously didn't give her enough sympathy. The GP rang me just now. I tell you, he's got it bad – any excuse to get in touch.'

'Would that I was in such demand,' O'Neil said.

'Keep your eyes peeled, Eloise. You might spot a fan.'

Ryan avoided O'Neil's eyes.

'That's one less problem for us to deal with.' O'Neil moved quickly on. 'Except we now have to prove his guilt without being able to interview him. Grace, we need time and date of death, where the body is now and samples. We're at his sister's house, available if you need us. Keep in touch if there are any further developments.'

'Don't work too hard.'

They ended the call.

*

Sophia's house was cold inside – in more ways than one – a chill cutting through them as they entered the premises. This was not a happy house. O'Neil began her search upstairs. Ryan did the same on the ground floor. As he'd seen through the window a few days ago, the kitchen was pristine, obsessively clean, not a thing out of place.

Montgomery was a woman who liked electric gadgetry. Cupboards were crammed with kitchen aids. On the counter, an espresso machine and a multi-purpose charge point for her devices. The home was marginally more interesting than Mark's. As Ryan moved through the living room, methodical and organized in his task, something he couldn't quite get a handle on began to bother him. It niggled at the edges of his consciousness for a good half hour as he continued to search, refusing to rise to the surface.

Pushing it away, he went into the hallway as O'Neil arrived at the bottom of the stairs. She was holding a sealed evidence bag in her hand and was deeply troubled as she showed it to him. The bag contained an image of a woman and a girl he assumed was Montgomery and her mother. O'Neil thought so too.

'There's something disturbing about her,' she said.

Ryan looked at her. 'Sophia or her mother?'

'Sophia. What a creepy kid.'

'You suspect she nudged her mother over a cliff accidentally on purpose. Your thoughts are coloured by that.' He glanced at the photo. 'I think she's kinda cute.'

'She might have been once. Not any more.'

Ryan didn't disagree. 'Anything else upstairs?'

'There's a camcorder in her closet. I left it for CSIs to

recover. There's a new team on its way.' They didn't want cross-contamination from Mark's flat. 'The camcorder is on charge.' The implication that Spielberg might be getting ready to use it again was worrying. Though how she'd manage without her brother's help was unclear, unless she was the killer, he the accomplice. 'If she sticks to her routine, next Sunday is the twenty-ninth, just four days away.' O'Neil pointed at the door facing them. 'What's in here?'

'I don't know.' Ryan gestured for her to enter. 'Why don't we find out?'

O'Neil opened the door. On the other side of it was a small office with a view of the front garden, an uncluttered desk, a chair and two filing cabinets. The surface of the highly polished desk was dust free. On it stood an Apple iMac, wireless keyboard, mouse and magic trackpad, a digital clock radio, a desk lamp. Four pens and a notepad placed with such care it might've been measured to ensure that it was truly plumb with the edge of the desk.

'Blimey!' O'Neil said. 'She must value order.'

'Above all else,' Ryan agreed. 'Check out the cupboard under the stairs. It's like a shoe shop. Several pairs all lined up in a row. Either she has a problem or nothing better to do than to tidy up. The whole house is like it.'

'Size?'

'Sixes and sevens.'

'Yes!'

'Thought that might please you.'

Ryan turned his attention back to the office. Bookshelves above the desk were similarly organized, filing cabinets too, their contents perfectly labelled, not a thing out of place. As he sat down to examine the computer, Caroline popped into his head and stayed there. Some of what he'd seen had seemed very familiar. The front door was a blurry image in his peripheral vision. It came into sharp focus as he turned to look at it.

'That's it,' he muttered under his breath.

'That's what?' O'Neil stared at him.

'This obsession with tidiness reminds me of Caroline. She's well ordered out of necessity, to protect her from harm—'

'Too right! Did you see the massive bruise on her arm where she'd tripped over the chair Newman hadn't replaced?'

'One more injury to add to her collection.'

'So what's your point?'

'Her blindness means she has no need for certain items at home, guv – mirrors, lights, that type of thing. Montgomery is supposedly mute and yet there are things here that are only useful to those who use speech to communicate: telephones, for a start. See that?' He pointed in the direction of the front door, to the thing he'd seen on the way in but not registered, the elusive thought he'd been trying hard to get a handle on.

'What am I looking at?'

'That's an audio entry system, perfect for a woman living alone, superfluous if you can't or won't talk. And the pièce de résistance ...' He clicked on the Applications folder in the iMac's menu bar, then double-clicked an application icon. 'See for yourself.'

'Speech recognition software?' O'Neil spelled it out, as if she couldn't believe her luck. 'You've got to be kidding me.'

'I happen to know it doesn't come as standard on this machine.'

'This is a great find, Ryan. Well done.'

Ryan clicked the Documents icon. 'We're going to have trouble with this lot. Every one of these files is password protected. We'll need help to unlock them.' As Ryan pulled open the left-hand drawer O'Neil saw his face change. She looked at him quizzically. He pointed at the *Simpsons* mouse pad inside.

61

Christmas had come and gone. Despite the euphoria of finding items that Sophia Montgomery didn't or shouldn't require if she didn't speak, the next few days were a pain in the ass with no sign of the woman herself and nothing to do but wait for others to carry out their tasks. Ryan wasn't feeling positive – and tomorrow was Sunday, an ominous thought if she was getting ready to kill again.

'Why so down in the mouth?' O'Neil asked.

'Technical support lucked out,' he said. 'I was hoping they would find incriminating evidence on Montgomery's computer, but it's clean. They say there's nothing in her locked files to tie her to these offences. Not a damned thing. She's as devious as we feared. I reckon she did her research on her brother's computer, removing it after his death.'

'Maybe the speech recognition software will give us something.' O'Neil was trying to give him a boost.

'Don't hold your breath. There are no active files on the application. Technicians aren't hopeful it was ever used. It wouldn't surprise me if she bought it to piss us off.' Ryan sat on the edge of her desk, trying not to look quite as glum as he felt. 'Any news on the camcorder?'

'It's old, which fits with the report we commissioned. Experts say it could be the one Montgomery used. Equally, it might not be. We'll probably never be able to prove it either way. It's another piece of circumstantial evidence to add to all the rest.' She reached into her drawer, handed him a report from Ne46 Technology.

He took it from her.

'Before you read that, and before the others return from lunch, I want to say how much I appreciated your support over Christmas. There hasn't been the opportunity to thank you properly. You were an absolute star.'

'What I get paid for.'

'So you keep saying, but I meant personally, not professionally.' Her eyes held a special thank you. 'The latter goes without saying or you wouldn't be here. I'm not sure I'd have got through it without you.'

Ryan didn't quite know how to respond. He wasn't used to such overt gratitude and was at a loss what to do with it. She'd helped him when Jack died and he was more than happy to reciprocate. He'd do anything for her. *Anything*. Right now, he dealt with her praise in the only way he knew how.

'You're staring,' he said.

'Go!' She pointed at his desk. 'You know I hate a slacker.'

Ryan got up and wandered away, a smile developing. When the enquiry was over, he'd ask her over to his place for dinner. He missed his seaside home and wondered when he might return to it. Still, the view through their office window was fast becoming one of his favourites. On the road below, there was no sign of Newman and Caroline. Grace was approaching from a distance, a tiny red ant making her way towards him at breakneck speed, unaware that he was watching from above. She checked her watch, quickened her step even more.

Why the hurry?

As always, when Ryan allowed his mind to wander from the subject of a murder investigation, ideas began to flow. Something Grace had said on Christmas Day intrigued him. Pulling his mobile from his pocket, he dialled the number for Jo Nichol. The telephone didn't ring out long. Ryan was surprised when it wasn't her who came on the line.

'Jo Nichol's phone.'

Male voice.

'Mr Spencer?'

'No, it's Doctor Blake, her GP. Who is this?'

'Detective Sergeant Matthew Ryan – Northumbria Police.'

'What can I do for you, Detective?'

'My enquiry will only take a second, sir. Can you put Jo on?'

'I'm afraid not, Detective. Ms Nichol died an hour ago. I'm here to certify death.'

Shit! 'I'm sorry to hear that.'

'Yes, it's very sad.' His response was clinical. 'Better here than in an anonymous hospital room surrounded by busy nursing staff. She would have hated that. Jo wanted to die at home with dignity and she got her wish. She was a brave young woman.'

'She was. I spoke with her recently. She didn't mention it to you?'

'Why should she. I'm a doctor, not a priest.'

'She wasn't in trouble,' Ryan said. 'She looked weak, but not particularly close to death—'

'The terminally ill often don't,' Blake explained. 'They're on high levels of medication. There's no need for anyone to die in pain these days. The medical profession aims to make patients

413

as comfortable and peaceful as possible, within the law, of course.'

'Were you with her when she passed away?' O'Neil was studying Ryan, intrigued by the conversation he was having and no doubt wondering where he was taking it. 'Doctor Blake?'

'No, Mr Spencer called me.'

'He's there with you? Could I have a word?'

'He left. He's rather upset. I gather they worked together. I said I'd wait for the undertaker.'

'In that case, do you have a moment to talk to me? I'd like some insight into Sauer's.'

'Whatever for?'

'I'm investigating the murder of multiple victims. It's a complicated case involving the disease. It would take too long to explain. Jo Nichol developed symptoms at around the same time as one of our main suspects.' Ryan failed to mention that his suspect was also dead. 'In no way am I suggesting that she was involved – she was ruled out of our enquiry some time ago – but it would help me to know how plausible it is in the latter stages of Sauer's to beat a man to death. We have reason to believe that our suspect, a male, was quite poorly.'

'He would be. These patients deteriorate quickly.'

'Which is why I'm asking.'

'I'm not qualified to answer that, Detective. I'm a general practitioner. You need to talk to a consultant.'

'I'm after your opinion, sir, nothing more. There are so few specialists, we've not yet managed to find one who is available to talk to us. You've had very close and recent contact with a sufferer. In my book, that counts; you have an expert opinion to give and I'd like to hear it.'

The GP hesitated.

Ryan pressed on. 'I wouldn't ask if it wasn't important. If our main suspect didn't have the capacity to kill, we may be looking in the wrong direction. Sir, we have reason to believe that another death might be imminent . . . possibly before the day is out. The perpetrator must be stopped. Not to put too fine a point on it, your advice, expert or not, may save a life.'

'I see your dilemma.' The medic paused. 'I won't give evidence on a witness stand.'

'Off the record is fine.'

'Then, in my humble opinion, and don't quote me on it, it's highly unlikely that a person in the latter stages of Sauer's would be capable of extreme violence such as you're describing. The disease is brutal, Detective. It saps strength and drains energy. Don't get me started on the physical deterioration.'

It wasn't what Ryan wanted to hear.

He thanked Blake and hung up.

He was about to redial when Grace let herself in.

'It's turning cold.' She took off her coat and sat down, a rueful expression on her face. 'Guv, sorry to be the bearer of bad news – Danish Police say Pedersen failed to identify Mark Montgomery as a suspect. He's not the man she saw.'

O'Neil eyeballed Ryan. 'Can this day get any worse?'

He felt her frustration and saw her head go down. His conversation with Blake had brought him to the same conclusion. Mark Montgomery was not the killer. Suddenly, the case they had built together began to crumble, every building block falling down around them, creating a cloud of confusion.

Ryan was every bit as deflated as the rest of them. A chill

ran down his spine as Grace's words taunted him. 'I need to make a call,' he said.

'This is not a good time,' O'Neil said. 'We need to regroup.'

'Later, I need to do this – Jo Nichol is dead.'

Grace and O'Neil were nonplussed. They watched him dial out, lost interest as he waited for the call to be answered, and went back to work. The ringing tone stopped, Dan Spencer answering with his full name. He was in a car. Ryan heard road noise in the background. He tried to lift himself out of the gloom and put on a professional front.

'Mr Spencer, it's DS Ryan. I just spoke to Doctor Blake and wanted to offer my condolences. I'm so sorry to hear about Jo. I know how close you two were. Is there anything I can do for you?'

'Nothing, thanks.'

'Are you sure?'

'I'm fine.'

'Do you need company? I could send someone round.'

'I said I'm fine. I'm heading north to see my mum. Thank you for taking the trouble to call.'

'No problem, as long as you're OK. You take care.'

I'm heading north . . .

Those three words were like a punch in the gut to Ryan. He swore under his breath as he put down the phone, causing O'Neil to raise her head. His eyes found hers. 'Pedersen was correct. Mark Montgomery wasn't the man she saw in Copenhagen. We fingered the wrong guy.'

62

'What a monumental cock-up.' Ryan was pacing up and down, angry for not having seen what was right in front of him, more so for allowing Sophia to get one over on him. 'Mark Montgomery was *Shdwman*. Dan Spencer was *dude1980*. Why the hell didn't I spot that? Sophia must have been laughing her socks off when I tried to implicate her brother.' He took a long, deep breath. 'Well, she won't be doing it for long.'

It took Newman less than twenty-three minutes to find out where Spencer's parents lived – an address in the village of Yarm, North Yorkshire – twenty more to find the identity of the caller the cinematographer was most in contact with. The DVLA were useful, British Telecom too, everyone keen to cooperate in finding the country's Most Wanted.

An hour later, police moved in and picked them up, a hard stop with a firearms team on the northbound carriageway of the A1. While they were waiting for the suspects to arrive under a police escort, in separate vehicles, Grace called the path lab. DNA comparison was complete. Scientists had identified familial DNA to that of Mark Montgomery at two crime scenes, proving an indisputable link to Sophia. The team had no doubt that a third, as yet unidentified sample, belonged to Dan Spencer.

Ryan stopped pacing and sat down.

The Ne46 Technology report O'Neil had given him was lying on his desk, waiting to be read. The company had already proved themselves invaluable. He couldn't wait to put their findings to Sophia Montgomery in interview. Even though he knew the gist of the updated document, he picked it up, his eyes skimming the words on the page.

As stated previously in our report dated Friday, 20 December, it was not possible to establish the exact type and brand of camera used from the sample DVD you asked us to examine. The camcorder now under analysis could be the equipment used. We are unable to say with absolute certainty that this is the case. What we can say is that the timer on the equipment is running seven minutes and thirty-six seconds fast . . .

Ryan shut his eyes, hoping for inspiration. He found it too. Throwing the report down on his desk, he got up suddenly. Feeling O'Neil's eyes on him, he punched a code into the safe and took out the DVD from the Whitley Bay crime scene, then shifted across to his desk under his boss's watchful gaze. Grace and Newman were observing too. The disk slid effortlessly into the computer slot as they gathered round.

'What are you after?' O'Neil wanted to know.

'I'll show you in a minute.' Footage of Fraser's flat uploaded on screen. Ryan could feel the tension in his chest as he fast-forwarded to the point he was interested in. O'Neil was standing directly behind him, so close he could almost feel the warmth of her body. When he got to the relevant section, he restarted the DVD to run in real time. On screen, the camera paused dramatically to dwell on the long-bladed knife glinting from the overhead light, before running on slowly and deliberately across the old tea chest the nurse used as a bedside table, Fraser's uniform shirt, his ID lanyard. Ryan paused the disk, rewound slightly, freezing the screen on the digital radio-alarm clock.

'Look at the time on the clock,' he said.

'Eleven fifty-one,' Grace said. 'So what?'

'Compare it to the DVD counter.'

'Eleven, fifty-eight – it's fast by seven minutes.'

'And thirty-six seconds, if we wait,' Ryan said triumphantly. He didn't need Technical Support to prove his point. 'I'd like to see Sophia try to wriggle out of this one.'

O'Neil reached forward, placed her hands over his ears and kissed the top of his head.

63

O'Neil offered Ryan the interview with their prime suspect, if he wanted it. No chance would he turn it down. There was, without doubt, enough evidence to convict: DNA, the camcorder, reams and reams of circumstantial evidence, all of which amounted to a watertight case. Despite the fact that Montgomery was refusing to speak, they had to go through the motions of questioning her.

Ryan cautioned her, making sure she understood that she'd been arrested and brought to Newcastle on suspicion of five murders: Paul Dean, Lord Trevathan (Leonard Maxwell), Michael Tierney, James Fraser and Laura Stone. Sophia didn't answer to her name or give her date of birth. She sat passively beside her solicitor, staring across the table, hands loosely in her lap.

O'Neil wasn't wrong . . .
Sophia was creepy.

'I'd like to take things chronologically.' Ryan sat forward, elbows on the table, Montgomery's file in front of him. 'Do stop me if you need to take a break. We'll probably need one too. We've been working very hard on this case. We didn't find your brother's computer, but I suspect you removed it from his flat. Actually, we don't need it because our technical support unit has examined the chat room he used to frequent under the username: *Shdwman*.'

Ryan opened the file.

'On the tenth of January 2013, *Shdwman* (Mark) had a fascinating conversation with another chat room user with a similar profile who called himself *dude1980*. We now know that *dude1980* was in fact your co-accused, Daniel Spencer. Spencer was a predator, not a chat-buddy to Mark. I thought I'd better make that distinction. I'm guessing you already know that, because you were doing some grooming of your own, weren't you?'

Montgomery's solicitor sighed. 'Is there a point to this line of questioning, Detective? If so, I'm not seeing it.'

'As I said to your client on the phone on Christmas Eve, we have an eyewitness who identified her loitering outside the British Embassy in Copenhagen (Denmark) at around three o'clock on Friday the twenty-sixth of July 2013.' Ryan waited for the brief to stop scribbling. 'Ms Montgomery was in the company of Daniel Spencer, who has since been identified by the same witness. This was just two days prior to the disappearance of Ambassador Paul Dean who was found dead on July thirtieth.'

More note-taking.

Ryan had eyes only for Montgomery. 'Daniel Spencer is talking to us, by the way. He's in the next room with my colleague. It might help your defence if you follow his lead.' Ryan winced, shook his head, a sorry face. 'Loyalty is not his specialist subject.'

She didn't flinch.

'We also found, within the chat room, a conversation between

Spencer and a woman calling herself *brokenkiss*. This is a complicated one, so listen carefully. The woman calling herself *brokenkiss* claimed that her father went to see a solicitor in order to stop his wife from having a second child.' Ryan switched focus to Sophia's legal counsel. 'To make this absolutely clear, the child she was referring to was Mark Montgomery, Sophia's late brother.' Ryan was back with the accused. 'But you know that, don't you, Sophia, because you are *brokenkiss*.' He paused for a response and got nothing in return. 'I'm getting there, I promise you. This lawyer didn't manage to swing a court order, despite being smart enough to eventually become Scotland's second highest judge, Lord Trevathan, whose body we found floating in the River Tay on December ninth. How am I doing?'

Montgomery didn't nod or shake her head. She didn't appear stressed or worried. No body language of any kind on display. She was far too cool a customer for that.

O'Neil glanced at him: *Must try harder.*

'You moved his body from the folly at huge risk. I can see why you did it. It's such a popular beauty spot and you didn't want anyone to find him before Police Scotland received your DVD. That wasn't part of your plan, was it? Your message was more important than the individuals concerned. I know this, because most killers dispose of victims to get rid of evidence. The body is, after all, a silent witness. You did the opposite. I have a theory about that. I think you see yourself as someone with right on her side, someone with a serious point to make – isn't that your endgame, Sophia? To make us all sit up and take notice. To send a clear message that you would and have been punishing those with an opposing point of view, blaming them for not supporting your cause. You said as much on the footage you sent. They deserved it, were the words you used in one form or another, to justify your actions.'

'My client doesn't speak,' the brief said. 'How could she possibly have told you that?'

'With respect, we all know that her mutism is discriminatory.' Ryan eyeballed his suspect. 'You may as well admit it, Sophia. We have video evidence of you talking to Spencer prior to your stop and arrest on the A1. Some of the vehicles that passed you in the outside lane were ours, a covert unit doing a job on you. You're not the only one with a plan. Before pulling you over, firearms officers saw and heard you yelling at Spencer to put his foot down. But I'll come on to that later . . .'

Montgomery feigned boredom.

'Do you have anything to say?'

She remained silent.

'Do you really think the people you killed were in the wrong? If so, you should think again. It certainly wasn't so in the case of Mr Tierney. Remember him? Nice man on the end of the line the night you threatened to throw yourself under a London tube train. He offered to help, didn't he? But nothing came of it. Michael Tierney didn't deserve to die, Sophia. In fact, he was so shaken by your call, he resigned his post that very night. Of course, you didn't know that he'd referred you on to Social Services. Why should you? His email' – Ryan pushed a sheet of paper across the table – 'was never acted upon. It wasn't his fault, Sophia. He did everything he could for you. I want you to go to prison knowing that.'

She was like ice, nothing touching her.

'Let's move on to Laura Stone, then. She didn't like Mark, did she? She wouldn't sign him up for her documentary, and you killed her for denying him a voice. Do you think he's at peace now because of it? I doubt that very much. I suspect he found out that you were using his computer. He may have been angry not to get his fifteen minutes of fame on TV, but I suspect he got over it. What he couldn't bear to live with was the guilt of what you were doing. Isn't that right? I suspect that's why he rocked himself off.'

The solicitor peered over the top of his specs. 'Evidence, DS Ryan.'

Ryan handed him the post-mortem report without interrupting his flow. 'For the purposes of the tape I am showing Sophia Montgomery and her solicitor a post-mortem report on Mark Montgomery.'

Sophia shifted in her seat – she wasn't expecting that.

Unable to help herself, O'Neil joined in. 'DS Ryan is a clever detective, Sophia. Remember James Fraser, the nurse you killed in Whitley Bay. He didn't deserve it either, did he? DS Ryan was the one who worked out that he was an innocent bystander, a nurse who happened to jog past your kill site at the wrong moment and was killed for it. At first, DS Ryan was prepared to give you the benefit of the doubt on that one, because even he couldn't believe that you were callous enough to kill a man who hadn't hurt you in some way. You've left his mother a broken woman. The only thing DS Ryan failed to spot in this whole affair was the assumption that your co-accused was ill, until we realised that he's just a drugged-up little thug who likes hurting people. I have to hand it to you: keeping him supplied was a great control mechanism. Where did you keep his stash?'

Sophia crossed her legs and let out a bored sigh.

'Carry on, DS Ryan.'

'We searched your house,' Ryan said. 'Nice place. I know exactly where you were standing when you called me on Saturday the twenty-first of December, when you told me to call you Marge.' Ryan held up the evidence bag containing the *Simpsons* mouse pad.

The brief glanced at his client.

Sophia ignored him.

'Or maybe you were sitting in front of that expensive computer of yours.' Ryan's eyes were on Montgomery now. 'You love gadgetry and technology, don't you, Sophia? I bet you watch *Click* on the BBC. Great show. I've got a good one for you, if you're into that.' He flicked through the file in front of him, removed another sheet of paper and then looked up. 'Ever heard of egocentric video analysis?'

She didn't answer.

'No? I'm not surprised. It was a new one on me too. Well, let me tell you that video technology has moved on apace in recent years, enabling us to ID certain characteristics of filmmakers from biometric signatures. Imagine my surprise when I was told that it's possible to extrapolate the height of the camera from the ground, even the gait of a person who might wish to hide their identity in criminal cases. Isn't that brilliant? Data can pinpoint with high accuracy the optical flow associated with such a person, each individual producing a unique pattern, much like a fingerprint. I reckon it's fairly accurate in your case. What do you think?'

'Five eight?' Sophia's brief almost scoffed. 'You'll have to do better than that, Detective. If my googling skills are up to scratch, although that height represents less than five per cent of British women, may I remind you that there are thirty-plus million of them. Can we move on?'

'Certainly. We found the video you made in Spencer's house, Sophia? The one you coerced him into making in exchange for drugs. He said you tried to upload it to YouTube and got knocked back on grounds of hateful content and threats. Shame. All that wasted effort. Nice that you got to star in your own movie though – a speaking part too!'

The suspect was done for – they both knew it.

There was a game of poker going on between accuser and accused. 'You should've got rid of your camcorder, Sophia. The counter on it is running fast by seven minutes and thirty-six seconds. Remember when you were filming in James Fraser's house? The discrepancy between the timing on your camcorder and his digital alarm clock is precisely that. What do you think the odds are of two pieces of equipment being that distance apart, down to the nanosecond?'

The solicitor lifted his pen, fixing Ryan with a stare. 'That doesn't amount to proof that she was there.'

'Her camcorder was, so was her DNA and James Fraser's firearms were found in the boot of the vehicle she was arrested in, along with Ambassador Dean's wallet. Spencer is a thief as well as an addict.'

There was anger in Montgomery's eyes.

'In my book, that is deeply incriminating evidence,' Ryan said. 'We'll let a judge decide, shall we? Oh, I forgot. I'm told that the tread pattern on a pair of her shoes matches the footprints we found in James Fraser's flat. She did her best to clean them up, but I'm certain we'll be able to prove conclusively that his blood is on them. Then there's the small matter of your photograph album. It's not looking good, Sophia.'

Montgomery was losing it.

'I don't suppose you care much, do you?' Ryan said. 'You're dying anyway. Forgive me if that sounds callous. The disease you inherited is nasty. Ordinarily, you'd have my sympathy. It must have been tough for you and your brother as kids, having a rare genetic disorder. Your mother knew about Sauer's, didn't she, and yet she put her needs above yours – and you hated her for it. You decided to play judge and jury. You killed her, just as you killed all the others. Granted, that's not what the coroner said – and now she's been cremated we'll never be able to prove it. But that doesn't mean it didn't happen.'

'Did anyone ever tell you how much you resemble your mum?' Ryan opened the file and took out a blown-up copy of the photograph O'Neil had found in Sophia's house. The likeness was astonishing. 'You must've liked her once.'

Sophia wiped a tear away.

'Your mother didn't agree with genetic testing, did she? She thought it labelled people. Oh yes, I know all about that. You go with what you're given, wasn't that her philosophy? She didn't care about you or your quality of life. All she wanted was to give birth. I'm not sure about my guv'nor . . .' Ryan glanced at O'Neil. 'But I understand where you're coming from. I've

64

It was rare for Ryan to feel sorry for a killer. A small part of him had done so during the latter part of a murder investigation that had led him in several directions before the truth was finally revealed. From a young age, Sophia Montgomery had lived with a death sentence, her vicious crimes motivated by hatred of a mother who'd put her own needs above all else. Faced with the same dilemma, Ryan knew he'd suppress his wish to father children.

But that was easy for him to say.

Still, a child's well-being must come first. No one asked to be born. Not Rebecca Swift, certainly not Sophia Montgomery. She'd suffered twice over: from the emotional fallout of being told she had Sauer's; from having to watch her younger brother go through a living hell. Whether her mother had told them that terrible truth high above the Filey shoreline, detectives would never know. Ryan would like to think that Sophia hadn't meant her mother to go over the edge. That her fall from the cliffs had been a tragic accident brought about by a kid's outrage, but deep down he didn't believe it.

She was evil!

Those three short words were the only ones he'd heard Sophia speak, delivered with such venom that any sympathy he might have had for her evaporated. The fact that she'd spend the time she had left on this earth incarcerated was of no real consequence to either of them. Ryan felt sure that she was already in a prison of her own making.

O'Neil had taken the view that the media coverage surrounding Laura Stone's documentary had been the flashpoint, fuelling a new and explosive anger to the point where Montgomery couldn't stop. Bizarrely, she would get her way. Her story had already raised the profile of an issue she felt strongly about. She and her accomplice, Daniel Spencer, were splashed across every national newspaper, a situation that would remain until the two were indicted and handed a life sentence in a court of law.

Anja Pedersen had been Ryan and O'Neil's solitary eyewitness. Without her sharp eye and attention to detail, Ryan was sure the investigation into the unlawful killing of four British citizens, at home and abroad, would have gone on longer – for months, possibly even years. He was grateful to the Danish librarian whose testimony would be pivotal to the case. Set to play a leading role in her own crime story, Pedersen would dine out on it for the rest of her life.

The cell door slammed shut on Sophia Montgomery. As campaigns go, hers had been an unprecedented success. After Ryan had done his stuff, she was rushed to court for a bail hearing, the car mobbed by waiting journalists keen to take her picture. She shooed away an offer to cover her face. Now she'd been caught, there was no point hiding. She craved the attention. As she stood in the dock while the Crown Prosecutor objected to her release in the most strenuous terms, she listened patiently. There was a moment when it looked like she might go free, but when the sitting magistrates were invited to clear the court, she knew she was in for a treat. A video, *her* video, appeared on the TV monitor in seconds, shocking a small but critical audience. Having finally made her screen debut, she was done. When magistrates remanded her in custody, she thanked them politely; maybe now people would think twice. Mark was gone. What else was there?

There was a final bit of housekeeping for Ryan and O'Neil. A murder file was being written up and submitted to the Crown Prosecution Service – someone else's problem for an elite unit like theirs. The panic alarm had been removed from the home of James Fraser's heartbroken mother. She, like Robert Parker and relatives of Lord Trevathan and Ambassador Paul Dean, had now been given permission to bury their dead. The search would go on for the body of Laura Stone. It was Ryan's wish to return the brilliant documentary maker to her loved ones in the Ardèche region of France.

She was out there somewhere.

Ryan scanned the waves crashing onto the shoreline within sight of his tiny Northumberland hideaway, willing the sea to play its part, praying that storm-force winds now battering the region would bring Laura home. Newman and Grace arrived, hand in hand, happy to have spent their first Christmas together as man and wife. They cared less that they had been working. Neither was ready to abandon their investigative skills just yet. Their considerable expertise was vital to the unit – that was the word according to Grace. She'd practically begged O'Neil to take them on permanently.

Whether she would or not was anyone's guess.

Caroline too had played her part. She and O'Neil were approaching from the south, Bob trundling along beside them, the historic remains of Dunstanburgh Castle in the distance. The two women appeared to be sharing a joke. Ryan hoped his twin was being discreet.

Suggesting they walk back to the cottage, Grace and Newman linked arms with Caroline. As the three walked off, Bob duly followed. O'Neil made no move to follow. She stared at Ryan, hands in pockets, hair flying in the wind – more alive than he'd seen her in weeks.

Intoxicating.

Her mood wasn't easy to read as they sat on the sand together, an intimate moment for such a gaping landscape: a sweeping stretch of empty beach, a dramatic sky and roaring sea. There were times when silence spoke volumes and this was one of them. A flock of gulls headed inland, screeching as they flew overhead. A grey seal pup limped up the sand, separated from its mother in rough conditions. Like Sophia, Ryan wondered how long it would survive.

As if she felt his pain, O'Neil turned to face him as it began to snow, heavy flakes landing on her head and eyelashes before melting away. 'You look like a kid at Christmas,' O'Neil said playfully. 'Close your eyes.'

Ryan was intrigued. 'What for?'

'Do it! I have a present for you.'

Ryan pointed at his chest. 'For me?'

She looked around her. 'I don't see anyone else.'

'Eloise, you shouldn't have. I didn't get you anything.'

'We can share.' She was trying not to laugh as she handed

him a bag of nuts and a bottle of Babycham in gloved hands. There was so much he wanted to say but somehow it seemed less important now. The courage and veracity she'd shown in the face of Newman's allegations was testament to the kind of woman she was. Not only had she closed the book on Forsythe, O'Neil had come out fighting and forgiven him for doubting her integrity. In Ryan's mind, that was all that mattered. The unit would go on.

Acknowledgements

Ryan and O'Neil began life on opposite sides of a disciplinary hearing in my stand-alone novel, *The Silent Room*. In *The Death Messenger* they're back, having joined forces in a new elite unit, the shadow squad. Writing these characters has given me great pleasure and I hope you enjoy reading this, my eighth book.

Many people put this novel together. I'd like to acknowledge the entire staff at Pan Macmillan: especially Wayne Brookes – to whom this book is dedicated – Philippa McEwan and Alex Saunders. Thanks must also go to my freelance editor, Anne O'Brien, a very special lady who had to push me to the limit to get this one right. She motivates me to lift my game with every book.

I'd like to thank all at A. M. Heath Literary Agency, my friend and agent, Oli Munson, on hand to offer advice at every turn, guiding me to make the right career choices.

A special mention here for Dr Charlotte Beyer who helped with translation of dialogue during a police interview. Appreciation must also go to Steen Hansen of the Copenhagen Police for helping me understand the Danish equivalent of British CID and pinpointing their location within that fine city.

Lastly, thanks to my wonderful family: Paul and Kate; Chris and Jodie; Max, Frances and Daisy. Much love as always to my partner Mo who kept me sane at times when I was losing the will to live. It's not all beer and skittles! Knowing she has my back makes a huge difference.

The Silent Room

BY MARI HANNAH

*The first book featuring DS Matthew Ryan
and Detective Superintendent Eloise O'Neil*

A security van sets off for Durham prison, a disgraced Special Branch officer in the back. It never arrives. En route, it is hijacked by armed men, the prisoner sprung. Suspended from duty on suspicion of aiding and abetting the audacious escape of his former boss, Detective Sergeant Matthew Ryan is locked out of the manhunt.

Desperate to preserve his career and prove his innocence, he backs off. But when the official investigation falls apart, under surveillance and with his life in danger, Ryan goes dark, enlisting others in his quest to discover the truth.

When the trail leads to the suspicious death of a Norwegian national, Ryan uncovers an international conspiracy that has claimed the lives of many.

The Murder Wall

BY MARI HANNAH

The first book featuring DCI Kate Daniels

Eleven months after discovering a brutal double murder in a sleepy Northumbrian village, Detective Chief Inspector Kate Daniels is still haunted by her failure to solve the investigation. Then the vicious killing of a man on Newcastle's Quayside gives Daniels her first case as Senior Investigating Officer and a second chance to get it right.

When Daniels recognizes the corpse but fails to disclose the fact, her personal life suddenly collides into her professional life. And – even worse – she is now being watched.

As Daniels steps closer to finding a killer, a killer is only a breath away from claiming his next victim . . .